FROM THE CASE FILES OF

HALSEY, PEASLEE, & LYDECKER

CONSULTING DETECTIVES

THE ELDRITCH EQUATIONS

AND OTHER INVESTIGATIONS

Praise for *The Eldritch Equations*

"The mystery story and the tale of terror were both born in the fervid mind of Edgar Allen Poe. When handled by lesser writers these tales can become pastiche, but in the hands of as fine a writer as Peter Rawlik these genes once again cross-fertilize into strange (and I dare say) rather wonderful fruits."
—**Don Webb**, author of *Building Strange Temples*

"Murder comes to the Miskatonic Valley, and someone has to find out whodunnit. *The Eldritch Equations* is an interstitial novel, and finds its place in between the genres of weird fiction and the detective novel. Rawlik's novel splices a touch of Dashiell Hammett into the literary DNA of Lovecraft's Arkham Cycle, and does justice to both." —**Bobby Derie**, author of *Sex and the Cthulhu Mythos*

"Looking for Lovecratian horror fiction the way it should be written, then Peter Rawlik is your man." —**David Conyers**, author of *Cthulhu Reloaded*

"From Asenath to Zabdiel, Rawlik conjures an imaginative kaleidoscope of Lovecraftian New England and its inhabitants, leaving no insane professor or harried investigator unturned. An utterly unashamed dive into the devious and deluded world of the Mythos, where the living, the dead, and the re-animated have a book they don't want you to see. And it may not be a good idea to answer that knock at the door..." —**John Linwood Grant**, author of *Where All is Night, and Starless*

Praise for *The Miskatonic University Spiritualism Club*

"Imagine Nick and Norah Charles [from the *Thin Man* films] up against cosmic horror, Lovecraftian lore, and traditional Christmas ghost stories, and you're not far off from Peter Rawlik's charming, funny, frightening, and moving *Miskatonic University Spiritualism Club*. Save this one for bedtime on Christmas Eve—you won't regret it." —**Shaun Hamill**, Author of *Cosmology of Monsters*

Praise for Peter Rawlik

"The coolest, most gifted Lovecraftian writer working today." —**W. H. Pugmire**, Author of *Witches in Dreamland*

"Rawlik rampages through Lovecraft country like a grave-robber on formaldehyde. . . not so much a writer to watch as one to keep under constant supervision, animal tranquilizers, and heavy restraints." —**Cody Goodfellow**, Author of *Radiant Dawn*, on *Reanimators*

"Is Lovecraftian pulp-punk a thing? Because that's what Rawlik's doing here, at its action-packed, cinematic best!" —**Christine Morgan**, Author of *The Night Silver River Run Red*

"Rawlik is one of today's great conjurors of mythos, magic, mayhem and monsters. Disregard the trail of green foul smoke that emanates when you open the covers of *Strange Company*, because buried (unburied?) inside are creatures that would just as soon cheat at cards as detonate the universe into dust. Monsters and mythologies pulled from the silver screen blend with great literary beasts, a battle that shakes the foundations of reality. Readers beware—these tales will suck you in with razor-tipped claws and fling you carelessly into the void." —**Philip Fracassi**, Author of *Behold the Void*

"Pete Rawlik is one of the most prolific and talented Lovecraftian writers put there. His work is a joy to read." —**Mike Davis**, *The Lovecraft e-Zine*

"Rawlik's *The Peaslee Papers* transcends mere Lovecraftian homage into an area all its own, spanning time and space, slipstreaming historical characters into the mix while diving deep into occult conspiracies that linger on the mind long after the last page is turned." —**Bob Pastorella**, *This is Horror*

THE ELDRITCH EQUATIONS

AND OTHER INVESTIGATIONS

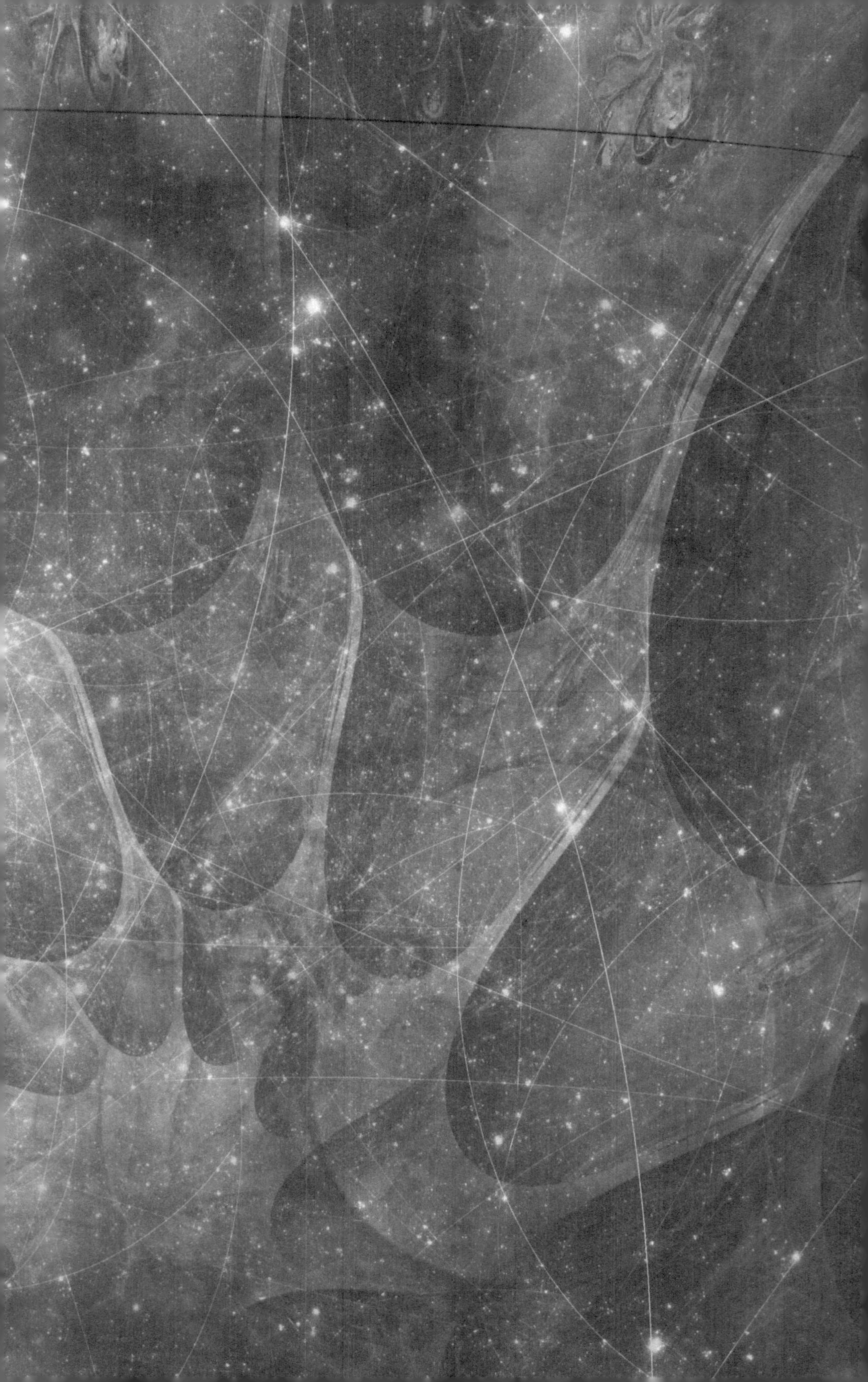

FROM THE CASE FILES OF
HALSEY, PEASLEE, & LYDECKER
CONSULTING DETECTIVES

THE ELDRITCH EQUATIONS

AND OTHER INVESTIGATIONS

PETER RAWLIK

JACKANAPES PRESS

Preview Edition — ISBN: 979-8-840893-80-7
First Standard Paperback Edition — ISBN: 978-1-956702-07-1
1 3 5 7 9 8 6 4 2

For Sal, who doesn't know, but should

**FROM
THE CASE FILES
OF**

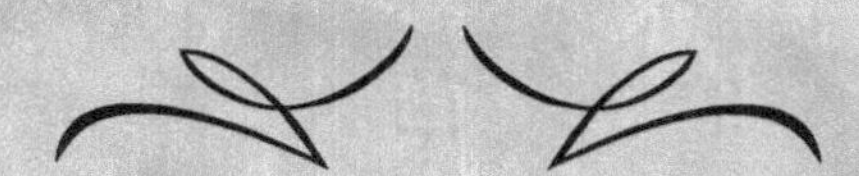

HALSEY, PEASLEE,
& LYDECKER

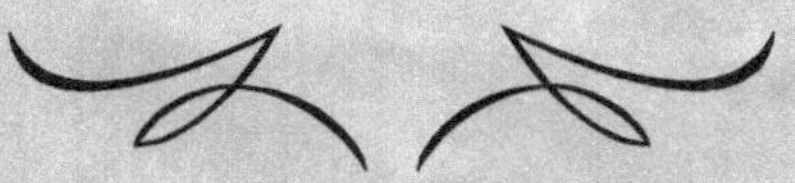

CONSULTING
DETECTIVES

CONTENTS

Our understanding of the world is based on numbers. Physical constants and the equations that handle them describe the behavior of our universe, whether that be the behavior of objects in relation to mass, or the time it takes for light to traverse the void. Mathematical constants help describe the space around us whether it be the length of an arc, the inclination of an angle, the area of a circle, or the volume of a sphere. Numbers help mankind explain the behavior of the natural world, and by extension the universe. Without numbers we would be lost. But some of these numbers, the numbers that we rely on to establish the laws of the universe, to rationalize the behavior of the stars and the spheres and the rain and the dust, are inherently irrational, undefinable and unknowable. Some call them transcendental. Our rational universe is but a pretext, a bit of numerical handwaving, wholly dependent on a set of concepts—irrational numbers—that we do not and likely cannot ever hope to understand. Is it any wonder that sometimes the so-called laws of the universe, seem to twist and bend?

—Robert Blake

The Potter Incident

October 16, 1928

"You're not going to shoot him, are you?" said Megan Halsey-Griffith as her partner, Robert Peaslee, removed a rather large gun from the trunk of their car and loaded it with what she thought were rather oversized shells. She looked over at the old man who was staggering away from the building.

"Let us hope that it doesn't come to that." He handed her a small box of ammunition for her revolvers. "But I would rather be prepared."

She took the box and cracked it open, emptying the bullets into her coat pocket. Behind them a bolt of lightning arced between the building and the sky casting a terribly pale glow across the landscape. Thunder rolled through the earth and Megan could feel the vibration in her bones. The sun seemed to be fading behind the preternatural storm clouds that had filled the sky, and the weak illumination that remained showed Megan and Robert what they already knew. The Miskatonic University Extension Building which stood on the southern edge of the industrial town of Bolton was being torn apart. One whole wing had been ripped to shreds, windows and walls were shattered, furnishings were being picked up by ferocious winds, a busted pipe sprayed water into the sky, but it never came back down. But all this devastation was nothing compared to that which towered just above the roof.

The tempest forming in the sky appeared as both a titanic storm and a dark Promethean god. There was a vaguely humanoid appearance, there was the suggestion of arms and legs, and a torso and head, but for the most part, it was like a whirlwind of black viscous tar, with a foul stench that was giving both Robert and Megan headaches.

Robert raised his hand, "I'll drive."

Megan threw him the keys, which he caught deftly. "I'm a better driver," she offered.

He nodded, "And a better shot, which is why I need you with guns in both hands." She couldn't argue with him and dashed over to the other side of the car.

Robert put his hand on the trunk and casually glanced back at the monstrosity towering over them. Soon it would be finished, and after that it would be much harder to stop. He reached back into the trunk and pulled out a bundle of five sticks of dynamite. He tucked the explosive under his arm and slammed the trunk shut.

Robert slid in from the other side as Megan slid into the passenger seat. She didn't say anything about the bundle of dynamite that he set down between them. "I'm going to take us around the back and into the courtyard. Hopefully we can reason with Mr. Potter before things get out of hand."

Megan looked up at the cyclopean juggernaut that was coalescing above them. "You don't think things are already out of hand?"

"Not just yet."

He stood on the gas pedal and left a spray of muddy earth behind them. As they whipped around the building, cutting between bushes and trees and what looked like a statue of George Washington, Megan Halsey-Griffith couldn't help but remember how she had gotten into this mess.

Had it really only been hours earlier that they had been in Arkham, sitting inside Griffith House, waiting for something—anything—to happen? It was hard to fathom that, but it was true. Time, it seemed to her, had a way of running together; for instance, it seemed as though it was only yesterday that they had filed the paperwork to create Halsey, Peaslee and Lydecker, Consulting Detectives. That had happened on the first of October, and in the more than two weeks since, they had only had a handful of calls. Those first few cases were not what the agency had been formed to handle and turned out to be rather pedestrian in nature, including: a cheating wife, a missing engagement ring, and a bookkeeper accused of embezzlement. Each case was handled swiftly, without incident, and established a steady, if paltry, stream of income. Not that they needed it—Megan was funding the whole operation out of her own pocket.

Being the scion of one of the richest families in Arkham granted Megan many benefits, with disposable income being chief among them, she thought. Still, there wasn't much in the way of expenses. Robert lived in Griffith House, and was paid a modest salary, while Lydecker—who wasn't much more than a talking head—had very minimal needs. He didn't eat or drink, and he couldn't really go out. The only thing he needed was a fresh supply of reanimation fluid, which was relatively cheap, and a steady supply of reading material. After they had solved their first few cases he had protested and demanded more pay, but Megan reminded him that his options were limited. If he didn't want to do this, he could always get a job in a sideshow.

Lydecker—a name he preferred over that of Clapham-Lee—was quite the brilliant mind. He may have been an adequate surgeon during the war and something of an evil genius afterwards, but in his role of integrating various quanta of information he was likely unsurpassed. Even Robert had been impressed, and had compared him to his wartime friend Hadrian Vargr, whose skill at observation and deduction had been crucial on missions for the Allied Powers. Robert had often told the tale of how Vargr and a man named Chan had helped rescue the chief of police after the Germans invaded Brussels, cheating the Kaiser out of a highly prized asset.

Adding to Lydecker's skills were those of Robert and Megan herself. Robert was a dogged investigator, and rather good in a gunfight, and Megan—who occasionally referred to herself as the Mistress of Mad Science—was better trained than any doctor at Miskatonic University, a better driver and an excellent ambidextrous shot. Some of this she had gained from study and practice, but she suspected that her unusual strength, constitution, memory and preternatural senses had something to do with her birth. She couldn't be sure, but all the papers and documents she could find suggested that her mother had conceived her after her father had died and been resurrected by Doctor Herbert West, a man who had made a career out of trying to cheat death. Lydecker had been both a colleague and a victim of West's. West had been punished accordingly for his many crimes against both man and nature—or so Lydecker believed. She hadn't told the disembodied head hidden in her basement that she knew that Herbert West was still alive, that she had seen him, spoken to him, worked with him—and even been intimate with him. Sooner or later, she would have to cross that bridge.

But dealing with people like West—and with things that were worse—was exactly why she had formed the agency. People—particularly those in Arkham and other towns in the Miskatonic Valley—needed someone they could call upon to stave off things the cops couldn't—or wouldn't—deal with. Robert had tried to do something similar, from within the system, but it had only made him a pariah. The cops wanted him—needed him—to do the job, but they were afraid of him as well. In the department he had been isolated; but in the agency, he had co-workers with similar experience to talk to, making the transition from the force to her burgeoning agency an easy decision. Though he really only had her to speak to for any length of time—Lydecker was a little too demented for a sustained conversation.

The lack of business beyond the mundane world of cheating wives and thieving bankers made her doubt herself, but then one phone call changed all that—a call from one Professor Rice. Rice had played some part in the Dunwich Horror, but afterward had retreated from the public eye, transferring to the Miskatonic University Extension in Bolton. It was a small campus, not much more than a single building, at which students who were employed full time at one of the many industrial plants and mills could still pursue coursework and degrees. Rice, an expert in Classical Languages, spent most of his days teaching Latin and Greek to aspiring veterinarians and German to chemists. It was in the course of his responsibilities as an instructor that he encountered something that had scared him enough to call Armitage, the man who had led the confrontation against the Dunwich Horror.

"Armitage isn't well. Dunwich—and the death of his wife—took its toll. He can't help me. But he said that Robert Peaslee could, that he and you might understand, that you might be able to do something to help me." Over the phone his voice sounded so distant, so small, so helpless. "I have a student, a boy named Potter, quite an excellent student actually, high marks and all, but lately... " He paused as if he didn't know what to say. "He had a seizure and started chanting something I didn't understand, then he sat up and shouted things that reminded me of what we had heard in Dunwich." He paused again. "Please, you have to help me."

He was right, of course—they did have to help him. No one else was really in a position to. So, despite the fact that Bolton was more than two hours away, they agreed to take the case (which meant that Megan agreed, and Robert would follow her lead). It took them an hour to pack overnight bags, but when Megan went to put the bags in the trunk Robert had waved her off. "The trunk is full. Use the back seat."

"What, pray tell, is in the trunk?"

Robert scowled a little, "Necessities, surprises. Things we might need."

Megan took in his cryptic answer with a shrug and turned her attention to watching the world pass by.

The Bolton Road—which connected Arkham to Bolton—was modern and smooth, a gently-curved strip which cuts through the rural countryside, filling the space between the two towns. Unlike the twisting roads that wind through the forests into the hill country of the northwestern portion of the state, the Bolton Road was sleek in nature and a proud monument to the surveyors, engineers and construction crews that built, designed and routed it. Here and there it paralleled the railway—at times almost sharing the same bed—and twice Robert played with racing a train that had come up behind and beside them. There were always trains coming in and out of Bolton, bring raw materials and taking away processed goods to be sold in Arkham and Boston and beyond. There were, in fact, not enough trains to transport both goods and people into and out of Bolton and so, out of necessity, the road appeared. The shimmering ebon scar raced through the land between the hills and through the small valleys from one town to the next bringing travelers and visitors and workmen and merchants. It was a menagerie of human-kind and automotive-kind all moving hurriedly together to get from one place to the next, existing in perfect symbiosis. These denizens of the road came in all different shapes and sizes and speeds, from trucks, sedans and buses to tractors and carts that should have stayed on the farm but had—for unknown reasons—been turned into makeshift caravans.

The sights and smells and peoples of the Bolton Road kept Megan entertained, at least until Robert casually put his hand on her knee. This wasn't the first time, but she wasn't about to let him get away with it unchastised.

"If we get pulled over should I let the cops open the trunk?"

He took his hand away and put it back on the wheel. He looked behind him instinctively. "Why would we get pulled over?"

"I tend to speed."

"That is why I'm driving."

"That's not the point, it's a hypothetical question. If we get pulled over, should I let the cops see what's in the trunk?"

"What do you think is in the trunk?"

"I don't know—that's why I'm asking."

Robert smiled but never took his eyes off the road. "There is nothing in the trunk that we don't have a permit for or can't explain."

"So, if we get pulled over I can show the cops what's inside our trunk."

He sighed. "Do you want to know what's in the trunk?"

"Only if you want to tell me."

"Would knowing make you happy?"

"That really depends on what you tell me is in the trunk."

"I'm not so sure that is true."

"Is there something in the trunk that will make me unhappy?"

"There's nothing in the trunk that makes ME unhappy."

"That's not answering the question."

"I am very comfortable with what's in the trunk, because I put it there. It is all properly packed for transport, and there is nothing that we need to worry about, from a safety or legal perspective."

She sat there in silence for a moment. "Are there guns in the trunk?"

"Yes, there are guns in the trunk."

"Is there ammo in the trunk?"

"Yes, there is ammo in the trunk."

"Are there explosives in the trunk?"

"There is a small quantity of explosives in the trunk."

"Are there knives in the trunk?"

"Yes, there are multiple knives in the trunk, including a Persian dagger."

Megan made a small noise with a hint of curiosity. "Ahuh." She let things stew for a moment and then probed for more details. "When you say Persian dagger, do you mean the qama or the peshkabz?"

"Does it matter?"

She shrugged, "Well maybe not to you, but to me the qama is more of a sword, while the peshkabz is more of what I think of as a dagger, something that would slip between defenses, rather than beat through them. The qama is something you might be comfortable with, while the other is more my style. Also, the peshkabz isn't technically from Persia. That particular item is from Afghanistan, and has a handle made from the horn of a goat inlaid with agate."

"I brought the peshkabz."

"Ahuh. And why exactly did you pick that dagger?"

"I know you like it, it's your favorite."

"Actually, the Javanese kris is my favorite."

"No, you like the kris, and it looks good, quite decorative and intimidating, but when you practice you always spend more time with the peshkabz." Robert smiled. "It fits your hand better and is better balanced."

"And you notice these things?"

"I do."

"Hmm," Megan was genuinely surprised. "You watch me practice?"

"I do."

"Careful there, sir, those are dangerous words, and you've said them twice."

"I'll say them again if you want me to."

"Am I supposed to take that as a proposal?"

"You can take it any way you like."

"If it was a proposal it was lacking in both romance and style."

"I never said it was a proposal."

"Well, whatever it was, it still lacked romance and style."

"That would make it much like this car."

Megan was suddenly offended. "What exactly is wrong with the Studebaker Commander? This is a very sturdy car, and quite powerful."

"I will agree that it is very sturdy and powerful, but I find it the complete opposite of stylish, and lacking any ability to spark romance. It is perhaps the most unromantic car I've ever seen."

Megan almost laughed.

"What's so funny?"

"This car, the Studebaker Commander, unromantic, the opposite of stylish, but still sturdy and powerful?"

"Yes."

"I bought it because it reminded me of you." He looked at her, and her eyes grew wide, and a playful smile crept across her face. She leaned over and kissed him, but only for a second. "Keep your eyes on the road darling."

He turned back and kept quiet for a full minute but then couldn't contain himself anymore. "I prefer the Hudson Silver Wing."

She nodded with a stern look on her face. "Duly noted."

Megan spent the remainder of the trip looking out the window, watching as the rural countryside gave way to the industrial town that was Bolton. Bolton was not a handsome place. She recalled that the town had been a planned community; it was built specifically to facilitate the needs of the industrial revolution, and the neighborhoods that consisted entirely of brick row homes provided evidence that her recollections were accurate. As individual buildings they seemed adequate, but the proliferation of them in vast replicated numbers linked the neighborhoods together into a tedious rusty red chain that repulsed and overwhelmed the eye's attempts to find any beauty in their architecture. There had been some attempt to break up the monotony by introducing small parks and clusters of shops and merchants, but it wasn't enough. She preferred the more natural way that cities grew, with houses built individually, each with its own character. The ugliness of the houses extended to the industrial areas as well. The factories and mills were great monoliths, testimonies to the bleak gods of corporate efficiency. Here and there she saw an odd symbol, a circle divided into quarters. At first, she thought it a kind of compass—or perhaps a surveyor's mark of some sort—but as they drove deeper into the core of the town it seemed to proliferate, particularly on public buildings. Slowly she came to realize that it was a stylized wheel that had been adopted as a kind of municipal coda. A symbol of progress, she supposed—but she shuddered as she remembered the book by Wells in which a utopian civilization had used the wheel to crucify their savior instead of the cross.

The only exception to the bleak industrial setting seemed to be a single facility that had somehow rejected the stark, dull-red brickwork in favor of something else. She could still see where the buildings of Delapore Chemical had once been like all the others—you couldn't erase the original completely—but the white paint and the murals of idyllic pastoral scenes did what they could to make things different. It was, in a way, an almost rebellious act and Megan wondered how such a thing had found its way into existence.

"It's a wonderful town," sneered Robert. "Just like I remember it." There was a touch of distaste in his voice.

"You've been here before?"

He nodded, "Back in '24. I had a meeting with Senator Henry Paget Lowe in the Eckert Building."

"I read about that case in your files."

He didn't say anything in response. Instead, he asked, "Do you know what I love about Bolton?"

"No."

"The people."

She looked out the window, a sudden realization crashing to the forefront of her thoughts.

"But there aren't any people." She thought for a moment. "Robert, I haven't seen anyone since we drove into town, not a one!"

"It's a weekday, Megan. Everybody is working."

"But what about the children? There should be children playing in the streets."

"School if they're lucky, the factories if they aren't."

A dour look crossed her face.

"You grew up in Arkham, which is mostly a college town with some merchants and a small port. For the most part it's an affluent area, one where kids were allowed, encouraged even, to play. In other parts of the United States—in places like this—child labor is a necessity, both for factories and families."

They drove on toward their destination, Megan lost in thought.

The Miskatonic University Extension Building was a two-story architectural nightmare that had obviously once been something else but had been retrofitted into an approximation of an academic institution. Oversized gates and windows had been bricked up into smaller, more human-sized openings. There was a titanic smokestack to one side, but beneath it was a smaller chimney that spouted smoke instead. In the lawn that surrounded the place one could still see the remnants of paths where draught animals had drawn carts from one side of the building to another.

As they parked the car, a middle-aged woman emerged from the building and trotted toward them. "Are you Mr. Peaslee?"

"I am," he confirmed as he climbed out of the car, "and this is my partner, Dr. Megan Halsey."

The woman paused for a moment; whether it was because Megan was a woman or a doctor was unclear. "I'm Laura, the receptionist. Professor Rice is waiting for you. If you'll follow me." She turned and hurried back the way she came.

Robert and Megan followed, but not without some reservations. She leaned towards Robert and, almost inaudibly, asked, "Are you sure you don't want something from the trunk?"

"You have your Colts?"

"Of course," she affirmed.

"I'm fine."

The inside of the building was even more of a retrofit than the outside. The floor was old brick—chipped and cracked through years of use—but polished smooth for use as an office. Above them, the lack of a ceiling revealed rough timbers that had been laced with modern pipes and wires. We're in a barn, thought Megan, not that she minded.

Laura led them at a brisk pace through the winding halls of the building and to the back. She opened a creaking door marked *Staff Lounge* and ushered them inside. An older man with an iron-grey beard sat in a wingback chair next to a divan occupied by the prone form of a young man. The man on the divan was not unhandsome, but he looked sickly. He was pale, and his hair was matted with sweat. His lips were cracked and although he appeared unconscious, he was clearly mumbling something. As they approached the old man closed the book he was reading. It was a something old, in a moldering leather binding accented with brass buckles. He slipped it inside the valise that leaned up against the side of his chair. Laura closed the door behind them.

"I'm Professor Rice," said the old man, extending his hand to Robert. "I'm so happy you could come. This is Andrew Potter," He gestured to the young man on the divan.

Megan bypassed the academic and knelt by the sickened student. He was running a fever, and even this close, his muttering remained unintelligible. "How long has he been like this?"

"What? Hmmm… He collapsed in my office yesterday. We brought him here and called for Doctor Loomis. He seemed to think that all the boy needed was rest and some clean food and water. We kept him here. His living conditions… the place is atrocious, filthy. Here was better."

"And the mumbling—when did that begin?"

"Last night, just after midnight. I called Armitage first thing in the morning, and then you right afterward."

Megan made a sound of agreement and then turned the boy's head. "And has he always had these bruises on his neck?"

"What bruises?" The old man came out of the chair and tried to see what Megan was talking about.

While he was distracted, Robert reached into the valise and removed the book Rice had tried to hide from view. He flipped it to the title page, and then thumbed through the body. He made sure that he didn't damage the pages or make much noise.

"I don't see anything of import," said Rice who was obviously annoyed.

Megan looked up, past the old man and at her partner. "What about you Robert, do you see anything of import?"

Robert snapped the book shut causing Rice to jump. "*The Restitution of Decayed Intelligence* by Richard Verstegan. A book on the practice of necromancy, historical mostly, the later chapters look like they contain some rites. Originally published in 1605; this copy rebound by The Restitution Society in 1714. At least that is what the back-end page says." He flipped the book back and forth in his hands. "They didn't do a very good job. "Oh, and this book—I don't think it belongs to him. The last page has a wax seal bearing the name Ralsa Potter."

Megan looked at Rice in the eyes. "You've been up to something Professor, you and Mr. Potter here, something that didn't work out the way you planned. Something you should have left alone." The old man shrank into himself. "You better explain things sir, and very quickly."

"It was Potter," the old man stammered. "He found me, sought me out really. He had read about the events in Dunwich. His family was from a small town on the outskirts of Arkham and was distantly related to the Whateleys. They called Ralsa Potter a wizard, and he use to correspond with Noah Whateley in Dunwich." He stopped thinking that was enough, but an evil look from Megan motivated him to continue. "When Andrew was a child, his mother had an incident—one not unlike what had happened in Dunwich, but obviously with less explosive results. When Andrew came of age, he inherited everything that his family had owned, including the library of Ralsa Potter. He wanted to understand what had happened to him, to his mother, his entire family. He thought I could help. He thought I could protect him, God help me, I thought I could protect him!"

"How exactly?"

"What?" The old man was on the verge of blubbering.

Robert pulled him to his feet. "How exactly did you think you could protect him?"

"The book said the Vach-Viraj Incantation would be effective, that it would keep us safe, but..." his voice trailed off.

"But you screwed it up. You got the pronunciation wrong. And something leaked through and took possession." Megan was almost yelling.

"Do you know what the first rule of necromancy is, Professor Rice?" Robert gave him a split second to respond. "I know it, so does my partner, but you don't—do you?"

Rice shook his head in a kind of panic.

"*Never bring up that which you cannot readily put down!* That is rule number one, first lesson, page one, paragraph one, sentence number one. But you didn't even bother to read the book, did you? You just skipped ahead and thought you would go right to the back. Do you even know what you brought up?"

"Andrew said it was the thing that had been inside his mother, the thing that had made him a prisoner and a slave in his own home. It was something black and nebulous, something that Wizard Potter had brought down to serve him. When the old man died it was left behind, and when Andrew and his family moved in, it latched on to Andrew's mother, and maybe even Andrew himself."

"How did they get rid of it?"

"There was a schoolteacher, and a man from Miskatonic University. They drove it out."

Robert was losing his patience. "I didn't ask who, I asked how."

Rice finally started crying. "I don't know. Andrew was just a kid, he couldn't remember." There were tears pouring down his face. "He was only a little kid."

On cue, the body of Andrew Potter rose up from the divan, screaming. "*He comes!*"

The voice was strange—tinny and strained, like a radio tuned in from far, far away. "*He comes from beyond the stars, from beyond the Hyades, from beyond the shores of Hali. He comes on the wind, the hungering, tearing wind.*" Then he opened his mouth wide and from that black, yawning maw came the most haunting of cries, it was a hollow, wind-blown sound that filled the room and forced the others to cover their ears.

Robert pulled Megan out of the way as the thing that was Andrew Potter lunged forward and grabbed at Professor Rice. Megan kicked back and caught the young man in the shoulder. It was a solid hit and should have knocked him backwards on to the floor. Instead, it knocked him upwards into the air where he floated, laughing.

"*He has come!*" The phantasmagoric man announced, and then the room exploded in a concussive blast that cracked the walls and blew out all the windows in the study. Potter floated out of the largest of the shattered windows, glass falling behind him like rain.

On the other side of the room, Robert was pulling Megan through the door and cursing up a storm. "Goddamn academics! Just because they can do something doesn't mean they should." He stalked down the hall and Megan followed. "If it were up to me, I would burn all these damn books." He waved the crumbling grimoire in the air. "And then I might throw the academics on top." He looked back at the aged teacher who was trailing behind them, almost limping along. Robert stopped and turned; he shook the book in the old man's direction. "You would be the first on the pile!"

Behind them they could hear the rumbling thunder that wasn't thunder and Potter's chanting in a voice as booming as the not-thunder in the courtyard. It only took a few more seconds for them to reach the parking lot. Robert popped the trunk and went about getting what he needed. Megan watched as Rice stumbled beneath a tree and collapsed.

That was how they had come to be in a car speeding toward some alien monstrosity on the outskirts of Bolton, with a packet of dynamite between them.

They whipped around the first corner of the building and Robert banked hard to bring them around the next one and into the courtyard. Potter was there in the sky, his arms outstretched like some abysmal deity. The darkness surrounded him, enveloped him, extruded from him. Megan had thought it had looked like tar, but it was more than that, and less. It was a nebulous sort of matter that flowed and spun in titanic vortices that seemed to open into the space beyond the sky itself.

"Remember when I said that I hoped I wouldn't have to shoot him?"

Megan had her guns out. "That's not what you said, but I get your meaning!" She rolled down the window and leaned out, pulling the trigger on both guns. There were sparks where the bullets should have hit, but not on Potter's body—rather, on the fluidic gas that spun around him.

"I can't get through," she yelled. The whipping wind drowned out the sound of her voice, but Robert understood what she had meant. He reached down, picked up the bundle of dynamite and handed it to Megan. She turned it over and over again in her hand. "Where's the fuse?"

Robert looked at her in shock and slammed his hand against the dashboard. "It's in the goddamned trunk!" He slid the car sideways to avoid a tendril of whirling debris. "Throw it! He yelled. "Throw it at Potter!" His left hand began rolling down his own window.

She did as she was told. Robert turned the steering wheel hard to the left as the dynamite arced through the air toward the thing in the sky. It was growing larger, more substantial. It wasn't even vaguely man-shaped anymore—it was more like an immense starfish with dozens of branching tentacles.

He took both hands off the wheel and forced himself shotgun-first through the window. He knew that Megan would take over driving. The spinning winds of darkness were full of mundane things; like a tornado might, it had picked up bricks and furniture, some small trees and bushes. He saw a lamp fly by, and then a tea kettle. He focused on the bundle of dynamite and waited for it to drift toward Potter, then he pulled the trigger and hoped for the best.

He saw the shot hit, saw the tiny spark, followed by a puff of grey smoke that vanished almost instantly in the roaring winds. He saw the dynamite shrink a little bit and then explode outward, and then the sky was full of fire and smoke that enveloped Potter. He screamed in agony, but only for a moment. Then he was gone, and the black, swirling vortices of impending doom began to fall apart and dissipate.

Megan was driving from the passenger seat, sliding the car sideways trying to line up for a clear shot out of the courtyard. But it wasn't happening—the ground was too soft, and the car was going too fast. She was sliding all over the place, doing her best to dodge obstacles. Then shock wave of the explosion hit, and the car was forced down into the earth where the tires quickly dug themselves in, stranding the car beneath the dying winds and the accompanying deluge of objects they had picked up.

Robert tumbled out of the window, scrambling to his feet and yelled "Run!" even before he realized that Megan had already popped the door open and was well on her way toward the tree line. She may have had a head start, but his legs were longer, and he caught up with her after only a few desperate strides. They dove for the dubious safety of some tiny knoll or clump of dirt, rolled to the side and then turned to watch as the sorcerous gale-force winds subsided, and the debris began to rain down from the sky.

It was a blizzard of bricks, rocks, wood and sand, and all other matter of material. It fell like a torrential downpour, pelting the car and creating a metallic staccato as if thousands of hammers were being taken to the Studebaker. Larger debris followed. A chair smashed through the front window. A steel beam plummeted through the roof. Megan and Robert watched as their vehicle was slowly beaten into so much scrap metal. Then came the desk, which landed plainly on the back of the trunk, making a scraping sound that made Robert cringe. There was a puff of smoke, and a burst of flames. Robert and Megan got up and ran around to the far side of the building, but they could still hear the trunk full of ammunition as it ignited and burned.

"Tell me there isn't any more dynamite left in the trunk?" Megan asked.

"There is no more dynamite in the trunk," Robert assured her. There was a sudden explosion, small but clear. When they looked back, they could see a cloud of black smoke rising into the sky. "That is not dynamite," Robert assured her. "That is the roll of safety fuse that we needed to set off the dynamite.

Rice came stumbling across the green, more emboldened now that all the work was done. "Is it over? Where's Potter?"

Robert jabbed a finger into his chest. "Potter is dead—probably incinerated, which is what you and everybody else would be if it weren't for us." He was obviously frustrated. "I suggest, Professor, that you stick to teaching and stop meddling about with things you don't understand." He walked away before his temper got the best of him.

Megan smiled at the old man. "All this is clearly the result of a freak weather phenomenon, and you're lucky that more people weren't hurt or killed." She took his hand and shook it, he seemed confused. "We will be sending you a bill. If you don't want the authorities and Miskatonic University to find out what really happened, I suggest you pay it." She followed Robert, catching up to him as he walked toward the road. He put his arm around her.

"Where are you going?" she asked.

"Train station."

"You have money for that?"

He nodded and put his hand to his chest. "Billfold right here." But there was something more, something larger.

"Robert?"

"Yes?"

"What happened to Laura?"

"Who?"

"Laura, the receptionist."

He pulled her a little closer. "Don't know. At the moment, not really my biggest concern."

"I suppose getting back to Arkham is your biggest concern?"

"Nope." He reached into his coat and pulled out the old leather-bound grimoire. "I should burn this."

"You should, but you won't."

"Why is that?"

"Because I want it," she was suddenly coy, "as a wedding present."

Robert stopped in his tracks and looked at her as she continued down the road. "You want to get married?"

She walked back to him, looked down at the ground and kicked at a rock. Then, looking up, she pulled him closer. "I do."

The Acquisition of Mariah Lieberman

October 26, 1928

Doctor Cyrus Llanfer, the acting head of Miskatonic University's library, was a nervous little man. He sat in the offices of Halsey, Peaslee and Lydecker fiddling with the hat in his hand and his left leg restlessly bouncing, a nervous habit he probably didn't even notice anymore. Across from him, in the more comfortable chairs, sat Robert Peaslee and his new wife Megan Halsey. They tried once more to explain that their other partner would not be in attendance.

"I'm sorry, Doctor Llanfer, but you've arrived without an appointment. If you had called ahead, we would have advised coming at a different time. You must understand that Mr. Lydecker is an invalid. He must keep a rather strict schedule. He cannot see you at the moment."

The old man snorted. "Mr. Peaslee, I'm a very busy man, very busy. If you assure me that whatever we discuss here is to be kept in confidence, I'll take you at your word. I know your father, and your brother. I assume you are as trustworthy as they." He stopped playing with the hat and gripped it tightly. "Of late, the university—particularly the library—has been experiencing some security issues that have resulted in stains on its reputation. You are aware, of course, of the death of Walter Gilman, and of that of Wilbur Whateley, and the subsequent Dunwich Horror. There have been other incidents." He reached into his valise and removed a rather thick file which he handed to Robert. "You'll find these detailed reports educational. At Doctor Armitage's urging, the library has authorized funds to institute new protocols to protect the collection, students, staff, and the reputation of the university. I would like to see a written proposal from your firm on my desk in the next ten days."

Robert handed the file to Megan, who flipped it open. There were sections on various security breaches, problematic students, and the rights of access that faculty, staff, students and the public had been accustomed to. There were even architectural drawings, floor plans and schematics of the library and adjacent buildings. Toward the back there were descriptions of various staff members, their backgrounds and skills. To Megan's mind it looked to be everything they would need to respond to Llanfer's request.

"This should suffice to get us started. If we need anything, we'll be in touch. Should we call you, or is there somebody else we should contact?"

"As I said, I'm a rather busy man. If you would contact Miss Lieberman…" but he never finished that sentence. "I'm sorry, force of habit. Miss Liberman is no longer with us. You can contact Mr. Alwyn; I'll be sure to instruct him to work with you." He seemed suddenly sadder. He stood up. "Well, I think that should get you started."

Robert Peaslee rose and shook his hand. "Thank you, sir. You won't be disappointed." He led Llanfer to the door.

"Dr. Llanfer," Megan called out. "Two questions before you go. Why the sudden urgency?"

"I don't understand, young lady. What do you mean?"

"The deaths of Wilbur Whateley and Walter Gilman happened quite some time ago. You could have initiated a new security system months ago. Why now? Why come to us without an appointment?"

He looked at her from across the room and was obviously a little perturbed by the question. "We had another incident earlier in the week. A member of staff had to be hospitalized… you'll find a report in the back."

Megan nodded. "Second question, what happened to Miss Lieberman?"

The old man was suddenly apoplectic. He put on his hat and buttoned his coat. "I told you, Miss Halsey—you'll find a report in the back!" With that, Robert showed him the door—there might even have been an apology. Though, if there was, it was doubtful that Llanfer had heard it.

"What's the deal with Lieberman?" asked Robert as he came back into the office.

Megan held up the woman's thin file, showing him the top page.

"Those are orders committing Mariah Lieberman to the care of the Sefton Asylum."

Megan nodded. "With payment coming from the University." She closed the file with a snap. "The papers are dated four days ago."

"I'm thinking we should go visit Miss Lieberman and see what we can learn."

"I'll get my coat."

········

"I'm sorry, but as you can see Miss Lieberman isn't in any condition to answer any questions. She's barely spoken a word since she arrived." Doctor Eli Loomis gestured at his patient and almost shrugged.

Mariah Lieberman was a middle-aged woman with dark hair and a thin build. Some might have called her striking, but that was before she was committed. The woman before them was a forlorn husk, with the vestiges of whatever beauty she once possessed clinging to her raggedly. There was something sad about the way she looked now, as if she was thinking about something that she had forgotten and still couldn't remember.

Loomis, on the other hand, was rather bright and young. A handsome man with clear eyes and a strong aquiline nose. Megan couldn't place his accent. There was a touch of New England, but a touch of the old world as well. Megan looked at his office wall, adorned with degrees from Harvard and All Saints College. To one side there was a picture of him with an older man and a young boy. She stood up and walked over to get a closer look. There was a strong family resemblance.

"Is this your father, and your son?"

"Ah, yes. Three generations of Loomis men. My father Donald is a physician up in Bolton. My son Samuel is something of a prodigy—ten years old and already preparing for a career as a physician."

"And you went to All Saints and Harvard?" He nodded. "Did you have the opportunity to study under Sir Roderick Glossup or Morton Prince?"

He stood up, surprised that a woman might have such knowledge. "Yes, yes I did."

"They're both proponents of hypnotherapy, Doctor Loomis. Perhaps such a course of treatment night help Miss Lieberman?"

He thought for a moment. "It might, but it also might damage her already fragile condition—drive her deeper into her own mind. It could leave her catatonic."

Robert stood up and put a hand on the Doctor's shoulder. "We need to know what happened to her. There must be a way."

Megan smiled. "The hospital is always in need of funds, isn't it Doctor Loomis?" She reached into her bag and pulled out a small packet of bills. "I would be very interested in making a donation." She placed the bills on the corner of his desk. "Is one hundred dollars sufficient?"

"Well—" he picked up the money, and seemed to weigh it. "These are special circumstances, and it would help to know what happened to her," he said, and shook the bills to make his point. He spoke again as the money rustled disappeared into a pocket. "To further her treatment and recovery, of course."

"Of course," Megan smiled as Robert gave the Doctor a friendly pat.

··········

It was about twenty minutes later that a nurse led the two investigators into an exam room where Mariah Lieberman was sitting, while Loomis stood behind her with his hands on her shoulders. The room was stark white with a single lamp hanging from the ceiling. It was all terribly clinical.

Loomis was smiling and speaking softly, but very deliberately. "She's under, and very receptive. She's talking but is very reluctant to speak about the day in question. "I've created the suggestion that she is not Mariah Lieberman—that she is a woman named Maria who was only seeing through Mariah Lieberman's eyes, hearing through her ears... I'm trying to disassociate her from the actual event. It should give her a sense of distance and security, make it easier for her to talk about it."

The two investigators nodded but remained quiet.

"Maria, can you hear me?"

"Yes doctor, I can hear you." Her voice was emotionless, almost monotonal.

"Maria, I want you to go back to that day at Miskatonic University. I want you to tell me what you saw, what Mariah Lieberman saw."

A look of distress came across her face. "I don't want to do that; I don't want to think about that."

"Maria," he was very stern. "You are completely safe. There is nothing to be afraid of. Now tell me what you saw that day."

Her face relaxed and became eerily calm. Megan thought perhaps nothing would happen, that the memories were too traumatic, but then Mariah opened her mouth and told them what she saw happen to Mariah that fateful day.

··········

Mariah Lieberman stared at the woman sitting in her office and sighed in frustration and apprehension. As Director of Acquisitions, it was her responsibility to supply books for the ever-growing library of Miskatonic University. Usually that meant negotiating with publishers; occasionally it meant dealing with individuals in possession of or with access to private collections of interest to the university. In her experience such individuals were rather pleasant, most of the time. The woman, who had been waiting for twenty minutes, was someone Lieberman had no desire to encounter. Her name was Phaedra Whateley and by all accounts she was a rather detestable human being.

She had been waiting twenty minutes because Lieberman was doing her best to delay any kind of interaction until after the rest of the office had left for the day. She may have to negotiate with the woman, but she would be damned if she would do it in front of the staff. No one really wanted to meet with the Whateley woman, but since Judge Zellaby had ruled in her favor and declared her the sole legal heir to the Whateley Estate one could, despite one's desires, no longer treat Ms. Whateley as a pariah. This was especially true given that the woman now owned the farmland in Dunwich, the ruin of a house that was once the familial manse, and the family library—which contained a veritable treasure trove of manuscripts both rare and dangerous. Henry Armitage, the Head Librarian, had seen that collection of ancient tomes, and briefly had possession of Wilbur Whateley's diary, until the judge had ordered it turned over to the estate administrator. By all accounts the library was extensive, damaged and in need of repair, and it housed perhaps the single largest collection of occult writings in New England.

Legally, the library belonged to Phaedra Whateley, but Henry Armitage wanted it—and the old man had made it clear that he expected Lieberman to make the acquisition happen.

So, Lieberman had reached out to Phaedra Whateley's lawyers and begun negotiations. There had been some back and forth, and a variety of concessions had been made, but both teams had eventually found a price and conditions they could agree to. Lieberman had expected to just sign the contract and then have Whateley do the same, but that idea had been rejected. Phaedra had demanded a meeting, without lawyers—just the two of them. They agreed on a time, and Lieberman had cleared her schedule. Even so, she hadn't expected Whateley to show up herself; she expected the woman to cancel at the last minute or send some attorney or another in her place. But there she was, sitting in the office, waiting patiently.

She wasn't an unattractive woman. She was an albino—apparently a trait inherited from her mother, with white crinkly hair worn long in a braid down her back. Her skin was creamy pale, her eyes were wide set and pale pink, an unnatural color reflected in her lips. She didn't have the Whateley chin, meaning that she actually had one—a strong one—with a powerfully set jaw line that reminded Lieberman of a horse. The equine comparison was not without merit. There was something about her build, the cut of her shoulders, the thickness of her thighs—Lieberman had seen sketches of her brother Wilbur, whose face had been goat-like, but Phaedra's face was thicker, more powerful. She was wearing gloves and a rather long and heavy coat, which gathered around her boots in rolls on the polished wooden floor. Mariah thought the coat odd; it was cold out, but not that cold—it was only October.

Just looking at the woman made Lieberman uneasy, she didn't want to talk to her, but she had to. If she was to do what Armitage had ordered her to, if she was going to acquire the books he wanted, then she was going to have to talk to Phaedra Whateley, sooner or later. Thankfully, just as she began to feel she had delayed the confrontation beyond the limits of civility, she saw the last clerk clock out and wave goodbye. Finally, she was alone. This part of the library, the Acquisitions Department, wasn't in the library proper; it wasn't even part of the night watchman's patrol. She took a deep breath, opened the door, and went inside.

"Miss Whateley, sorry to keep you waiting." As she shut the door behind her, she closed the window blinds as well, just in case someone did come back. It's not that she wanted privacy; she was embarrassed—ashamed, really. This meeting made her feel dirty, unclean. Phaedra Whateley was the last member of the decayed Whateleys, a family that had—rumor held—committed unspeakable acts of depravity. She was afraid that being seen with this woman might taint her somehow.

"That's quite alright, Ms. Lieberman—or is it Doctor?" Her voice was reedy, like a bassoon.

"Doctor Lieberman, please." There was a scent about Phaedra; it got into her head and rattled around in there. It reminded her of a girl she knew in college. Her name had been Cheryl and she had worn lavender and rosewater. They had walked along the sea in Connecticut, eaten lobster rolls in the shadow of the dunes. That had been a long time ago.

"Not at all." Phaedra smiled as Mariah took her chair. "I understand from my lawyers that all the paperwork is in order. Is this true?"

"In a word, yes. All that's left is to sign one last document finalizing the agreement."

Her guest made a queer sound—a clicking noise—and then slid a slip of paper across the desk. "This is a check from a bookseller in California, a man named Geiger. He's offering a substantial amount of money, as you can see."

Lieberman glanced at the slip of paper and nodded. "I know of Mr. Geiger. He's a shrewd businessman. If you are looking for more money, I'm afraid I'll have to speak with Doctor Armitage." She slid the check back.

"I'm sorry. You misunderstand me, Doctor Lieberman." She pulled out the contract and flipped it open. "It's not about the money—I share Mister Geiger's check with you only to make that clear. It's the other considerations, those outlined on this page that concern me." Suddenly there was a sheet of paper in her hand. "I need to make sure you and the university understand them."

Lieberman reached out for the contract and brushed the woman's pale white fingers. They were warm—electric—like Cheryl's. Cheryl was always warm. Her lips were like small fires, and her eyes had smoldered when Mariah looked into them. When they embraced in the dark, naked beneath the sheets, Cheryl's nipples had felt like burning coals.

She read the page, and distractedly recalled the details—including the concessions she and her legal department had previously agreed to—aloud.

"You want the books restored and to be designated the Whateley Collection."

The strange woman nodded slightly.

"And access in perpetuity for any member of the Whateley Family."

"Yes, as long as they can properly prove a relation."

"And you personally want full access to the library, including all the special collections."

"Is any of this a problem?"

Mariah Lieberman looked into those eyes—those pink eyes set in alabaster skin. She suddenly realized how exotic, how strangely beautiful, the woman was. "No, I don't think so." Her lips seemed to glow.

The smile on Phaedra Whateley's face grew larger. "Good. Then there is no reason not to sign, is there?" She flipped the contract to the last page. Lieberman could see where Whateley had signed, and the space where she should as well.

"Not at all." Mariah Lieberman took her pen from the well on the desk and with a flourish signed her name across the bottom of the page. Instead of handing it across the desk, she stood up and walked around the desk. She knelt down next to the woman and placed it gently in her hands, letting their fingers touch again.

This close Mariah could see the way Phaedra's neck arced, the curve of her bosom, the width of her hips. It was all so alluring, so reminiscent of Cheryl. In an instant, Mariah realized that Phaedra Whateley wasn't repulsive at all—exactly the opposite, really. "Miss Whateley—Phaedra—after a transaction of this size, it is customary to celebrate. Could I convince you to have dinner with me this evening?"

Phaedra Whateley stood and glowed at the woman. "I'm supposed to be visiting Judge Zellaby in the hospital tonight. He was very helpful in establishing my claim to the Whateley estate. You are correct though; we should celebrate, you and I."

Lieberman felt her heart quicken. "I followed the case, I even read the court documents, strictly professional interest of course, so that I knew whom to approach for the books. And," Mariah paused here—a hopeful pause—then asked, "Didn't the judge have a breakdown of some sort?"

"His doctors say that he has a nervous condition. They claim he is overworked. I think they aren't very good doctors."

Mariah Lieberman stood up, her mind remembering some things about the case, details she had forgotten. She was suddenly very curious, she wanted to know all about this captivating woman before her. "The other heirs challenged your claim. Said that your birth certificate was fake. That there was no proof that you were even a Whateley at all. How did you convince Zellaby that you had a right to the entire estate?"

The albino woman smiled, "I'm not just any Whateley. I'm Lavinia's first child, Wilbur's older half-sister, the result of my grandfather's first attempt to find a suitable partner for my mother. I was an embarrassment, really—not what he had expected at all. He sent me away to live with relatives in Ashborough. I don't think anyone in Dunwich ever knew I even existed."

"But that's my point. With only a dubious birth certificate how did you convince Zellaby that your claim superseded all others?"

"Oh, that was easy." She stood up and began to unbutton her coat. "I showed the Judge incontrovertible evidence." The coat fell away, and the evidence she had shown to Judge Zellaby, she now showed to Doctor Mariah Lieberman.

What resided there beneath Phaedra's coat was the most beautiful thing she had ever seen, and she screamed when she saw Phaedra in all her true glory. She screamed in awe, in devotion, and in adoration of it. She screamed because she had no words to describe what she saw, for there were no words. She screamed because it was the most natural reaction a human being could have, and because she could do nothing else.

She fell to the floor but couldn't take her eyes off the body of Phaedra Whateley: what was there, what was within, and what was beyond. The thing that was beneath Phaedra Whateley's coat writhed with tentacles of living light, and pulsing fronds that reached out and played over Lieberman's body. With each touch Lieberman's brain, her spinal cord, her nerves were flooded with impossible sensations. She saw the agonizing shrill of her own screams, she tasted the bitter-sweet paleness of Phaedra's hair, she felt her cold and damp fear as it washed over and enveloped her like a wave at the beach. The word 'synesthesia' floated to the surface of her mind, but only for a moment. She understood what was happening to her, and for just a brief second, she even thought that in doing so she might have an opportunity, a chance, a way to stop it, to survive it—to perhaps even control it. But that moment was lost as the luminous entity reached out and enveloped the body, mind and soul of Mariah Lieberman.

And then she was lost, and there was only the screaming, and clawing at her own flesh, trying to feel something familiar, trying to feel something human, trying to hold on to her humanity, to tear out what was left and hold it in her hands. It was only then that Phaedra Whateley closed her coat. But that didn't stop the librarian from screaming; that only ceased when her throat became raw, and her vocal cords tore apart. After that, all she could do was sob. She was still sobbing the next morning when the staff found her. She was curled up on the floor, and the contract for acquiring the Whateley Collection still on the desk, the signatures all very proper.

············

Postscript by Roman Lydecker

The Whateley Collection was delivered to Miskatonic University in early November 1928. Under the direction of Miss Stanley, the individual books were assessed and prioritized. It is estimated that preparing all four-hundred-and-thirty-six books for limited circulation will take approximately four years. The university has made the restoration of the Whateley Collection a priority and has budgeted accordingly. In order to accelerate the project, the library is seeking donations through the venerable bibliophilic charity known as The Restitution Society.

As part of their revamped security protocols for the library at Miskatonic University, Robert and Megan urged that the contract with Phaedra Whateley be honored, and an identification card granting her full access to the library in perpetuity was included along with the check that was delivered to her lawyers. Armitage objected of course, but conceded when it was made clear that not doing so would put the university at more than just legal risk. The training manual for clerks and other staff now has a section on dealing with special visitors. There is a picture of Phaedra Whateley posted at the reception desk. They like to think they are prepared for when she visits.

As for Mariah Lieberman, Doctor Loomis was right—the hypnotherapy session caused her to withdrawal even further. One week after Megan and Robert's visit she took a spoon and before anyone could stop her, she dug out her own eyes. Since then, she has been sedated, so that she could hurt neither herself nor anyone else. But the drugs don't stop her from dreaming, and when she sleeps Mariah Lieberman's hands and arms seem to embrace some long-forgotten lover. Every so often she cries out a name, but staff aren't sure whether that name is Cheryl or Phaedra, not even her doctors can tell.

Perhaps even Mariah Lieberman does not know.

The Man Who Wasn't There

Megan Halsey

January 25, 1929

It was in the first week of January, about four months after our firm was hired to improve security at the Miskatonic University Library, that the night watchman called and summoned me. By all rights Robert should have gone, and indeed he was requested, but he was out wandering the city, a victim of his inability to sleep. Therefore, it was I that drove down to the campus security office in the cold, well after midnight, to confront the intruder that had been ensnared by our improved measures. In this case that had been to vary the route used by the guards during their patrols. It was in actuality very simple. We had developed ten versions of the nightly patrol route and staff were assigned to follow a different one each night, meaning that the entire set would be run through in ten days. However, as there were only seven days in the week, the application of a particular pattern to a particular day of the week was always shifting. The idea was to make the pattern of guard visits difficult to predict, and sure enough, somebody had been caught by our deviously simple plan.

That someone was a twenty-two-year-old male whose wallet identified him as Curtis Harvey, a student of Engineering at Yale. We were more than one hundred and fifty miles from New Haven, which suggested Mr. Harvey's intrusion into the library archives was a casual prank more than a little suspicious. What also piqued my interest was the box of files he had been attempting to depart with. It had been a box full of files and notebooks from a student project almost three decades old. To the guard it was just a jumble of old notebooks and papers, but to me what was in that box was nearly invaluable, and incredibly dangerous. I looked at the box, trying to figure out who he was and why he wanted this particular box.

"Are you sure you don't want to wait until morning?" the security guard asked, pulling me out of my own thoughts.

"Hmmm? No, I don't think so," I muttered. "The sooner we question him, the less time he'll have to come up with a plausible story to explain what he was doing down there." I picked up two thin notebooks out of the box and tucked them under my arm. "Now is as good a time as ever."

I walked into the small holding area where he sat calmly in a simple wooden chair at a simple wooden table. He was as the security guard had described. Young, large but not brutish, handsome in a midwestern sort of way, with dark hair and dark eyes, and very large hands. The holding room was warmer than the others, fueled by a small wood-burning stove that sat in the corner. I made a slight detour as I approached the table and opened the damper on the stove to fan the flames inside. Then I sat down at the table in the second wooden chair and made to introduce myself. "Mr. Harvey, my name is Megan Halsey. I'm in charge of library security. I would like to know exactly what you think you were doing in the library basement tonight."

The young man looked at me as if he knew me. "I have told the guard that I had gotten lost earlier in the day and fallen asleep amongst the stacks." His voice had a particular accent to it, one that wasn't Connecticut in origin, though I couldn't place it.

"And why were you carrying this box of notebooks?"

He shook his head, "I wasn't. I found that box on the floor just moments before the guard found me."

I tossed the two notebooks on the desk between us. "So, these don't mean anything to you?"

He looked without touching them. They were old shabby things bound in cheap leather that had long since been chafed and frayed and torn. Random pieces of paper peeked out from the edges, some obviously pages of the books themselves that had become unbound; others were ephemera too large to be entirely concealed. On the side of each, someone—likely an industrious cataloger—had adhered paper tags identifying the contents. One said

WEST
Laboratory Journal
Summer 1903

The other said

CAIN
Laboratory Journal
Spring 1903

Harvey shook his head. "They're just some old notebooks. They mean nothing to me."

I nodded disappointingly and then picked them up off the table as I stood up. I walked over to the stove and tore the first few pages out of the journal belonging to Cain. Harvey showed no reaction and seemed entirely disinterested. He showed no reaction as I opened the stove door and shrugged as I fed the pages into the fire. When I threw the rest of Cain's book in after the rest, he still showed no reaction.

"I told you Miss Halsey—I don't have any interest in those books."

I threw the other journal in after the first. Harvey flew across the table diving for the stove and the book that I had just tossed in. He went to push me out of the way, but despite his size and youth he was no match for my training. I caught him on the back of the head with my elbow and then used his momentum to swing him around and sit him down on his rump with his face toward the stove. I held him there as the pages quickly caught and turned into black brittle sheets of ash tinged with an ember edge.

With one arm across his neck, he cursed at me. "Damn you. Do you know what you've just done? How much time and effort you have just cost me?" He coughed. "You had no right!"

I relaxed my arm and used my knee to push Harvey to the ground and raise me up at the same time. "That journal," I said straightening my shirt, "was written by Herbert West, as part of his time here at the university. As such, it is part of his academic file and the joint property of West and the university."

Still prone Harvey growled over his shoulder. "You stupid cow, *I am Herbert West!*"

It was a lie. Herbert West was a much older man, shorter, thinner, less muscular, with a mop of unkempt white hair. I had of course read of the advances in plastic surgery achieved by Gillies and Mowlem, but the techniques that would have been needed to transform West into Harvey were unheard of. It was impossible that this man was who he claimed to be, and I told him so.

He laughed as he staggered to his feet. "Not impossible Miss Halsey." He brushed himself off. "How could you think such a thing? After all, you yourself are the product of what was once thought impossible."

He was not wrong on that point, and even knowing the facts that had brought about my birth lent credence to his claim. I reached out to him with my mind—I had since childhood had some ability to sense the reanimated, to touch their minds, even to influence their behavior—but with this man there was nothing of that. He was alive, and therefore when it came to my extrasensory perception he didn't even exist. I pointed at the table and gestured for him to sit. "Explain to me how this happened," I pointed up and down at his body.

He wandered slowly back to the other side of the table, nursing his chin as he went. He sat down and smiled, there was blood in his teeth. I hadn't realized I had been so hard on him. "I won't bore you with the details," he offered. "Let me just say that my old body had become compromised. A change needed to be made or else the world would have been denied one of its most brilliant scientific minds."

"You refer to yourself?"

He bowed his head, "Of course."

"When you say your original body had been compromised, this was some side effect of the reanimation process?"

Harvey's face went pale. "No, not at all. Given proper care and maintenance, the reanimation reagent appears to bestow indefinite life to its subjects."

I shook my head, "A semblance of life."

"As you say," he conceded my point, "No, the loss of my body was the result of an experiment in which I applied the reagent to . . ."

"I would rather not know the details," I cut him off. "You transferred your mind to Harvey's body, how?"

"Well not at first. My first host was less than ideal—a hobo, chosen simply because I was desperate to escape my rapidly deteriorating condition. I didn't do it alone, of course; I had read about the theory of mental transmigration but had no skill in it. Thankfully, a friend of mine knew someone who did—someone who was more than willing to assist me, for a price." He sniggered a bit.

"What is so funny?"

"My rescuer, the person who taught me how to . . ." then he stopped and seemed to reconsider things. "It is perhaps better for me to not reveal too much. Not my place to disclose a lady's secrets." He looked at me as if I he was holding the world's greatest secret. "Anyway, after inhabiting the rather obnoxious hobo, I travelled down to Yale to visit my friend Alberto Balsamo. I had hoped he might find a way to restore my original self. Sadly, he had moved on. Fortunately, I discovered that Mr. Harvey was highly susceptible to the mental transference process. It's a good body. Young, strong, rather handsome in its own way. It will do until I find something more suitable."

"Why bother, if, as you say, it's a good body?"

He sighed. "There is something lacking. The hands and fingers lack dexterity; their coordination is poor. It's likely related to what Thorndike calls motor memory; the muscles are trained for coarser work. I am like a mouse trying to sneak around in a bull's body, lumbering through the china shop. I need something more graceful, something with more delicate hands." He held out his large heavily calloused hands. "At least until I get my own body back."

"And how exactly do you plan to do that?"

He looked at me suspiciously. "You know how, Miss Halsey; you saw what was beneath that mansion on Long Island. I will clone myself, and when the time comes, I will displace the mind of the child with that of my own, and Herbert West will live once more!"

There was a knock at the door, a signal I had been expecting. I excused myself and exited the room as swiftly as possible. Outside I was greeted by Doctor Charles Hoffman, a member of the faculty who had rights at Sefton Asylum. He was flanked by two rather large orderlies and a charming young woman, none of whom I recognized.

"You heard?" I asked Hoffman.

He nodded. "More than enough. A strange and fascinating delusion. We'll admit him immediately. It will be a most fascinating case." He turned to the woman behind him. "What do you think, Barbara? Ready to take one on by yourself?"

The young woman smiled. "More than ready, Doctor Hoffman."

Hoffman suddenly realized his manners. "I'm sorry," his finger wagged between myself and the woman called Barbara. "Doctor Megan Halsey, meet Doctor Barbara Bishop. Barbara is my new assistant, freshly minted form her internship at St. Mary's."

I nodded to her and offered my hand, "Miskatonic University?"

She shook her head and my hand, "No, Women's Medical College in Philadelphia. And you?"

"Shrewsbury in Oxford." I lied; it was a force of habit.

"Do you practice with your husband?" She blushed a little. "I mean professionally."

I laughed to set her at ease. "In a way. We work together as consultants."

"Oh, specialists." She seemed genuinely excited. "What fields?"

Hoffman could no longer bear my avoidance of the subject. "Really Barbara, Miss Halsey doesn't practice medicine—she and her husband are private detectives." He suddenly guffawed. "You two are married, aren't you?"

I smiled, "Most recently, and the last time I checked our license was still valid."

"Good, very good," muttered Hoffman. "Now, we will take good care of Mr. Harvey. Do you think that will be of any help to us?" He gestured at the box of notebooks and files.

I tossed the journal I was holding in with all the others and shook my head. "No, I don't think so." I rummaged around and pulled out another notebook. "Some kind of clerical error—the top two books did belong to Herbert West and his classmate Daniel Cain, but the rest of the file is just full of junk. Look for yourself." I furled the book open. "Just blank pages."

"Useless, then," muttered Hoffman. "Well, thank you for calling us. We shall take it from here."

I picked up the box, and as I did Barbara touched my arm. "I hope you don't find this too forward, but I would love to sit down and speak with you about your work. I find it a tad fascinating."

"Of course, but unfortunately my husband and I are leaving. We're spending the month in Palm Beach. Can I call you at Hoffman's office when we get back?"

"That would be wonderful," she said.

And with that I left the security office, the box of ersatz documents tucked under my arm. I brought them home with me and spent an hour in front of the fireplace burning the contents. I had seen the box before, and the clerical error that had filled it with blank files and notebooks had been mine. This was just one example of my—well, both Robert's and my—attempts to destroy certain records held by Miskatonic University. It was a slow and tedious process, but we had, over the last few weeks, made sure that some of the more dangerous experiments and procedures performed over the past few decades would never be repeated.

That in the process I had been able to confine Herbert West to the Sefton Asylum seemed to be a rather special bonus, and I went with my husband to Florida feeling rather pleased with myself.

I shouldn't have.

It was in late January that I learned what happened while I was away. We had been back in Arkham for a few days, and I was on campus for one thing or another and saw Hoffman in the library. I then remembered that his assistant, Doctor Barbara Bishop, had wanted to sit down with me. I caught Hoffman's attention and asked if he could convey a message to Barbara for me.

He sighed and replied in the negative. "Barbara isn't with me anymore; in fact, she's gone back to Philadelphia." He sighed. "I think she took the death of her patient very seriously. Too seriously."

I was confused. "What patient?"

"That boy, from Yale, what was his name—Harvey. The one you called us in for. Poor fellow, his condition deteriorated rapidly, just after you left. A new year is often difficult for our patients; they are often left out of family festivities."

I was in shock but managed to mutter out a request for an explanation.

"That first week was rough on the ward, and more so for Harvey, who had taken to his bed and become nearly catatonic, chanting some strange sounds that I hesitate to even suggest were words. Barbara stayed with him all night and then sometime in the morning she cried out. The orderlies found her on the hallway floor unconscious. She couldn't remember what happened, but we all supposed that Harvey had reached through the bars and assaulted her. She had these strange bruises on her throat that looked like fingerprints."

"And what of Harvey—was he still catatonic?"

"No, he was awake, but his mania had metamorphosed. He no longer thought he was Herbert West. Instead, he thought he was Barbara Bishop." Hoffman raised his eyebrows in a kind of academic fascination. "Quite an interesting case, really. I wish that he was still around to study."

"You don't have Harvey at Sefton anymore?"

"No—sad, really. I had arranged to meet with Harvey and was on my way in. Apparently at the same time, an orderly was bringing Harvey out of his cell. There had never been any indications of violence before—the orderly had no reason to think there would be now. Harvey broke free and threw himself against the window of the upper floor. He fell into the bushes right in front of me. The doctors say he would have survived the fall, but the plate glass severed an artery and he bled out before anyone could do anything about it. Barbara sent me a note the next day resigning. I wanted to stop her, plead with her to stay, but she had already left the night before."

My hands were shaking, "The note, was it handwritten?"

"No," said Hoffman, 'Which is odd because Barbara always had such beautiful handwriting—rare for a doctor. She was very proud of her handwriting, described it as 'delicate'." He paused and smiled awkwardly. "Funny."

"What?"

He shrugged a little with his hands. "When Harvey fell from the window, he didn't die right away. I was there with him, and he said the most curious thing. I hadn't thought about it until just now when we were talking about Barbara."

"What did he say, Doctor?"

"He said—at least I think he said—'He wanted me for my hands. Can you imagine that? He wanted me for my hands. My delicate hands.' Isn't that an odd thing to say before dying? The transference to the new personality must have been utterly complete."

I cannot recall saying anything else to Hoffman; I just ran off and left him. Three days later a detective in Philadelphia sent me a newspaper clipping about the deaths of a Mister and Misses Bishop in the town of Glenside during an automobile accident. Their daughter Barbara survived and was reportedly recovering with friends in an undisclosed location.

I suppose I should have done more. I could have killed West or warned Hoffman. I could have done something more than just play the dilettante detective. A woman is dead because of me—because I didn't do what should have been done. That changes today.

THE ELDRITCH EQUATIONS

PART ONE

A PROBABILITY OF MURDER

First Report

Robert Peaslee

"Your name, sir?"

I didn't really need him to answer. I knew who he was. It would have surprised me if anyone in Arkham didn't. His name and picture had been in all the papers, and I had seen him about the University and other venues over the years. I recognized him through the smoked glass in the door when I went to answer the bell, even though he was noticeably haggard—disheveled, even. His brown suit hung on him loosely, and his face was gaunt and pale, too pale even for early February. Through the window it was hard to say where his face ended. If it weren't for the toss of brown hair, and his eyes, which were tinted pink from lack of sleep—a condition I knew well—I might have lost that face amongst the snow-covered hedges of the rear yard.

The firm of Halsey, Peaslee, & Lydecker had established itself in the lower level of Griffith House. The house itself fronted on West High Street, but the gardens and the crushed oyster shell path that cut through them extended all the way to West Saltonstall Street, and it was here that we hung the small porcelain placard advertising our presence. It took some effort to reapportion the old floor plan to meet our needs. The upper level of the house consisted of four guest bedrooms; the ground level held the master bedroom, kitchen, library, conservatory, and other rooms, while the lower level housed our offices, work rooms and the small apartment of the Kreitners, a trusted couple that acted as staff. Given our line of work, it took a great deal of effort to keep house for the three of us—particularly for Doctor Roman Lydecker.

Once, Doctor Roman Lydecker had been a brilliant and skilled surgeon by the name of Eric Clapham-Lee, but that had been before the war—and before he had met Doctor Herbert West, or Megan Halsey. He had died during the war; a plane crash had beheaded the man. This made him a candidate for the depraved experiments of Doctor West, who had succeeded in bringing both body and head back to life. Years later, Clapham-Lee had become a most terrible adversary, not only to West, but also to me and Megan Halsey. This had been after he had assumed the identity of Roman Lydecker, a professor at the Hall School in Kingsport. It was in the midst of battle that Megan Halsey had blown a hole in Lydecker's chest and destroyed his heart. The act had put his body down. The head, however, had lived on, and despite my objections Megan had not only allowed it to live but had made it—him—a partner in our firm. Indeed, for all intents and purposes, Lydecker—posing as a rare adult victim of poliomyelitis—was the brains behind our brawn (or, if I am allowed a small and morbid joke, "the firm's head") so to speak. It was to Lydecker that we gave the credit of solving all our cases. The reporters and public seemed enthralled by the concept of a sickly detective who could not leave his home, whose agents scoured the city and countryside for clues, and who wasn't afraid of ordering the use of force to bring about justice. The Potter boy up in Bolton, the Dunwich Foundlings—a few other cases—all tied up nice and neat by Megan and me, and explained away with elaborate stories conceived by Lydecker, with himself cast in the lead role. It was a convenience, really, to let the public think that Lydecker was a genius and we his mere factotums. It was to Lydecker that we gave all the credit, and therefore it was Lydecker that our clients asked for by name, even this young, haggard and pale man that stood in our receiving room.

"Lydecker . . ." He let the name hang there for a moment, then clarified, "I would like to see Doctor Lydecker." He paused and looked at me with, strange violet eyes. "You're Robert Peaslee."

I nodded. "And you are Frank Elwood. You are unexpected, sir. It will take me a few minutes to make Dr. Lydecker presentable. You will wait here, please." It wasn't a request. I gestured towards a blue leather chair, and he reluctantly sat down. I smiled politely and then vanished behind the bright green door that led to our consulting room.

Formerly dedicated to billiards, our consulting room was a rectangle about twenty feet by twelve feet. I emerged through the middle of one of the short walls, opposite the well-stocked mahogany bar. Behind the bar there was a red door that led to both the storeroom and the room where the furnace sat. To my right, along one of the long walls, was a long sofa adorned in brown leather and flanked by a pair of matching chairs, and lamps. There were no windows in the consulting room, and these lamps, accompanied by the rectangular brass ceiling fixture that had once lit the billiards table, provided all the light in the room. Beneath the hanging brass fixture, three yellow chairs sat in a semi-circle in front of Lydecker's desk. The desk itself, a purely a perfunctory piece of furniture, sat in front of the short wall. To my left, along the other long wall, was a second door beyond which was a hallway that led past the stairs and to the servant's quarters. Past that door the wall turned, and then there was the door to the elevator. Ostensibly, this was to allow our wheelchair-bound partner Lydecker to travel from his rooms on the third level to our offices below. There were two bedrooms on the third floor supposedly dedicated to Lydecker and the equipment that kept him alive, but they were actually Megan's private study and laboratory.

With a practiced hand, I stepped inside the elevator, and closed the door behind me. Instead of engaging the lift I pressed a small button concealed in the woodwork. There was a whirring sound and the back panel of the elevator slid open. In a single step, I was through to the rooms that made up the true residence of Doctor Roman Lydecker. His wheelchair with its mannequin body in a fatuous blue suit sat to one side. In the far corner sat the hydraulic pump and the cylinder of pale, green-tinged fluid that it kept in constant motion. Lydecker, or what was left of him, sat on the table with his neck immersed in a small circulating basin. He wore glasses, wire-framed circles secured by loops behind his ears. He was reading a book. As I approached, I could see that it was Margaret Murray's much-maligned magnum opus, *The Witch-Cult in Western Europe*. The volume was set up in a small electro-mechanical contraption that turned the page every two minutes, a necessary invention given that Lydecker had no hands with which to turn the pages himself.

I cleared my throat. "A student, from Miskatonic University."

His eyes never left the book. "Another one?" He spoke slowly and carefully.

"It *is* a college town," I offered. "He's frightened. He has reason to be. His name is Frank Elwood, of the Kingsport Elwoods. You have read all of the newspapers for the past year thoroughly, so you must know what happened to him and his friend."

"That was months ago. The affair of the Witch House likely concluded with the death of Walter Gilman."

"There was that spot of bother at the hospital during the aftermath of the Dunwich Horror, that led to the arrest of Doctor Hartwell. If he is here related to that, I would think you and Megan would be interested. After all, Hartwell was—is—in the same line of research as the two of you."

His eyes turned and glared at me. "Robert!" His voice bubbled and wheezed. It had taken him years to learn how to move air through his throat without lungs, and on occasion he still had trouble, particularly when he was excited or angry. "Very well." He sighed and resigned himself to what came next. I lifted him out of his bath and wrapped the stump of his neck in a towel. Then I carried him over to the wheelchair, lowered the stump and towel into the neck of the suit and strapped it into place, giving the leather wrappings a strong tug to secure them. I did up the buttons on his shirt, then tied his cravat in the regency style, his preferred manner, and then stepped back. It was a fine deception. The gloved hands gripped the armrests and were secretly pinned in place. The legs and arms of the dummy were visibly bound to the frame of his chair, which created a kind of spectacle that drew the eye, and thereby forced people to look away. A bit of cleverness that Megan had devised. I had been in the war, and I had my share of comrades who had become invalids. In my opinion, Roman Lydecker looked the part, and the wheezing voice simply added a touch of authenticity that we couldn't manufacture if we tried.

Pleased with my preparations, I pressed a small button by the side of the door. This sounded a gentle tone on the second and third level, letting Megan know that we had a client. My other partner summoned, I rolled my charge into the elevator, opened the door, and then positioned him behind the desk.

Megan Halsey, my partner both in business and love, wandered through the door. "Are you two prepared?" asked my wife. She paused as I nodded and Roman let out a short sound of affirmation. "Good, then let us get this show on the road, and see what the day brings us."

She sat down on the couch at the back while I went through the door to the receiving room. Elwood was sitting where I left him, still moon-faced and with that worried look in his eyes. I ushered him through and sat him in the center yellow chair while I took up the chair to the right of him. As I sat, I made introductions. "Doctor Roman Lydecker, may I present Mister Frank Elwood. Mister Elwood, Doctor Lydecker."

Frank Elwood rose and extended his hand, but then realized that his gesture couldn't be reciprocated. He withdrew his gesture and sat back down both nervous and embarrassed. "I suppose I should start with the death of my friend Walter Gilman."

Lydecker gasped out a question. "Is it relevant?"

"Yes. Yes, it is." He affirmed. "At least in a way. He was the first, you see, the first to die. It was back in May. I was there the day he died, and I saw how he died. I saw the rat—the abomination named Brown Jenkin—chew through his chest. It was a terrible thing to witness, and I'll admit that I was shattered to the core. It has taken months of therapy, all graciously supplied by the university, but I've finally gotten over the nervous shock. Indeed, I went home over the summer to Kingsport and there decided to reject the grades the University had assigned me for my work that spring. I was determined to earn my degree on my own merits, and not benefit from the death of my friend, though I must admit things have not been easy. Apparently Professor Upham is taking a break from teaching this year, so I've had to take a few elective courses to make up the credits, which will take me to this June. Of course, the university is waving all my fees. I'm sure the administration just wishes to put all this in the past, which is what I want as well." He was wringing his hands. "But then in January I saw a newspaper clipping. My classmate Richard Jacobi had been killed in an accident out at the mill, a tragedy to be sure, but the newspaper report said that it was simply an accident. Then, last week I found out that Fritz Long died on New Year's Eve—he had been in an accident that ejected him through the windshield of the car he was driving. The article claimed he died instantly, and I really didn't think much of it at the time except to note it as yet another tragedy. But I have my doubts now. Yesterday I saw this."

He reached into his pocket and handed me a newspaper clipping. It was dated a week earlier, but it looked older. It had been folded and mishandled far too many times. The ink was smudged, but it was still legible. "Edward Fritch, killed while walking in the woods out by the reservoir. Article says he slipped and fell down a hill and broke his neck. Animals had apparently been at the body."

Elwood was shaking. "You see? The evidence is incontrovertible."

"I'm sorry Mister Elwood, I do not see," Lydecker hissed. "Three of your schoolmates are dead, but Miskatonic University is a large college, some rate of expiration must be allowed for, expected even, amongst the student body."

Elwood nodded. "It's not quite that simple, Doctor Lydecker. Gilman, Fritch, Jacobi, and Long—we were all students together under Professor Upham. There were only twelve of us. Now four of us are dead. Do you understand what that means?"

"You have incredibly unlucky classmates?" My tone bordered on the flippant as I asked the question. Like Lydecker, I was not certain there were connections to anything amiss at Miskatonic University. My wife had a different understanding of the situation.

From the back of the room, Megan rose from her seat and stalked across the room. "Luck has little to do with it Robert. The odds of four healthy people in the same class dying accidentally are preposterous." She took the chair on Elwood's left. "Outrageously so."

Elwood was trembling. "Even if you alter the baseline assumptions by discounting Gilman's death, the numbers are still impossible to accept. I've been left with no other explanation but to suspect foul play. The probabilities simply don't allow for accidental death."

I cast a puzzled glance at Megan, who looked at me as if she expected me to understand. Fortunately, my puzzlement was interrupted by the wheezing voice of Doctor Lydecker.

"It is an interesting problem, Mister Elwood. You are correct in your assumption; those odds are extremely difficult to reconcile. Not impossible, but difficult. We shall investigate this situation for you. In the meanwhile, you shall reside here under our protection."

I was still puzzled. "What exactly are we investigating?"

It was Megan who cleared things up. "Mr. Elwood and the rest of his surviving classmates are under threat. Unless we help them, they will each, in all likelihood, soon suffer some sort of fatal accident. But they are not accidents. There is a strong possibility that these are homicides."

Elwood had a frantic look on his face. "There can be no other explanation, the odds are against everything else except a probability of murder!"

"Have you been to the police?" My question wasn't just academic. If the authorities were already investigating these deaths as murders, then we could be stepping on someone else's toes. I knew from personal experience that the local cops could be very territorial and weren't above some heavy-handed retribution.

"I spoke to a Captain Fricasse. He said he would make some phone calls." Elwood's voice was trembling—he was truly terrified, or at least believed he had something to be terrified of.

"Robert?" Lydecker wheezed.

"Phil Fricasse—been on the force for fifteen years. Unimaginative. Not above taking a bribe, particularly from local rumrunners, but not from out-of-towners. Prefers to keep things quiet if possible. It's unlikely that he followed up or questioned any of the official reports."

"And Professor Upham?"

Now it was Megan's turn to supply background. "Hiram Upham, Chair of the School of Mathematics—but it's likely that he earned that position by default, being the oldest and most tenured member of the faculty. By all accounts a mediocre administrator but an excellent instructor and researcher. Published widely and prominently, most recently last year. The paper providing mathematical proof refuting the Bohr-Heisenberg theory of quantum mechanics gathered notes of praise from Bose and Szilard. Faculty gossip has it that he is working on a paper with Nikolai Tesla, something to do with movement through four-dimensional space."

Elwood moaned. "Historical Evidence for Non-Linear Motion Through Fourth Dimensional Space. Gilman and I were doing some supporting research in the library on the subject before he . . ." There was no need for him to finish the sentence.

Lydecker sighed. "You, Gilman and the others were all students of Upham's?"

Elwood nodded. "For Gilman and I, he was our academic advisor, but for the others he was just an instructor, we were all in his Calculus D class.

The coursework involved far more differential geometry than calculus, it was quite an esoteric course of study, really. If Gilman hadn't died, I wouldn't have passed. Not exactly the kind of calculations one needs as an actuary."

"You're in insurance then?"

"My family is, in a way. My father and grandfather work for the East Coast branch of Taney Mercantile Casualty . . ."

Megan cut him off. "You review claims for losses of freight at sea. We've used them at Griffith and Son. You're familiar with actuary tables, which is why you suspect your friends have been murdered."

"It is more than a suspicion; the probabilities don't allow for an alternative."

I reviewed the notes I had been taking. "This class you took with Upham—you said there were twelve: you, Gilman, Richard Jacobi, Fritz Long, Edward Fritch—who were the rest?

"I can't remember all their names. There was Leroy Beaumont, Nathaniel Kaye, Scott Home, and Abraham Alder. The rest I never really knew that well." A light dawned in his eyes. "We could ask Professor Upham for a list."

Lydecker's response came as both a snort as a statement. "So as far as you know all the others could be dead."

The blunt observation hit Elwood hard, and he seemed to shrink back into his chair. "Yes, I suppose that is true."

Megan stood up and took a short quick walk around the room, something she did to help buy her time while she formulated a thought. "Does anybody know you're here?"

He shook his head. "I was so afraid. I didn't even think to talk about it to anyone but Doctor Lydecker."

She smiled. "That's good, and we're going to keep it that way. Mrs. Kreitner will make up a bedroom for you, the Central Suite, which overlooks the back garden. There's a study just across the hall where Robert and I can stand watch at night. I'll accompany you to classes. Both Robert and I are well known on campus, but I will cause fewer potential problems."

I let loose a low frustrated sighed. Our work at Miskatonic always ran the risk of an encounter with one of my family members. I gestured to Megan, "You and Elwood should see Upham and get that class list and see what you can find out about the other students. I'll consult the State Police and see what their files have to say about these four accidents."

"Three accidents," shot back Elwood. "Gilman was murdered."

"As you say," I replied and made a gesture of frustrated acceptance. There was some enmity building between Elwood and myself. I had a nagging dislike for the young man who seemed intelligent enough but presented himself as something of a victim. It was a position I was not unfamiliar with, but—whereas I had bettered myself and risen above that station—Elwood seemed to revel in the role, embracing it even. His demeanor suggested an unwillingness to move beyond victimhood, and it was this unwillingness that was likely creating the animosity I felt toward our newest client. It was possible that he sensed that. I was sure that Megan did.

She broke the tension by suggesting a change of subject. "Before we go anywhere, we are all going to sit down and eat some lunch. I believe Mrs. Kreitner has prepared a stew of some sort."

But our new client still had one more piece of business to discuss. "I'm sorry, it may be rude, but I need to know . . . I'm not a wealthy man . . . my family isn't poor, but I'm not . . ."

Lydecker sputtered out an interruption. "Mr. Elwood, we are not at this point in dire need of funds. Miss Halsey's family fortune pays our rent, and our contract for implementing new security measures at the University library is substantial. We therefore find ourselves in the position to be charitable."

The look on Elwood's face conveyed that he hadn't understood what exactly was said. I slapped an arm around his shoulder and smiled. "Today's your lucky day, Frank. The services of Halsey, Peaslee and Lydecker just became free of charge."

With that settled, we moved upstairs to the kitchen.

Second Report

Robert Peaslee

When it came to meals, we had rules in Griffith House. The dining room was only used for formal dinners only; all other meals were had around the small table that sat in a bright alcove off the kitchen. This was at the insistence of Megan, who had spent too many years eating institutional food prepared by faceless cooks at the Hall School in Kingsport. She wanted to see what was going into her food, and who was making it. In her mind, this was the more civilized way to dine, with the people who prepared your meals, and surrounded by the sights, smells and sounds of what went into its preparation. It was for this very reason she avoided fancy restaurants and instead preferred open kitchen diners that cooked in sight of their patrons.

Our cook, Mrs. Sheila Kreitner, was Irish, but her husband was Jewish-German, and consequently our meals reflected that strange combination. Cabbage, potatoes, and beef sausages abounded, but some ingredients were rare. It wasn't that she couldn't prepare such dishes—her bacon-wrapped scallops fried in butter were the most tender I have ever had—but Mr. Kreitner, despite not exactly keeping kosher, never developed a taste for pork or shellfish in his youth. If it seems strange for a household to bend its tastes to that of one of its servants, you must remember that we are a strange household, and we had asked much of our staff: including the keeping of frightful secrets, and the mending of terrible wounds. Our lives were in their hands, accommodating some dietary peculiarities was the least we could do.

Of course, Dr. Lydecker did not dine with us. He had no need for solid food, no way to digest it, and to allow him to join us at the table would have raised more questions than we were comfortable answering. It had only taken a moment or two for me to set him back in his nutritive bath before coming up the stairs to the gallery hall and cutting through the kitchen. I paused to grab a roll out of the basket that sat on the butcher block and then dodged a playful flick of Mrs. Kreitner's dish towel as she shooed me out of her kitchen.

The meal, in addition to the hot buttered rolls, consisted of a stew of chicken and apple sausages, potatoes, carrots and cabbage from our own root cellar, all in a stock thickened by a saffron-spiced rice. It was a hearty meal, fitting for a cold December day, and I like to think that Hadrian Vargr, my former colleague who was something of an epicure, would have enjoyed it immensely despite its rather modest ingredients and preparation. I certainly did, and I knew it to be one of Megan's favorites, at least during the winter season. Mr. Elwood seemed wary at first, but after a modest and careful spoonful his eyes widened, and he devoured the steaming bowl in good form. Mr. Kreitner, who had been working on something or other in the attic, soon joined us, and sitting next to his wife he casually stroked her hair, and she smiled in response. To see that after all these decades of marriage they were still in love filled me with hope. The marriage of my own parents, and Megan's as well, having been torn apart by forces beyond their control, were not exemplary models for us to follow—particularly since we had engaged in battle with the very forces that had destroyed them.

"Your father works at the university, doesn't he?" Elwood managed between spoons. "He helped me get through the worst of things back in May."

We have a strict policy of not talking business during meals, but this wasn't precisely business; it was family, an equally forbidden subject. Elwood didn't know that, though his expression changed as he noticed the mood at the table subtly shift, growing colder. I forced a smile. "Both my father and my brother are on the faculty at Miskatonic." I dabbed a stray bit of stew off my lips. "Father used to be an economist, but he has followed Wingate into the study of the human mind. He has had a great deal of experience in trying to understand injuries to the human psyche, though not so much success in repairing them. I suppose one must start somewhere." I let the sadness that held sway in my heart slip out. Despite resolutions to the contrary, I have never been able to bring myself to reconcile with my father. I knew that what happened to him wasn't his fault, but whenever I looked at him, I couldn't see the man that was my father—instead, I saw only the weird and frightful thing that once hid behind his face.

Suddenly, I was off my lunch, though there wasn't much left in the bowl. I threw my napkin on the table and announced, "I should be back by five. You two need to get that class list." They just stared at me as if I had committed some sort of social sin. "What?"

Megan smiled. "It's Sunday Robert, the university is closed, and I would suspect that the State Police might be operating on a minimum of staff today as well." She reached over and touched my hand. "You'll take Mr. Elwood back to his room, gather up some of his things and then bring him back. By the time you return, Mrs. Kreitner will have his room made up and I'll have his schedule figured out." I could feel the heat of her fingers on the back of my hand. "We can start fresh in the morning."

I tried to shake off my melancholy mood by forcing a smile. "My apologies, I apparently have lost track of the day. Mr. Elwood, where exactly do you live?"

"The university gave me a room in the East Dormitory." He saw my look. "I know it has a bad reputation, but it's quite a bit better than the last place I was living in."

"The last place you were living in got your best friend killed." The sarcasm of my remark was so palpable it practically hung in the air, but Elwood merely smiled.

"My point exactly, Mister Peaslee. After that, what could be worse?"

The university was only three blocks away, but the freezing cold made the short walk seem inadvisable. One look at the roads outside, slick with ice, made me rethink using the car, a burgundy-paneled Heron Silver Wing. So, at a little after one, Frank Elwood and I donned our winter coats and marched into the cold. It was not as bad as all that, really, and the trek towards the school was downhill—slightly downhill. We made better progress walking in the tracks of those who had gone before us than using either sidewalk or street, both of which were, as I suspected they would be, rife with long patches of ice. We were grateful that there was little wind, and what there was came from behind us and not from the frigid Miskatonic River. Sometime in late November a whole flotilla of ice sheets had drifted down from the slower and colder upper tributaries and made the whole harbor impassible. It also created a source of near-Arctic cold whenever the wind blew past the miniature ice floe. With such conditions making the short trek far more arduous than normal, we reached the East Dormitory just before two, and were glad to be in the meager shelter that the building provided. Though, truth be told, I estimated the temperature to be just above sixty degrees—better than the overwhelmingly freezing cold kept at bay outside, but hardly comfortable. A quick glance about the lobby of the building validated this conclusion; I noted the numerous students wrapped up in sweaters and blankets as they went about their business inside what passed for a residence.

Elwood's room was nothing to speak of, little more than a brick-and-mortar cell. There was a window, but the paint had long since flaked away and the frame was loose and would have allowed a draft if the occupant hadn't stuffed the gap with newspaper. I had lived in worse, but not since the war. Elwood had little in the way of possessions. A few notebooks and some class texts all fit into a single satchel. His clothes we shoved into a battered suitcase, and still had room for his toiletries bag. That was all of it, there wasn't anything else to take. He hadn't any thing of a personal nature. No photographs, no pictures. There was nothing decorative or of intrinsic value.

I mentioned it and he just shrugged. "I had things once: a family photograph; an album of pressed flowers that my sister made me; my journal. I left them all behind in the Witch House after Gilman died. Never could muster the courage to go back inside." There was sadness in his voice. "I suppose they are still there, waiting for me."

As we made our way out of the building, we encountered a small group of students coming in. When they saw Elwood, they crossed themselves and said a quick prayer. One went so far as to spit in his direction. I moved to do something about it, but Elwood put a hand on my shoulder and pulled me back.

It wasn't till we were outside and marching down the street that I broached the subject with him. "What was that all about?"

He kept walking, but I could tell he was trying to process his thoughts. I let him find his own time, both with the pace of the walk home, and the decision to explain why other students were afraid of him.

"They think I worship the devil."

I laughed, but then realized Elwood wasn't joking. This was witch-haunted Arkham, and I knew from personal experience what that meant. "Seriously? But how could they. . . you were the victim!"

He looked back at me with those strange violet eyes and sighed a long sigh, and his breath curled up in the air behind him like a trail of smoke. "After Gilman died there was an academic inquest, a lot of our fellow students were interviewed. Some of Gilman's papers and ideas were made public, all out of context of course. Yes, we had consulted some of the books in the restricted section of the library. Yes, we had gone out to the dolmens north of Meadow Hill. Yes, we had rowed out to the island off the Garrison Street Bridge. And yes, we had made copies of the queer markings we had found there. But it was all in the name of science. Walter proved that. You can ask Professor Upham."

I asked him what exactly Walter Gilman had proved.

He paused again, breathing contemplative clouds of steam as we walked on in silence.

And then—just as the anticipation and the crunch of our footfalls on the icy, snow-slick streets threatened to drive me to madness—he told me.

Third Report

Frank Elwood

It was towards the end of March that Gilman seemed to have a breakthrough and his understanding of the higher order mathematics we were studying crystalized. He was still failing Psychology, but the hours he had spent working on Riemannian equations had finally paid off. He developed an intuition about those formulae and was able to solve them with ease. He had even instituted a kind of shortcut for cancelling and substituting entire sets within the transformation.

Professor Upham had scoffed at the procedure, but after having seen it applied more than a dozen times, he acquiesced to formally review it, and, if it was proven valid, to aid in its publication. At the same time, there emerged in Gilman an almost total comprehension of fourth dimensional geometry and the mathematics that supported it. These subjects had been the source of much difficulty amongst the rest of the class, me included, and to see Gilman excel where he had once floundered engendered not only awe, but in some a small modicum of jealousy. All of this led up to a sort of academic crescendo, a culmination of Gilman's knowledge and understanding, some of which seemed beyond the ken of even Professor Upham.

It was on the last Thursday of the month, when Upham opened the class with a discussion of the curvature of space and the application of Riemann manifolds in understanding the shape of those curves, that we could see just how changed Gilman was. Upham went so far as to propose a model, a three-dimensional analogue to the four-dimensional fabric of the universe. This, he expounded, was the current best theory that explained the diverse behaviors of the universe as observed by scientists such as Einstein, Planck and Bose.

All through this exposition I could see my friend grow more and more agitated. His left leg began to bounce, and the fingers of his left hand were tapping the tabletop. As Upham continued Gilman stopped taking notes and held his pen at the ready, desperate to ask a question. When the elder academician finally did pause a bevy of hands went up, Gilman's included, but he simply couldn't wait to be called on.

"Surely Professor, that can't be the best model." He was openly contradicting our esteemed teacher but seemed oblivious to the faux pas he was committing. "I can think of at least three alternatives that would demonstrate the same solutions but in much more elegant manners."

I'm not sure if what happened next was because Upham felt upstaged and wanted to embarrass Gilman, or if the man truly wanted his student to shine. Either way, Pr. Upham stepped off the elevated stage, walked over to where his vociferous student was sitting, and handed him the chalk. "By all means Mister Gilman, feel free to explain yourself."

The whole class tittered with amusement, for they expected Walter to meekly apologize and allow the lecture to continue. Instead, Gilman defiantly snatched the chalk and marched up to the blackboard while Upham retreated to the back of the room.

"The problem with this model is that it is—by its very nature—rigid. It may be curved, and some points may be closer to one another than others," he drew lines between various points on Upham's sketch, "but this would not allow for various effects predicted by Einstein's concept of a Space-Time Continuum. Specifically, it would disallow non-linear travel from one point in space to another." He paused to begin sketching a twisted conical image. "Only if we allow for the flexibility of the underlying fabric—a fabric that can be bent and twisted, or even rolled—not as a constant state, but rather only achieving flexibility when subjected to the proper conditions, do we begin to account for all of the possible states of esoteric behavior that waves, particles, matter and energy seem to exhibit."

He moved on from sketching and began inscribing equations around his model. "Here we begin with the rigid-state equation you provided us, Professor, but as you can see," but of course we couldn't see, not at first—his hands were flying across the slate, moving faster than we could comprehend, "if we transform the base manifold like this, and move from a fourth dimensional equation to a fifth, the entire system becomes flexible, malleable even, perhaps even without the need for significant energies. Which in itself opens up an interesting corollary."

He paused and stepped back so we could see the entirety of what he had written. In its own way—a way that can only be understood by mathematicians and perhaps physicists—it was beautiful. There is, as I understand it, a science of poetry—orthometry—in which verse is studied, dissected and analyzed in order to understand what made it so beautiful. This was the opposite of that, not the science of beauty, but the beauty of science. It was the poetics of math, and the equation he had written was both an abstract sculpture of fourth and fifth dimensional geometrics and quantum physics, and a silhouette of the true nature of the universe. All of us gathered round our tables could see that, could see the elegant and fantastic truth that Walter Gilman had just unveiled, and we became frantic to transcribe the eldritch equations into our own notes so that we might keep them and on occasion allow ourselves brief glimpses of their elegance, and remind ourselves of the magnificent outré universe that we resided in.

Amidst the frenetic transcription I caught sight of a furtive glance that passed between Gilman and Professor Upham. It seemed to me that Walter had made his point and wished to release control of the class back to its rightful owner, but Upham was having none of it. Gilman had begun this thing and Upham wanted to see where it led, despite his student's desire to cease.

Unable to find relief, Walter reluctantly continued. "You will note that implicit in the malleability is an energy requirement that is not at all substantial. Indeed, the levels of expenditure are well within those values regularly achieved in the human brain during periods of extreme stress. This suggests—or at least *I* will suggest—that it might be theoretically possible, and supported by this manifold," he quickly scratched out a set of numbers and variables, "to fold two areas of space together, merely by thinking about it." He continued to scribble on the slate. "It should be noted, as shown by this equation, that these two areas are not subject to any real limits of Euclidian measurements. Energetically, it is just as easy to fold points in space between galaxies as it is to do so, say, from one room to another. Though, admittedly, in both cases a linkage must be built between both locations, and while this linkage is relatively expensive compared to the requirements of folding space, it is energetically neutral." He circled a balanced equation. "This bridge through the stars might be costly to create, but once used and disassembled there would be no energy loss. This might seem to violate the laws of thermodynamics, but remember: we are not operating within our own universe, but in the spaces above and between it. In such space, the transformation of energy from one state to another should be extremely difficult, and losses to heat, light and the like should be limited," he swirled a curve around a set of calculations, "which also means that a biological system—plants and animals, even humans—should be able to survive the transition across the bridge."

This began a murmur of amusement that travelled through the class, and I even saw Upham smile, but Gilman wasn't amused. He continued his strange and tangential calculations and moved to one side, so we could see the proof he was providing. While we took it all in, copied it all down, and tried to comprehend it, he continued to speak. "Now just because transitioning the bridge is not inimical does not mean that travel via this method is without risk. It is likely that the vast majority of planets and similar points in space have extremely dissimilar atmospheres and conditions that would be intolerable and even instantly fatal to physiologies such as our own, or to any physiology whatsoever. Conversely, it is also likely that there does exist, given the size of the universe, a myriad of places in which the atmosphere and physical conditions are favorable to physiologies like or similar to our own. If we were able to fold space between such places and generate the transitioning bridge that penetrates the enclosing layers of both manifolds, then it is reasonable to assert that a human being could visit another habitat, even one that is extragalactic. By the same token, the reverse is true—a being of alien nature could use the same technique to travel to Earth." He paused and then seemed to realize that he had forgotten something. "It is important to note here that while the invagination of space and the bridge itself likely require a conscious mind for creation; they are stable and sustained until actively unmade. Additionally, there appears to be no requirement for the object transferred to itself be sentient, opening the door, so to speak, to the transfer of cargo or even animal life across the bridge."

By this time, few of us were listening, and I watched as Alder put down his pen and stared slack-jawed at the numerical symbols that had been laid out before him. "There's a bridge . . ." he whispered.

"A bridge to the stars," echoed Long.

I don't think Gilman heard either of them, for he just kept talking about more and more tangential subjects. "There does appear to be a set of concerns, states in the bridge that might create issues. The first is a weakness here in this descending, recursive factor. This suggests that at some energy states, and given the level of energy needed to create the set of desirable and stable states, the transition might not be instantaneous, but rather tremendously extended, though still energy neutral. In other words, the transferring object would not age but subjectively would experience a passage of time on the order of years if not centuries. An experience that, if inflicted on a conscious individual, would likely incur some degree of mental instability.

"The second concern expands on the concept that energy cannot be transformed in the transition. And I stand by this assertion, that spontaneous transformation is unlikely. However, given that the bridge space is tolerable to biological systems, it might therefore be home to a native fauna, or one that has adapted to that in-between space. Such beings might be obligate predators, particularly on objects transitioning between places in normal space, which by their very nature would appear as highly energetic and therefore desirable consumables."

"A bridge," I heard someone mutter behind me.

Gilman was oblivious to the susurrus coming from the class, whom he had long ago left behind. I suppose I was the only one that had deemed it important enough to continue to listen to him. "The third concern is the transformation of the bridge itself. If one were to apply a significant amount of energy here, perhaps in the form of a fluxing capacitance, the bridge might become unhinged from either of its terminal ends and move either *dup* or *owen* along a fourth dimensional slippage. Such a slippage would almost assuredly result in the bridge forming a recursive loop such that both terminals occupied the same physical space but different temporalities. Such tunnels in time would be extremely energetic, and—unlike the spatial bridges—highly unstable and unsustainable. They would only exist for moments, and while they might be just as hospitable as the structures we spoke of earlier, this calculation implies that their energetics might be forced into a diametrically opposing state to the energies and objects around them. Imagine a phosphorescent fish swimming against the river current. While this is not intrinsically dangerous, when coupled with our theoretical predatory native fauna, it might be seen as a meal too tempting and obvious to let pass unpursued. In other words, time travel might be possible, but inherently dangerous."

I laughed a little, but I was the only one. Everyone else including Professor Upham was enthralled, entranced by the flow of hundreds of equations and matrices that had flowed out of Walter Gilman's mind. In his hand, he still held the piece of chalk that Upham had challenged him with, but it was little more than a stub now, and there was more chalk dust covering his hands than existed in that little fragment of soft rock. Embarrassed, he tossed the shard onto the lectern and brushed his hands clean with a small towel that existed for just such occasions. But I was the only one noticing these tiny details; everyone else was either trying to copy what was on the board or was simply marveling at the complex beauty of it. Thankfully, the bell rang, marking the end of class and breaking whatever spell Gilman had cast over us. Conditioned by years of Pavlovian repetition, the bell caused notebooks to slam shut and students to slowly shuffle out; headed to either their next class or the library to begin work on whatever assignments they had due.

I hung behind, waiting for Walter, and gave him a pat on his back as he gathered up his belongings. I meant to say something encouraging to him but was interrupted by Professor Upham before I could even begin.

"Interesting work, Mister Gilman," praise from Upham was rare. "Very interesting. It would seem my faith in your abilities was well placed. Though I had my doubts, given your performance up until now. These equations, barring the phantasmagorical commentary you provided, are intriguing."

"Thank you, Professor. I didn't come up with it alone, though. Frank provided critical input and kept me from going down some dead ends."

It was a lie, or at least a half-truth, and given the look that Upham gave me he knew it. "I expect a full paper expanding on these concepts by the end of term, gentlemen. Do that, and explain away a few lingering inequalities and remainders, and I'll forget your earlier lackluster performances."

Gilman opened his mouth to say something, and the look in his eye told me it was going to be rude. "Thank you, Professor," I hurriedly interjected. "Thank you very much."

As I pulled Gilman away and through the door, I cast a backwards glance. Professor Upham was staring at the slate blackboard with an expression that I had never seen upon his visage before, and I heard him speak in a tone I had never heard him use. "A bridge to the stars . . ."

It troubled me a little that someone as worldly and brilliant and imaginative as the Professor could be awestruck.

Fourth Report

Megan Halsey

It was just after ten in the morning when our client, Frank Elwood, and I knocked on the door of 507 W. Miskatonic Avenue, the home of Professor Hiram Upham. We had, by that time, already been to Miskatonic University and the School of Mathematics and been rebuffed by the staff. Apparently Professor Upham hadn't just taken a break from teaching, but had also ceased coming to the office. From what we could gather, this had been going on for weeks and was a secret that his staff and faculty were keeping from the rest of the college. He was still in charge, he still issued memos and signed forms, but he hadn't actually left his home in weeks. So we made our way back up the hill to an address not far from Griffith House.

It snowed overnight, and as we left I was struck by the beauty of Griffith House and the surrounding grounds as they—blanketed in soft white powder—glittered brightly, caught in a sunbeam that broke momentarily through the melancholy grey of the firmament above. The same could not be said of the streets of Arkham, which had been subjected to the staff and plows of the Public Works Department and now stood relatively clear of snow and ice. This had made our walk a bit easier, though it was still bitterly cold, and the fingers of frigid air cut through our coats and made us shiver. As we stood there on the doorstep huddled in the shade of the bushes along the house that provided a momentary windbreak, happy to be out of the biting breeze. When an old woman finally opened the door, she didn't bother to ask us any questions, and instead hustled us inside quickly and with nary a word. We didn't wait for a verbal invitation and gladly followed her out of the foul weather and into a warm and pleasant foyer.

The woman introduced herself as Mrs. Murry, the housekeeper. When we asked if we could see Professor Upham she hesitated for a moment and a strange look stole over face, as if we had asked for something ridiculous. A moment later her look of puzzlement turned into a forced cheerful smile. "Of course. Why don't you wait in his study, and I'll let him know you are here." She opened a paneled door and directed us inside.

Following her lead, I entered the room and I saw what I had expected. There was a large oak desk with several neat piles of paper and a few books along the edges. The chair behind it was of brown leather and well worn, while the two in front were covered in olive cloth and of lesser age. One wall consisted entirely of shelves filled with books and small examples of geometric figures. Behind the desk was a rather large window with filing cabinets on either side, another set of which framed the door we had just come through. The remaining wall was decorated with photographs, some decades old, which I could see had been taken at various locations throughout the university and Arkham. I may not have gone to Miskatonic University, but I had spent a significant portion of my childhood in the town and knew its sights, even those that had long ago been erased by progress. Those frozen shadows of memories framed a rather plain wooden door through which Mrs. Murry had passed a moment before. Crossing the room to the door, I could hear Mrs. Murry and another voice speaking. I made sure to look deeply engrossed in study of one of the pictures as Mrs. Murry's voice grew closer to the door. After a minute or so the door opened, and the housekeeper strutted out, clearly unhappy.

Another voice called to us. "Come into my laboratory, please. I'm in the middle of some very interesting work." The voice was deep, cracked and you could hear the age in it.

Professor Upham's lab was nothing like the one that I kept hidden behind the laundry in the basement of Griffith House. Where mine was full of glassware, burners, ice baths, and chemicals, this one consisted primarily of chalkboards and tacked up scraps of paper. The walls were nothing but slabs of slate, and these were covered with hundreds—if not thousands—of mathematical symbols drawn by hand in various colors of chalk. They were laid out in lines to form equations. Some were only a few symbols long; others were vast, unwieldy things that stretched from one board to another and then curved down around the edges. One complex monstrosity seemed to begin at the very top-left corner of a board and then ran across the top, down the side, then backwards across the bottom, only to shoot up the other side, near to where it had first started. This loop repeated over and over again, spiraling down on the rectangular workspace like a weird mathematical whirlpool. With each successive loop the markings became smaller, and tighter and more esoteric until at last, towards the center of the board they were reduced to mere ghostly impressions of actually numbers and symbols. It was perhaps a kind of mathematical shorthand of the Professor's own devising.

The dividing frames of wood were filled with pages—some torn out of books, but most scribbled on in pencil in the same furious script that had made the symbols on the various chalkboards. In the center of the room there was a large worktable covered with a mass of unkempt papers and books that kept them in place. These volumes were unfamiliar to me, but I made a mental note of their titles, which included *The Algebra of Mohammed ben Musa*, *Liber Abacci*, *De Thiende*, and a five-volume set of something called *Mecanique Celeste* that was tattered and worm-eaten.

Behind this table laden with academic chaos sat an older man who was perhaps in his mid-sixties. Square glasses perched on a hawkish nose and framed wrinkled blue eyes. Even in the chair I could tell that his left hand was trembling, but his other hand seemed steady enough. He wore no suit coat but did have a sweater vest over a white shirt with black buttons that matched the color of his pants; the whole ensemble was easily two decades out of style.

He looked up from his work on the table and smiled. "Mr. Elwood, so nice to see you again. I hope your coursework is going well."

"Doctor Roy's class on Probabilities in Complex Systems was kind of boring," Elwood forced a smile, "but boring is nothing to complain about."

"Yes, I suppose given what has happened, boring might be something to cherish." The old academician let loose a short chuckle. "You're not here to complain about your classes, Mr. Elwood. For that you would have made an appointment, and you wouldn't have bothered to bring Miss Halsey."

My ears perked up. "I'm sorry, Professor Upham—are we acquainted?"

This time he let a full laugh. "No, but I knew your father, Alan. He and I were very good friends. I was a pallbearer at his funeral. Of course, this was all before you were born." There was something soulful in his tone. "It was a shame what happened to him after . . ."

"My father is dead, Professor Upham. We should leave it at that." I was polite, but firm. "We were hoping you could provide us with some information—the student roster from the class Frank took with you last year."

The old man looked at me as if I had just asked to see his mother's secret recipe for the world's best chocolate cake. "An irregular request. A very irregular request indeed." He pushed his chair back from the table but never stood up. It was only then that I saw the wheels on either side of his armrests. He rolled across the floor, out of his laboratory and into his office. All the while he was whistling a tune that I recognized but couldn't place. As Elwood and I followed him, I tapped out a chord from the same piece of music.

Upham was suddenly elated. "Are you fond of du Hond? I myself only discovered him in the last few months." He paused and looked me in the eye. "I find his work . . . soothing." He whistled louder as he rolled over to his desk and began flipping through one of the piles of papers on his desk. The whistling became discordant, shrill, and then suddenly peaked and stopped. A smile grew across his aged face and revealed a set of yellowing teeth.

"Spring Semester, Calculus D. Twelve students, it's always twelve students, did you know that?" The question was rhetorical at least I thought it was. "Dozens apply but I only take twelve, and not at random either—well, not entirely." He pulled a file out and waved it about with flourish. "A dozen names, handpicked by me, one for each of the first twelve letters in the alphabet." He handed me a page, and for the first time I saw what I would later come to think of as a list of victims.

Spring Semester Calculus D

Abraham Alder | Leroy Beaumont | Arthur Campbell
Nicholas Dallas | Frank Elwood* | Edward Fritch
~~Walter Gilman~~ | Scott Home | Gerald Ingalls
Richard Jacobi | Nathaniel Kaye | Fritz Long

The strikethrough of Walter Gilman's name was in red ink, the same as the star next to Elwood's. The old man saw me staring, as did Elwood.

"Mr. Elwood never took his final exam, but in light of the circumstances the administration has granted him a passing grade." He smiled at Elwood. "I have no doubt you would have passed, Mr. Elwood. No doubt at all."

They were distracted by sentiment, which is why I needed to be professional. "What can you tell me about them, Professor—any of them unusual? Special? Did somebody stand out as a troublemaker, or as particularly quiet?"

"You mean besides Gilman." He looked at the list and I could see that he was trying to put names to faces. "Edward Fritch scored highest on the final exam. Arthur Campbell and Abraham Alder had some sort of a disagreement. Richard Jacobi was involved as well. Something about a girl I think, Josephine Merrill as I recall. I had her in one of my Freshman Algebra courses. Pretty girl. Of course, at my age, they are all pretty girls."

I wasn't sure if he was just being truthful or purposefully lecherous. "Can I borrow this?" I didn't wait for him to respond and grabbed a red pen from his desk. I crossed out the names of Alder, Jacobi and Long, and I made sure that Upham saw me do it. "Three of your students are dead, Professor. Think the Administration will do anything for their roommates?"

"Three dead?" Upham shook his head. "That can't be right."

"It was in the papers, Professor." My voice was slow and direct. "Mr. Elwood is very concerned. He's in danger. He has asked me to help him, to protect him."

Upham's tremors seemed to grow. "I don't . . . I don't read the papers. Not since Dunwich. Doctor's orders." He laughed again, but it was a sad, scared laugh. "I spent ten days in a bed in St. Mary's back at the end of October. Nervous exhaustion, they said. Apparently, I've worked myself sick." He seemed to grow small. "At least that's what Doctor Peaslee says."

At the mention of my father-in-law's name my stomach clenched. "Doctor Peaslee?"

"Nathaniel Wingate Peaslee, My psychoanalyst. We've made real progress over the last few weeks. I'm eating better, my blood pressure is down, and I'm sleeping better at night." He smiled nervously. "I've had to give up coffee, my pipe and my nightly glass of scotch. Frankly, things are kind of boring, but—as you said, Mr. Elwood—that might be something to cherish. The alternative, at least according to Dr. Peaslee, is a plot, six feet under, and that is something that I would like to put off for as long as possible."

I nodded. "That's a sentiment I can get behind, Professor Upham, and one I would like to apply to Mr. Elwood a well. If you think of anything else that might be helpful, please don't hesitate to contact me." I handed him one of my cards, thankful that it only had my maiden name and our corporate initials. I didn't want Upham to know that his doctor was the father of my husband. It would have made things messy, complicated. And while complicated was my business, I didn't need that kind of complicated in my personal life.

He took the card in his trembling hand and spoke in that deep but cracking voice. "Of course, of course." He sat up in his chair, trying to be something more than he was. "Now if you please, I would like to get back to work." He turned and rolled back into his laboratory, whistling that strange, haunting tune.

Elwood and I said our farewells and left the man's office. Mrs. Murry was waiting for us. There was a young boy with her, half hiding behind her dress. "He's not a well man." Her voice was a little sad. "He hasn't been for a while now. He had an episode last year. He spent a couple of days in St. Mary's in late October. His health has been deteriorating. He hasn't been able to walk for months."

Elwood opened his mouth to say something, but I put a hand on his and made sure my voice was the only one that Mrs. Murry heard. "I'm sorry, we shouldn't have bothered him."

"No, you shouldn't have," I was surprised to hear the young boy speak to an adult so boldly. "He's a great man, a brilliant scientist. He's going to save the world."

"Alexander!" His mother was clearly embarrassed and scowled at the child.

"It's all right," I said. I didn't wait for an apology—I just rushed Elwood out the front door, back into the cold.

It wasn't until we were a block away, the wind whipping at our bones, that Elwood spoke again. "Did you see those calculations on the blackboards?" He paused; his teeth chattered.

I stopped and looked at my client. There was fear and confusion in his eyes. "I did."

"I may only be a student, but those calculations were meaningless." I started to walk away, and Elwood rushed to catch up. "Those blackboards, all those calculations and symbols—it's meaningless. He's been spending months writing on the walls, but it's all just nonsense."

"So, what if he has?"

Elwood stopped. He just stopped there in the street and stared at the back of my coat as I walked away. Then I heard him say words I had heard spoken in Arkham before. It was a sentiment which was far too common in this city. "He's insane, isn't he?"

I kept moving forward, heading home to Griffith House. I didn't bother to look back.

"He's as mad as a hatter."

Fifth Report

Robert Peaslee

It was late in the afternoon when I came in out of the cold. The sun was low on the horizon and cast ominous shadows through the clouds. I left my coat on the brass hook by the door and made my way into the consulting room where I could hear Megan talking to Lydecker, who was propped up behind his desk. She had pulled a rolling blackboard out of her lab and had written a list of names on it. Frank Elwood was on the couch in the back. I could see he was upset; his name was on the list.

Abraham Alder

Leroy Beaumont

Arthur Campbell

Nicholas Dallas

Frank Elwood

~~Edward Fritch~~

~~Walter Gilman~~

Scott Home

Gerald Ingalls

~~Richard Jacobi~~

Nathaniel Kaye

~~Fritz Long~~

I flipped my notebook open and compared what I had written down at the police station with what was on the board. I shook my head disapprovingly. "You are not going to like what I have to tell you."

Megan let slip a short, sarcastic laugh. "Are you pregnant?"

"No." I shot back.

"Am I pregnant?"

"What? No!" I was annoyed—amused, but annoyed. "At least, I don't think so." I paused. "Are you?"

She shook her head. "No. What did the cops tell you?"

I flopped into a chair, still flipping through my notebook. "The State Police have records of the deaths of Long on Aylesbury Pike on New Year's Eve, Jacobi right here in Arkham on January 7 in a lumber mill down on Water Street, and Fritch on January 21 out in the wilds west of Arkham."

I heard Elwood let loose a small cry, but the creaking voice of Lydecker drowned him out. "I assume you noticed the pattern?"

I frowned. "Yeah, and based on that I found another death. You can cross Nicholas Dallas off the list. Coast Guard found him in Kingsport Harbor on the 15th of January."

Megan was crossing Dallas' name off when Elwood suddenly appeared behind me. I hadn't even heard him stand up. "What pattern?"

Long died on New Year's Eve. Jacobi on the 7th. Dallas the 14th, and Fritch on the 21st. Every seven days, every Monday, one of your classmates has died." I made a gesture of conciliation. "So, you can officially count me as a believer. Someone is killing off your classmates." I looked at the revised board.

Abraham Alder
Leroy Beaumont
Arthur Campbell
~~Nicholas Dallas~~
Frank Elwood
~~Edward Fritch~~
~~Walter Gilman~~
Scott Home
Gerald Ingalls
~~Richard Jacobi~~
Nathaniel Kaye
~~Fritz Long~~

"So, if the pattern holds, then there should have been another murder last week." Megan was stating the obvious, but someone had to. "And another one today." She began reciting names off the board. "We have to find Alder, Beaumont, Campbell, Home, Ingalls, and Kaye. At least one of them is dead, and the others are all in grave danger."

"You're mistaken, Megan," Lydecker hissed. "I think you will find that both Mister Ingalls and Mister Alder are already dead. Ingalls on Christmas Eve, and Alder last week." His eyes darted back and forth across the list.

"Megan, please rewrite the list placing the names in three columns but keep it alphabetical from left to right."

Megan nodded and with a quick flourish cleared the existing list and then with a fluid hand rewrote it as Lydecker had insisted. In moments, it appeared as he had requested.

~~Abraham Alder~~ | Leroy Beaumont | Arthur Campbell

~~Nicholas Dallas~~ | Frank Elwood | ~~Edward Fritch~~

~~Walter Gilman~~ | Scott Home | ~~Gerald Ingalls~~

~~Richard Jacobi~~ | Nathaniel Kaye | ~~Fritz Long~~

Lydecker wheezed and then began explaining what he had deduced. "Gilman was the first to die. Then I suspect Ingalls, followed by Long on New Year's Eve, then every seven days after a new victim, but in a very specific pattern. A pattern that kept this list balanced: Jacobi, Dallas, Fritch, and Alder." He paused and gasped for air. "Mr. Campbell should die tonight—that is, if my analysis of the pattern is correct."

"Why haven't we heard anything about Alder and Ingalls?" Megan pondered aloud.

It was Elwood's turn to offer an explanation. "I think they graduated, left town, perhaps even the state." He paused and let that sink in. "Five of my classmates are confirmed dead, another two are likely so. And the cops don't even know about it." A light dawned in his eyes. "How do we save Arthur Campbell?" We all just stood there in silence. "Campbell is going to die tonight." The young man's voice was tinged with worry, but I wasn't sure if it was for his classmates or for himself. "Arthur Campbell is going to die tonight!"

Megan put a hand on his shoulder. "Do you know where he lives? How to get in touch with him?" Elwood shook his head. "I'll call campus security. We have some pull with the university maybe we can get addresses, or a copy of the student directory."

He pulled away from her. "I'm tired, and I need to study. Would you mind terribly if I went to my room?"

"What about dinner?" Megan queried.

The look on his face was full of melancholy remorse. "I'm not hungry. Eating just doesn't seem important right now."

"I . . ." Megan let her thought die. "Mrs. Kreitner will leave something in the kitchen for you."

I'm not sure that Elwood heard her as he wandered out of our offices. We listened as he climbed the stairs and they creaked under his weight.

It was odd to have someone else moving about and making noise in Griffith House. It was an old house, built not for our motley band of barely human adventurers, but for a family. The house had a personality all of its own, and I knew that from the first day I had lived in it. I knew it didn't particularly like me. When Megan came home, when she and I moved in, I thought things had gotten better. The house seemed comfortable. Then we moved Lydecker in—I think that's when the house turned sour. Not at first, but slowly, over the course of weeks and months. Is that even possible? Can a house grow to hate the people who live in it? Can it long to be something else, to belong to someone else?

I suppose it must be true, and this is why—on occasion—as I walk the streets of Arkham, I am afraid. There are so many houses, and I think that for too long they have hated so much. If a house can learn to hate, can a whole town? Does Arkham hate the people who live in it?

And—if so—what will it do when that hate finally grows too great to contain?

Sixth Report

Roman Lydecker

The following represent my attempts to reconstruct the events that led to
the deaths of Frank Elwood's classmates. They are based on what records
and evidence were gathered by local law enforcement agencies, and that
were made available to me after the application of considerable influence. In
places, I have taken the liberty of speculating on certain issues, sometimes to
the point of fancy. I apologize if my literary license has gone one or two steps
too far.

24 December 1928

By all accounts, Gerald Ingalls, age 25, had been a fine student. His record
at Miskatonic University showed satisfactory grades, and only included one
letter of reprimand, but this had been during his freshman year, when most
students are still trying to test the limits of what they could get away with at
college. Ingalls went too far once, but only once. Either that, or he learned how
to be more discreet. The young man had studied engineering at Miskatonic
University, but, despite his grades and glowing recommendations from his
professors, he had not pursued any of the opportunities that had come his
way, instead returning to his family home to take a position in the family
business, which for the last fifty years was the buying and selling of tobacco.
It was a trade that made his family well off, but one that Gerald himself had
expressed little love for.

Still, that had not stopped him from taking full advantage of his family's
wealth, as evinced by the party they sponsored on Christmas Eve. The Ingalls
bought modest presents for all the children in town and supplied all the tables
and chairs for the potluck that gathered beneath the tree in the town square.
The Ingalls supplied the tree as well, and by doing so bought themselves the
right to decorate it as they saw fit. It had become a competition amongst

members of the Ingalls family, only one of whom was selected each year to handle the yule décor. This season Gerald had been awarded the task, and he had brought in professional decorators from New York to help him. Two weeks of designs, another week of crafting what couldn't be bought, and then over the last few days his workers and he had followed the plan to exacting detail, even bringing in icicles and powdered snow to decorate the branches.

It had all been done under the strictest of security. A fence had been installed around the green, and then lined with yew trees to keep prying eyes from seeing the spectacle. There were fifty balls, all hand-blown Italian glass, in three different colors. Garland wreaths encircled the tree from base to tip. Carved birds were secreted on branches, staring with tiny glass eyes that caught the light in a multitude of facets and reflected it back like twinkling stars. It was a cavalcade of lights and metal and glass, and Gerald was sure that it was much better than the one his sister had organized last year, even if her star hadn't tilted like his.

The little imperfection ate at Gerald. The staff had tried to fix it, but no matter what they did the damned thing just kept leaning over. Not much, mind you, but just enough to be more than noticeable. He was sure that he could fix it. He had brought a ladder and a pair of pruning shears. It wouldn't take much, just a minute or two. A snip here, a snip there was all that was needed, or so he had convinced himself.

Gerald Ingalls would never get the chance to solve the problem. He would never get to use the ladder, or the shears. He barely saw the shadow that came out of the darkness and knocked him to the ground. He hit the frozen earth hard, first with his lower back, and then the back of his head followed with a muffled, meaty smack. The woolen hat he wore suppressed the sound of his head hitting ice, and it prevented his skull from shattering, but it could do nothing to warn him of the mortal danger he was in as he sat up in bewilderment—nor could the hat do anything to halt the shears came at him from the darkness again, and again, and again.

An hour later, the patriarch of the family, frustrated by the disappearance of his son and the growing crowd of townspeople eager to see the display, unlocked the gate to the town green and let the citizens of New Milford see what was waiting for them behind the fence and the rows of decorative yews. They found the young man, though it took a moment for the crowd to register how fully involved young Gerald had become in the process of decorating. A collective gasp rushed through the townsfolk as they witnessed Gerald's final touches: his fingers hung like icicles from the branches; his entrails wrapped round the tree like garland strands; splashes of blood had frozen to the tree, and they glittered in the light of the display like a vast array of crimson stars amidst the branches. The real show piece, though, was the new crown of the tree. Gone was the crooked star, replaced by the watchful and somehow mischievous head of young Master Ingalls—his eyes were two twigs of berried mistletoe, and his mouth was affixed in a wide grin, a caricature of holiday cheer that welcomed the townsfolk to enjoy the new display. Gerald Ingalls had done what he had wanted—he had finally finished decorating the tree. And yes, the head was on straight—perfectly so.

31 December 1928

As he rounded the turn, Fritz Long put his foot back down on the accelerator and took the speed of his 1925 Nash Ajax up above sixty miles per hour. It wasn't a safe thing to do; the Nash began to shake at 65. Nor was the Aylesbury Pike designed for such speeds, but he was running late. He was already an hour late to Arkham and there was still an hour of driving ahead of him. He let out a huff of frustration. He had left Aylesbury on time, even a little early, but an accident barred the way out of town: a truck had broken an axle just by Dean's Corners, and the rough-looking men who had come to help seemed more intent on transferring its cargo than clearing the road. Long had recognized a few of them as members of the Perkins family—notorious moonshiners, and prone to violence. So Long had chosen to be patient rather than risk the ham-fisted wrath of Timothy and Alexander Perkins. His patience had cost him, and his girl Liza was going to be none too pleased over him being late, but he could feel the weight of the small box that was in his coat pocket and knew that the ring inside would make everything better.

He was wrong. Elizabeth Larson would never see that ring. In fact, she would never again see Fritz Long.

As the road wound round the edge of Billington's Wood, queer shadows fell from that rumor-haunted forest, reaching across the road like hungry arms, only to be banished by the light that cut through the dark like an avenging blade. Long had always hated this stretch of road. Even in daylight the trees seemed too close together and the underbrush seemed too thick to be normal. The vast majority of it seemed dead, with some hints of green scattered amongst the browns and greys of that heinous and drab stretch of road, but Long couldn't believe that the sparsity of such fresh leaves could support the tangle of vines and briars that lined the roadside and grew unchecked into the wood itself. It was a terribly lonely stretch of country, and—in Long's mind—more disturbing to the psyche than that of the Blasted Heath, where almost nothing at all dared to grow. He wondered to himself which was worse: a land so barren that nothing would take root, or one so fertile that everything bloomed to vast unnatural proportions, filling up all the available space, like some unchecked mutation? He preferred desolation to this unchecked and cancerous growth.

Lost in thought, he took another curve and caught the shadow standing there in the center of the road. It was a man, or at least the shadow of a man. What was the idiot doing in the middle of the road? Long slammed on the brakes, he felt the tires lock up and then begin to skid across the road. Time slowed and the milliseconds seemed to stretch as the car sped toward the figure in the road. Headlights struck the shadow, revealing its true nature. It was a man and Long could see the folds of the dark coat, the slouch hat that nearly hid the face—a face that he thought for a brief moment that he recognized. It was impossible, though. What we *he* be doing out here?

Then the car hit the shadowy figure. The headlights shattered, and the illumination they had generated faltered and then vanished. The front end crumpled, as if the Nash hadn't hit a person at all, but something far more substantial. Fritz Long, unfettered by any sort of restraining device, was launched from his seat, his skull cracking the windshield and allowing the rest of him to follow through the shattered glass, the shards tearing and slicing his flesh. Ejected from the car, he flew over the hood and tumbled hard against the road, breaking his spine and both his legs.

The next day the coroner would confide to the investigating officer that he hoped that Fritz Long had died on impact. It wasn't that his other wounds were particularly painful; if he had survived, the spinal cord injury had likely made him unable to feel anything below the neck. He would have bled to death in an hour or so anyway, and his wounds were so extensive that it was unlikely that any physician could have saved him. What the coroner had been referring to was the fact that moments after being ejected from the car several other vehicles, trucks mostly, came through the scene and either didn't see Long in the road, or didn't care. He was run over at least three more times before a car hit some debris from the Nash and spun out of control, landing in a ditch and knocking the driver unconscious. The driver of that vehicle, Thomas Burton, a member of the notorious Perkins Gang, was arrested and charged with manslaughter, though this was really just leverage used to try and turn him on his fellow moonshiners.

The ring that Long was going to give Elizabeth Larson was never found, at least not by the State Police. Presumably it's still there, lying on the side of the road in its fancy box, forgotten by everyone to whom it had ever or would ever mean anything. Just another piece of roadside detritus, to be swallowed up by the forces that bury such things in the midden piles of roadside swales—a forgotten diamond in the rough.

January 7, 1929

Richard Jacobi wasn't supposed to be in the Burke Mills Lumberyard after hours, but his own apartment was just too cold to stay in. The landlord had promised to do something about the heat, but the oil burner in the basement seemed to break down every other day, usually in the morning, which gave Mr. Robbins the landlord time to fix things—and by "fix things" he meant banging on the pipes with a heavy wrench while cursing at the various women who he felt had ruined his life. This time the burner had failed in the evening, and Robbins had decided that the time had finally come to call a professional, and despite the late hour one had indeed agreed to come out, but the diagnosis was not good. A number of parts were needed, and there was a significant amount of labor involved. It could be fixed, but it would take a day, maybe two at the most. So Richard Jacobi, astronomy student had sought refuge in his place of employment. Most of the yard consisted of stacks and stacks of semi-finished boards—some uncovered, some underneath open-air sheds, none of which would have made decent shelters. Instead, Jacobi had gone into the main office, where a small Franklin stove could be used to keep him warm. A small desk lamp was sufficient to allow him to study, and he had spent hours reading Denison Olmsted's erudite *Observations on the Meteors of November 13th, 1833*. It was somewhat tedious but informative towards his own work collating the observations of the stone that fell over Arkham back in 1882. It was an ambitious project, but one he hoped to resolve soon. There were just a few manuscripts left for him to look at: four sets of notes by those who had actually recovered the infamous object and brought it back for study. This quartet of pages was enshrined inside a cabinet of what Professor Armitage had designated the restricted section of the Miskatonic University Library. It had taken him weeks to obtain the necessary permissions to gain access, and now his appointment was scheduled for the very next day. If all went well, he believed his thesis might be complete by the end of the month.

He would never keep his appointment with Armitage, and never would finish his thesis.

There was a coffee pot that sat on the stove; it was an old, battered thing made of some metal or other. It had been painted once, but now only a few flecks of blue remained on its battered and patina clad body. The contents, now poured into his own cup, had been a particular strong brew, one that

Old Man Burke bought from a merchant on the far side of the river. It came from a place near Sumatra that Burke called Mondo Island, and it was a thick, dark and rich with a bitter taste that even copious amounts of sugar could not mask. Staring at his cup Jacobi could not help but think of the darkness as a metaphor for the soul of the bitter old man that was his boss, Eliphas Burke. Surely, thought Jacobi, all that remained of any human decency had long since fled the old man, leaving only a dark abyss swirling with black grains like dread memories of past transgressions concentrated into flecks of pure human malignancy.

It was a wild, almost indecent fancy, and Jacobi pushed it from his mind as fast as he could. He had always had such thoughts, and for a while had collected them in a journal with the intent of one day assembling them into a volume detailing his observations of the human condition, but that had been years ago. Now the only things that filled his notebooks were observations of the heavens and the things that fell from them. The stars were his life, and he hoped he could find a way for them to become his occupation. Miskatonic had a decent observatory and a fairly well-known graduate program, it would be easy to stay in Arkham if he had to.

The desk lamp flickered and somewhere in the yard one of the portable saws—a large one—kicked on and filled his ears with a familiar metallic squeal. His first instinct was to douse the light and hide, but just as he wasn't supposed to be there neither was anyone else. Certainly no one was authorized to operate the saw at this hour, in the dark, in freezing temperatures. It was dangerous; hell, that saw was always dangerous. Against all logic, but completely consistent with the folly of youth that conveys to young men the idea that they are immortal, Richard Jacobi left the warm comfort of the office and went into the yard to investigate.

They found him the next morning. The official report would say that he had been drunk and had fallen into the saw by accident. What the report couldn't explain was how he had been cut twice, once lengthwise and then again across the abdomen.

January 14, 1929

Nicholas Dallas was drunk. He hadn't intended to be, but someone had spiked the punch and he and several others at the party had consumed more than their fair share. Now he was staggering down the streets of Kingsport, the sounds of the ships in the harbor guiding him toward the ship that he had been contracted to. He hadn't ever expected to follow in his father's footsteps—going to Miskatonic University was supposed to keep him away from all that, but things hadn't worked out as planned. His father had taken ill, too ill to fulfill his contract and too ill to pay off the debts he owed, debts that weren't just about money. His father's illness forced young Dallas to take his father's lot in life and his place on the trawler that ran out of Kingsport Harbor and out to the fishing grounds, but it wasn't fish that would fill the boats holds when it returned—fishing was merely a cover. The trawler's real business was opium, and occasionally silk. They'd been smuggling for years, and the local cops had never even come close to catching them. Despite his success, Dallas found the whole thing distasteful—a necessary evil that he would rather not be part of. He had a degree in chemistry, and a job waiting for him up at a plant in Bolton that was his ticket out of smuggling. He was going to leave this world behind, and he would take his parents with him. He didn't know that after tonight he wouldn't have to worry about his parents or smuggling ever again.

The road sloped down toward the harbor, and the old stones that comprised it were slick with frost, which made walking more difficult than it should have been. The ship sailed at dawn, and dawn would bring exhaustion and regret. He hadn't meant to be out as late as he was, but the party had been very entertaining. At one point, Laura Masterton had dragged him to a dark corner, supposedly to talk, but neither of them had factored in the perfect storm of booze and the longing created by two years of separation. The dim twilight of the corner gave them the excuse they needed, and within moments their bodies and lips were pressed together, their hands fumbling drunkenly—almost independently—all over each other. It was just like old times. Like when they had been in high school, sneaking into the locker room at the public pool. They had never courted, never even been out on a date, but there was an unspoken attraction between the two of them that always led to passions flaring. It was nice to think about Laura, to hold her, to remember her breath against his neck. It made the cold go away, it made all the fear and frustration that filled his life seem inconsequential. Maybe it was time he finally asked her out. They could go walking, just walking. She would make a fine wife. If he could just talk to her, really talk to her. Perhaps they could go to a concert, or a moving picture.

His stumbling gait had brought him closer to the harbor. He could see the ships, their masts and the funnels swaying gently with the waves. The cold December wind that blew off the bay was only a gentle breeze, more bracing then freezing, but that was just for now. Dallas knew that the weather this time of year was fickle and that the forecast for tomorrow was high winds and high seas. Which meant that he was looking at the potential for hypothermia, with a side of seasickness. There was nothing worse than watching your lunch churn into the prop wash as you hung your head over the stern and tried to massage some sense of feeling back into your fingers and toes. It could happen to the best of sailors. Not to him, of course, or to his father, but his Uncle Ross—it had happened to him during the winter of Twenty-Three, and it had cost him two fingers on his left hand. Given what would happen to him in the next few minutes, Nicholas Dallas might have preferred the loss of a few fingers.

A shadow rushed across his path, startling young Dallas out of his drunken reverie and setting him off balance. With a twist of one foot and a turn of another he was suddenly no longer upright, and the world gained a different perspective as he looked up from the street level. His backside would be sore, he supposed but he was grateful that he hadn't hit his head. He chuckled at his good fortune and cast an intoxicated look up at the figure that had sent him all catawampus.

"Give me a hand up, would you?" He stretched out his right arm and felt the stranger grasp it with both hands. In a fluid, almost effortless motion, he was lifted from the cold street, but oddly he couldn't feel his feet gaining any traction on the ground. He looked down and in utter terror found that the ground, the street, and the city itself were receding away. He was rising into the air like a child's balloon, rising higher with each passing second. He looked up and into the eyes of the man who had lifted him up. What he saw there was inevitability and Dallas began to scream for help, struggling fiercely against his captor. Despite the struggles, his attacker remained unmoved and steadfast, rising to even greater heights—its eerie silence in direct contrast to the screams of Dallas—and drifting out over Kingsport Harbor.

How long Dallas struggled against the shadowy figure cannot be said. Likewise, whether he escaped from the thing or was let go cannot be known. What is known is that he was found on the morning of the sixteenth, his body bobbing between the quay and a moored sloop. They would have found him sooner, but no one was evening looking for a body. His family assumed he was out to sea, and the captain of the fishing trawler had sailed without him, having no time for crew who were tardy, and no desire to pause and tell the harbor master of the young man's failure to report.

The body of Nicholas Dallas was a terrible thing to behold. It was recognizable as human, but limbs were bent in odd directions, and the chest was caved in, while the belly was distended. The autopsy found that nearly every bone in his body had been broken, the result of some tremendous force acting on the corpus of the young man. Though he would never say so on any official record, the coroner speculated the young man had been carried up to some great height, and then hurled downward with tremendous force, encountering some rigid object along the way. On the official report he listed death by falling caused by misadventure; it fit the evidence provided on a superficial level. The police investigation fared little better. Flabbergasted, the local authorities decided that the poor man had wandered up the lofty heights of Kingsport Head, and, in a drunken stupor, fell over the edge. The fall would have sent young Dallas tumbling over the cliffside before hitting the beach and being washed around the harbor. It was a plausible theory, and one that satisfied nearly all concerned, even the boy's father, who had no desire to urge an investigation into his son's activities. The only person who voiced any objection was a young intern in the morgue from Miskatonic University who couldn't understand why the body of Nicholas Dallas was so mangled, but his head was untouched, unblemished, without even a bruise. Surely if the man had fallen from the cliff his head would have had some evidence of damage. It was a conundrum he voiced only once, for the look he got from the coroner made it clear that his opinion was neither wanted, nor needed.

January 21, 1928

Edward Fritch stared out at the vast wasteland that was the Blasted Heath and tried to understand what all the fuss was about. It was a tract of land much like any other in the state: a plain of low plants that stretched out for hundreds of acres in either direction, bounded here and there by forested woodlands and the occasional farm, or—in this case—the remnants of farms. Over the last few years, Essex County and Arkham had slowly been acquiring the entirety of the area with the plan of building a reservoir to feed the future demands of the city and its outlying villages. No one lived here anymore, the last few farmers had moved out two years ago when the final survey had been laid out. One would have thought that would have been the end of the matter, but it wasn't.

There were rumors that the soil was bad, and that the trees that grew along the edges, thick and twisted and misshapen, were diseased. The rumors were unsubstantiated, attributed by most to the surveyor who worked throughout the area in 1926. Fritch personally thought the man spent too much time listening to too much backwoods gossip, and then spread too much of it himself.

Whatever the cause, the county had contracted with the university to carry out a scientific study of the land to allay fears about potential soil contaminants being transferred into the waters of the future reservoir. The university assigned the work to the International Society of Limnologists, a multi-disciplinary committee formed three years earlier to showcase the merits and potential of Limnology—a ground-breaking new field of science that was best described as the oceanography of lakes. Limnology involved a variety of disciplines including chemistry, biology, and naturalism to study the holism of a freshwater body. Miniature expeditions to various regional lakes and streams had already been undertaken, and the university established a long-term investigation of Hangman's Slough on the southwest side of town. The knowledge gained concerning the seasonality of flows and nutrients and the responses of various invertebrate populations was astounding. At least Fritch thought so. He also thought he Blasted Heath Reservoir project presented a similar opportunity and showed great promise There may not be any water flooding the lands yet, he thought as he surveyed the area, but through careful selection of samples and experimentation the laboratories of Miskatonic University just might be able to tell the committee something about how the waters and soils of the area would interact.

Fritch had been dispatched to collect samples. The drive to the unkempt patch of land that sat between the river to the east and Billington's Wood to the north felt like an eternity spent in the shoddy and rust-covered car borrowed from the university. It was a cold day and the wind cut right through the carriage of the car, making Fritch shiver violently. This had better be worth it, Fritch thought as he surveyed the landscape before him.

To the west and south, the low rocky hills that the natives called the Cotoahaad, rose. Under the planned designs, these would form the western boundary of the reservoir. There would have to be some earthwork, but all in all it wouldn't take much to seal the valley off, and then pump the water in from the Miskatonic River. Borrowing engineers from the Scituate Reservoir in Rhode Island, the Blasted Heath Project was likely to avoid significant pitfalls and progress much faster than previous ventures. The university team just needed a few tests and studies to put these damned unfounded fears to rest and squelch the insidious rumoring stemming from the area's history.

And that meant sending Fitch out on days like this. Not that he minded. He was, after all, eminently qualified. He had been at Miskatonic University for six years, since he was seventeen. In that time Fritch earned enough credits to graduate with degrees in chemistry, physics, biology and agronomy, but he never actually bothered to apply for graduation. Fritch's education was completely free—the result of his grandfather's dealings with the University decades ago. Fritch vaguely recalled that his esteemed ancestor sold them some land or something, with the stipulation that his descendants could attend for free. No one expected one of those descendants to be a professional student, but Fritch was, and he was good at it. Even more, he was quite adept at manipulating the system. He knew the student handbook by heart, knew the ins and outs of campus life, politics and government better than any professor or administrator, and he was adept at applying for grants and scholarships. Thus, he found himself not only with free tuition, but also complementary room and board paid through various scholarships and the grant monies from various college programs assured he was well taken care of. Even this job of collecting samples of sediments, plants and rocks came with a small stipend, but only because Fritch had known to invoke an obscure departmental rule.

Unfortunately, his ability to quote academic chapter and verse wouldn't save him on this desolate day in this sparse place.

Fritch suddenly paused; he had heard a stick crack somewhere behind him. He turned to look, but there was nothing there. The low brush hid a myriad of animal life including mice, rabbits, foxes, and the occasional badger, but nothing large or clumsy enough to snap a stick.

He scanned the landscape and while he saw nothing overt, he did notice that the entirety of the wild land had suddenly become still. The wind ceased to blow, the sedges stopped swaying, and the Blasted Heath suddenly froze—though it had nothing to do with the temperature. The flow of time itself ceased, and the clouds above paused their slow crawl to the east, their shadows now permanent stains on the fabric of the earth. And there in the gloom he finally saw it—saw it move, and saw the umbra face of death as it came for him, tearing in terrible silence across the sedges.

He dropped his samples and listened to them as they clinked and tumbled through the branches and onto the frozen earth below. He didn't turn to run; he did not even think of escape. He stood transfixed by the doom that came for him. It was, in a way, a beautiful thing—terrible, in the way that the angels in the Bible were terrible, a being at once awe-inspiring and terrifying. It was a fragment of divine wrath that clawed through the air towards him, and as it finally and inevitably struck a fatal blow he knew at last what had been missing in his life. In that last second of his existence, he ceased any semblance of faith in rationality and embraced the mysterious nature of the universe that all of the sciences had failed to explain to him. He no longer believed; he knew, and that was more than enough to set his mind at peace.

Two hunters out of Bolton found him the next day. If it hadn't been for the ravens, they might have missed him entirely. The birds had been at his eyes and face, but something larger had torn open the abdomen and removed all the organs. The game warden blamed it on a bear and posted a bounty. He never did read the coroner's report that came two days later. If he had, he would have seen that Edward Fritch's organs had not been torn out by a bear. The coroner ruled out any animal at all being involved in the attack. In his expert opinion, whatever—whoever—removed the organs did so with a precision far surpassing any surgical technique the aged physician had ever seen before.

January 28, 1929

Abraham Alder stood on the shore at Martin's Beach and stared out at the roiling ocean, contemplating his future. The beach was covered with tufts of foam that rolled across the wet sand like tumbleweeds in a desert. He loved walking along the beach in winter. It was a lonely, contemplative place where he could clear his mind and focus his thoughts. He honestly thought that if more people took the time to be alone—to just be alone and listen to themselves rather than the cacophony of voices and noise that cluttered their daily routines—then they might actually begin to understand themselves. It was an idea he developed after reading Thoreau's *Walden*. He couldn't bring himself to embrace the concept of simple living—the universe was too wondrous to not explore it—but he made time to shut out the world and just be alone and think. Which led him to places like this, lonely places where few people chose to tread. It hadn't always been so; once this place had been a holiday getaway during both summer and winter, but that had been before a terrible tragedy had killed a dozen or so bathers, all in front of the eyes of hundreds of other beachgoers. The horrible fluke accident was not the fault of the local hotel but that had not stopped the steady decline of tourism to the area. Now the old Victorian hotel stood nearly empty, despite reasonable prices and excellent views. Tales were told comparing Martin's Beach to Innsmouth, misinformation and nonsense promoted mostly by resorts and hotels at other nearby towns in an effort to hold the town under as it drowned. It made Alder sad that people would be so cruel, but on the other hand it left the beach for him to enjoy alone.

It would be the last time he ever had such a pleasure.

Alder found he wasn't the only person on the beach. He frowned at the realization and tried to make out the distant shape. He could see a figure in the distance, a blurry shape with a large coat blowing in the sea breeze. He paused in his walk and looked down at a tangle of driftwood that had washed ashore. Stripped of bark and cured by the sea into a pale grey, it was strangely beautiful, and though it was entirely natural, it seemed somehow alien, transformed by whatever esoteric trials and tribulations the ocean had subjected it to. Alder had often thought that the waters of the Atlantic strange and had seen the most common of objects transformed by time and the elements cast upon its shores.

Satisfied with his introspection he stood up and took a step forward. He was no longer alone. The figure that had seemed so far away was now mere feet away, but it was no clearer in resolution than it had been. Alder thought he could see a face, a familiar face at that, but it was so blurred. He squinted, thinking the salt breeze had interfered with his vision, but the image just jumped and skipped about, as if purposefully avoiding identification. He opened his mouth to say something, a greeting of some sort, but as he did his world turned upside down.

The figure in black (or was it a black figure?) swirled and dissolved into a shadowy mist that streamed through the air and into his gaping mouth and down his throat. He gagged, and his body reflexively tried to vomit, but his throat was full and instead he fell to the sand clawing at his throat. He tried to scream but couldn't move any air from his lungs. He spasmed and bucked in agony and then raised his arms up in a desperate bid to attract someone's attention, but to no avail. In less than a minute he was dead, his body contorted and twisted.

When the beachcombers found him the next morning, they barely recognized him as human, and thought perhaps he was some sort of mannequin, or doll. It was only when the crabs crawled out of his mouth that they realized he was flesh and blood and not some piece of flotsam from some long-forgotten wreck. The investigators understood the error, though, and none of them could explain why Alder's skin had turned grey and had the cracked consistency of old driftwood.

Through Limitless Abysses

Frank Elwood

I woke this morning in a cold sweat, my heart racing, my lungs gasping for air, my fingers clutching at the sheets. For a moment, I didn't know where I was—the surroundings were unfamiliar—and then I remembered. I remembered that Robert and Megan had taken me in, given me shelter, and offered to protect me from whoever was killing my classmates. Griffith House was nice and warm, even clean, a significant step up from the campus housing or the Witch House.

I had dreamed about the Witch House. Not surprising, really, but I feel compelled to mention the dream here. We talked about Gilman earlier in the evening, and I had been reading his copy of Hermann Weyl, trying to understand his application of Riemann surfaces to understanding the structure of the universe. He had argued that space was a four-frame manifold and showed the math to prove it. He also suggested that this allowed for one-dimensional tubes, wrinkles or folds in space-time. Gilman had made notes in the margins disputing this; he suggested that the universe was a pentad and that fact allowed for two-dimensional or even three-dimensional tubules. Here Gilman had invoked Schwarzschild's radial coordinate system and drawn two lines asymptotic to each other. One he had labeled "Space" and the other "Time", and then posed a question, "As the space and time radii approach each other, does space becomes time-like or does time becomes space-like?" It was typical of Walter to think like that, to simplify the most complex of concepts and reduce it down to a rather simple question—at least for physicists—which nobody had thought to answer yet.

I'm sure it was the reading that set the stage, put things in my brain into motion. As I think about it, I've never been much for dreaming. I met a man once who considered himself a great dreamer and he had such marvelous stories to tell, but I myself am not such a man. I dream, but my dreams are small things: about my mother and father, about a girl I once kissed, about the dog I grew up with and buried. Small dreams, yes, but small dreams are good dreams—befitting a man of my standing—and there are hardly ever any nightmares. I will not say that the events in the Witch House did not disturb my mind, any man who had watched a rat with a human face chew its way out of their friend's chest would surely suffer, but Doctor Peaslee helped me as best he could. Over the course of many therapy sessions, he taught me how to control my dreams when I needed to—when Walter and Keziah and the Brown Jenkin wormed their way into my psyche. They were only memories, churned round in my mind by whatever events of the day had brought them to the forefront. Bad days bring bad memories, and those make bad dreams.

But last night's dreams were not bad—not nightmares—at least not in the traditional sense. They were more like a memory, something Walter had described, something he himself had seen while under the influence of that accursed hovel that we had called home. Gilman told me of the things he saw, of channels of multichromal spectra inhabited by queer geometries that led to worlds graced with extraterrane architectures untold distances from our own. Of course, I had at the time dismissed these as fever-induced ramblings, but after what came later, I realized there may have been more than just madness to those stories.

Thus, last night, when I too stood on the threshold of an enormous, yawning vortex—its cacophony of color playing over me like a titan's kaleidoscope—my mind was not unfamiliar with the imagery. This is not to imply that I was not wonderstruck. It seemed as if great vistas were suddenly opened up to me, as if I had been forever lurking at the threshold of something more, something incredible and wondrous, and only now was I aware that it was even a possibility. And I was not alone; all around me, vast numbers of forms—fantastical fusions of geometries and fractal crystallizations—swarmed into and out of that spectral chasm. I tried to watch what happened to those that entered, but the nature of the vortex was such that they were accelerated beyond my view almost instantaneously. So instead, I turned my attention to those forms leaving the maelstrom.

The multitudinous swarms of shapes seemed to branch off in dozens of directions, and while some headed past me, others streamed away. It was only then that I noticed that there was not just one vortex, the sky was full of them. They were not innumerable like the stars, but there were more than I could easily count. And towards these, the vast majority of shapes seemed to fly.

"Ninety-seven gates," said a high-pitched voice.

I looked for the source and saw a small figure standing in the darkness nearby. Other than the fact the newcomer was three feet tall, the darkness obfuscated most of its other features. Peering harder into the dim space it occupied, I could just barely see its glossy black eyes reflecting back the illumination shed by the vortices overhead.

"I'm sorry?" I hadn't meant it as a question, but that is how it came out.

"There are ninety-seven gates from Earth to places beyond. That cluster over there, is for local travel—Mars, Venus, Jupiter, Saturn and Neptune. The rest are for other star systems—Altair, Epsilon Eridani, Polaris, and a few distant galaxies you don't have names for yet." He paused and seemed to laugh; it was a chittering sound. "Ninety-seven gates. A joke. A prime number, the twenty-fifth prime number—at least in base ten. They liked their jokes."

I dared to ask another question. "Who did?"

"What—oh—the makers, of course. The First, the Elder, called by their slaves the Q'Hrell." The chittering sound again. "You could call them that if you want to."

There was an implication there, something I should have understood but didn't. "Because I am a slave, and you are not?"

The voice from the darkness turned cold and the dark eyes narrowed. "Oh, I am a slave, but you are their slave, while I belong to—something else. Let it never be said that I do not know my place."

And then he stepped forward out of the darkness and into the light, and I could see what he was, and I knew his name. "Brown Jenkin!"

"He doffed his top hat and clicked his heels together, bowing his head down, but never taking his eyes off me. Those terrible eyes, inhuman eyes, set too far apart to belong to a man, and too close together, too forward facing to belong to a rat. His nose twitched, and I caught a glint of his yellow teeth.

"And you are Frank Elwood, companion, confidant, fellow student to the late Walter Gilman." He bowed his head a little further. "God rest his soul."

"Your false sympathy does you no good here, monster." My eyes were searching for a weapon, casting about frantically and finding nothing.

"False sympathy? On the contrary, my dear boy, I had only the utmost respect for Mister Gilman. He was a promising student, very skilled—an adept, one might say. Far superior to Mistress Keziah."

"And yet you killed him!" There was nothing with which to defend myself and I could feel my panic rising.

"I had been wronged. My Mistress—the Witch Keziah Mason—had been killed. The rules of vendetta had to be enforced, otherwise she might have come back." He flipped his hat back on and slid a clawed finger along its brim. "Not even I wanted that."

"So, she is truly dead?"

He chittered. "Dead, oh yes, quite. I'm quite sure of it. My agents in the Dreamlands can find no trace of her, and I have spent years searching through limitless abysses for any remaining trace of her. She is, I think, truly dead."

"Years? It has been only months."

"Surely sir we do not need to have a discussion on the meaning of time and relative dimensions in space?" He glared at me. "Or do we?"

"No, of course not. I get your meaning."

"Excellent. Let us be on our way then." He turned to leave.

I was suddenly confused. "I'm sorry?"

"Don't be sorry, boy—let's just go." There was a hint of exasperation in his voice.

"Go, I'm not going anywhere with you. Why would I go anywhere with you?" I was shouting now, panic filling my mind with flapping wings.

He reached into his waistcoat—was he wearing a waistcoat and jacket, or was that hair?—and pulled out a gold pocket watch. He looked at it, looked back at me, and then at the watch again, and then back at me. "I seem to be ahead of myself, or at least ahead of yourself." He tucked the watch away. "No matter. Time for your lessons."

I was suddenly frustrated, anger quelling the flapping panic and turning it into bemusement. Brown Jenkin suddenly seemed less frightening, and more amusing, than he had before. More like an absent-minded professor than a demonic creature of the night. I had no time for this, no desire to continue speaking to this absurd daemon. "No," I said.

He took a step toward me, and I stepped back. He spoke with a somewhat imploring tone, imploring but with a touch of frustration. "Look, this is the way of things. I am the teacher; you are the student; there must always be a teacher and a student. You have a gift, boy, the same gift Keziah had, the same gift Gilman had. Now admittedly you aren't as adept as Gilman, you'll need to work harder, and so will I."

"What gift? What are you talking about?"

"Hmmmph!" The little rat man exhaled. "I am either very early, or you are running very late. What time is it?" He suddenly waved his hands. "No, never mind that, you'll just confuse the issue even more. Look down there, boy." He was pointing away from the sky.

I couldn't see anything at first, just a kind of miasma of blue and green and brown, of darkness and light, but then things began to resolve themselves, and the longer I looked, the harder I looked, the more I could see. A river and a town, and farm fields and trees, and buildings, and small things moving about that I knew were people. "It's Arkham," I exclaimed.

"Yes, Arkham. City of Trees, Witch-Haunted Arkham. Tell me, what else do you see?"

As if a switch had been turned there were suddenly small multi-colored lights scattered throughout the town. There weren't many, but they were there, some were violet, some green a few red, and one so dark I thought it was black. But that wasn't possible; light can't be black.

"What are they?"

Brown Jenkin peered down and sighed. "Those are the dangers you face. They are everywhere. Watching, waiting, scheming, and more. The old man looking to be a young man again, the thing that sleeps in the waters, the blind man who saw too much, the family that was grazed by time, and there—see that there? The man of dust. He's waited a very long time to live again. They thought they killed him, twice now, but he's more resilient than they think. It'll be interesting when he meets up with the old man. They used to be friends, you know, but that was centuries ago. Things have changed since then, and they are both desperate and weakened by circumstance. People are going to get hurt when they finally cross paths. Best to be gone from here by then." He stood up and waved me on. "Best to be going."

"I'm sorry, no. I'm not going anywhere with you."

Suddenly any pretense was lost. The rat surged across the distance between us and grabbed me by the throat. "You think this is a game, boy? You think you can just throw your hat in the ring and play? That there aren't rules to abide by? That you don't need to be educated in the way of things? How are you going to travel through the limitless abyss, and see the universe for all its wonder and terror and glory, without me? I'm the best thing you've got going for you. The other? The calculus, he's just as weak and inexperienced as you are. He can't help you, even if he wanted to. And believe you me, he doesn't want to help you at all. Quite the opposite, really. Quite the opposite. So get it through your skull that you are coming with me!"

I pushed him away. "No, and you can't make me, can you? This place, whatever it is, you can't hurt me here, can you? You can't do much of anything at all, just talk." I stared at him, and he seemed to shrink back. "You talk big, but you're really small, aren't you? You keep talking like I need you, and maybe that is true, but . . ." and then it dawned on me. "You need me. You need someone to latch on to, to serve. Someone to give you power. You have all this knowledge, all this know-how, but you don't have the power itself. You need me."

"Yes, you mealy-mouthed little stain, I need you, but you need me as well. There is no denying that. You may think that you know what you're getting yourself into, but you don't."

"You know, I am honestly glad that I have no idea what you're talking about. But whatever it is, I'm not afraid of it, not in the slightest."

He slunk away, his eyes locked on to mine and squinting as he backed into the shadows from whence he came. "When you fail, when your friends fail you, when you finally embrace your fear, and it threatens to swallow you whole, you know where to find me." And then he was gone, and I was left once more standing by myself on the edge of that yawning chasm of spectral madness.

But I wasn't alone. There was a woman there—or at least it looked like a woman. She was tall and thin, with a large chin and pale skin. She wore a long beige-colored coat that enveloped her thin frame. It moved here and there, rustling in a breeze I could not feel. Her hair was long and seemed very fragile, I could not discern a color as I was too distracted by her gaze. Those strange pink eyes bored into me, made me feel exposed and vulnerable, as if every thought and deed was available for her casual perusal. She spoke and her voice was both the crystalline and cosmic, singing of the celestial spheres and tumultuous crashing and cracking heard at the end of the world. "You should have listened to Brown Jenkin!" And then she threw her coat open and let me see all that she was.

That is when I woke screaming, covered in sweat, my heart like a drum in my chest. I saw it just for an instant, saw what was there beneath the skin, what she hid, what she was, what she will be. In that instant, I saw it in all of its glory and wonder and for a moment I regretted not going with Brown Jenkin. But then I was awake, and the moment was gone.

I wish I could tell you more, I wish I could tell you how beautiful she was, I wish I had the words, the education, the understanding to explain it, to write it down. But I don't. And even if I could, I only saw it for a moment, a brief glimpse at divinity, a mere sliver of godhood, a single peek—a momentary glance at the gnosis of the truth is not time enough for the mind to adequately grasp the enormity of such a concept. That is all I had, though, and the more I think about it the more I believe that not seeing was for the best. Sometimes it is better just to believe, to have faith. Sometimes it is better not to know.

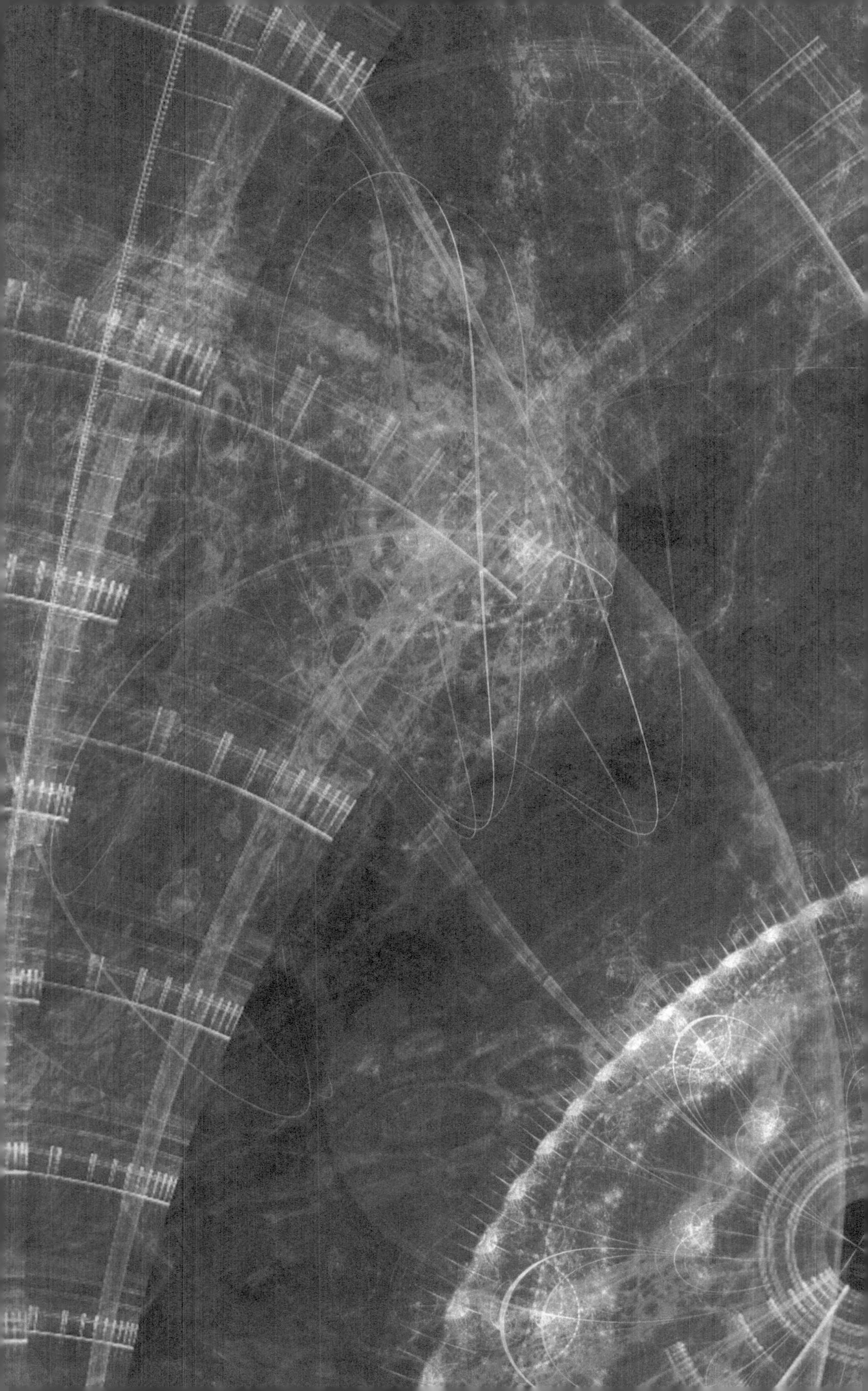

THE ELDRITCH EQUATIONS

PART TWO

DEATH OF AN OUTLIER

Seventh Report

Megan Halsey

"Peaslee!"

The booming voice that echoed through the house belonged to Phil Fricasse. He was standing in our receiving room demanding to see Robert. This, despite the fact that I had already informed him that my husband was gone, bound for Vermont on the morning train. This bit of information didn't seem to matter to the man who continued to bellow for my husband to come out and—between outbursts—take long, obnoxious drags off of a fat, greasy-looking cigar. He stood about five and a half feet tall, which I'm sure was a source of much ridicule for a cop. His hair was black, neat and slicked back using Dapper Dan. His nose was large and hooked and sat between two beady black eyes. His skin was olive. His coat was reddish-brown wool fringed with white fur down the lapels that ran down the front. The coat made him look bigger than he actually was, particularly around the shoulders. To me he looked like a stoat, a small weasel that thought of itself as more dangerous than he actually was. If you took away his badge and he grew a pencil-thin mustache he would look like one of those Italian mobsters whose photographs haunted the pages of the papers in Boston and New York.

"Peaslee!" He bellowed again, and this time Mr. Kreitner peered in, just to make sure I was safe. I waved him back. Fricasse wasn't anything to get excited over.

"Lieutenant Fricasse," I was standing between him and the door to our consulting rooms. "I've told you Robert isn't here, and Doctor Lydecker won't be seeing anyone for several hours. If you want answers to questions, you can ask me."

He took a long drag on that disgusting cigar and blew the smoke in my general direction. "Last night you called campus security, you asked for a copy of the Student Directory, and when they said no you asked for the contact information for some very specific students."

I smiled and shrugged. "Is that a crime, Lieutenant?"

I saw a vein throb in his forehead. "Last night a Miskatonic University student was killed, violently murdered. We're investigating everyone associated with the case. One of the names you asked for last night is part of our investigation." He pointed his cigar at me. "So, you are going to tell me exactly why you are so interested in Arthur Campbell."

"We have a client." When lying to the police it is best to stay as close to the truth as possible. "He has information that would have been of value to Mr. Campbell." Fricasse was frowning. "It might have even prevented his murder."

Fricasse was gawking at me. There was a light in his eyes, something dark and illuminating at the same time. "Who said anything about Arthur Campbell being murdered?"

"You said," but then I realized that he hadn't said that at all. "The murder that happened last night, the Miskatonic University student who was killed. What was his name?"

"Why do you want to know?" The detective was almost laughing. "No, don't bother. It would only be a half-truth. You and Peaslee, you have a reputation. You know that, don't you?" The cigar wagged in my face in a somewhat triumphant manner. "*Her* name was Josephine Merril. She was twenty years old. A junior, she studied Art History. She was Arthur Campbell's girlfriend." He paused for effect, inhaling and billowing a cloud of smoke. He stepped through the cloud, pacing now as he warmed to the subject. "'Was' being the operative word. They had been dating for two years. Campbell had bought her a ring. She broke it off back in October and started dating somebody else. Campbell didn't like that. Witnesses say he was a frequent visitor to the street outside her apartment. His friends say he was trying to get back together with her. Her friends say she was afraid of him. That he has a temper." He brought the cigar up to his mouth and took a long drag off of it. Exhaled. Paced through the ever-expanding cloud. "You would have to have a temper, to do what he did to her."

"And what was that?"

"Meat cleaver to the chest. Cracked her ribcage wide open. Took her heart out." He took a breath. "At least that is our theory. We'll know more once we find it."

"Find what?"

"Her heart. He took it with him." He took steps toward the door, ominous and deliberate steps. He gripped the handle and the door creaked open. "At least we think he did. We haven't found it yet, but we will. I assure you, it's all just a matter of time." He stalked out into the morning sun and left me standing there to close the door behind him.

As the latch clicked, I turned, and Elwood was there. He was supposed to be in the office. I hadn't heard him come through the door. "Elwood . . ." But I never got the rest of the words out.

"Josephine Merril. He said that Josephine Merril was dead." His eyes were wild, and he ran a hand through his hair as he paced back and forth frantically, like a caged animal.

I tried to place a hand on his shoulder to calm him, but he shrugged it off. "You knew her?"

He nodded. It was just the barest of movements. "She was an art student but was petitioning to change her major to Mathematics. She hadn't studied much in the way of numbers until she came to Miskatonic. Then she took a Geometry class—basic stuff, really, but needed by artists to understand things like perspective. Turns out she had some natural talent. Not like Gilman mind you, but still a talent. She had this uncanny knack for being able to envision and then render three dimensional objects in two dimensions but creating the illusion of three dimensions. She was also quite fascinated by the Cubism movement, Pablo Picasso and the like, though her professors discouraged these studies as grotesque." He paused and looked thoughtfully into the space behind me. "She wasn't a particularly pretty girl, but Campbell didn't care about that. She was bright. She used to hang out in the library, borrowing math texts and making small talk with the Math majors. That's where we all met her. We were all surprised when she started dating Campbell."

"Why was that?"

"We had expected her and Alder to become a couple." He stared at me as if that needed no more explanation, but the look on my face must have made it plain that I didn't understand. "Alder and Merril, they were both Jewish, and obviously Campbell was not. Then, when it became obvious that they were dating, well, that only made things more difficult. Campbell's mother is the chair of the local chapter of the Daughters of the American Revolution, not the most welcoming of organizations." I could almost taste the sarcasm. "She tried to pay Josephine to stay away from her son. Even went so far as to file a complaint with the Dean of Students. Rumor has it that the university has a secret quota for limiting the number of Jews at the school and holds them to very different academic standards." There was a melancholy sadness in his eyes. "Mister Ford may have issued an apology for the things that were published under his name in *The Dearborn Independent*, but there are plenty of others who are unrepentant in their prejudice."

I began walking into our consulting room, and he followed. "Do you think it's possible that Campbell killed Merril?" As the words left my mouth, I suddenly realized there was another question. That my simple query was part of a larger postulation. "Is it possible that Campbell is our killer? That he is the one who has been systematically hunting down your classmates?" I walked over to the board and added her name below all the others, and then crossed it out.

~~Abraham Alder~~ | Leroy Beaumont | Arthur Campbell
~~Nicholas Dallas~~ | Frank Elwood | ~~Edward Fritch~~
~~Walter Gilman~~ | Scott Home | ~~Gerald Ingalls~~
~~Richard Jacobi~~ | Nathaniel Kaye | ~~Fritz Long~~
~~Josephine Merril~~

"It's still alphabetical," Elwood remarked. I hadn't noticed, but he was right. An odd coincidence, or something more? Upham had said that he had chosen his twelve students in alphabetical order. What were the chances that a thirteenth would have a last name that started with M?

Elwood was staring at the list. "It doesn't make any sense." He was fidgeting, running his fingers against each other as if he was counting at an incredibly fast pace. "She wasn't in the class. Why is she dead if she wasn't part of the class?" He began pacing in a tight circle. "Set theory. Someone is killing members of Upham's class. Merril has been killed. Possible explanations. Merril was part of the class—no." He wandered away from the board, toward the back of the room. "Merril's murder has nothing to do with the other murders—unlikely. Merril was murdered, but all the other deaths were accidents—also unlikely. She wasn't in the class. Why is she dead if she wasn't part of the class? False assumption. The murders have nothing to do with Upham's class—possible. Possible." He flopped down onto the couch along the back wall. "Unlikely, though." His hands kept touching themselves. "Outlier. The theory is sound, but incomplete. We're missing something. Something important, something that connects Merril to the others, something that makes—made her just as much a target as everybody else."

He was shaking.

"Calm down." I said. "We'll figure it out."

With those words, everything changed. He looked up at the board, eyes blazing with the impotent fury that washes over someone who wants war and violence and vengeance—anything but peace—and yelled, "Don't tell me to calm down! Just shut up and let me think." He rose up out of the chair and took a step toward me. As he did so he raised his arm and cocked back, loading it for violence. His second step forward continued his preparation as his hand clenched into a quaking fist. A third step and his fist came crashing down at me.

Instinctively, I raised an arm to block his strike, and then blinked. Just for a moment. I waited for the blow, but I never felt it strike. But I heard it. Behind me, he smashed his fist into the blackboard and shattered it. In a blink of an eye, he had crossed the entire room.

"Elwood," I muttered, walking toward him, "how in the hell did you do that?"

There was a strange odor in the air, like electricity and burnt hair. Slowly, with my hand held out as if I were approaching a scared dog, I reached out to comfort him.

He stood there panting, trying to calm himself down. At his feet, the shattered slate and shards of the wooden frame were settling. A small cloud of chalk dust still hung in the air. He unclenched his fists and looked at his palms. There were traces of blood, four little crimson crescents, in each palm where his fingernails had dug in.

"I don't know." His voice was breaking. He was holding his hands out, and for a moment, just for a moment, I thought I could see through them, as if they were only partially real, like a projection in a cinema. I thought it was my eyes playing tricks on me, but then Elwood gasped for he saw it too. "What is happening to me?"

All I could do was watch as my client broke down and crumpled to the floor. He knelt there beside the shattered stone and pieces of wood, staring at his hands. He was trembling, and sobs of fear and confusion filled the room. A wave of emotion passed through him as if it were something physical and as he shuddered, I saw him—saw his entire body, clothes and all—fade away, just a little. I could see the floor through his body, which had become somewhat transparent, almost insubstantial. It was as if for a moment he was made of gauze or fine silk. It was brief, but I saw it and I can safely say that it was no illusion or trick of the light.

"*What is happening to me?*" He pleaded.

I could say nothing, because for the life of me, I did not know.

Eighth Report

Roman Lydecker

Monday, February fourth, eight thirty-two in the evening. Josephine Merril was tired. She had spent most of the day in a studio, her hands caked with clay. She had been trying to finish a sculpture for one of her classes. Normally, this in itself wasn't very tiring, but because it was February, the clay was too cold, and too stiff. It wouldn't do what she wanted, wouldn't stay where she wanted. Nine hours of standing on a small stepladder and she had finally gotten the ears where she had wanted them. All that was left was the nose, which she could finish tomorrow, she thought as she put on her coat. Tomorrow, her sculpture would be done.

Josephine Merril never did finish that sculpture. In fact, if any one of a number of events had lined up differently, Josephine Merril would be alive still. If she had changed her mind about leaving, if she hadn't been so tired, if the clay had been more cooperative, if the studio had been a little warmer; if any of these had worked out differently, she might still be alive.

On the way out of the building she said goodnight to her friend Bernice Crockett. According to her, Josephine Merril left the university quadrangle at eight forty-five, heading north on West Street. She crossed Church Street, skirting the jewelry maker on her right and the old wooden church on her left. The church had been abandoned for half a century. Local whispers said that the place was haunted, and that the haunting was the cause for the congregation finding a home elsewhere. The wind would have been blowing off the river that night, and it would have whipped right through the old church belfry. One can imagine the low, soulful, wailing sound that would have emanated from that moldering edifice. At this point in her ill-fated journey Josephine would have quickened her pace and bundled her coat tighter, but not because of the wind.

At the next corner at the intersection of West and Main she would have taken a right. There's a small shop on the corner, an art gallery. In warmer weather Josephine would have stopped and admired the pieces displayed in the window. She would have picked a painting, studied it, and noted the quality of the brushwork. If there had been a sculpture or a bronze statue, then she might have taken the time to admire the craftsmanship, she would pay particular attention to detail, or the lack thereof. She was an art student, and the logical assumption is that she would have stopped and looked, at least when the weather was warmer. Instead, she would have found that storefront dark and the store long closed.

As she walked down Main Street, Josephine would have found most of the shops resembled the gallery she'd just passed; their windows dark and their doors locked, closed early by proprietors eager to get home before the night turned unbearably frigid. Merchants are like that, diligently setting and advertising hours, only to ignore them at the first sign of inconvenience. The locksmith and gunsmith were both dark. The dance school was still lit, a great chandelier hung illuminating the warm brown flooring, and reflecting off of the walls of mirrors. It was as warm and inviting as it was empty. Next door the pet shop was also lit and in its storefront window a cat and her kittens snuggled to keep warm. In the center of the block was the music store where one could buy sheet music, a variety of instruments, and even phonographs. There was an upstairs apartment, but between the smell of the animals and the cacophony of discordant sounds that emanated seemingly at random from the music shop, it was difficult to rent. Only someone with little money who didn't plan on spending much time at the place would have bothered to reside there. It was perfect for an art student like Josephine.

The door to the upper level was in the small vestibule that formed the entryway to both the music and pet stores. Hers was the middle door, the one without a window, the one with the lock that tended to stick, particularly in cold weather. The windowless door led to a narrow corridor that led all the way to the back of the building and then switched backed into stairs. The light was out. Josephine had asked her landlord to fix it—three times, actually—but the old man had simply forgotten about it, though he never forgot to come by for the rent on the fourth of the month. She climbed the stairs in darkness, and they likely creaked beneath her weight, not because she was a large girl—on the contrary, she was slight—but rather because the stairs were old, their risers separated from the nails that held them to their runners. There was a landing at the top of the stairs and a window that overlooked the street. It was from here that she could see the crowds of people shopping and strolling down Main Street, and it was here that she had always looked out at the bench across the way that squatted in the shadow of a great brick warehouse. It was on that bench that Arthur Campbell had waited for her while she dressed for their dates. It was the same bench he had sat on waiting for her to come home after she had told him that she never wanted to see him again. She liked that window, she liked that bench, and—to hear her friends speak—she liked that landing, particularly the door that led to her apartment. Where the door on the street had been windowless and plain, the door on the landing was large, thick and ornate. It was more of a gate than a door and comprised five oaken planks bound together by wrought iron straps that had been shaped into small spirals at all four corners. At one point, it had been painted gold, and you could still see some traces of that, but now it was green, a warm welcoming verdant that for Josephine meant that she was home. That door, the size of it, the iron strap, the second lock that used the same key as the door below, it always made her feel safe.

She never even got the key in the lock. The door opened as she reached for the handle, surprising her and rendering her defenseless.

Based on police reports, here is what happened: her killer came at her from the front, from inside the apartment. The first blow was to her right shoulder, which shattered her clavicle, and cut deep into her chest. The second strike was across her face, which left a gash in her cheek. The third blow was to the chest and had cracked her ribcage open. After that—the report suggests—multiple blows were used to expand the opening in her chest and then to cut out her heart.

The coroner's report generously claims that Josephine was dead after the third blow; this is pure speculation. The many wounds found on her hands and arms suggest she struggled for some time before she died. It is even possible that she saw her own heart in her killer's hands.

Mr. Daniel O'Bannon came to collect the rent at the usual time of nine thirty. Late by polite standards, but Mr. O'Bannon is not generally considered a polite man, nor does he tend to keep polite company, and so he came at a time which was convenient for him. He found the body halfway down the staircase, the head dangling at an impossible angle. It is surprising—given his line of work—that Mr. O'Bannon called the police as quickly as he did, and a testament to the gruesomeness of the crime that he was compelled to do so with such haste.

It should be noted that Miss Merril had left the rent in an envelope on the side table just inside the door. She paid in full, just as she always had. Josephine Merril was punctual and polite, even after she was dead.

Ninth Report

Robert Peaslee

I don't sleep, not since Dunwich—not since Megan brought me back. I'll pretend, close my eyes and lay there until Megan drifts off, then I'll get up and go down to the library, or the office, or maybe even for a walk. Megan doesn't mind. Neither do I, I suppose. It's better than the alternative. And it's not all bad. I still get to dream sometimes. Loss of consciousness is key and very once in a while I'll get hit in the head and knocked out by an accommodating suspect. Occupational hazard. When I'm out, I see things, things that do not always make sense right away, but maybe sometime in the future they become clearer, more understandable. It's not prophecy, or seeing the future, or anything like that; it's more like intuition. Lydecker thinks I've tapped into something Jungian, a kind of collective unconsciousness. I don't agree. I think that my subconscious is working faster than my conscious brain can understand. It needs time to catch up. So, I walk, and I try to process. I walk even when it is bitterly cold. I walk the streets of Arkham, a dark detective searching for solace, trying to understand the madness that is held within his own head.

That's why I was out that morning when Fricasse came to the house. I headed north, without any particular destination in mind, letting my feet decide where to go. This night that took me to familiar grounds, and I soon found myself standing on the outskirts of Miskatonic University. More specifically, I'd come to the five hundred block of Crane Street, where I once lived, and my brother and father still resided. It had been a long time since I had spoken to either one of them, and even longer since I had been home. My memories of the place were shadowy at best, I was very young when my father's change occurred, and our mother took us to live with relatives. By the time my father's native personality returned, I was grown and the formative years that would have bonded me to the man had passed. He was my father, but I barely knew the man. I ran away to the war rather than deal with what had happened and let my brother deal with it instead. He had actually known the man before his metamorphosis, spent time with him, did things with him. He seemed generally fond of the man, but more than that, he seemed to want to help. Wingate had grown up to become an expert in psychoanalysis, a professor at Miskatonic University, driven I suppose by a desire to understand what had happened to our father.

The old man must have thought he had made some progress, because he followed Wingate into the field. I knew that others thought Wingate accomplished: he was a prolific author, and supposedly an excellent lecturer, but something of a taskmaster when it came to his assistants. Rumor had it that students called my father The Old Man, and my brother L'Enfant Terrible. Sometimes they conflated the two and just called them The Terrible Old Man. I always chuckled at the idea that some people were afraid of my father and brother. Once, maybe, my father could have struck fear in me, but I had—more frequently lately—seen him around town and there was nothing to fear there; he was just old. He was just an old man who had been through something horrible, something that destroyed him, and his family—including me.

So, there I found myself, standing on Crane Street at three in the morning staring at the house of my father and brother. There was a light on in the study and someone was moving about, but who it was I couldn't tell, at least not from the street. Then my feet took me where they wanted to go, and I found myself on the walk to the front door. One step and then another and then—before I realized what was happening—I was halfway to the front porch. I must have paused for a moment because that is when I heard the voice of my brother.

"Hello, Robert," he called from the porch. He was sitting there in the dark in a chair. I hadn't even seen him. "It's good to see you. Good to see you trying." His voice lacked emotion; it was detached, almost clinical. He wasn't speaking to me as a brother, but rather as a patient. I wasn't surprised—I tend to do the same thing in difficult situations. I suppose falling back on our professional training is one way to stay in control. "I've seen you walk past before."

Was that true? I supposed it was. "I guess I've been working up the nerve."

He nodded. "Hannah thought you might come by soon. She said you were married. Anybody I know?"

"Probably. Alan Halsey's daughter, Megan."

He gave me a puzzled look. "I thought she was dead."

"To paraphrase Twain, the reports of her death were greatly exaggerated."

He nodded again. "Have you seen Mother lately?"

"No, but I did get an invitation to her wedding."

"Do you want to come inside?"

I thought about it for a moment. "Wingate, why are you sitting outside in the freezing cold, in the middle of the night?"

He thought about it for a moment, "The old man has been up all night in his study, correlating documents and observations. When he can't sleep, I can't sleep. Sitting on the porch, even in winter, is a way to calm myself. Kind of like the trances Indian mystics put themselves into." He grinned a little. "At least that's what I tell myself. It probably just keeps me from getting perturbed."

I laughed a little. "Do you think he'll see me?"

"Let's find out."

It had been decades since my feet had been on those steps, and back then they hadn't creaked under my weight. Somehow though just taking those steps and walking across the porch brought back memories I had long since partitioned away. As Wingate—my brother Win—opened the door, I hesitated.

Win spoke. "It's all right, Robert, you've come a long way. Take a moment if you need to."

Something about his tone and demeanor set me at ease. I steeled myself and stepped forward, into the house and into the past. Win closed the door behind me as I took everything in, memories firing as I looked around. Very little had changed in the intervening decades. The fabric on the sofa and loveseat were a little more worn but other than that it was like I'd been here only yesterday. The furniture was still the same, and still in the same places. The walls were still the same color, and the floors still needed to be refinished. My eyes darted to the stairs, and I noted the missing finial that I had broken off sliding down the bannister when I was four.

From across the parlor, I could hear someone rustling papers and muttering from the room that had been my father's study. I will admit a momentary feeling of trepidation. When I last heard such sounds, they had been generated by something that appeared to be my father but had none of his memories or his personality. I knew that things had changed since that frightful day, but the little boy who had been so afraid of the alien thing his father had become was still hidden inside me, and he was still afraid. After all these years, after all the horrors I had witnessed—and disposed of—I was still afraid of the thing that had once worn my father's face. I was terrified that it might be there still, lurking on the threshold of my father's mind, waiting for me to return before re-emerging to renew its reign of horror. Steeling my resolve, I strode forward, rapped on the door twice, and—not bothering to wait for a response—opened it and went inside.

His back was to me. He was huddled over his desk shuffling papers together and muttering to himself. He was a lot older than I thought he would be, and a lot thinner. The clothes he wore hung loosely on him, and I couldn't help but think they had been bought for a much larger man who had wasted away to become a shadow of his former self.

Journal of the American Psychological Society. Murchison's a stickler for grammar, and I had to redraw all my sketches in ink, but he's promised for this first piece to appear in the fall, and the follow-up next summer. Years of work and it all comes down to fifteen pages of text and a dozen or so drawings."

"Dad," I said, "It's not Win. It's Robert."

He stopped what he was doing and straightened up. As he turned around, I could see tears welling up in his eyes. Seeing his face and the thin gray hair that framed it, he looked even older than I had realized, but I could also see something of the man who had once been my father.

"Robert Keezar Peaslee," there was a sense of astonishment in his voice, "I thought I would never see you again. Your sister said . . . it doesn't matter. Thank you. Thank you for coming. I've missed you, son."

"How are you dad?"

"I'm good, surprisingly good. It's important to know I'm not alone, and working on things like this helps." He waved his hand across the papers on the table.

"It's a paper of some sort?"

"A summary of my dreams with crude illustrations of some of the images I repeatedly have seen. I think I may have tapped into what Jung calls the collective unconscious. These things I see in my dreams, I think they're some sort of memory shared by all mankind but buried deep and only brought to the surface by some sort of traumatic event."

I could see that he was serious. "Trauma—like the event that took your personality?"

"Yes," he looked like a bird bobbing his head, "but possibly not. I've been working on the theory that it wasn't the replacement of my personality that caused the trauma, but rather its return. Semantics, perhaps—but perhaps not." He looked thoughtfully over the written pages and illustrations. "I need to do more research." He paused, and I saw his face abruptly change. He was suddenly very serious. "Have you seen your mother?"

"N—no," I stammered out.

"Good," his response was smug, almost joyful. "She doesn't deserve you in her life. You understand that, don't you? Wingate and Hannah disagree, but you understand, don't you? She betrayed me, betrayed us, betrayed her vows."

Wingate was suddenly at my side. "Dad, we've been through this. Mother did the best she could, but when you were changed, when you were gone, it was so hard. She needed her own life. She just couldn't live with the thing that you became. It wasn't what she agreed to. I don't think anybody could have lived with the thing you became. I don't think anybody should have to."

Our father slumped into a large wingback chair that took up a corner of his office and sighed. "I don't know about that. I don't remember it, none of it. I'm being held responsible for things I have no memory of. As far as I'm concerned, one day I had a loving wife and family, and the next I had lost it all, along with five years of my life."

"Dad—" Wingate started but was cut off.

"I understand," he waved his hand in frustration. "You all suffered from losing me, but you had your lives. You lived them; they may not have been what you wanted but they were at least yours. I lost those years, lost them completely. Even the journals I kept during those years were lost. The only things I have to help reconstruct my missing years are a few letters, some newspaper articles, and financial records. Extensive financial records that suggest that, despite my change in personality, I still made sure that the family was taken care of." He paused, stood up from the chair, and turned away. "One might think that would have bought me some good will, some time—a respite of some sort. Instead, your mother divorces me, and when my old personality finally comes back, she refuses to see me. She gives me no chance to reconcile."

"Dad, we've been through this," moaned Wingate. "Mother was hurt just as much as you were. Perhaps even more so. After you signed the papers, she didn't want to have to live through it all again."

He turned back around with a stern look on his face. "I didn't sign those papers. That's not my signature. I don't care what the witnesses say." His hands were shaking. I could see he was getting agitated. I started to think that this was a mistake.

Wingate slowly walked over and took his arm. "Dad, you need to stay calm. Remember what the doctor said." As he finished that sentence, I watched my father's knees buckle and Wingate suddenly take all of the weight. I stepped forward and took his other arm. Our father was still speaking, but I couldn't make heads or tails out of the words. "Help me get him back into the chair."

We manhandled him back into the large wingback chair he'd just risen from, his dead weight making the task far more difficult. We tried to be careful, but he ended up flopping backwards and bouncing his head off the padded backing—not hard, but he moaned a little and scowled some more. Wingate propped him up with some pillows. Apparently, this was something of a routine.

"I'll get your medicine, Dad," Win said sadly, and then motioned for me to follow him into the kitchen.

As my brother puttered about in the kitchen, I spoke up. "Is he always like this?"

Win sighed. "He has good days and bad days, mostly good days. The medication helps. But when he gets agitated, especially about mom, he gets apoplectic. His blood pressure spikes, and he becomes uncommunicative. He's still there, but he can't talk or really move. The doctors think of it as a kind of hysterical paralysis. But we're getting it under control." He stirred something into a cup of water, turning it chalky green. "He used to be much worse. For a time, he was the exact opposite."

"What do you mean?"

cannabis and *bufo* toxin helps alleviate the symptoms. He's responded well to treatment, and with each dose the symptoms seem to get less severe. Maybe a year from now he'll be completely cured."

"I'm sorry, Win," I said, not really knowing what I was apologizing for.

He nodded. "We all made decisions. You, me, mom, Hannah. Somebody needed to stay with dad. It might as well have been me. I don't mind it, really. He's a good man who is trying to understand something that is beyond him. I've helped him the best I can, and I must admit I've profited from it. My entire education was funded by the university's children of staff tuition program. I had a vested interest in keeping him employed, and I reaped the benefits. So, did Hannah, albeit with only a bachelor's degree." He stopped stirring the glass. "The only person who didn't benefit from this is you, of course—but why should you? You ran away."

There it was—the anger I was waiting for, just not from where I expected. I didn't say a word. I just turned, picked up my coat on the way out and left. Suddenly the cold wasn't so bad. I half-expected for one of them to call after me, but my father was still paralyzed, and my brother had made his true feelings very clear.

I wandered through the dark streets, making my way around the southwest border of town, strolling alongside Hangman's Slough, and then into the old cemetery that it passed through. Strange waters run here, I thought, catching sight of the babbling brook, strange and ponderous in the moonlight. What foulness would such waters be tainted by? Would they taste bitter or sweet? I've heard the grave described in both ways. It was not unreasonable to suggest that waters might pick up some aspect of that which they have passed through. Like people, flowing waters are the product of what they have encountered in the past, and the impacts they have on their downstream journeys are shaped by such contacts and contents.

It seemed that my father's past was an awful and bitter poison, and that my brother lived with it for far too long, absorbing the toxic miasma of my father's broken past and shattered personality and becoming something that wears his own kind of mask, hiding his own discontent—discontent that was not so different than my own. Strange how we both took different paths, and, in the end, we both have similar regrets. Thankfully, Wingate will stay far away from the darkness that taints my life. Having one Peaslee son haunted by the cosmic horrors lurking just beyond the veil is enough.

A sudden epiphany: I was somewhat jealous of Wingate's life. Not his life as it was now, but his future. He had one, while I had only the moment and the past. His was a good, normal job, and someday a woman would scoop him up. He would have kids, and then—in a flash—he would be celebrating grandkids. Then a retirement. A normal life. I, on the other hand, was under no delusion concerning my chances. Megan and I had been lucky so far, but sooner or later that luck would run out, and our days as crusaders against the darkness would be over. It was, I thought solemnly, only a matter of time.

Tenth Report

Robert Peaslee

Though it took me some time, I eventually saw Arthur Campbell that very same day. But first, I had to avoid Fricasse, who was not my most favorite of people. I saw him arrive as I was approaching the house just before eight. He was cursing so loudly I could hear him all the way down the street. I had no desire to deal with the man, and I knew that Megan was more than capable of handling his fury. So I did a quick about-face and whipped around the block toward the back end of the house, entering through the other door and waiting for the man to leave.

After, I sauntered into the office, only to find the blackboard shattered and Frank Elwood kneeling on the floor in obvious distress. Megan caught my eye and her look clearly said that I shouldn't interrupt. So, instead, I went up to the kitchen and took advantage of the pot of coffee Mrs. Kreitner had placed on the stove and helped myself to the tray of muffins she had just taken out of the oven. She scolded me for spoiling my appetite before breakfast. I assured her that no one else would mind. The fare that our resident cook produced was very different than what I'd grown accustomed to when I lived above the bakery. Back then I had a wider variety, but my choices were a day old. Mrs. Kreitner—I never could get used to calling her Sheila—took particular pride in making sure we always had fresh baked goods to go with our meals, but always in small batches so there was no waste. If anything did survive from one day to the next it was quickly whisked away by her husband Alex, our gardener and handyman. He told his wife he was going to use them in the bird feeders, but I knew the birds would most likely go hungry; Alex was very fond of his wife's baking, even when it was a day old.

It was about five minutes after I sat down that Alex came in to join me. The coffee seemed better than usual, and Sheila's dried currant muffins filled the room with a rather delectable aroma that served as a tantalizing appetizer to actually tasting the warm and moist cake that the fruit made both tangy and sweet. It was, I reflected between sips of delicious coffee, an odd turn of events for my life: being married to Megan, living in this place, Sheila cooking,

Alex looking after the house and garden. I couldn't have predicted it. It's not what I set out to do, not a place I ever expected the path I set myself on would lead me to. Is it strange to find comfort and normalcy in the terrible things in the world, the monstrous things that people don't talk about, and the things that must be done to keep them at bay? I wonder if it is it strange to find those things normal—as I do—but the normal things in life—like marriage and families and creating a home with Megan—disturbing? I have a living disembodied head in my basement, but the thing that bothers me the most is the idea that Megan pays other people to take care of us. Somehow, I'm more comfortable with the fact that my wife can reanimate the dead than I am with an old woman cooking me breakfast. Humans are strange creatures; our capacity to embrace and normalize the unnatural may be our greatest strength—and our greatest weakness.

Not long after I finished my last muffin, Megan and Elwood wandered in and sat down. Elwood was still visibly shaken, a condition that Sheila noticed and thought she could rectify with her universal cure-all—food and coffee. Unbidden, she slid a small plate containing one of her muffins in front of the young man and patted him on the shoulder. I half expected her to say something calming—"There, there, dear" would have been appropriate—but she didn't. Whether that was of her own volition or due to a surreptitious, preventative signal that had been issued by Megan, I could not say. All I do know is that the mood in the room had suddenly changed. We were accustomed to trouble in our house, but Frank Elwood seemed to have more than his fair share, and we had yet to figure out a way to extract him from it.

We normally don't discuss business at the table, but, after we had finished our food and sat there sipping our coffee, we did just that. The Kreitners had wandered away to attend to other household matters. This provided Megan with the opportunity to inform me about Josephine Merril and the detainment of Arthur Campbell as the prime suspect in her death. After some discussion, we decided that I would try to see Mr. Campbell. First, I would have to determine who his lawyer was. If representation was lacking, I was to retain one for him. Then, I would inform legal counsel of the information we had concerning the deaths of Elwood's—and Campbell's—classmates so that doubt could be cast on Campbell's guilt. The easiest way to do this would be to provide an alibi for Campbell at the time of Merril's murder, but finding a link between Merril and the other victims, and then providing an alibi for those murders might do as well. That process might entail several days' worth of work. Meaning Campbell might be in custody for an extended period. We agreed, given the state of things, that might not be the worst place for him.

I was still working out the details of the plan in my mind and taking the last slug of coffee from my cup when I heard the front bell ring. It was an odd sound as we rarely have guests in the house; most clients who approach the front door are directed by a small but prominent sign to the back entrance. I exchanged a quick glance with Megan, who seemed just as curious as I about our caller and waited for Alex to bring us the identity of our caller. Even in the kitchen, I could hear him speaking to someone and then ushering them in out of the cold. There were a few footsteps and then Alex's own gait down the hall towards us.

"A young woman to see you, Miss Megan, on a personal matter. I've put her in the library." He seemed a bit unsettled. "I think she's from Innsmouth. She says her name is Waite, Asenath Waite."

At the mention of the woman's name a look of elation appeared on Megan's face, and she sprang from her chair and sped down the hall. She moved so quickly that she didn't notice that she wasn't the only one to react to the identity of our guest. Elwood reacted as well, but where Megan appeared delighted, the emotion that seemed to overwhelm our client's countenance was something that I could only describe as dread. I noted it and followed my wife at a reasonable pace.

I found them in the library greeting each other most excitedly. Megan was standing in front of me, so I could not see our guest. There was a hug, and some words that amounted to having not seen each other in ages, and then Megan stepped aside, and I saw the woman that called herself Asenath Waite. She was a petite thing, slim, not unattractive, but not what one would consider pretty, either. She wore a stylish ebony dress, with white lace fringe around the neck, cuffs and hem, accented with a triple loop of black pearls. She had dark hair cut into a kind of bob, a rounded face and olive complexion with large, dark eyes—set just a little further apart than the norm—that she had rimmed with rouge. One might have thought her a sloe-eyed Scandinavian, or perhaps southern European, but I knew Alex had been correct in his assessment of her. She, or at least one of her ancestors, was from Innsmouth. You could see it in the skin folds. If you didn't know what to look for, you might miss it, but the clues were there. Around the eyes there were crow's feet, and behind the ear, set back from the jaw line, some odd wrinkles of flesh, and in those the hint of the squamous. It was just a few patches of rough skin, but to the residents of Arkham they spoke volumes.

No one said anything publicly about Innsmouth, for years it had all been innuendo and rumor. Even after Federal agents descended on Innsmouth and seized control of it, the official line was that the town had been taken over by criminals engaged in the smuggling of liquor. Few made mention of the fact that many of the men of Innsmouth had taken foreign wives who went about in public with veils. These women had been brought back from the islands of the south Pacific, and were under the law, classified as not White. This meant that under the anti-miscegenation laws of Massachusetts those marriages were illegal and both parties subject to arrest. It had been a practice amongst merchantmen that the state had long turned a blind eye to. In recent years grousing by people like Coleman Blease, the former Governor and now Senator from South Carolina, had spawned new interest at enforcing the law, and perhaps enacting new legislation at the national level. The official motivation for the Innsmouth raid may have been smuggling, but there was plenty of gossip that suggested punishing the town for decades of interbreeding was the real reason. I and Megan both knew that there were darker motivations behind what had happened in Innsmouth.

"Robert," said Megan, dragging me out of my thoughts, "this is Asenath Waite. She was ahead of me at the Hall School. One of my dearest friends. Asenath, this is my husband, Robert Peaslee."

She stuck out her hand in the most unladylike fashion and I took it gently with both of mine, cupping it in a rather fashionable manner. "It is a pleasure to meet you Mr. Peaslee. I can see why Meagan married you so abruptly. You have your father's good looks, but a much better physique."

She was rather forward, but I ignored it. "You know my father?"

"The infamous Professor Peaslee, the man who forgot himself? Indeed, I had the pleasure of meeting him once or twice."

"Is my father really considered infamous?"

"Well, he's not famous in the traditional sense now, is he? And he did have a habit of traveling in rather suspect circles, at least during his ordeal. He met with Crowley, and Monkfield Cabot I believe, and even with my father, so yes, I would call him infamous. He may have returned to his scholarly life, but once you've tarnished yourself it is very hard to get yourself clean."

"Your father?" I struggled with a memory. "Your father was Ephraim Waite, but that would have been decades ago. You would have been . . ."

"Just a small child," she cut me off. "A wee slip of a thing, as they say, and let us leave it at that. I would rather not discuss my age."

I opened my mouth to say something, but Megan cut me off. "Robert, would you ask Sheila to make us some refreshment?"

"Of course, and then I'll be on my way out to run those errands we discussed."

She smiled and nodded as I walked away, but I could still hear her as she spoke to her friend. "Not that I'm not happy to see you, Asenath, but I know you. You're not here out of the blue just to visit. Why are you here?"

"Megan, I understand that you're the owner of Crowninshield Manor and you're looking to sell." Whatever was said after that was lost as I walked back into the kitchen and out of earshot.

Elwood was still there nursing his coffee. He looked up at me meekly. "Your wife knows Asenath Waite?" There was a tone in his voice.

I shrugged, "Apparently. Is there something I should know?"

"She has a reputation. Lately she's been out seen with Edward Pickman Derby. He's fifteen years her elder."

"Derby. He's a poet—didn't he write *Azathoth and Others*?"

"*Azathoth and Other Horrors*, originally," he corrected me." Published back in 1908 by Witch Hill Press, but when Arkham House reprinted it in 1918, they added six poems that the first edition left out and changed the title to just *Azathoth and Others*."

"And this man is disreputable?"

Elwood shook his head. "No, she is. Before she met him, she was a regular attendee at meetings of the Lastheneia Society." He said this as if it was supposed to mean something to me, when I didn't react his eyes grew wider, and he explained in hushed tones. "It's a sorority of sorts. They say their goal is equal education for women, but the rumor is that they're really devotees of Sappho."

"I'm sorry?"

Elwood took my question the wrong way. He thought I didn't understand what he was implying. "You know," his eyes darted about to make sure we were alone, "lesbians."

It was all I could do to keep from laughing in his face. Instead, I sent him to his room to study and assured him I would not be long. It was only when I was out of the house and well down the street that I let my amusement at Elwood's prudishness finally reveal itself. It was only a smile at first, but by the time I took the first turn and headed down toward the river I was engulfed in a full chuckle, one that I failed to suppress until I reached the bridge over the Miskatonic, and suppressing it then only to avoid having to apologize to any passersby for my unusual demeanor.

At the Police Station, it was more work making sure Fricasse didn't see me than to find out who his lawyer was. That answer was nobody, so it was another quick trip down the street to the offices of Oliver Chancellor. The scion of a well-to-do Boston family, Oliver came from a long line of New England and New York attorneys and had served our small firm quite well in the months since our formation. Oliver knew that our business dealt with things that police would rather ignore—or bury—and he had the forethought to avoid learning to many details. Such knowledge, he suggested, would interfere with his ability to carry out his duties. It was a peculiarity of the law that I conceded to his expertise. In fact, I admit to a nostalgic longing for the days when I had the bliss of such ignorance.

Our first task was to eliminate Fricasse's ability to interfere with my investigation, something Oliver accomplished with ease. The man, quite the prodigious professional, was handling more cases than he should have, including one that involved one of Oliver's junior partners. Oliver simply arranged for his subordinate to meet with Fricasse over some minor point of legalese and then to keep him busy. In the meanwhile, Oliver would establish himself as Campbell's representation, and I as his faux hired associate.

Back at the station, things went smoothly and within the hour we were ushered into a small room to meet with Campbell. The young man was obviously shaken, his eyes were bloodshot and his hair unkempt. His clothes were soiled and torn. There was a bruise on his chin. As a former cop, I recognized the tell-tale signs of an over-enthusiastic detective. Such methods had been a routine part of my own interrogation process—hell, they still were. Sometimes the only way to get the information you need out of someone is to apply some physical persuasion. But I wasn't a cop anymore, and looking at things from the other side—it just made me feel sorry for the kid.

Oliver introduced us, calling me his investigative assistant. It sounded better than hired muscle, but that was the implication and Campbell knew it.

Campbell stared down at the table between us and shook his head. "I can't afford a lawyer. Neither can my father. Besides, I haven't done anything wrong, I never touched Jo. I loved her. Why would I kill her?"

Oliver opened his mouth to speak, but I put my hand on his and took over. "Let's be clear, Campbell. The cops don't care about the truth—they're more interested in making things look neat and tidy. The public doesn't care for complicated. They prefer simple, and nothing is simpler than a lover's quarrel that escalated into assault and somebody dead. It's quick, clean and straightforward. The Chief of Police will sign off on it, the District Attorney will serve it up, the Judge will buy it, the Jury will cook it up, the newspapers will chew it up, and feed it to the masses as if the squawking public is their starving hatchling and they come bearing the pre-digested goods. Now, I know—I personally know—that you didn't have a thing to do with killing Miss Merril, and that makes me and Mr. Chancellor here the only real chance you have of getting out of here alive. We're offering you our services—free of charge. All you have to do is help us figure out why Josephine Merril was murdered, and you weren't."

That got his attention. "Me murdered, what are you talking about?"

I flipped open my notebook. "What do Abraham Alder, Nicholas Dallas, Edward Fritch, Walter Gilman, Gerald Ingalls, Richard Jacobi, and Fritz Long have in common?"

"What? Alder, Dallas, Fritch . . . nothing. We all took Calculus D with Professor Upham, but other than that nothing I can think of, why?"

I closed my notebook and looked at Campbell. I tried to be compassionate. "They're all dead, Mr. Campbell, all seven of them. We thought you would be number eight, but Miss Merril was killed instead. Rather odd, don't you think?"

Campbell went quiet, but his eyes spoke volumes. He wanted to say something but was too scared to open his mouth. I'd seen that look many times. Whatever he knew that might help us might also damn him. He would need time to work things out, to weigh the options, but in the end, I knew he would tell us. Whatever secret he was hiding couldn't be worse than being convicted of homicide.

It was Oliver's turn to take the lead. "Now that you have representation, the rough treatment should cease," he pointed up and down at Campbell's discomfiture. "We will be back tomorrow, perhaps you'll be more willing to discuss things then."

We stood to leave, purposely going slowly, giving him the time he might need to come to a decision. We were almost out the door when his voice broke the silence.

"Josephine wasn't my girlfriend." He was almost sobbing. "Check under her bed, there are boxes she kept her old schoolwork in. Look at it, that should make everything plain."

I nodded. "I'll be back tomorrow." I told him the truth, but when the door closed behind us, I developed this horrible feeling that I would never see Arthur Campbell ever again. I turned to Oliver to say something but before I could, a terrible noise erupted, as if a rhinoceros was blowing its nose.

"PEASLEE!" It was Fricasse, our ruse to keep him busy had lasted just long enough. "What in the Sam Hill do you think you are doing here?" He came storming down the hallway almost bowling over smaller officers and staff. I ignored him, turning away as if I hadn't seen or heard him, and headed for the nearest exit.

I felt Oliver's hand on my back, gently pushing me forward, and his voice at a near whisper saying "Go!" Then louder, "Lieutenant Fricasse, just the man I wanted to see. I suppose it was you who roughed up my client? And why exactly are you holding him? Have you any proof at all that he was involved in this horrific crime? Or is it all your evidence just circumstantial as usual?" He paused, but only for the briefest of moments. "I'm talking to you Lieutenant! I want answers, or do I need to go see Judge Hand?"

"Wait. What? No." Oliver had successfully interceded between me and the unpleasant Fricasse. My jovial mood from earlier in the morning threatened to return as I smiled at how easily the task was accomplished, but I couldn't help wondering if that was because the Lieutenant was easily distracted, or because Oliver Chancellor was an expert in the art. As I plowed out the door and into the cold, I hoped it was the latter. It was, after all, what he was paid for.

Eleventh Report

Megan Halsey

It was nearly midnight before Robert returned to the house the second time. The first had been hours earlier, after he had spent time talking with Arthur Campbell. He had returned from that meeting with only the most tenuous of leads, and one that was not readily available to us. Which is why Robert had to wait for nightfall to take any further action, and that gave us the opportunity to sit down for yet another of Mrs. Kreitner's fabulous meals. Tonight's culinary creation consisted of baked potatoes topped with pot roast and drenched in thick mushroom and Remmer's gravy. Robert and Frank devoured the meal with relish, while I found the dish slightly heavier than I preferred. Thankfully, the Brussels sprouts sautéed in bacon grease and almonds were more to my liking, as were the brandy-braised cherries we had for dessert.

Only then did Robert excuse himself and head for the garage. Over the last few days the streets had been cleared and were now more than suitable for automobile traffic, and Robert did so love to drive the Silver Wing. Besides, Robert was planning a bit of unscrupulous behavior and having a quick way in which to vacate the area would be highly advantageous. The downside was that the car was rather distinctive, and if spotted it would be linked to our firm rather quickly. I offered to go with him—to act as his driver while he carried out his nefarious task, but he declined. It would do no good for both of us to be picked up by the police. As much as I hated to admit it, he was right.

I did go to see him off, though, and there in the garage he asked after the visitor I'd had earlier in the day. "What did Asenath Waite want?"

I leaned through the car door window and kissed him on his forehead. "She wants to hire us. She's having an event, and she needs some extra security. Nothing we can't handle."

He shook his head. "I'm not doing any more academic dinners or sorority mixers. Those don't ever end well. Need I remind you what happened at the Ba Ghay Sin House?"

I caressed his cheek and smiled at him. "It's nothing like that. She's getting married, she wants us to make sure things don't get out of hand during the reception."

"Isn't that a little outside our realm?"

"Asenath isn't from Arkham, and she doesn't know a lot of people in town. She knows and trusts me." I gave him my best coy look. "I said we would do it."

He rolled the window up and drove off into the night, while I went to try and make sure our houseguest was still comfortable. After the scene earlier there was no predicting what could happen if Frank became agitated.

Thankfully, Robert returned sooner than expected—and with three large boxes that he had recovered from the apartment of Josephine Merril. Robert, Frank and I sat at the table in the consulting room with Lydecker at his desk pretending to supervise.

"Did you have any problems?" Lydecker wheezed.

Robert shook his head. "No, but I think someone was there before me, the place seemed out of sorts, as if it had been carefully searched and then put back together carelessly."

"The police? Fricasse and his cronies?"

"I don't think so. They wouldn't have tried to conceal what they had done." He popped the lid off one of the boxes and took out a handful of papers. I did the same to another and motioned to Elwood to do the same with the third box.

Mine was full of the administrative detritus and trivia that comes with being a college student. There were progress reports, bills, receipts, cancelled checks, letters from various university departments and colleges. I have heard tell of fans of the game of baseball who can be handed the statistics of a game and then envision the actual play. This box was like that; it provided enough detail to see how young Josephine had moved through her college career, the accomplishments, the failures, the roadblocks, and the leaps that moved her forward. It all seemed rather sad, a sullen testament to her life as a student. I threw the papers back inside with an obvious sense of frustration.

Robert handed me a sheet of paper. "She had talent, I think." It was a figure sketch done in the style of one of the old masters—all wispy lines that implied motion and light and shadow. He followed it up with a study of the musculature of a horse's leg. Then he passed me another. It was a sketch of a classroom done from the back. There were ten figures seated in front of a black board. An older man was off to one side, while a younger man stood at the blackboard. None of the seated students were identifiable, their faces were all turned away, but the old man's face was clearly rendered, and easily identifiable. It was Professor Upham, there was no doubt about it.

"Josephine Merril has been in Professor Upham's classroom," I said definitively.

"He told me she wasn't a student," Robert told me with confusion in his voice.

I tossed the classroom sketch on to the desk. Elwood eyed it as if it were a revelation. "There's a small room at the back of the class. It's used to house a continuous-slide projector for guest lecturers. This . . . I think this would be the view from the projection window."

"At least now we know the truth," Robert muttered.

"Which is?" Lydecker gurgled.

"That Josephine Merril was killed because she was observing the class."

"We know something else," I added. All eyes turned to me with rapt attention. "Whoever killed her knew that she was back there watching."

"But why is Arthur Campbell still alive? Why was Josephine killed in his place? The pattern clearly points toward Campbell." Lydecker's continued gurgling raised a valid point.

"Because Josephine was doing more than just auditing the class," interjected Elwood. "She was doing the work for Campbell." He threw several pieces of paper onto the tabletop. "The pages on the left are in Merril's handwriting, an analysis of an obscure proof that we had been assigned to review. The pages on the right are the same document typed up with Campbell's name as author, and with a high grade from Upham." His hand traced the mark from the professor. "I had thought Campbell was out of his depth in the class, but his grades seemed to contradict that opinion . . . but it wasn't Campbell, was it? It was Merril all along."

Lydecker wheezed and said what we were all thinking. "It would seem that we have evidence of a number of academic crimes. Miss Merril was auditing a class that she hadn't paid for, and Mr. Campbell was having his classwork done for him by Miss Merril." He paused and then spoke again, "That explains his reluctance to talk. I wonder how real the relationship between Merril and Campbell was? It might have all been for show, a ruse to conceal their academic misdeeds."

"It gives Campbell motive," suggested Robert.

"To kill Merril, but not the others," I shrugged in frustration. "We're missing something, it wasn't just being in the class. What else do all these people have in common?"

"You don't know, Megan?" You could hear the gloating as Lydecker wheezed and gurgled. "The answer is right there on the table. You put it there."

We all looked at the seemingly unimportant pages that had accumulated in front of us. "I don't see it."

Lydecker smiled, and I swear he was being purposefully smug. "Mr. Elwood, not counting Miss Merril, how many students were in your class?"

"Twelve, but we knew that."

"And how many people are in the audience in Miss Merril's drawing?"

He looked at the picture, we all did. There was a moment while we counted, but Elwood answered, "Ten."

Lydecker was smiling more now. "Who is that young man in front of the chalkboard?"

"There's no detail to the face, but Upham almost never let someone else take control like that. It only happened once that I know of—when Walter explained his weird theory about multi-dimensional space, and how it could be folded and bridged." He looked at the sketch again. "The equation on the board, I recognize it, it's the one that Walter wrote. The figure lecturing the class is Gilman!"

"Professor Upham's class consisted of fourteen people. Himself, the twelve registered students, and Miss Merril, for a total of fourteen. This sketch is from Miss Merril's point of view, so we know where she was. Professor Upham is off to the side, and Walter Gilman is at the chalkboard. There are ten people seated in the audience, but there should be eleven. Who do you suppose is missing?"

Elwood looked again, and then pointed. "This is me, or at least the back of my head." He shifted his finger around. "Alder, Long there, and Jacobi over here, Fritch down in front, next to Dallas. That makes this Ingalls. I look of understanding came over his face. "Campbell isn't in the picture; he must have missed class that day."

"I propose to you that Arthur Campbell is still alive because he was not present on this very day, and that Josephine Merril, is dead because she was."

"And so were all the others," I added.

"But that would make Professor Upham a target too, wouldn't it?" Robert had a point.

"Look again," instructed Lydecker. "All of the students appear to be busy copying down what Gilman has written on the board. Even Merril recorded it in this sketch. Only Upham isn't recording what Gilman has proposed."

"So, Campbell isn't in danger, he never was." Elwood sighed in relief.

"No, but this tells us something more," Robert shot back. "It tells us that the killer knew who was in the room that day, and who wasn't. And that includes Campbell."

I frowned, "That eliminates Professor Upham, he definitely didn't know Merril was there. Besides he's confined to a wheelchair. Has been for months."

"Our quarry has made a mistake," announced Lydecker proudly. "If he had saved Miss Merril to the end we might still be in the dark about his motives, but by killing what we thought of as an outlier, he has forced us to reassess our assumptions about the murders and the man behind them. We've reset everything, and in doing so we've learned a little bit more, maybe enough to prevent any further deaths." He paused and then continued, "Unfortunately, I need to ask Mr. Elwood to do something that will put us all in greater danger."

I felt my face screw up. "What exactly is that?"

"The equation on the chalkboard, the one Walter Gilman wrote. Can you explain it?"

"Why does that put the rest of us in danger?" asked Robert.

"Our unknown suspect is killing everyone who has had a copy of the equation and has the mental capacity to understand it." His eyes shifted back to Elwood. "Tell me, Mister Elwood, what is it that makes this equation so important that someone would kill to keep it a secret?"

The Walker in the Inbetween

I had thought the dream of Brown Jenkin an aberration, a nightmare brought on by the events of the day and the murder of my former classmates. Alas, whatever triggered the intrusive and invasive manifestation of those nocturnal phantasms—of Brown Jenkin and that other strange visitor—into my dreams is persistent, and for the last several days I have suffered from increasingly fantastic imaginings—though imaginings may not be the best word to describe such events. Megan Halsey bore witness to the strange event a few days prior in which I appeared to become partly insubstantial, or at least somewhat transparent, and I cannot help but think that event is related to my continuing hallucinations and altered state of mind. Still, I keep my concerns to myself and have not informed my hosts, who are themselves occupied with more pressing matters. The ever-stoic Robert left Wednesday morning in response to a phone call from a potential client, and Megan had begun working with Mr. Chancellor to liberate Arthur Campbell from the clutches of the police who wrongly blame him for the death of Josephine Merril. Thus, I was left alone to deal with my nightly descents, not—as I have started praying for each and every night—into the sweet womb-like abyss of sleep but instead into near maddening vistas beyond any human understanding.

The conversation on Tuesday night could once more be to blame for my mind being focused on Gilman, for it was just before I retired that the chair-bound Lydecker asked me what it was about Gilman's equation that made it worth killing over. I couldn't answer him, at least not then. I had to think about it. It has been four nights since the question was asked, and only now do I realize that the answer may have finally become clear to me.

That first night I found sleep elusive, and for some time lay in bed reading a text on relativity, until at last my eyelids began to droop and I nearly dropped the book. I can recall that the early portion of slumber was uneventful, filled with the common dreams of a common man, but as the night progressed that condition slowly changed. My dreams returned me to my childhood home which was being slowly invaded by the strangest of visitors, who manifested themselves as wild geometric shapes. Now, I had seen such things in nightmares of grand abstract vistas before, but here, in this setting, they were wholly out of place, intruding in the imagery of my childhood home, floating through my bedroom, hovering in my kitchen. It was all very unnerving, and I found myself cursing at them and even going so far as to pick up a straw broom and chase after them, swinging wildly and swatting them when I could—to no avail, really, for the blows I inflicted did little but send them careening across the dreamscape, puncturing the walls of my fantasy.

It was through this process that I myself tore down the bulwarks of my dreaming mind's carefully constructed illusion and exposed that which lay hidden beneath, or at least that is how it seemed. My room, the kitchen, the house all faded away and I was left standing on a great empty plain of unending visual static. And yet, while I knew that the terrible scintillation that I stood upon was eternal, unending, a forever of nothingness, I also somehow knew that there was more. There, beneath my feet, if I strained to see, to peer through the ever-shifting colors that danced chaotically, I could see—what? What was that? Things, things that cast weird shadows against that sometime-translucent barrier. There were a myriad of shapes and forms, not unlike the strange geometric invaders I had tried to repel before, but here they were different. They were warped and twisted, rendered two dimensional and then shattered by the barrier into silhouettes that only hinted at the form of their maker. They were endless, and in their numbers just as varied, as they moved together in a pulsing flow, driven by an unknown and unseen current.

There were other shapes as well. Through the pulsing curtain I could discern monstrous shadows moving in packs against the flow of everything else, as if they were primeval hunters lean and hungry for whatever prey that might satisfy their awful need. They were terrible shadows, and I hoped against reason that the long, sharp daggers that jutted from their mouths were merely a distortion of something far less menacing—though as they banked and curved, their shadows growing and shrinking, I felt that their existence hinted at something more horrible, more terrifying than I could glean from this obscured glimpse.

My observation of the stalking predators was interrupted by the presence of another shadow, one immensely larger than any others. It was a cyclopean thing, larger than a city bus, and it moved on eight great legs that despite its size seemed to creep across the thin barrier that separated myself from that queer shadow world. It skittered and paused, and its monstrous head seemed to be looking at me with an unnatural radiation—a kind of not-light that could pierce whatever it was that stood between us. As I looked at it and wondered what it was the shadow form changed before my very eyes, shrinking down into a smaller, almost human shade. I say almost human, for while it had arms and legs and a head, those apportionments were grossly exaggerated, bloated in some places and shrunk tight in others. It had huge spatulate feet that sat beneath articulated legs. Its arms ended in fat, bulbous fingers that gripped something thin and tenuous that seemed attached to a circular device, colored an odd reddish hue, that I could not identify. But most terrifying of all were the eyes that pulsed within its oddly-crested head. A shadow shouldn't have eyes, but this one did. It had dead eyes that glowed like silver orbs and seemed to hold the dark wisdom of the ages. Those eyes burned into mine, and I swear I could see a mouth open and laugh a most inhuman laugh, one that I could feel as well as hear.

I remembered my elective coursework on the folklore of New England under Doctor Wilmarth, and in particular one of the legends that haunted some backwoods village in Maine. There were stories of a shadowy bugaboo or troll, a killer of children that some scholars referred to as The Dark Laughter or Laugher, making no distinction between the monstrosity and the sound it made. According to Wilmarth, it was to this bit of local folklore that Reverend Ward Phillips was referring to when he mentioned the "Cloyne of Condeskeag Plantation" in his *Thaumaturgical Prodigies of the New English Canon*. Was this the thing that stood before me now? If so, what was the impetus that had dragged this thing from the depths of my memories and into the nightmares spawned by my subconscious?

Why that terrible shadow entity had drifted into my vision, I could not fathom; nor could I explain why it suddenly drifted away, only to be replaced with something far more terrifying. If the shadow cast by the Clown had been cyclopean and alien, then the thing that strode forward to replace him was titanic and, shockingly, human. The head, arms, legs and torso were all correctly proportioned, even down to fingers that seemed to reach out and touch the barrier between us. It towered over all other shapes and shades, which scattered as it stepped, and I seemed to detect the slightest indication of a ripple in that unseen flow that served as a media for the things beyond. It lacked visible eyes, but it was watching me. It looked at me and I looked at it, and I was filled with the certainty that I knew this vast apparition. I reached out and placed my hand on the barrier that separated me from this dweller inbetween, desperate to test its ability to keep us separated. I thought of that space-that-was-not-space beyond the shimmering wall as something inbetween everything else, whether that be space and time or life and death or here and there, it was simply the inbetween. My hand on that barrier felt peculiar, for it was neither warm nor cold, and although it was most definitely an impediment to my movement, it seemed infinitely fragile, as if a single blow could shatter it to pieces. My desperation gave way to sheer terror as the immense thing beyond the wall brought its own hand up and placed it on the opposite side, dwarfing mine. Indeed, I was little more than a speck in comparison, a mote in the vast darkness of that shadowed form. Helpless to move, I bore witness as the vast five-fingered silhouette closed, tearing the barrier into tissue-like ribbons with no hesitation or effort. There was no sound, but I knew I was screaming. As that scintillating field was torn to shreds, I saw what was beyond. I recognized the titanic being as something that was impossible, as something that shouldn't have existed, and I screamed.

I screamed until I awoke, panicked from what I had seen push through the barrier. As the dream faded a bit from my memory, I sat there in bed, cowering in fear. After a while I felt an almost overwhelming sense of gratitude. I was, I suppose, grateful that I could not remember exactly what it was that I had seen. The dream did not leave me entirely, dogging my thoughts as I spent the rest of the day nearly alone. Robert Peaslee was called to Bolton that morning, and Megan Halsey dedicated herself to freeing Mr. Campbell from incarceration. Mr. Lydecker was unavailable but given his condition this was not surprising. The Kreitners were around, but busy. Mrs. Kreitner was in the kitchen for most of the day, while her husband was working in the attic, dragging the accumulated detritus of the last century out of storage to be reviewed and potentially disposed of. This activity, while not overly noisome, was somewhat bothersome as it was taking place above my guest room, with the objects being arranged in the hall just outside my door.

I had considered ignoring my studies and staying at Griffith House all day. However, the new semester was just underway and the one class I had left to complete my degree was meeting for the first time that morning. In my reasoning, it was better to go to class and then the library, doing any necessary reading or coursework, than to stay hidden at Griffith House listening to sliding and scuffling of Mr. Kreitner's tireless efforts. With my mind made up, I set off at once to the college

Professor Lake's class on Evolutionary Theory was an elective course, designed to round out my education. It was not a core course, and I hadn't expected it to be the highlight of what was left of my academic career, but frankly I found that first class confusing and not at all what I had expected. From the title I had expected a review of Darwinian Theory, but instead I found the syllabus rife with work by Lamarck, Leclerc, Cuvier, Ray and Paley. This was not, as I thought, a review of Darwin's concept, but rather an exploration of alternative ideas and theories, some of which were generally discredited. Frustrated, but resigned to what would essentially be my last class, I spent the afternoon in the library reviewing the required reading list and checking out what volumes I could. Surprisingly, I was granted a copy of the third volume of Georg-Louis Leclerc's *The Histoire Naturelle* which dealt with humanity. This was not an original copy from 1749, but rather a reprint done by the Restitution Society dated in 1880. There was an entire shelf full of copies of this volume, many of which appeared to suffer almost identical damage in having large numbers of pages excised from the rear of the binding. Never one to be dissuaded, I searched through the copies until I found one that was not vandalized and chose that one to study from.

It was only hours later while in the comfort of Griffith House that I began to peruse Leclerc's book, which had been produced as part of his role as director of the Jardin du Roi in Paris but at the expense of his role as the Comte de Buffon. A new forward made mention of the condemnation of the book by the Faculty of Theology at the Sorbonne, particularly those sections that had been influenced by the studies of his distant cousin, Francois-Honore Balfour. It was these chapters, constituting more than a hundred pages at the end of the text, that the Restitution Society had restored in this volume. Intrigued, I flipped through the book to examine the restored sections that had been systematically excised from the other copies. How this one had escaped such blatant expurgation I did not know, but I soon understood why it had been removed.

Leclerc had included Balfour's collection of terrifying folk tales concerning the origin of mankind which he had distilled from Balfour's own work, a rather minor occult treatise called *Cultes des Goules*—which purported to be a concatenation of the beliefs of dozens of terribly vile witch cults that Balfour had investigated both in Europe and Asia. Here were presented the creation myths of the Tcho with their queer amphibious ancestors the Miri Nigri. So, too, were mentioned the beliefs of some unnamed Tibetan cult and the black ooze that seeped up from the depths of the earth to walk like men. Likewise, the belief systems of the Thule were detailed, with particular attention given to the so-called Efts of Ubbo-Sathla, who dwelt for thousands of years in shapes akin to tadpoles until finally metamorphosing into what could only be described as protohumans.

As I read these unsettling accounts, I moved to the relative comfort of the bed to continue my perusal. Looking back, it was perhaps inevitable that I would finally fall asleep while reading, the book falling to my chest and my mind racing back to that strange dreamscape. The wall of light and shadow remained shattered, and a gaping hole existed where once there had been none. Unbidden and slightly fearful, I stepped through and entered the

Inbetween. It was a strange fluidic space, and, almost immediately, I felt the gentle flow of whatever ethereal fluid formed the basis of its being. All around me I could see the things that swam within the Inbetween; they were no longer shadows, but they were not recognizable as any specific kind of life either. Indeed, it would be hard to describe any of the things I perceived in that ebbing flow, save perhaps in the most surrealistic terms. Perhaps I should say that what I saw there was reminiscent of the semi-organic beings depicted by Salvador Dali in *The Apparatus and the Hand*, or perhaps a work by the cubist Pablo Picasso.

Even stranger than the creatures that surrounded me, was the fact that they seemed oblivious to my presence, not only traversing near me but passing directly through my body with apparently no ill effects to either them or I. Each time one did pass through me there was a strange sensation, reminiscent of the feeling one gets when a chill runs up your spine, but nothing else. This was the case with things that were substantially smaller than I was, perhaps only the size of my hand or less. The other larger entities were not in sight, and for this I was grateful as I had no weapon or tool with which to fend them off.

Intrigued by the ethereal landscape around me, I allowed myself to be caught by the gentle flow and began to slowly drift away from the cracked plane that had allowed me entry. As I did so, I became aware of other things—larger things in the distance. Like the small things that had encircled me, these far-off forms consisted of both organic and geometric shapes fused together in a most surreal way, and not in any consistent manner. In some cases, human or animal torsos were fused with polyhedral limbs; in others, vast cubes were surmounted by flailing tentacles or eyes. The size of these entities was also open to debate. The whole area lacked landmarks of any sort for reference, and thus it was difficult to say if something was far away and titanic, or much closer, and of reasonable size. More than once did this lack of perspective motivate me to veer off my course and avoid one thing or another that I felt could be a threat.

It was only when I decided to return that I realized that my mistakes had been many. With no landmarks, no perspective, I had no clear idea on how to return to my starting point. As I glanced around, I could not readily see that enigmatic crack in reality from which I had left one universe for this Inbetween. At first, I simply tried to walk back in what I thought was a straight line, but how was I to recognize any particular direction? Indeed, how was I to know that I had travelled in a straight line in the first place? My only clue was the flow of the medium that surrounded me, and thus I strode against that gentle current, and the myriad and multiform inhabitants therein. It was not as easy as I had thought it would be, and in many ways reminded me of my visits to the beach and my attempts to stand up against the flow of water as it returned to the ocean after crashing forward as waves. It wasn't impossible, but it was slow and tiresome and sapped the very strength from my legs. Thus, I moved slowly against the tide, still uncertain of my path or destination and growing ever more tired with every step.

It was only after an indeterminate amount of time later—as I paused to rest—that I saw that I was no longer alone. Those lean shadows that had so frightened me when they were on the other side of the wall had returned, and they were more fearsome now than they had been before. They were fast, lean and sleek. That they were akin to sharks or some other predator seemed obvious. They wheeled in the atmosphere like a pack of winged wolves circling ever closer to my position, and it should be noted not only in two dimensions, for while my perceptions had been to describe my condition as if I were floating along on the surface of a stream, the truth was that it was more like being suspended in the ocean: with things moving not only around me, but also above and below, and even perhaps in directions I could not yet describe, for there was—perhaps—the idea of yet other vectors in addition to the three I was accustomed to.

These terrible hunters whirled in great arcs, coming closer and closer with each pass, testing my defenses and slowly coming to realize that I had none. This taunting and testing allowed me to observe their features more closely and I shuddered when I saw those gaping maws lined with crystalline geometries and terrible blue cylinders that ended with sharpened tips, like massive syringes designed to drain their victims in the most rapid manner possible. The rest of their morphology was equally terrifying. Behind their broad muzzles full of prismatic fangs sat what could only be described as a multitude of faceted eyes which, despite being of varied size and shape, all shared the same dead blackness. The bodies were shards of glass strewn together in a form that was reminiscent of both wolves and the aforementioned sharks. I thought for sure that these monstrous houndfish would be the death of me, but suddenly they broke their pattern and scattered into the distance.

I whirled around to locate whatever it was that could scare off such predatory monstrosities. I knew I did not have to see what was approaching—my lizard brain already knew what it was, and it was screaming a warning, but that part of my mind was not fast enough to reach out and stop me as I turned and saw infinity incarnate. It was again that titanic semi-anthropomorphic shadow, now made even more terrible by the fact that it was no longer concealed behind the wall. This gargantuan monstrosity walked across the landscape of the Inbetween without regard for anything that stood in its way or for any of the potential threats that it might encounter. It walked as if a man might through his own yard, without care or fear. To say it was a man does not do it justice, for, while the outline was indeed man-like, there was a complete lack of anatomic or physical detail. In place of these expected features was instead an endless void filled with the very cosmos itself; I could see its body was full of glittering stars and the hints of entire planetary systems. Only when it stopped and tilted its vast Brobdingnagian head to focus two glowing violet stars that seemed to function as eyes in my direction did I stir in panic from my melancholy despair and begin running against the flow once more.

It was here that I learned another secret of that queer dimension, for the crack in the wall had been only steps from my position, but was not visible from below, above or behind. It was as if the broken doorway was possessed of only two dimensions in a universe of vastly more. I dove for what I thought of as refuge, crawling backwards away from the entryway as something I did not understand reached through and tried to grasp my diminutive form. I backed away even as that massive hand clawed at me, and I could not help but feel that there was something terribly familiar about it. Whatever it was the realization of the truth seemed just beyond me, or at least beyond my consciousness. I suspect that perhaps my unconscious mind was able to make the connection because once more I woke screaming and grasping the blanket for whatever infantile comfort it could provide.

I spent the early part of that day drowsing in my room, caught between waking and sleep, but not fully in either. Eventually—driven by hunger and thirst and other needs—I roused myself and made my way down to the kitchen. Mrs. Kreitner made me coffee, toast and eggs. She had some shopping to do and needed her husband to help carry some of the heavier items. As Robert was still not back from Bolton, and Megan was working on freeing Campbell, I was, by late morning, left alone to shuffle aimlessly about the house.

This was not perhaps the best situation for me to be in. While I was not trapped in the house, I was somewhat isolated. I tried to study for Professor Lake's class, but my eyes and mind would not focus. I stared at the pages of Leclerc's book for hours but made no progress, and eventually tossed it onto my desk in frustration. I wandered backed down to the main floor and found myself browsing through a selection of phonographic recordings, settling finally on a recording by the Miskatonic Valley Philharmonic of several compositions by du Hond. It was an interesting choice; du Hond was a founding father of the Impressionist atonal movement, and his strained dissonance was reminiscent of Debussy. The strange chords and progressions seemed an appropriate accompaniment to the visual surrealism that was intruding into my dreams.

After the Kreitners returned, I ate a light dinner and retreated to my room. I was exhausted from the lack of sound rest during the previous two nights and hoped that by retiring early that I could offset the debt of sleep that I had incurred. Immediate sleep was not to be had, so instead I read to lull my overactive mind. I chose J. W. Dunne's *An Experiment in Time*, a rather speculative and more philosophical examination of how time might influence and be influenced by human consciousness. It might seem an odd read to some, but for my mind—filled as it was with the intricate symphony of high-level mathematics—it was in its own way soothing. So soothed, I fell asleep pondering Dunne's central question concerning time. Is time yesterday, today and tomorrow, or are these static states and it is only by moving through them that we perceive the passage of time?

It did not take long to once again emerge in the dream realm of the Inbetween, though this time it was remarkably changed. Somehow or another I had entered an area of that cool, pale realm in which the residents, those queer amalgamations of both the organic and inorganic, were dramatically reduced in stature. They were still as plentiful as before, sometimes as individuals, sometimes in groups, and sometimes in great shoals, only much smaller than they had been before. Indeed, some were so small that their characteristics seemed almost undefinable, too small to bring into focus. They swarmed around me as if they were some kind of insect, and I an animal that had inadvertently disturbed their nest. I could make out those lean and hungry predators, though, they were large enough in comparison to everything else to discern, but still too small to pose any real threat. Though at this thought my mind wandered to the piranha of the Amazon and the marabunta—the army ants that are rumored to strip the jungle bare as they move through it. With these thoughts in my head, I grew wary and moved slowly away from the larger swarms.

I had expected eventually to wander out of the diminutive zone and find myself once more back in a milieu in which everything was more sizable, but as I marched the hours passing and the flow of the ether around me little more than a gentle breeze, I saw no evidence of things returning to a sense of normalcy. Though how was I to know what was normal? My experience in this dream reality was limited; what I was seeing could be perfectly normal. I had no perspective by which to judge.

I stumbled on that thought, for it seemed somehow important to me, but my attention was soon drawn elsewhere. In the distance I could see a small pack of predators circling, wheeling around a point that to me was barely visible. Interested, I began slowly walking toward the display, which was farther away than I thought. As I moved closer, my ability to discern the small thing that was the focus of unwanted attention grew, and although I still could not tell what it was, it seemed vaguely familiar, and I immediately took pity on it.

Increasing my pace, I ran into the midst of the swarming hunters and with a swing of my arm sent them fleeing from my presence. I looked down at the strangely familiar Lilliputian figure, but it too was fleeing. I reached out, but it was fast, faster than I thought it would be, and it dodged to and fro searching for refuge. Suddenly it did a strange little twist and vanished as if it had never been there. I looked down and saw a hole in the very fabric of the material that made up this dimension. My prey had taken refuge there. I could see it, just barely, cowering. I reached down, my hand was too large to fit inside but I still shoved a couple of fingers down trying to capture or at least touch it. I heard something that sounded like a bird screaming and ashamed withdrew my fingers. I peered once more into that crevice of unreality but inside there was nothing, nothing at all. My quarry had vanished, but I didn't understand where it had gone to.

Sighing with frustration I marched on, against the flow which as I have said was barely noticeable, like a soft breeze and nothing more. For some reason I was still hopeful that I would emerge from this strange shrunken section of the continuum and find myself back where things were more proportionate. As I walked the small things that populated the place scattered before me and I sighed again, sadly this time as a sense of melancholy came over me. I did not like disturbing the tiny replicas of the organisms that dwelled here. This was their world, not mine. They should not have need to fear me. But they did, and I suppose rightfully so. One had to look at things from a different perspective. I was huge compared to them, and it might not be wise to get in my way. Who knows what damage I could do, even intending none?

It was again that thought of perspective that caused me to pause and think. There was something nagging at me. A fetal thought—not yet fully formed—was growing and trying to claw its way out of the womb of my brain. It was there, I could feel it, but just as it was about to come to the surface I was torn from my dream and jolted awake. This time, instead of cowering in fear, I cursed the waking. I was denied something just then, and I truly felt that if I had just had another moment I would have come to a great realization, an epiphany that would have explained much and left me no longer frustrated or fearful.

I spent the early part of that day frustrated and frantic, flitting from one project to the next, desperate to find distraction from the nocturnal visions that haunted my waking mind. I lingered in the library perusing volumes at random. The first volume I picked up was Richard Verstegan's *Restitution of Decayed Intelligence,* which I immediately set back into place, for I had no real interest in the subject matter. After browsing a little more, I was surprised to find that a volume on the 1807 Weston Meteorite included not only the chemical analysis carried out by Benjamin Silliman and James Kingsley of Yale, but also the analysis of its observed trajectory by Nathaniel Bowditch. As a pioneering actuary and former President of the Essex Fire and Marine Insurance Company, Bowditch had been required reading at Miskatonic, for he had written an astounding number of papers on a variety of mathematical subjects including Lissajous figures, celestial mechanics, and financial risk. His treatise on celestial navigation was now considered the standard work on the subject. Fascinated, I was tempted to plan a trip to Weston to visit the impact site, only to learn that the area had been inundated by the Weston Reservoir and the associated aqueduct.

My planned excursion frustrated, I cursed the Olmsted Brothers—the engineering and design firm that had planned the reservoir and associated grounds. It was only then that I recalled that this was the same family firm that had been chosen to build the reservoir outside Arkham, and whose forebears had in the past been party to New York's Central Park, Brooklyn's Prospect Park, Boston's Emerald Necklace, and the 1893 Chicago World's Fair. It was only as I listed off these major accomplishments in my head that I realized that the same family had been involved in projects closer to home. Indeed, I recalled a youthful visit to one of my aunts in Providence where I saw plaques commemorating the work of the Olmsteds on Swan Point Cemetery, the adjoining Butler Hospital, and the connecting Blackstone Boulevard. Indeed, it seemed that through their work on landscape design, the Olmsteds had come to permeate the American psyche, haunting it in a way not unlike some *genius loci,* but on a far grander scale. The Olmsteds did not so much concern themselves with the spirit of a place, as with its potential—not what it was, but rather what it could be. It seemed antithetical to the very nature of the natural world, and yet the family name and firm had become synonymous with the precepts of conservation.

After noon, I put on my coat and stepped into the back yard in the hope that fresh air would help refresh my mind and at the same time rouse me from the shroud of exhaustion that was slowly dragging me down into slumber. It was only my intent to be gone a few minutes, an hour at the most, and so I failed to tell either of the Kreitners where I was going. I was only going to be within the walled garden adjacent to Griffith House itself—a mere stone's throw away.

There is on the grounds of Griffith House a winding path that leads from the back of the house—the offices of HP&L, through the garden and to Saltonstall Street. It was this main footpath, and only this path that Mr. Kreitner had shoveled clear of snow and ice, revealing the slate work beneath. From this trail there appeared several less-formal pathways, though, given the accumulation of snow, it was hard to tell the difference between planned routes and those that had developed by simple chance or the intersection of various features. Regardless, after I had reached the gate to the road I turned back and instead of staying on the cleared path I took a step off into the unblemished snow and into the garden proper.

There was something inherently peaceful about the grounds. Draped in vast snowy shrouds the trees and shrubs seemed to swallow the noises of the street and neighborhood creating an eerie but almost relaxing hush, not unlike the sound of water lapping at the shore, or a breeze blowing in the trees. Indeed, so enticing was the sound which was not a sound that I wandered further into the garden, and soon found myself surrounded by what could only be thought of as "white noise." The further I went, the denser the plantings became and soon I was surrounded by terraces of a near monochromatic garden. The only shades I could see were the white of the snow, the pale blue of the ice, and the soft grey shadows that were cast by both. Even the sky had turned that same foggy color, and any trace of a rooftop or chimney had been obscured by the ancient, enshrouded trees.

It was in that nearly colorless milieu that I began to become increasingly uncomfortable, for it seemed hauntingly similar to the landscape of my nightly adventures. I turned around and began to follow the trail back to the main path but after a dozen or more steps realized that I had somehow missed a turn. Instead of reaching the familiar and normal slate rocks that led to the house, I instead found myself surrounded by an area in which the very definition of things began to fade. The thin traces of lines that defined depth and objects began to blur into a kind of fog. The ground at my feet seemed to dissolve, and though I tried to trace my own tracks—these too were suddenly gone. My head spun and the world with it, I closed my eyes and held my head as I fell—not to the ground, but to nothing—nothing at all.

With a sense of trepidation, I removed my hands and opened my eyes, but I knew where I was without seeing, for I could feel the familiar current against the form that was not my body but my dream body. The fact that I was surrounded by the swarming masses of tiny abstract figures flying, floating and swimming in a vast nothingness only confirmed that I had awakened in that queer nightmarish landscape that had drawn me in the three previous nights. Only this time I had entered it while I was very much awake.

Or had I? Was it possible that I had fallen asleep? Was I perhaps still in the library in a warm chair with a book open in my lap? Had I slipped and fallen on the walkway? Was I now lying injured, my lifeblood leaking out into the ice of the path? Could I have simply sat down beneath a tree and been lulled to sleep by the near silence and peace of the deeper parts of the garden? Anything might be the truth; I had no way of telling. All I knew was that I was once more in the realm of the Inbetween where the indigenous species had shrunk down to being rather miniscule in size, and there was little to no definition of any kind of structure or landscape.

At least there hadn't been previously. Before me there appeared what could only be described as a low wall of thickness that seemed to have some kind of distinction from the rest of the great white space. I walked toward it and it seemed to be at eye level, and it ran linearly as far as I could see. It was, as I have said, more opaque than the rest of the area, and as I studied it, I could see that it held within it a trace, a modicum, a hint of color. Indeed, as I strained to peer into that cloudy material, I could see what might be described as a ribbon of multicolored reality which I quickly realized was the real world, viewed not through a window or door, but through a terribly thin but incredibly long slit. I was able to see only a cut of the real world with the colors transitioning from one to the other, but without any real context or shape to explain the transition. It was therefore nothing more than a riot of particolored ribbon, the origin of which could only be surmised based on tenuous supposition. Fascinated, I began walking along and examining the transition from one shade to the next; pondering what was beyond, encased within that misty translucence.

It was not long until something broke the pattern and a fully-fledged object appeared. It was tiny, so tiny I almost missed it, but it was there and what it was was inarguable. There, embedded in that opaline wall, was a small figure. Like a miniature doll it stood between the ribbon of the real world and the outer shell that kept me from reaching in. I studied it, deliberated its very existence, for it seemed so much like the small figure that I had seen the night before. There ewas again that overwhelming feeling of familiarity, that I should know what this thing was—and that it was not a thing, but a person—a person that was of some import to me.

Driven by those feelings, I reached out and put my hand against the wall. It was firm, but I could feel within it a kind of weakness. I pushed, gently, and the crystalline material cracked beneath the applied pressure. I pushed harder, and the wall shattered and fell away. The tiny figure backpedaled as my hand cleared away the shards. There was a high-pitched whine that seemed to echo in my skull, but it was not so much a sound as a memory of a sound. A memory that this had all happened before, that I had seen this scene played out previously.

And then I remembered.

Mr. Kreitner burst into my room just before dawn. I had been screaming in terror, much as I had been the previous nights. It was to be expected, given the events of the previous year and the mounting stress I was under. I asked about the garden and when I had come inside, but Mr. Kreitner could not remember me going out, or coming in. Indeed, it had begun snowing late yesterday afternoon and had not yet let up. If I had been outside there would have been evidence by the back door, at least some dampness, and he assured me that he had seen no evidence of any such intrusion.

He left after that, and so he did not see me crawl out of bed and discover that I was not in my nightclothes, but rather in the clothes I had worn outside during the day. He did not see as I stumbled over my coat and boots and the puddle of frigid water that had accumulated on the floorboards. He did not see me fall to my knees and cry over the sudden epiphany I had over what I had seen in that unnerving Inbetween.

It is indeed an inbetween, perhaps between our world and another, perhaps between our three-dimensional world and realms where multi-dimensions are prevalent. Perhaps it might even exist between time itself. That might explain things; indeed, it might be the only explanation for what I have experienced. The thing that walked Inbetween, that monstrous titan that had so terrorized me those first two nights, and the tiny figure that seemed so familiar that I had pursued, and I suppose terrorized—they were both *me*, translated through time and space and viewed from different angles. It was all just a matter of perspective.

I wonder what the future may hold. What unearthly vistas might this ability open up before me? Walter had told me of his dreams, of being able to walk between worlds. Could I achieve this? Could I go further—build bridges, not between worlds, but between the present and the past and even the future?

It seems cliché, but perhaps only time will tell.

The Delapore Solution

Robert Peaslee

Sitting in the dark with the great factory looming about me, its pneumatic systems wheezing, its hydraulic pumps gurgling, I could not help but take a moment to reflect on how I had come to be in this particular situation. Not that I had much choice—I was, after all, tied to a chair, unable to move, and gagged so that I could not call for help. As if anybody could hear me in the vast steel and glass caverns of Delapore Chemical—as if anybody who heard me could, or would, intervene. If Megan had been with me things would have been different, but she wasn't. She was back home in Arkham taking care of our current case, that of Elwood and the murdered college students. I was on my own and in it up to my eyeballs in was what the French would have called "merde" and Megan would have called "the shit." So, with nothing to do but wait, I examined the lines of fate, luck, and circumstance for hints or clues, starting with the offer I just couldn't refuse.

It was only three days prior that I had been summoned from Arkham to the industrial town of Bolton, more specifically to the office of Toussaint Delapore, the head of Delapore Chemical. Normally, I would have delayed initiating a new case; we were, after all, embroiled in a matter with Frank Elwood, but Mr. Delapore promised a hefty retainer and invoked the name of Hadrian Vargr—a former colleague during the war to whom I owed more than I could say. There was also the fact that I had history with Delapore Chemical. Many years ago, I had found a connection between the people who were running Delapore and the manufacture of a refined version of Herbert West's reanimating reagent. I put an end to that and found out later that the villain in the matter, Senator Henry Paget Lowe, had been killed in a fire at his woodland cabin—the only problem being that they never found his head. Now, normally I wouldn't have been worried about such things, but this was Bolton, and my review of files I found while working that case revealed that the legacy of Herbert West had lingered long after he had moved on.

Toussaint Delapore was an amiable man, not at all what I expected. Younger than I had thought he would be, thinner too, and darker than I expected. In common parlance he was a mulatto—not that it mattered to me, but I was surprised that such a man had come to control an enterprise such as Delapore Chemical. It was probably an interesting story, but I didn't think it was relevant to the case at hand, so I never asked about it. What I did ask about were the various pieces of primitive art, including a number of *veve* that I recognized from a case file I had read concerning a man called Castro in New Orleans, and another from New York involving a man named Papa LaBas.

Toussaint smiled, almost chuckled. "I am a houngan, Mister Peaslee. Not a very good one, mind you, but for the people of the Bayou d'Ys I did what I could. I serve the loas: Dhamballah, Ti Malice, Agou L'Ephant, Ghede Doubye, and the Black Madonna, and in turn they serve me. Is that a problem?"

I shook my head slowly, "Your money is still green, but why not just call on your gods for help?"

He snorted as if what I had suggested was ridiculous. "You Europeans and your white Jesus Christ, you invoke him for everything—war, business ventures, good days at work, sporting events, even for your meals. He is a very busy god, and you all give him very little, but very little from so many is still so much. He is a very rich god. My gods are not so busy, and not so rich either. They demand payment, and those payments can be very dear, more than I am willing to pay. But you, Mister Peaslee, all you want is money, and of that I have an excess." He slid a check over and I looked at the surfeit of zeros that were on it. "I assume that will be enough to get you started."

I took the check, folded it and tucked it into my pocket. "What exactly do you need my help with, Mr. Toussaint?"

He stood up and gestured out the window that overlooked the factory floor. "I inherited all of this, and it turns out it has been rather profitable. The company holds patents on a number of food additives, stabilizing agents used in aviation fuels and ordinance. We have even developed a method for distributing the phage cure for bubonic plague, though Doctor Arrowsmith is still looking to extend shelf stability. Despite these successes, the factory I inherited was something of a shamble, crumbling in places. It was dreary and dirty, its safety record was deplorable. It employed women and children of little skill to work dangerous jobs with no protective equipment and for little pay. I have been trying to change that. We no longer employ children and have redesigned equipment so that we don't have to. We do still employ women, but now everybody from management to staff gets proper training and protective clothing. We've gone from two twelve-hour shifts to two eight-hour shifts, and we close on weekends. The other businessmen in the area thought I was insane—so did my managers. But we've seen an incredible result. The rate of injuries and accidents has gone down, and productivity has increased dramatically, and this has more than offset any rise in salaries and other expenses. My little experiment has paid off handsomely."

"I applaud you, sir, but that still doesn't explain why I am here."

"I'm coming to that. We set up an advisory committee to pass ideas up from staff to management. They suggested that the entire factory and its grounds are kind of drab even depressing. If we cleaned them up it might make staff happier. I couldn't argue with them. So, we've embarked on a beautification project both inside and out."

I nodded, "I noticed that the last time I came through a few months ago."

"Yes, the Olmsted Brothers may be expensive, but they certainly do seem to know what they are talking about. Anyway, after they finished one project several months ago, they submitted a proposal for the second phase, which included twice the amount of some materials as needed. Lumber, concrete, copper wire, other construction materials. When I questioned the increase, they informed me that they had suffered an inordinate amount of theft during the first phase and needed to build that into future estimates. When I mentioned this to my managers, they admitted that something similar was happening to our chemical stores. Someone is stealing from me, Mr. Peaslee, stealing from this company, and I want you to find out who and put a stop to it."

"Surely your managers or your staff have some clue as to the culprit?"

"On the contrary, they are stumped. We've taken to measuring our stocks every night and then again in the morning. Chemicals, equipment, even food has gone missing from locked rooms, from locked containers almost every night. We've posted guards, but they don't see anything, and then when thefts are discovered they become indignant and quit." He pulled a handkerchief from his breast pocket and wiped his brow. "It is really most frustrating."

"Have you witnessed any of this yourself?"

The look on his face would have made a lesser man blush. "Of course I have. I sat up all night in a supply room waiting for the thief to show up." He threw the piece of cloth on his desk. "They took what they needed out of a small lab on the other side of the complex."

"Do you have a list of what they've taken?"

He nodded and handed me a sheaf of papers. One page was glassware and equipment. Another was foodstuffs raided from the commissary: meat mostly, but a few vegetables and loaves of bread. The last page was chemical components broken down by date. It was a long list, but while the number of events was extensive, the variety was low. The thief was routinely taking the same chemicals, and ones that I was rather familiar with.

I handed the list back. "I need to go and check on a few things in the neighborhood, but in the meanwhile, I would like your staff to work on consolidating all of your chemical stores—everything that is on that list—into a single location. Don't explain why, don't try to hide it. In fact, do the opposite. Make sure that everyone knows that you're putting everything in one room. Can you do that for me?"

Toussaint nodded. "Anything else?"

"I'll need an office with a phone, directions to the nearest cemetery, a gramophone, and someplace I can get a block of ice."

"Then you know what is going on?" He seemed elated.

I tapped the list of chemicals that had been stolen. "I have an idea Mr. Toussaint. I have an idea."

I visited two cemeteries that afternoon, and two more the next day. The evening in between, I stayed at a hotel—the same hotel that I stayed at the second evening. On the morning of my third day, I walked into Delapore Chemical and sat down in the small office Delapore had assigned to me. I sat there with my feet up on the desk reading the local rag. The *Bolton Bulletin* wasn't the *New York Times* or the *Philadelphia Inquirer* or the *Boston Globe*—it wasn't even the *Arkham Advertiser*—but as local papers went, it more than filled its pages with gossip and small-town intrigue. At just after eleven in the morning Toussaint Delapore stormed into the room and demanded to know what was going on.

"I'm doing research." I didn't bother to look away from the paper.

"Research! You're reading the newspaper."

"Mmhmm. Do you have a pencil?"

He reached into his pocket and threw a pencil on the table. "The *Times* says doing the crossword is a sinful waste of time."

"I'm not doing the crossword, Mr. Toussaint; I'm finding evidence to support my theory." I laid the paper down and circled a small article in the farm report.

Toussaint craned his head around and read the small headline aloud. "Ten cows stolen from Carr Farm. How exactly is that related to the theft of chemicals here?"

"Carr Farm is just over the hill to the west, Mr. Delapore—they are your neighbors. They are having the same kinds of problems you are having—thefts. I find that intriguing, don't you?"

"I suppose," he conceded, "but what is the connection between the theft of chemicals and the theft of livestock?"

"Chemicals aren't the only thing you've lost, Mr. Delapore. You've lost vegetables and bread, and most importantly some meat. You'll note that you lost apparatus first, glass bottles and the like. Then some chemicals. Then some meat. This pattern went on for quite some time. In fact, you only lost the bread and vegetables in the last few weeks. Which I suspect is unrelated, an opportunistic theft."

"I'm sorry?"

"One person stole your glassware, chemicals and meat. Another has used those thefts to cover up their own takings of vegetables and bread, the latter is most likely your own cooks."

"My own cooks . . ."

Whatever he was about to say was interrupted by the ringing of the phone. I lifted the receiver "This is Robert Peaslee." I paused and let the person on the other end report the information I was expecting. "Thank you, sir. I appreciate the information. I'll have this problem resolved within the next day or so." We exchanged a few more pleasantries and then hung up.

"Who was that?" Asked Toussaint.

"Gladeview Cemetery. Just to the east of here. They had an unauthorized disinterment last night."

A puzzled look crossed my employer's face.

"Graverobbers," I said. "Bolton has a rather long history of graverobbing, but it's been particularly frequent since you've been having your own thefts. You and your neighbors should really talk more often. You might learn a thing or two."

"Missing cows, grave robbing—how is this connected to the missing chemicals and equipment?"

"And the meat, don't forget the meat." It was hard not to laugh. "If I told you, you wouldn't believe me. In fact, I think that you would probably fire me, and I really want to solve this case for you. You might say I have a vested interest in it."

Mr. Toussaint sat down in the chair on the other side of the desk. "I'm paying your bills, Mr. Peaslee. So please fill me in."

The irony that I was suddenly in charge even though he was paying my salary and I was in a building he owned was not lost on me.

"I think your thief is a vampire."

Toussaint stared at me and then reported the word with a kind of uncomfortable lilt. "A vampire?"

I stood up and put my hands out to try and keep him in his seat through sheer force of will. "Not your traditional vampire that Stoker wrote about—these sort of undead creatures need fresh meat and blood to survive. They can resurrect the undead and can be turned into dust and back again . . . well, ashes, really."

"So, not vampires, but rather dust vampires."

"Look, I know how this sounds. I warned you that you wouldn't believe me."

"On the contrary, Mr. Peaslee. We have a long tradition of the undead in my faith. I'm just surprised that this was the first thing you came up with."

"As I said, I have a vested interest. I've dealt with one before."

"Do you know what you're doing?"

"I think so."

"Then I'll leave you to it."

I really did think I knew what I was doing.

It was my third night in Bolton, or my fourth morning—take your pick—but this time I wasn't in the hotel. It was just after midnight as I left the main office, the gramophone, and the block of ice behind me. I was walking through the vast edifice that was Delapore Chemical, stopping every so often to listen to the Magnavox loudspeaker as it droned out static and background noise from the microphone, which was locked in the open position. Delapore used it for broadcasting announcements or reading the morning's news. In the afternoon he paid a woman to read from a book, they were just about halfway through S. S. Van Dine's account of Philo Vance solving the case of Margaret O'Dell's murder. Hearing Vance's adventures over the intercom reminded me of the days when I served Philo in a capacity similar to Van Dine's, and for a brief moment nostalgia threatened to overwhelm me. I found myself thinking about how my life would be different if I had stayed with Philo Vance, but then I shook that melancholia off. Vance was an egotist, in love with himself more than anything else. I would have been lost inside that world. Van Dine seemed more suited to what Philo needed—a silent partner willing to let him pontificate and bluster and record it all in adoration. I was more suited to action without accolades. Once, Megan had called me a Ronin—a masterless samurai with my own code of honor. It was an assessment I couldn't argue with.

An hour after I began my rounds, I caught the first hint that I was no longer alone. Somewhere on the main floor a window creaked open and then slammed shut. I hid myself in a dark corner and tried to home in on the action. There were footsteps, dragging footsteps and then a door unlocking. This was followed by more footsteps, maybe four or five sets. What I didn't hear was the sound of anyone speaking or breathing, despite spending several moments straining to do so. This put me at an extreme disadvantage. With a modicum of caution, I worked my way through the darkened factory floor and towards the intruders.

I was careful, I was quiet, I was circumspect. I came upon them, hid behind some crates, and then peered through a small gap as they worked their way through the factory. As instructed, Delapore had left all the doors inside unlocked, which should have raised some suspicions, but they didn't seem to mind. It only took them about twenty minutes to find the central location where their target supplies had been relocated, and I had shadowed them all the way. It was one-thirty in the morning, I just had to keep them in the building for another half-hour. There were only four of them. It would be easy. I was so sure of myself; I never heard the fifth thief come up behind me and hit me in the head with something hard.

When I awoke, I was tied to a heavy chair. The first thing I looked at was the clock on the wall. It was only a few minutes before two. I had been out for more than twenty minutes. Somebody behind me made a groaning sound and another figure resolved itself from the darkness, turning to look at me.

"Mr. Peaslee, yer finally awake." He had a queer New England accent, as if he was from the more remote portions of Massachusetts, but I knew that wasn't true. He was an educated man, just long removed from his original time.

I nodded, and I tried to speak but discovered my mouth was gagged.

The looming figure stayed in the shadows, but I could still see his eyes, old, deep-set eyes, that exuded age and forbidden wisdom. "I'm not a fool Mr. Peaslee. I know what ye are, I can smell it. I'm not going to risk ye knowin' the incantation to put me and mine down."

His compatriots chuckled. I looked at them for the first time in the light. They were hideous misshapen things. Human, but not quite whole, with large chunks of flesh missing and the remnants of muscle, bone and viscera showing through. I grimaced at their incompleteness.

"You will forgive my failures; I am still perfecting my formula for preparing the essential saltes needed for resurrection. Still, my compatriots are happy—they prefer living like this to the alternative." He withdrew a large blade from his belt. "I'm sure you will agree, when I bring you back in a few years."

I looked at the clock. It was just a minute past the hour. It was time, and yet nothing had happened.

The blade came closer. I went up on the balls of my feet and lifted the chair off the ground. I swung it round, knocking the knife out of the threatening hand. A fist caught me in the head, and then a hand was on one of the chair's legs. I was thrown off balance, and in a second, I was on the floor. It was enough.

All around me the Magnavox speakers were suddenly sputtering more than just background noise. There was a repetitive sound, a kind of low cycle that I and any other person from this century would recognize.

My opponent and his servants didn't notice. "You're only delaying the inevitable, Mr. Peaslee." He stumbled to his feet just as my recorded voice came over the intercom.

IS THIS THING ON?

I could remember sitting in the recording booth in Arkham. The shellac disk had even picked up my breathing. I could hear the change jingle in my pocket.

OK THANKS

I heard myself take a deep breath, then I began speaking.

OGTHROD AI'F

The man with the knife screamed and ran for the door, the others tried to follow but I kicked at the first one and brought him down in the doorway. It was just a minor inconvenience, but it was enough. My recitation of the spell accelerated.

GEB'L—EE'H
YOG-SOTHOTH
'NGAH'NH
AI'Y ZHRO

There was a terrible roll of thunder and then a flash of lightning. The creatures on the floor screamed and then collapsed into a pile of dust. That was all that remained of them—a pile of dust and the lingering odor of an ancient tomb.

The foreman found me the next morning. After he untied me, we inspected the rest of the factory. We found a small pile of dust by an unlocked door, there wasn't very much of it, certainly not enough to account for an entire body. A hand, I thought. I could just make out the fingers.

An hour later, Delapore came in and together he and I gathered the ashes and then poured them into a vat of nitric acid. We didn't bother to watch them dissolve. Back in the main office, I apologized for ruining his gramophone. It had sat for hours in a pool of water, and while the mechanism was still functional, he and I could see where the wood and veneers would soon be warping and separating. I took my recording and put it back into its case.

"You used ice to block the winding mechanism, so that it would start after the block melted. Ingenious, but you could have asked for a timer," chided Delapore, "we are a chemical manufacturing company. We have things like that."

I shrugged. "The fewer people that knew my plan, the fewer moving parts, the less chance there was of failure."

"One of them got away."

"The leader, the one that has been called Doctor Asche. He should be readily identifiable now, though—he's missing a hand, perhaps a whole arm."

Delapore suddenly had a faraway look in his eyes. "A one-armed man. I knew someone like that before. He was named Michaels; I think he sold shoes."

"He'll be on the defensive now, and on the run. I very much doubt he'll ever bother you again."

Delapore nodded in agreement. "I have to say, Mr. Peaslee, you get things done. Well worth the money." He handed me an envelope. "Your train ticket back to Arkham for this afternoon. You have several hours before you need to be at the station. There's a quaint little café just a block from there. Can I interest you in some brunch?"

I closed my valise. "I would like that, Mr. Delapore. There are some things that I would like to discuss with you."

He opened the office door. "Please, call me Toussaint. This conversation, is it business or pleasure?"

"Business, I'm afraid."

Toussaint closed the door behind us and paused to lock it. "Too bad."

We did discuss some business, I swear, but we never did make it to that café, and I barely made my train. It would seem that Bolton is beginning to grow on me.

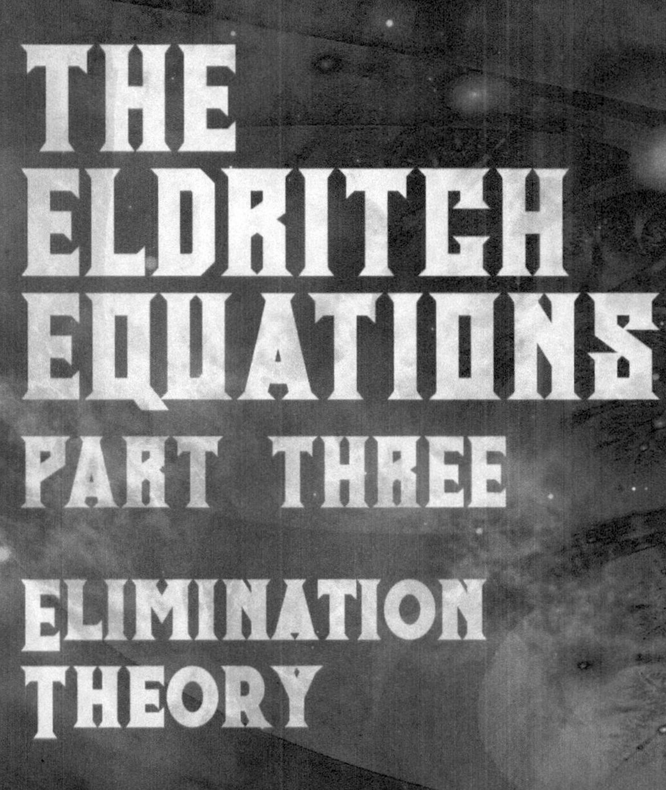

THE
ELDRITCH
EQUATIONS
PART THREE

ELIMINATION
THEORY

Twelfth Report

Megan Halsey

It was on the afternoon of February the ninth that Robert Peaslee returned from Bolton. Not long after his return our attorney secured the release of Arthur Campbell from jail and delivered him to Griffith House. It had been days since I had seen Robert, but we had little time for socializing. It was a Saturday, and if the pattern held, come Monday someone else was going to die.

Campbell was made comfortable in the library, and kept separate from Elwood, while we made a flurry of phone calls to the still-living members of Upham's class. Robert was purposefully vague concerning the issue at hand, and instead of specifics suggested that it would be in the subject's best financial interest to come to Griffith House at eight that evening. Surprisingly, they all agreed and we—I, Robert, and Lydecker—set about preparing what we were going to say to the assembled students. Ultimately, we settled on the truth being the best course of action, with only some minor prevarications. Lydecker would do most of the talking; he was, after all, the most imposing of all of us, and his condition as a paraplegic engendered a certain level of respect, even amongst those who weren't familiar with our work.

It was after dinner, a meal we shared with both Campbell and Elwood, that the first of our guests arrived. Nathaniel Kaye was a shorter man, with a round face framed by two overly large ears. From his first word of greeting, I could tell that he was not from New England, but rather from Philadelphia. The way he ordered his whiskey with "wa-der" rather than "wat-er" confirmed my suspicions shortly thereafter. I set him in the yellow chair to the right of Lydecker, with Campbell in the blue chair to the left and Elwood along the wall on the couch. He nearly gulped the drink Robert had mixed him, as if he had been pining for one the entire day. He nursed the remainder of it, swirling it gently with his left hand.

"What is all this about?" he queried in a casual manner.

"Mr. Lydecker will explain everything once the rest of our guests arrive," offered Robert. "Just a few minutes, I'm sure."

He looked around and for the first time noticed both Campbell and Elwood. He seemed to recognize them, and even proffered a small wave to Campbell, who nodded back noncommittally. I had the feeling Kaye was going to say something, but just then the bell rang and that seemed to dissuade him.

The man at the door who introduced himself as Scott Home was not what I had expected. Mr. Home was a tall and thin man, and his accent—when he introduced himself—was clearly from the British Caribbean. Indeed, as he came through the door and took off his winter coat his manner of dress betrayed his heritage, for it seemed entirely divorced from the realities of Massachusetts weather. No self-respecting New Englander would have worn a white linen suit with the tie replaced by a cravat, certainly not in February. He asked for a bumbo, and—when neither I nor Robert admitted to knowing how to make it—he stepped over to our bar to show Robert the basics. It had something to do with rum, sugar, and grenadine. Just as he was searching for some nutmeg the bell rang again and I went to answer.

Leroy Beaumont was an older man, or at least that is what I thought. The clothes he wore, though fashionable, seemed a size too big for him. His hair was prematurely gray, his eyes surrounded by wrinkles. He walked carefully and spoke with a crack in his voice, as if his vocal cords were rusty from use. I sat him near Elwood. When I asked him if he wanted a drink, he fished in his pocket and pulled out a bottle of bromo-seltzer and then asked for a glass of water.

Home was still mixing his drink and regaling Robert with tales of a small island called Redonda, which I gathered was somewhere near Montserrat. I darted between the two and snatched the decanter of water in one hand and a small glass with the other. Home never missed a beat; he just kept talking. As I returned, I caught Kaye rolling his eyes as Home made some point or another that was supposed to be humorous but apparently wasn't.

I placed the glass on the table next to Beaumont and then poured some water from the decanter. He smiled at me weakly and then picked it up in shaking hands. For some reason I felt compelled to touch him on the shoulder to reassure him that whatever was wrong, everything was going to be all right. But he and I both knew that was a lie. I regretted it immediately and then walked over to Lydecker's desk. I surreptitiously pressed the button that lit the light on the faux elevator indicating that our employer had arrived.

I walked over to the gate and drew it back, and then opened the door. Lydecker was there—or at least his head was—topping off a simulated body resting in a wheelchair. I carefully rolled him out, my eyes darting to and fro, making sure that all the straps were in place. He wheezed dramatically as we crossed the threshold and took up a spot behind his desk. Although I couldn't see them, I knew his eyes were inspecting the people in the room, analyzing them as best he could from even the most innocent of mannerisms.

It perhaps went on a moment longer than it should, for I saw several of our guests begin to squirm under his gaze. I was just about to prompt him when he opened his mouth and began to speak. "Thank you all for coming," he wheezed. "I appreciate you all being prompt."

Home put down his drink with a bit too much force, transferring attention to himself. "What's this all about, old man? In our financial interest? Did someone die? Were we all named in someone's will?"

Lydecker glared. "Indeed sir, a great many people have died. Walter Gilman, Gerald Ingalls, Fritz Long, Richard Jacobi, Nicholas Dallas, Edward Fritch, Abraham Alder, and Josephine Merril. Eight individuals in total, and in that order."

Beaumont let out a little gasp. Kaye's eyes grew wide. Home picked up his drink and swallowed the last of it down.

Lydecker continued. "You are all well versed in mathematics and statistics. I do not need to explain the probability of such an event being merely random. Someone is murdering students of the class you all took with Professor Upham."

"Merril wasn't in that class," interjected Kaye, "and Gilman was killed in an accident at his boarding house."

Arthur Campbell stood up; his voice broke as he spoke. "Merril and I had an arrangement. I wasn't any good at numbers. I paid her to secretly attend class by hiding in one of the observation booths. She wrote my papers and tutored me." He sobbed a little. "She even went to class when I couldn't"

Lydecker gurgled, "And that, Mr. Campbell, is likely why Miss Merril is dead, and you are still alive. As for Gilman, it is true that he died well before the others, but he must be included for statistical purposes. More than sixty percent of the students in that class are dead. A highly unlikely scenario. Our conclusion is that there is a high probability of murder."

"Why would anybody murder a bunch of college students?" Home's voice was incredulous.

"We think it was something you saw," I shot back, letting Lydecker observe the unconscious responses our guests were having. "During class on March thirtieth, in an impromptu discussion, Walter Gilman wrote an equation on the chalkboard. We think everybody who saw that equation is in jeopardy."

Kaye was looking at the floor. "What about Professor Upham? Why isn't he here?"

I nodded. "We talked to Upham, and made several inquiries. In early September of last year, he was diagnosed with exhaustion, and shortly thereafter relieved of his teaching responsibilities. In late October he had a minor stroke and spent almost three weeks in St. Mary's. Not many people knew about this because much of the university was busy helping out in Dunwich. As a result of his stroke, Upham is confined to a wheelchair, and seems to be having some cognitive issues. We think his condition has eliminated him as a potential victim, much in the same way that Campbell's absence from that day's class has protected him."

"What you're saying," intoned Beaumont, "is that Home, Kaye, Elwood and I are all potential targets of a homicidal maniac."

"Yes," exhaled Lydecker.

"But what you're not saying," Beaumont continued as he stood up, "is that one of those same four people is likely the killer."

"That is a possibility," gasped Lydecker, "not certain, but still a possibility."

Beaumont sat down slowly, sinking back to his seat and contemplating the situation, but this allowed Home to rashly speak up. "Why are we here, what's the point of all this? I mean you can't just have called us all together to tell us we're going to be murdered, and maybe one of us is the murderer, for absolutely no reason. You have some kind of plan?"

Lydecker rasped out the plan. "We have a house, a very secure house. We want to take you all there and protect you. The murderer has been following a pattern—he kills on Mondays. If we can get you to this place of safety, this safe house, without being followed, then maybe we can protect you, and at the same time frustrate him enough that he makes a mistake."

Beaumont was back on his feet, "You're using us as bait. Why don't we just get in our cars or on a bus or a train and get as far away from here as possible?

It was my turn to inject some reality into the situation. "While most of the murders have been committed around Arkham and its environs, Gerald Ingalls was killed in his hometown of New Milford, Connecticut. This, coupled with some of the rather bizarre manners in which the murders were perpetrated, leads us to believe that distance is not a deterrent."

This didn't seem to make a difference to Home. He marched past the others and grabbed his coat. "Nonsense," he said loudly, and in his mouth the word was almost a swear.

Robert put a gentle hand on Home's shoulder. "It's not nonsense. You can deny all you want, but come Sunday at noon we will be leaving for the safe house with or without you."

He pulled his shoulder away and stomped out the door, slamming it behind him.

Beaumont stood up and nodded his head solemnly. "You'll have to forgive Scott; he's always been a little hot-headed."

"It's understandable, but surely you can see the wisdom in what we are proposing?"

"There's so much to consider. Frankly, it's all a bit unbelievable." He moved quickly to the coat rack. "It's like being told there's a new Jack the Ripper and you're destined to be one of his victims, but the only solution is to lock you in a room with other victims and wait for the murderer to kill one of you." He buttoned his coat, fumbling with the last button. "It's not very appealing. Quite a bit to think about."

In an instant, he was down the hall and out the door.

"Well, count me in," announced Nathaniel Kaye rather jovially rubbing the back of his neck. "The odds to catch this fellow seem better if we stick together. Just let me run home for the evening. I'll pack a bag and a book, put some things in order, and be back no later than eleven." He turned to Lydecker. "Thank you, sir. I appreciate everything you've done here."

Robert walked him out of the building. I could hear them arranging details as they went.

A minute or so later Robert returned with a sigh of exasperation. "At least we convinced one."

Lydecker turned his gaze toward Robert. "Don't count on what Mr. Kaye said as the truth. Did you see him rub his neck as he spoke to us? A classic tell. He was lying to us. The easiest way to get out of the room was to tell us what we wanted to hear."

There was a moment of silence that was broken by Campbell, "Looks like it's just Elwood and me, then."

"No, Mr. Campbell," corrected Lydecker. "As it stands now, only Elwood will be going to the safe house. The terms of your release mean that you must stay here in Griffith House. Besides, we have made it quite clear that we think your lack of academic attendance has eliminated you as a potential victim."

He lowered his eyes and meekly proffered, "What if you're wrong?"

"Indeed," grated Lydecker, "if I am wrong, then you are either a victim, in which case we will have an opportunity to identify and capture the killer, or . . ."

"Or what?" Campbell's eyes focused on Lydecker.

"Or you could be the killer and your compulsion will betray you." Lydecker smiled a very rare smile. "Either way our case will have resolved itself."

Thirteenth Report

Robert Peaslee

Come Sunday morning the car was packed with enough supplies to last three days, including Megan's favorite guns, a significant amount of ammunition, and a selection of knives. Mrs. Kreitner had been up most of the night baking almond cookies and chocolate cake. She also packed a picnic basket with cold fried chicken, and another with a loaf of bread, salami and a block of cheese. Somewhere there was a jar of yellow mustard. The trunk of the Hudson Silver Wing looked like we were going camping for a week instead of just hiding out for two days, but as we had not told our housekeeper where we were taking our guests, she—as she always does, bless her heart—planned for the worst.

At half past ten, I had the sneaking suspicion that the only people going on this little adventure were to be Megan and Elwood, as none of the other three had arrived, or even phoned. I was happy to be proven wrong when—at just after eleven—the bell rang, and I discovered Scott Home standing there carrying a small overnight bag and mumbling apologies for his behavior the previous night. I settled him in the library with Elwood and told him we would be leaving promptly at noon. Campbell was upstairs in one of the guest bedrooms, as we had thought it best to keep him isolated until after the car left. He protested a bit, but after Megan threatened to return him to jail, he relented.

I hadn't even made it back down the stairs when I met Megan coming up with Leroy Beaumont. He had an overstuffed suitcase in one hand and a valise in another. Given his frail appearance I was surprised that he was able to handle both. I offered to help but was immediately denied. I took Beaumont to the library and let Megan return to the office. As Beaumont entered, Home stood up and greeted the man with a firm handshake and then a hug. They sat next to each other, thoroughly ignoring Elwood's presence. I made a mental note to mention this to Megan.

At ten before the hour, I moved the bags our two guests had brought with them to the car, and then drove it around to the front door where the rest of the party waited. Beaumont, Home and Elwood fit comfortably on the bench seat in the back. I looked up and down the street one last time and saw nothing worth noting. Megan came out dressed in her trench coat, which did a modest job at hiding the guns she was wearing. I gave her a look that told her that I thought she was overdressed, but that I knew she needed to be careful. She just smiled and kissed me.

"There's something going on with Elwood. The other two don't seem very fond of him."

She nodded as I continued. "If things get rough, I expect you to find a way to come home, no matter what."

"It's my plan, and we've been in worse situations. I can handle myself."

"It's not you I'm worried about."

She kissed me again and slid into the driver's seat, closing the door behind her.

As she pulled away, I heard a voice yell out "Wait! Please!" It was Kaye, running down the sidewalk with a small suitcase.

I thumped the side of the car and Megan applied the brakes. I went around to the front passenger door and opened it. "You'll have to sit with your bag on your lap."

Kaye nodded as he ducked into the car. "Thank you," he said. "Thank you, thankyou, thankyou."

I slammed the door behind him and watched the car drive down the road, winter clouds roiling in the sky. As I turned, I saw movement at an upstairs window and caught a glimpse of Arthur Campbell. I wasn't sure what made me more uncomfortable—the look on Campbell's face, or the fact that my wife had just left to spend the next two nights with four men.

Crowninshield Manor may have only been a few miles away, but for our plan to work, I had to stay away and let things play out, and let our killer underestimate Megan. I might as well have been in another state. I kicked a clod of frozen earth in frustration, scattering it over the snow.

Fourteenth Report

Megan Halsey

It's late Sunday night, just before midnight. Everyone else is asleep. I took a nap just after we got to Crowninshield. I've also consumed the better part of an entire pot of coffee. All things considered, I should be good till morning. After that, I'll have to struggle through the rest of Monday. The day went rather well; we left Griffith House on time, and I drove through Arkham and the surrounding countryside in a manner purposefully designed to confuse anybody who was following us. The truth is we're only a few miles from our starting point, but we spent more than two hours on the road. I'll admit that I even got turned around once myself, but only for a few minutes.

I've installed our guests in the basement, which isn't as terrible as it sounds. This part of the house was once the staff quarters and the kitchen. It's fully furnished and is heated by a very large and very old central fireplace. Barring some small windows, there is only one way in or out, which is the central stairwell of the house. This makes it rather strategically sound. I've shut the door at the top of the stairs, and the one at the bottom, and I've set myself up in a comfortable chair with a thermos right in the alcove right there by the door. I plan to stay here for the rest of the night reading my copy of Hemingway's new short story collection, which has been languishing on my shelf for almost two years. It will be nice to have some peace and quiet after the raucous argument that occurred earlier in the evening.

Robert had warned me that there was some enmity between Elwood and Home and Beaumont. I had thought it would have been something to do with Elwood's reputation as a possible witch, but it seems that is only a rumor amongst those who don't know him. No, the conflict between Elwood and the other two is firmly rooted in an academic debate concerning the economy and the sustainability of the stock market. This is a disagreement that apparently has been going on for some time.

When it comes to the economy, Elwood is apparently a conservative alarmist. He feels that the current rise in the market is driven by unwarranted speculation supported by unsecured loans, and that this is dangerous. Home disagrees and believes that risk is necessary to create new capital, but that risk will be made whole by the ever-increasing value of the market. Here Elwood invoked the Federal Reserve Board's warning about an excess amount of credit being located in highly speculative loans, a comment which led to a dip in the market earlier in the week.

Home laughs this off, calling the Board a bunch of old women still managing money using techniques from the last century. As for the market dip, Beaumont suggests that it was caused by the Bank of England raising its discount rate by one percentage point. Beaumont meant for this point to counter Elwood's argument, but Elwood seized the idea and used it to bolster his case. If the actions of the Bank of England can have such an immediate impact on the American Exchange, then it must be understood that the Exchange is not insulated, but rather global in nature and therefore subject to global influences. The American reserve might be cautious and conservative, but if a foreign power were to suddenly act wildly in either a conservative or liberal manner, whether by reflex or on purpose, the result might be catastrophic for global markets. He suggests that wheat markets in the United States, Canada, the Argentine and France are particularly vulnerable. This was followed by a bunch of incoherent yammering that invoked—amongst other things—J. P. Morgan, the Dawes Plan, Calvin Coolidge's plans for an increased naval force, and even the political theories of my father-in-law.

I let this heated argument go on for half an hour or so before putting an end to it by serving the cold fried chicken that had been sent with us. There was a half-hearted attempt to restart the discussion after they finished eating, but I subverted this by asking Nathaniel Kaye what he was reading. Kaye's nose had been buried in a book since he had gotten in the car and he had barely said two words since. He'd even abstained from the economic slugfest.

"Herman Hesse's latest, it's called *Steppenwolf*. It tells the story of a man named Haller, an intellectual who is unhappy with his life and society as a whole. He feels himself torn between his more spiritual thoughts and his baser, more animalistic urges but cannot find any compromise between the two. He's just met a woman who understands him and promises to help him become better adjusted."

Home chuckled, "A romance, then."

Kaye shook his head, "I don't think so. Every time Hermine shows Haller a manner in which others are able to relax, he finds her suggestion bourgeois indulgences. I'm not even sure Hermine is real; she could just be a figment of his imagination."

Home lit a cigarette. "Typical German literature—all mysticism and myth wrapped up in nationalism and romance. Their time would be better spent working toward paying their war reparations."

That seemed to me an opening for another fervent discussion, so I intervened once more. I withdrew a deck of cards from my jacket and shook it in front of the four of them.

"Anybody for Bridge?"

They played for about three hours while I cleaned up the remnants of dinner and wandered the halls and various rooms of the basement. There was something odd about this whole level of the house. My footsteps echoed more than I thought they should have, and some of the rooms are oddly shaped. It is I suppose just a result of centuries of haphazard modifications and renovations, but someday when I have more time, I would like to undertake a more detailed survey. I am sure of one thing though, the basement extends well beyond the walls of the house itself, particularly in the direction of the river.

I'll give another update in the morning.

·········

Late morning, almost ten. Nothing significant to report. Everybody was up before dawn. Elwood has been walking back and forth down the halls for the last few hours. He asked me about the architecture and renovations. I think he has noticed the same thing I did last night. There is something not right about how this floor fits together.

·········

Just before noon. It took him some time, but Elwood has made a map of the entire basement and there is a gap in between the walls of two rooms on the outer edge. It's only about six feet wide, so not a bedroom or anything like that. Probably just an old closet or dustbin.

·········

It didn't take long for us to tear away the plaster and wood that had been covering the old door. I was wrong; the space we uncovered wasn't a closet, but rather a set of steps cut into the earth itself. They descend to a whole other sub-basement. No wonder our footsteps echoed. I have the lone flashlight, and Home is making some torches out of broom handles, rags and some grease that he found accumulated in the moldering kitchen. Normally I would be wary, but this is just the kind of thing needed to distract these four from their worries. We will embark on our expedition as soon as we finish lunch.

···•··•··•··

If you have found this manuscript, please return it to my husband, Robert Peaslee, at Griffith House, Saltonstall Street, Arkham, Massachusetts. It has been ten days since we descended the stairs into the darkness below, seven days since our food ran out. We have lived on mushrooms and a queer species of blind and furless rat that we roast and eat whole.

Just kidding.

The stairs only went down one level and opened up into a warren of tunnels and storerooms carved out of the earth. The walls and floors aren't quite rock, but neither are they clay. Everything seems centered round a single large chamber with a rather substantial pool of cool clean water. There's a hole in the wall that the water flows out of. I think this once was a kind of limestone cave through which a natural spring feeds into the Miskatonic River. There's a pulley system and some remnants of chain along one side, suggesting that this room may have once been used to smuggle goods in and out of the house. Judging by the age of everything, it probably predates the revolution. Beaumont suggested that the place was once a ritual chamber for the worship of sea monsters that would come up out of the ocean and through the river. The chambers scattered around were for holding young female sacrifices captive until the fish men could have their way with them. It took me a whole minute to realize he was joking. If only he knew what I knew.

The rooms are not without their attractions. To go along with the air of mystery, there is the expected accumulation of detritus, including old crates and bags, bottles, various tools, and bits of metal. We could spend hours down here just rummaging around through what was once trash and is now a kind of memory of things lost. Unfortunately, the flashlight and torches won't last that long. I gave everyone fifteen more minutes and then I herded them all back upstairs.

. . . .

Kaye asked me what was for supper, and I opened up the basket and laid out the bread, hard salami and cheese and told him to help himself. He looked at me for a moment, and I knew he was trying to work up the nerve to ask me to make him a sandwich. I think perhaps the guns I'm wearing made him think twice. Everybody is sitting around eating and drinking a bottle of wine I smuggled out of the house. I think we're going to get through this.

. . . .

If we all survive till midnight it will be a miracle. Home left the room to use the facilities and when he came back his glass of wine was empty, as was the bottle. He immediately accused Elwood, who was still nursing the first glass I poured for him. Kaye suggested that he had finished it himself before he had left, but Home was adamant that there had been some left. Elwood offered what was left in his glass but Home just looked at him and said something that I didn't catch. Elwood just stood there in shock. I could see the anger building in him, and I thought for sure that they were going to come to blows, but Elwood just shook his head and turned away.

That's when Beaumont sucker-punched Home in the kidney. Home never saw it coming and crumpled to the floor. He vomited a bit. Elwood just kept going down the hall. I think he grabbed the flashlight and went down the newly discovered stairs. Beaumont walked away in the other direction, leaving Home to stumble to his feet and head off to the room he had claimed as his own.

I asked Kaye what happened. "Home called Elwood a dirty kike. It's not true. Elwood not even remotely Jewish, but Home was just looking to insult the man."

"Then why did Beaumont get involved?"

Kaye looked at me as if I had asked the stupidest question ever. "Because Beaumont is half Jewish, on his mother's side. He's rather sensitive about it."

"But aren't you Jewish?"

He nodded. "Yes, but I'm used to it. Leroy, not so much."

I told Kaye, Home and Beaumont to stay in their own rooms for a while. I need them to cool off while I go get Elwood.

··•••••····

It was easy to find Elwood—I just had to follow the light. I explained to him that we only had a few more hours to go to make it through this thing, and I needed him to come back upstairs. I wanted everybody in the old kitchen where I could keep an eye on them. I've settled in Kaye and Elwood. I'm going to let Home and Beaumont cool off for a few more minutes before I drag them back. I'm starting to feel very tired. Everybody is very tired, and, after what just happened, I think nobody trusts anybody else. I know I don't.

Fifteenth Report

Megan Halsey

Looking back, the words preceding reek of hubris. I cannot believe how quickly it all fell apart, and how badly things ended up—how many people died—and that I myself was forced to kill one of them. But I'm getting ahead of the story.

Kaye was the first to die. He had been dead for quite some time when I found him, for hours at the least. Which of course made no sense. I had just seen the man at dinner. How could a man who I had seen less than an hour earlier be so cold and so stiff? Startled, I felt a noise escape my lips. It was more a gasp than a scream, but the result was the same—it alerted the rest that I'd discovered something problematic. Footsteps echoed as the others came running. Home and Beaumont got there first, Elwood a few seconds later. That matters because in those few seconds Home had already made up his mind.

He turned away from the grisly scene of Kaye's death to look at Elwood, and there was anger in his face. "You did this," he muttered. "I don't know how, but you did this. You killed him!" And then he lunged at my client.

I thought for sure that he was going to smash Elwood across the face, but Elwood moved out of the way so fast that he just seemed to vanish. Home, driven by momentum, tumbled to the ground and smacked his head against the wall. Beaumont knelt down and helped the man up. Home, however, wasn't having it, he pushed back against Beaumont and knocked him on his ass.

"Keep your hands off me," he growled, staggering to his feet.

Home had barely gotten up, and was still bent over when Beaumont came up quickly and, with a swift but deliberate movement, kicked him in the throat. Beaumont may have meant to kick him in the chest, but Home was moving and so was Beaumont's target.

I heard something crack and Home's eyes went wide. His left hand went to his throat. He was gasping for air. There was a terrible gurgling sound as he fought for breath, it was only when he realized that he wasn't getting any air that panic set in.

He flipped over on his back. There was a terrible fear in his eyes and a grimace on his face. His hands, clawing at his throat, drew bloody lines in his flesh. His body contorted, unnaturally thrashing about, desperate for air—for breath—but his throat was crushed. There was nothing he could do.

I tried to help. I pushed Beaumont out of the way and fumbled at my belt for my knife. I pushed Home's hands away and ripped open his shirt collar. The blade slipped into the flesh. I cut slowly, carefully, methodically. The blood welled up and formed a small pool before it began running down the side of his throat. Air bubbled up through the blood, which I thought indicated some measure of success, but when I pulled back, I realized that his chest wasn't rising. He had gone still. His arms, his hands, his eyes had all stopped moving. Just like that, in a matter of minutes, Nathaniel Kaye and Scott Home were dead.

I looked at Beaumont, "You killed him." I don't know why, instinct perhaps, but my hand went to my gun.

And then Leroy Beaumont—the man who looked so much older than he actually was, the man with the ancient and somehow faraway eyes—did something that I wasn't prepared for, something I could never have been prepared for. Leroy Beaumont stepped sidewise and simply vanished into thin air.

It happened so gradually that it took me a moment to recover, to understand what had happened, what I had seen. Beaumont had nervously edged away and towards his left. I drew back the hammer on the pistol and with its CLICK he took a full step and disappeared. I swore loudly as I realized that our killer had been revealed and was getting away. It took me another second to realize that the game was still afoot—Frank Elwood was still alive and very much in danger.

I bolted from where I was crouching, gun in hand and screaming Elwood's name. I saw something move by the stairs leading into the sub-basement. It was Beaumont, or something that looked like Beaumont. As he descended the stairs with a preternatural swiftness, he seemed to be almost insubstantial, like a ghost or a curtain of thin cloth floating in the wind. I followed, taking the stairs two at a time and praying I did not fall or twist my ankle.

There was light shining up the stairs from the lower level. It was too bright for a flashlight or a torch, so bright that it seemed almost blinding. As I stumbled out of the stairwell and into the main room, I saw Elwood. He was floating in the air above the water. Rays of light streamed out of his body, pouring out from beneath his clothes. He was an angel, radiant and glorious.

Beaumont was there too, a dark and devilish shadow creeping toward the luminous figure that was Elwood. There was a knife in his hand, held menacingly. I didn't see how Beaumont was going to reach Elwood as the two were separated by both distance and elevation. Beaumont stepped off the edge as if he was going to go into the pool, but instead he vanished again—but only for an instant. He reappeared mere feet from Elwood, as if stepping out of a doorway in the air.

"Beaumont, NO!" I screamed, but he lunged forward with the knife, and I pulled the trigger. The noise echoed around the room in a deafening boom, like thunder rolling through the countryside. The knife plunged into Elwood but passed through him, as if the man wasn't there at all. The same thing seemed to happen to my bullet. It sped straight through Beaumont as if he wasn't even there. I fired again, and again, to no avail. The three of us were stalemated. Beaumont couldn't hurt Elwood and I couldn't hurt Beaumont. But stalemate was perhaps the wrong word, for I did not enjoy their immunity.

Elwood warped in on himself and then unfolded out of space mere feet from where I was standing. "Nice to see you, Miss Halsey. Or Missis Peaslee. Whichever do you prefer?" He didn't bother to let me answer. "It doesn't matter. In a minute or so it won't matter in the least." He took a menacing step forward.

I raised my gun. From across the room, Beaumont blinked out and instantly reappeared behind Elwood. "Please," I said, "stay where you are."

Elwood shook his head. "You do what you need to do. You can't hurt me." And then he winked at me.

As I saw Beaumont raise the dagger above his head, ready to plunge it down into Elwood's back, I pulled the trigger. Elwood, his speed somehow magnified, sidestepped the bullet and I watched as the projectile penetrated Beaumont's chest. He seemed truly shocked that the bullet had struck him. Blood bloomed, a stain spreading across his shirt. He crumpled to the ground. I went to kick the knife away, but it wasn't in his hand. I scanned the floor, but it was nowhere to be seen. I turned and saw Elwood walking away, the dagger lodged in his back.

He was stumbling forward. I ran to his side and put my arm around him.

He was pale, almost white. He looked at me with strange, haunting eyes. "Fast enough to dodge a bullet, but not a dagger." He forced a smile. "You solved the case."

I smiled back at him half-heartedly. "You're going to be fine," I told him. "The wound isn't very deep. A couple of weeks in bed and you'll be right as rain."

He moaned. "I hate St. Mary's"

"No," I said, "you'll stay at Griffith House. My guest."

"Thank you," he whispered, smiling. His eyes focused on something in the distance and then rolled back into his head as he lost consciousness and collapsed in a heap to the floor.

Which was for the best. I called Robert, and together we staged the scene and crafted the narrative to keep things simple for the cops. Fricasse was annoyed, and wanted to hold us as well, but he was hard-pressed to come up with a charge to raise against us.

There was a question of motive. Why had Leroy Beaumont killed all of his classmates? We never mentioned the strange powers that both Beaumont and Elwood had developed. We chalked it up to madness. "Arkham. It's just the way things are."

Fricasse frowned, nodded and started to walk away. He paused and turned back to us. "Too many witches, if you ask me," he said knowingly. "Too many witches." Then the night swallowed him up and we were left to find our own way home.

A Plague of Grimoires

Robert Peaslee

"How much do you know about the *Necronomicon*?" Scott Goudsward asked me as he unlocked the door to one of the Tabularium's many work rooms. We were in the basement of what used to be the old Marsh Library and used by the main library for storage and for restoration projects. We were on a secure level, passing through security features—multiple locks with different keys—I had installed myself. It wasn't an impenetrable set of features, but without the keys it would take almost an hour to pass through the four doors that had gotten us here. The keys were meant to be assigned to different library staff members, but Goudsward had them all on one ring. I wasn't surprised that the staff had found a way to essentially negate everything done to protect their precious books. Most of them never wanted me working there in the first place.

"Not much," I said, purposefully misleading him. "A grimoire of some sort, written in Greek. Rather rare." The door opened, and he invited me inside. The room smelled of age and dust, and, curiously, a hint of vanilla. A light sputtered on and chased away the darkness. The only piece of furniture in the room was a large table, perhaps ten feet by five feet, which left only about a three-foot walkway between the wall and the edges of the table. The table was oak, simple in design, and stained black. As we drew closer, I saw that the stain had rubbed away over time and use to reveal the natural color of the wood and its grain beneath. I wondered for a moment how something so large could have been fit into the room, but then I saw that there were actually sections to the massive piece. It could be broken down into smaller more manageable pieces.

Occupying its surface were dozens of leather-bound tomes which had been carefully laid out to assure that none touched another. Each had a small white card upon which a few words had been typed. The books were old, so old in fact that if I were to use the words ancient and moldering, I would not be exaggerating. There were some bound strictly in leather with straps that were tied together; others had iron clasps and hinges. The lettering and designs on some were long faded, but still retained noticeable silver or gold stamps on their spines or covers. Some were thin, perhaps a hundred pages, while others seemed voluminous, easily as thick as the length from my elbow to my fingertips.

"Not exactly," Goudsward chuckled, he seemed pleased with himself. I remembered months earlier when we started this security project, he was rather upset about the whole thing, particularly limiting access. "The original, the *Al Kitab al-Azif*, was written in Arabic around the year seven-hundred and thirty, by a man using the name Abd Al-Azrad, from which the more common but corrupted name Abdul Alhazred comes from. Around nine-hundred and fifty, Theodoros produced a Greek translation and first used the name *Necronomicon*. Other translations followed, including one in Latin and another in Bulgarian Cyrillic. In the late fifteenth century, versions printed in German began to appear. Olaus Wormius produced a corrected Latin version in sixteen-hundred and twenty-four. This appears to be the definitive work and is the basis for most future translations in French, Italian and German. Doctor John Dee created a partial English translation for Queen Elizabeth. From these, literally dozens of versions have been produced."

"I see. But it is a grimoire, correct?"

"In the sense that it contains spells, yes. But the majority of the book is a description of Al-Azrad's travels to the forbidden places of the Middle East and what he found there, coupled with an exploration of ancient regional mysticism." He paused and thought for a second. "One might consider it akin to T. E. Lawrence's *The Seven Pillars of Wisdom*—an adventure, a bit of romance, a healthy dose of mysticism, and a dash of sorcery."

"A dash of sorcery?"

"Well maybe more than a dash. Enough to gain the condemnation of the Patriarch Michael Kerularius and Pope Gregory the Ninth. Crusaders in the thirteenth century were ordered to burn any copies they found. A difficult task considering that not many crusaders could read."

"While I appreciate the condensed history lesson, what does that have to do with me and all of these books?"

He shut the door behind him, "We have a new curator, Miss Stanley. Very efficient, very thorough. She wants to write a treatise on the *Necronomicon* and its imitations."

"What do you mean by imitations?"

Necronomicon Ex Mortis, for example. That is essentially a medieval grimoire but has little relation to the real book. Then there is the Raed Valente's version, based on cuneiform tablets recovered from the Sumerian city of

Uruk; interesting but wholly anachronistic. Then there is the copy preserved on goatskin scrolls in Aramaic and purported by some Gnostics to have been consulted by Jesus himself, nearly seven hundred years before it was supposedly written. But not all fakes are ancient. Just before the war, Landon d'Osty released a version in Belgium subtitled *The Wanderings of the Mad Arab*. It was actually story and captured the fundamentals of Al-Azrad's travels, if not the sorcery and associated heretical demonology. Very popular if I recall, particularly in Paris, but then the French have always had a fascination for the outré."

"So, these books on the table are what, exactly?"

"Having you been listening? These are all the books in the library that have laid claim to the title *Necronomicon*."

"Which Miss Stanley is going to research and write a treatise on."

"Exactly."

"And I'm here why?"

Goudsward's eyes drifted down to his feet. He didn't want to look me in the eye. "She's new, we don't know her very well. Her credentials are impeccable. Armitage vouches for her."

"But?"

"Llanfer and the rest of us don't trust her."

"So, you want me to do what exactly?"

His eyes shifted to mine. "What you are good at, what you've been hired to do. Make sure she doesn't steal anything."

· · · • · • · · · ·

It doesn't matter how much you pay me; I have always hated babysitting jobs. Despite this, I was pleasantly surprised to discover that Jane Stanley, whom I had met before, albeit only briefly, was a rather pleasant young woman with a professional demeanor. She had a narrow countenance highlighted by a pair of round, wire-rimmed glasses that made her look slightly like an owl. She carried a small valise in her right hand, and in her left was a rather battered copy of a Pent & Serenade auction catalog. As she noticed me waiting for her in the work room, her face pinched into a frown.

"Good morning," I said with a perfunctory tone.

She nodded reluctantly, "Good morning Mr. Peaslee." And that was all we said to each other for hours.

I sat in the corner reading Esther Forbes' *A Mirror for Witches*. The author was somewhat local, and I have seen her speak in Boston. Her previous novel was a romance, but this one was an examination of the witch trials. I found

Forbes' novel an interesting if somewhat overwrought fictionalization of the subject. I must admit that my knowledge of the actual subject was rather limited. As I read, I occasionally glanced up at my charge and her work before returning to my book. The only sounds I was making were the semi-regular whisks of the pages turning, or so I thought. In contrast, Miss Stanley was rather noisy. Her pages were much larger, and she seemed to slam books around in frustration. Further, she expressed her emotional state with long, breathy sighs that lingered and disrupted the quiet of the room, like a wheezy locomotive gasping along the tracks. I did my best to ignore her until she seemed to actually want my attention, and, more importantly, my assistance.

"Look at this, would you?" She had laid out three books side by side, their covers closed. For all intents and purposes, they seemed to be three copies of the same book, each a rather slim volume bound in cloth without any adornment. "Three copies of Joachim Ferry's *Notes on the Necronomicon*, a kind of abridged version produced at the turn of the century. These copies were printed in 1920 by the Restitution Society."

Suddenly I was paying more attention. I had heard the name of that organization before.

"At first glance they look identical, but here on the spine they are numbered in roman numerals—One, Two, and Three."

"I would have thought that the numbering was a volume identification. Some sort of set, maybe?" I offered this without trying to be critical of her skills.

She shook her head, "I thought that as well, but I've gone through the pages and compared the text and the illustrations. They appear to be identical—some minor splotches of ink here and there, but nothing significantly different."

"Perhaps a printing number, then? Or maybe the numbering was added later by a previous owner or overzealous collector."

"They all appear to have come from the same collection. Look here on the back-end page—a blind stamp for the Library of Cyrus Hook. Have you ever heard of him?"

"I have. The Hooks were one of the founding families around here. I think the Cyrus Hook mansion burned down around 1870." I flipped all three books opened to their back endpapers and confirmed that all three bore the same stamp.

"How does that make any sense? Three books proclaiming to be part of a family library that burned down fifty years before they were printed." Stanley sighed in frustration.

"Well, I don't know about that—but how these books differ is suddenly rather obvious."

She nearly knocked me over as she rushed to see what I was looking at. Even then I don't think she saw it right away. When she finally recognized the differences, she let out a little squeal. The endpapers of each volume were architectural drawings of a building, and they were very similar—but there were subtle differences. Some doors were in different places; stairs were oriented differently; some walls were missing, while in other places there were more.

I think we both figured out what we were looking at almost at the same time, but she said it first. "They're floorplans for a building." She flipped to the back endpapers of each book in rapid succession. "Six floors. And this one at the front of volume two is the ground level—see, it has doors in the outer walls. Which means it has two more upper stories and three more below ground."

I nodded. "Which explains the lack of windows and exits in these three pages."

She was ducking under my arm to look at the designs and almost giggling. "This is incredible! I wonder where this building is, or even if it was ever built."

I looked at the print that she had decided was the main floor. It seemed familiar—very familiar. It was a sizable building with a large central room surrounded by smaller spaces, some of which seemed too large to be offices. The two upper levels mirrored the ground floor. The whole thing seemed to be overbuilt, buttressed for more weight than I would have expected. It wasn't a manufacturing plant, or a warehouse. I flipped to the first lower level. Much different than the ground floor. You would put the boiler over there, and that would make that room storage for the cleaning staff.

Suddenly, I had it. I let out a little yelp of excitement. "I know exactly where this building is."

"You do? Where?"

I was grinning as I pointed down at my feet. "We're standing in it. There's been a few cosmetic changes, but this is a blueprint for the old Marsh Library."

Her eyes narrowed and she shook her head. "That's impossible. We're in the basement. There aren't any stairs that lead down from here." She was pointing at the stairwell. "These stairs don't exist."

I shrugged. "That may be true. Maybe they didn't build the lower levels, or maybe they've been sealed off, but these are the designs for this building." I looked where she was pointing. "Besides, those stairs don't go down to the lower levels." I scanned the page with my finger floating over it. Then I found what I was looking for and I pounced. "See, over here, off the boiler room. There's a side alcove with another stairwell to go further down."

She looked at the page and then back at me. "Why would you limit access to the lower levels to going through the boiler room?"

"Probably because when it was built it wasn't originally the boiler room. Possibly because what is down there is just building facilities. Foundations, plumbing, storage, that sort of thing." I pointed at a sealed off section. "That, for example, is probably a cesspool."

"If it's so ordinary, why hide it in a copy of a book very few people would have an interest in?"

"Maybe the binder was just cheap and used whatever paper he had laying around."

"If that were the case, he could have turned it over and used the reverse side. But look these were specifically set so that they could be read, and preserved, in secret."

I waffled "Perhaps."

A huge grin filled her face, "There is one sure way to find out."

"No," I was firm. "I'm here to make sure you don't steal or damage anything while you do your work—not to go traipsing about in dark sub-basements. We solved your book binding mystery. That will be the end of it."

The light went out of her eyes, and she settled back in to looking at her books and taking notes. I returned to my chair and my book, but try as I might, I couldn't get the idea out of my head. She was right—it didn't make complete sense. My reasoning was logical but unsubstantiated. My eyes drifted from my book to the floor. What was down there?

I stood up, threw my book on the chair and walked over to where she was working. Carefully, I flipped open volume two to the back endpage. I studied it for a moment and then looked her in the eye. "You wait here," I said sternly, "I'll be gone for two minutes." She tried not to smile as I left the room.

I was back in a minute and a half. I picked up my book and sat back down, pretending to read.

It took her a full thirty seconds to break the silence with a questioning screech. "Well?"

"There is a door in the back of the boiler room. Old, very old. Thick oak, with an ironwork latch. There is a padlock, also old. Rusted. I don't think anybody has been in there for years."

"Oh," she seemed depressed.

I reached into my pocket and slid what was in there across the floor. It left a trail of flaked iron behind as it came to rest at her feet. It was the padlock. She picked it up and stared at it.

"It fell apart when I touched it."

"Does that mean we can . . ."

I cut her off before she finished her question. "Tomorrow. We need flashlights, and a few other things. I'll get them all together tonight, and we'll go first thing tomorrow morning." I looked at her outfit. "You do have something more suitable to wear? Maybe some overalls?"

She nodded, and I could tell she was doing her best to contain herself. I didn't bother to tell her that what I really wanted for tomorrow was a bigger gun.

· · · • · • · · · ·

The next day—Friday, February the fifteenth—came earlier than I wanted, and I left Megan at home to tend to Elwood. She kissed me as I walked out the door and gave me a sideways glance at the large cloth bag that I was carrying with me. She knew I was up to something, but also knew that if I wanted her to know I would tell her.

"Be careful," she asked of me.

"Always," I told her.

There was a look.

"I try."

Her eyes rolled.

"If I'm not home by midnight . . ."

She nodded, "I'll bring the cavalry."

"A small amount of explosive should do, one maybe two sticks of dynamite."

"Is that your answer to everything?"

I shrugged, "It's worked so far."

She closed the door in mock frustration.

I arrived at the Tabularium by eight that morning. The staff waved at me as I walked in. Nobody even questioned my bag, let alone stopped me to search it. I was relying on that, even though it was in complete opposition to every recommendation in the newly established guidelines concerning building security. Stanley was waiting for me by the door to the basement. She was wearing a long skirt, a light sweater and heels.

She saw my look of disapproval and kicked a small bag sitting at her feet. "I'll change when we get downstairs."

While she did that, I set about unpacking my bag and setting up in the boiler room. I had two flashlights, chalk in case we needed to mark things, twenty feet of rope, a hammer and a chisel, some miscellaneous tools, and a belt that held my gun and a supply of ammunition. This last piece was discreet enough to fit under my coat and not really be noticed.

Which apparently was not the direction that Jane Stanley had decided to go. I had never really considered what Stanley had looked like. The hair bun, glasses and layered sweater and skirt had cast her permanently into the realm of academics which included spinster librarians and frumpy schoolteachers. I had never considered that there might be more to her than that. Her choice of outfit made it clear that I had been substantially underestimating the woman. She was wearing dungarees and a plaid cotton shirt, along with tight fitting leather gloves and a pair of well-worn boots. It was as if she had stepped out of a western as the epitome of the rough and ready cowgirl. Across her chest she wore a thin bandolier fully outfitted, including a small pistol the make of which I didn't recognize. What I also recognized was the fact that she was rather well-proportioned. Not that I have a tendency to notice these things about women. Megan is well-built, feminine but strong—stronger than she looks. Miss Stanley was missing most of the curves that were in fashion these days, but in their place was a compact physicality that, in a man, would have made him wiry. It was a very different definition of attractiveness. Still feminine, but not weak.

She noticed me staring. "I grew up mostly in Colorado, working at my uncle's hotel. We know how to work hard, and how to dress for it."

"And the gun?"

She looked down. "The smallest one I had. An Ortgies semi-automatic, made in Germany. It's proved itself rather reliable in competition."

"You shoot competitively?"

"No, Mister Peaslee. I hunt, deer and bear, mostly. The Ortgies is simply for protection."

Put in my place, I left it at that.

The door put up a little resistance, but not much. Rust cracked and crumbled, and the accumulation of paint that had coated the hinges fell away in flakes as the wooden door swung open for the first time in decades with an audible and ominous creak. There was a small burst of cold air, as the atmosphere from below suddenly mixed with one that it had been partitioned from for so many years. It brought with it a smell of damp, of mold, of aged stone and rotting wood.

A shower of dust fell from the door jamb and Stanley coughed a little as she flipped on her flashlight. "Ready?"

I flipped my light on and pointed it down the stone steps. Everything seemed stable enough. "Stay behind me, but not too close."

The stairwells in the upper levels were magnificent examples of architectural design, combining the need for moving people from one floor to another with air flow and elegant windows which ran from floor to ceiling to provide light. Over the years, the administration had embraced the idea that these spaces could also function as galleries, and so were home to some of the more durable pieces of art in the University collection. The combination of artistry, architecture and functionality had made the steps a place for reflection, if not completely quiet contemplation. These steps down into the darkness bore no relation to their cousins. They were dank and poorly wrought things, cut from the stone of the earth itself, but they showed little wear. Indeed, the edges were almost uniformly crisp, and seeing an occasional chip here and there was noteworthy.

It was twenty steps down—two flights—and those were uneventful, save once when I slipped on a bit of accumulated sand. Thankfully, Miss Stanley had been close enough behind me to steady me before I fell. It surprised us both when we found, built into the wall at the bottom of the stairs, an electric light switch. Emboldened, we turned it to the on position and watched as a long hallway full of crudely mounted lamps sputtered into view.

Stanley paused and examined one of the bulbs. "They haven't made these kinds of bulbs in more than twenty years."

I pointed down the hall. "That might explain the two decades of dust accumulation."

We walked cautiously down to the first door, knowing from the map that it led to the largest of rooms.

"Shall we?" I asked putting my hand on the doorknob.

"By all means."

The door opened with ease, and I could see the light switch just inside. I flipped it and once more the lights sputtered to life, though this time one grew brighter, popped and then went dark. We went in without hesitation.

The room was large, maybe a thousand square feet, with support columns in a regular pattern throughout. Next to each column was a large cement cistern. Pipes followed the columns down into the top of the cisterns, and then more pipes came out of their bottoms and then ran to the side of the room where they joined a larger pipe that plunged through the floor. We could hear water running through the pipes and then the cisterns and then to the central sewer. Each pipe only carried a little flow but once they joined up, it seemed immense.

I turned to Jane Stanley and smiled. "Plumbing. A crude septic system, still operational after all these years." I thumped one of the concrete tanks. "They don't make them like this anymore."

Stanley glared at me disappointedly. "Maybe the lower level will be more entertaining." She reached into a pocket and pulled out a cigarette case and a box of matches.

I put my hand on hers. "Better to wait. Decades of decaying sewage—there might be accumulated pockets of gas down here."

She nodded and put the cigarettes and matches away. "Well, are we going down or not?"

Where she led, I followed. I didn't bother to mention that the level that we were on only vaguely resembled what we had seen on the map.

The steps down were just as old as the first set we had come down, but showed even less wear than the first flight we descended. The switch for the lights was in the same place, and as they sputtered to life, I was wholly unprepared for what was revealed. The entire floor was one large, cavernous room, the effect of which was exacerbated by the nearly twenty-foot ceilings. As on the other floor, there were immense columns supporting that ceiling, but between those columns, for as far as we could see, were rows and rows of cases of wood and glass. They were of mismatched construction, style and size. None were under five feet in height, but some reached nearly to the ceiling. Some were thin, and others were immense constructions that would have spanned great walls. Some were plain or roughly hewn; others were incredibly detailed and ornate, with carved adornments and reliefs. But neither of us were that interested in the woodwork. We were too busy looking at the contents—thousands upon thousands of books that filled the shelves as if this place were a forgotten library, a floor that had once been stocked but then somehow forgotten. The only distraction from this vast forest of literature was the familiar large pipe that came out of the ceiling and gurgled and churned with the wastewater that drained from above.

The room with all of its books was a librarian's dream, for it held an impossible number of texts that seemed to have gone untouched for decades. Yet there was one curiosity. The books were not randomly distributed—each shelf seemed to hold multiple copies of the same volume. Different shelves held different volumes, some large, some small, but all neatly arranged as if in a publisher's warehouse.

Without a word Stanley went straight to the shelves and began shuffling through them. After a moment or two she turned to me and shook her head. "This isn't possible." Then she began frantically walking down the aisles flipping open copies of each book and muttering to herself, over and over again, "Not possible . . . not possible . . . ."

She turned the corner and then another. I could still hear her, so I wasn't too worried. I followed anyway.

It only took me a moment to realize that the shelves formed a kind of labyrinth. I took out my chalk and made a mark on a shelf. This place wasn't very large, but if things went wrong, seconds might be critical. I could still hear Miss Stanley, but she was babbling, getting farther away with each passing moment.

Desperate, I called out to her. "Jane, stop! You're going to get lost. I need you to talk to me and tell me where you are. What are you looking at right now?"

There was a silence and then I could hear her voice in the distance. "*The Ethics of Ygor.* Five copies. It looks like they just rolled off the press."

"No, you don't understand, I need to reach you!"

"NO!" She was shouting, "You don't understand! This is impossible. Here are two copies of *Restructor Omnium Rerum*, and three of *Remnants of the Lost Empire* by Dostmann. Here are copies of *The Imperial Dynasty of America*, and a stack of Poe's *Worm of Midnight.*" She paused again, and then I heard her voice choked with sobbing emotion. "I think these are copies of the *Song of Xeethra.* But that's impossible. All of this is impossible."

I heard her move down an aisle and tried to follow the sound but could not tell exactly how far she had moved. "Stanley, stop!" I ordered. "Where are you exactly?" As soon as the words left my mouth, I knew they would be useless.

She was gasping, almost hysterical. "I've found *The Unfathomable Ruse* and Von Junzt's *Uber das Finstere Lachen.* Over here, this is a stack of editions of *The King in Yellow.*" She was moving again, and I cursed softly. Why wouldn't she just stay still?

De Umbram Regni Novem Portis?"

"I can't say that I have."

"Most people, even librarians, haven't. Extremely rare—most copies are thought to be fakes, but even those are considered terribly valuable. Priceless." She paused. "I'm looking at two copies."

I took a left, then a right. I could hear her breathing.

"I've found the *Necronomicon.*" There was suddenly a sense of calm in her voice. Her steps had become slow and deliberate.

"Miss Stanley—Jane—what's happened?"

"The shelves, they're full of them. Like stars in the sky, thousands of them—all you have to do is look and you see more. They're everywhere." She was ranting. "It's not possible. How is this possible? It's not possible. It's a lie. This whole place is a lie. An abomination. It shouldn't exist!"

She paused for a moment and then said three words that seemed totally disconnected from what we were talking about. "The Restitution Society."

Then there was a sound—a simple yet terrible sound that struck fear in my heart. It was a singular scratching sound that was followed by a kind of low crackling. I knew that sound and it filled me with dread as I listened to it grow and spread. I looked at the ceiling and could see the flickering light and shadows that were coming from wherever Stanley was. A moment later the smell finally hit me. It was an undeniably familiar smell, acrid but sweet, comforting but at the same time engendering caution. Never before in my life had I been so afraid of the smell of fire.

"Stanley," I screamed, "what have you done?"

She was laughing and then she was running. I could hear books being pushed out onto the floor; I could hear the fire spreading. And I could hear Jane Stanley going mad!

"This shouldn't be here, shouldn't be here, shouldn't be . . ."

The light from the flames grew brighter on the ceiling, and that gave me a kind of map to follow. Still marking my way with chalk, I sprinted down the aisle, turning this way and that, moving closer and closer to the danger, to the flames, to the rapidly growing inferno. I ran till I felt the heat, till I could see the light leaking underneath the shelves and through the seams between cases. I ran until I could hear Stanley shrieking in madness close by. And then, with her mere feet away from me, I found the smallest of shelves and I threw my entire weight against it. It barely budged, but I had known that it wasn't going to be easy. I stepped back and hit it again. This time the case behind shifted forward a few inches. I hit it again and again and again. On the fifth time, with my shoulder battered and bruised, the far case toppled and the small case that I had been beating on fell over, allowing me access to the aisle on the far side. As I clambered over the jumble of broken glass, cracked wood, and disheveled books, I saw Stanley.

She was kneeling on the floor. Her head was down. In one hand she held a mass of torn up papers that were blazing like a torch, with the other she was opening a book, fanning open its leaves. As I watched, she brought over her makeshift torch and lit the book aflame. Then she opened up another book and started to light that on fire as well.

"Jane!" I screamed with panic in my voice.

Whether it was my presence or my tone, she snapped out of her mania and stood up in a quiet kind of fear. Now that she wasn't focused on setting fires she could see where she was, and how much danger she was in. Behind her was a raging bonfire, a pile of tumbled books that she had set ablaze and then had forgotten about. That fire had spread, as fires do, to the cases on either side, running like some kind of living thing along the ancient dry woods and oil rich stains. The bonfire behind her and the small blaze in front of her combined with the now burning bookcases on each side meant that she was essentially cut off. Not entirely, though—if I pressed, I could still make my way through and reach her, as long as she didn't panic.

The flames leapt suddenly from the bookshelf on her left to a stack of dry pages and they went up in an instant. Sudden heat cracked the glass of the bookshelf, and the sudden influx of oxygen created a kind of explosive tongue that curled out and licked at the crazed librarian.

She screamed and pulled away. She successfully dodged the burning tendril but had forgotten that in her hand she held an ersatz torch. As she twisted away, she brought that hand in and moved her head down. It was a natural kind of reflex, but in this case a tragic one. The flames that smoldered on the curled-up pages jumped into her hair. Her tresses went up in an instant, as did the cotton of her shirt. She screamed. It was a horrible, soul-numbing scream, as much a thing of fear as it was of pain. She dropped the torch and began beating at her head with her hands. All that accomplished was to spread the fire to her sleeves.

I stumbled down the fallen shelving and swiftly took off my coat. I covered my head and leapt through the small fire that was between us. My intention was to use my coat to smother the flames, but in her panic, she began spinning around, screaming in agony. I could hear the sizzling of her flesh as she continued to try and beat the flames out. In her madness she ran from me, she careened through the bonfire she built, falling through the flames. I could still see her, but only for an instant. The flames swallowed her up. I knew she was still alive, but I couldn't see her, and I didn't dare risk making my way through the inferno as it continued to spread.

I screamed her name, but only once more. Then I was jumping back across the small blaze and climbing over fallen shelves. I followed my chalk marks back, weaving my way through the maze of bookshelves as behind me the fire spread from one shelf to the next, from one aisle to the next, the still-smoldering ashes accelerating the flames, allowing them to jump entire sections, moving almost as fast as I was. It ran, and I ran with the hellish heat at my back and the crackling flames growing into the dull roar of an inferno. If I looked, if I cast a glance to either side, I could see the flickering tongues lapping at my heels, as if I were a runner in some kind of marathon—only the race was for my life, and the competition would literally kill me.

My breath was ragged, I could feel my sinuses crack from the heat, and sweat was pouring down my back but evaporating before it could soak my shirt. I wrapped my coat around my head tighter and ran faster, hoping that I could stay ahead of the conflagration.

Then I was out. I burst out of the entrance to the labyrinth like a shot and fell, rolling across the floor. As I tumbled, I could see the ceiling, the dance of terrible light and shadow, the black smoke that was billowing up, slowly but inevitable filling the room. I crawled away, desperate to get up and out.

Maybe it was all my years as a soldier, or as a cop. Maybe it was my training, or my innate humanity, or it could have just been my contract with the university, but I knew I needed to do something. I could have just run, saved myself, and let everything else burn. It would have been easy. It would have been consistent with what Megan and I had been slowly doing over the last few months. All of those tomes should be destroyed, and Jane Stanley had done me a favor by setting that blaze. It was just that her efforts were too enthusiastic and too grand in scale. Her conflagration was too big, too noticeable, too damaging. The books would be destroyed, but so might the building and anybody working in it. Given the amount of kindling down there, some firemen might perish as well.

I stood up, mounted the first stair and then withdrew my gun. I took careful aim and fired at the drainage pipe. The first shot connected and punched a small hole in it. Brown water spurted out and onto the floor, spreading like a thin mud. I fired again. Another hole. A third shot and the pipe buckled, a gushing torrent pouring out. Satisfied, I turned and made my way slowly and steadily up the stairs. At the main floor I pulled the fire alarm and calmly walked outside with everyone else. Nobody ever bothered to stop me. In the confusion of staff and students evacuating and emergency personnel rushing in, nobody looked twice as I walked off campus.

Later that afternoon, after I had cleaned up and thought things through, I did go back to campus and sit down with staff. I admitted to being there, but I never mentioned going down to the lower levels. There were some questions about Jane Stanley. I admitted I was watching her work but that she had left the work room just before the fire broke out. I had thought she had gone to powder her nose. I never mentioned anything about the sub-basements or what we found there. They told me that the fire had broken out in a sub-basement that had originally been built to provide drainage. They suspected that an accumulation of debris and methane had spontaneously ignited and then blown out the interior plumbing, and it had been hours before they had actually turned the water off. This had caused the level below the boiler to flood, and even the basement level where Stanley and I had been working now had an inch of water in it. The fire department had declared the whole area off limits, and the University was bringing in an architect to assure that the structure was still sound, and coordinate drainage and reconstruction. Very preliminary time estimates suggested that it might be weeks or even months before anything below the ground floor could be accessed safely. In the meantime, teams of librarians would be going into the upper levels and recovering documents and books for storage elsewhere.

I reminded Llanfer that Stanley and I had been working on rather rare books having to do with the *Necronomicon*.

He frowned and suggested that perhaps I would be willing to go down and extricate those volumes. I agreed, knowing it might give me an opportunity to be a little creative with what I was able to rescue. I suggested that, given the fragility of such volumes, that time was of the essence. If possible, I would go down tonight, after the fire department left. I would leave what I found on a table in one of the conference rooms on the main floor. Llanfer agreed wholeheartedly, pleased with my eagerness.

It was after midnight when I piled the last of the books on the table. I had conveniently dropped one out of ten books into the filthy waters that had risen to a depth of six inches. This included all copies of Ferry's *Notes on the Necronomicon*, which had contained the secret blueprints of the building that had led to the forgotten levels and initiated the disaster that had cost Jane Stanley her life, and had essentially condemned the Tabularium.

Satisfied, I made myself ready to go, but I could not bring myself to leave without taking one last around. With torch in hand, I wandered back down to the first basement and began walking the halls, wading through the sewage and trash-filled waters aimlessly. No, not aimlessly. I had a purpose, though I didn't want to admit it. I was drawn toward the boiler room and the door that was behind it, the door I had forced.

It was still open, but there was no manner in which I could descend the stairs; the rising flood waters had filled the staircase with not only water, but with a mass of burnt and waterlogged books. Even if the flood waters receded it would take an excavation team weeks to clear the debris that clogged the steps. I sighed, but whether that was a sigh of sadness or relief I could not say. I turned away, but as I did, something moved.

A skeletal hand shot out of the accumulated filth and grabbed my ankle. It was a black and unwholesome thing, the tattered remnants of something undead. I pulled back, but it refused to let go. I heaved myself away from the stairwell and in my efforts to escape I dragged the creature out of the darkness and into the light. I will not let the irony of the situation go uncommented on. I knew that my condition was not much different than that of this thing that had risen out of the pit to claw at me, and yet I was disgusted by it. As it clawed up my pant leg it revealed itself as a tattered revenant of black flesh hanging over a red musculature. It moaned as it came at me, its barely functional hands clawing for my face.

I pushed it away, but it refused to let go. I turned and gagged as the smell reached my senses and filled my sinuses and mouth with the scent of blood and burnt flesh. I nearly retched and reflexively grabbed the thing by its jaw, clamping the mouth shut. Then with all my strength I gave it a quick twist and heard the neck break. It was only then that it finally slumped to the side and stopped moving.

It was as I tried to extricate myself from its entanglement that I noticed the fragments of clothing that still clung to its form. A plaid flannel shirt and the rivets of dungarees around the waist. Its hair had all burned away, as had most of the flesh on its face, but I thought for a moment that those eyes and those teeth were familiar. If I had been a lesser man I would have screamed as I recognized what I was holding, but I had seen too much horror, suffered too much pain, and survived too many tragedies to feel anything other than resignation. I was, I suppose, no longer human. At the very least, I had lost too much of my humanity to feel anything other than numb in the face of such grotesqueries.

The boiler was still on, the fire still burning, as it was needed to keep the upper levels warm and dry. I opened the gate and loaded the body of the thing inside. I used a poker to shove it all the way in. I watched, the oven door spitting out smoke and flames like a tiny gate to Hell itself. The cadaver steamed a bit as the heat drove the moisture out of it, but then, as the remnants of clothing and skin rapidly dried out, it finally caught fire and began to burn. In time, all that would remain would be ash and a few bones, and an open case file that listed Jane Stanley as missing. I closed the oven door and went back upstairs.

As I walked home through the dark Arkham streets, not truly feeling the cold wind blowing, I looked at the sky and the stars that were perhaps the only witnesses to what I had done. At home I showered, ate a meal and drank a glass of scotch. I sat in the library in the dark, occasionally looking out the window at the moon, that great cyclopean eye that stares unblinking down on the world. It sees all, but I wondered if it ever bothered to pass judgement on what it witnessed. I poured another scotch and tried not to think about what I had done and what kind of man I had become.

The Entitlement of Jane Grimm

Megan Halsey

When the doorbell to our offices rang, I found myself in the position of having to answer it myself. The Kreitners were out for the morning visiting various establishments in an effort to replenish our larder and diminished supplies. Robert had been moody for the last few days, the fire at the college had affected him immensely, and was ill-suited for company. For obvious reasons Lydecker cannot answer the door. So, it was I who opened the door and greeted the woman who stood there.

She was a very large woman, not obese, but tall, easily over six feet, and with a broad face and shoulders and a muscular build. Her face featured large eyes, a large flat nose, and a mouth that seemed wider than normal. Her skin was of an olive complexion which made me think that she was of Latin origin, maybe not entirely but at least somewhere in her family tree. She wore a respectable outfit, comprising a white shirt tucked into a pair of grey trousers. Over this she wore a matching grey wool suit coat. It didn't take much for me to realize that she was wearing men's clothes. Even her shoes had been made for a man. The reason was obvious. The clothes did little to hide her physique; even the men's suit barely hid her build.

"Can I help you?" It was a stupid question, the only reason people come to our door is when they need help, but it was the best way to break the ice.

"Is this Halsey, Peaslee and Lydecker? My name is Grimm, Jane Grimm. Toussaint Delapore said you might be able to help me." Her voice was deep, her accent mid-western.

I nodded, "You've come to the right place. Please come inside."

I led her into our consulting rooms and sat her on the couch, mostly because I thought the chairs would be too small for her. I offered her a drink, which she declined. I thought about bringing in Robert or Lydecker, but I wanted to hear her situation first.

"As I said, my name is Jane Grimm. Toussaint and I know each other from the circus—we both had once worked for Doctor Lilith L'Avenza, but then Toussaint came into money and I . . . I got tired of being on the road. I found a place, not far from here. Bought a house, I made a life for myself. I work out at the Point, at the fairgrounds." She paused as she struggled to explain herself. "Last year, my mother died. She was a trapeze artist, she never told me anything about my father. Anyway, the lawyers sent me all her possessions. There wasn't much, but the papers included my birth certificate. It identified my father as a man named Alfred Jermyn. There were some newspaper clippings, they told how Alfred Jermyn had been killed by a gorilla he was meant to be taming. That story also related how Alfred had been a member of the British aristocracy."

"Your mother was married to your father?"

"There was a marriage certificate, and his name is on my birth certificate. But my mother's papers . . . she contacted the family lawyers. Alfred Jermyn already had a wife, and a child, a boy called Arthur."

"So, you are illegitimate. You have no claim to the family title, but they might still be kind enough to grant you an allowance, just to keep you quiet."

She agreed with me, "You would be right, except Arthur Jermyn has been dead for years. He committed suicide. He doused himself in oil and set himself aflame. I am the last living descendant of the Jermyn Family."

"You've asserted your claim?"

"Yes, but to no avail. The Brightholmes refuse all my letters, and my attempts at having my legal representatives intervene have been fruitless. The Brightholmes' solicitors have kept this out of the courts for months. I'm running out of resources, patience, and options."

"I'm sorry, who are the Brightholmes?"

"A family of the British aristocracy. My great-grandfather Robert was married to a daughter of the Seventh Earl of Brightholme. In absence of a legitimate heir, they've laid claim to the Jermyn properties through this marriage." She opened her valise and produced a file. "I've made a copy of all my paperwork for you to review."

I put my hand up. "I'm sorry, Miss Grimm. This is all very interesting, but I'm not sure what we can do for you. We're private investigators, not lawyers."

She nodded, "I understand, I—it's just that the Brightholmes, well some of them anyway, are here in Kingsport. They have a vacation home, they come for the Spring Regatta. I thought maybe you could help me gain access, somehow arrange a meeting. I just want to understand why they refuse to talk to me."

"Let me look this over, discuss it with our lawyer, and see what I can do." I took the file. "I have to warn you, our services aren't inexpensive."

"Toussaint," she caught herself, "Mr. Delapore has assured me that he will cover your expenses for me."

I was a little surprised. "That's very kind of him."

"Yes, yes, it is. We have a long history together. Before he came into money, he was a carnival mystic for der Zirkus L'Avenza. Called himself Doctor Crocodile. Kind of silly really."

"And you, what did you do in the circus?"

"I was Amazona, the Strongest Woman in the World," she flexed her arm in demonstration. "Not much of an act, but I also did an acrobatic display. That was much more satisfying."

My curiosity was aroused, "Were you any good?"

She nodded half-heartedly. "I wasn't bad. Amongst strong men acts I was above average, and as an acrobat I was proficient, maybe even better than most. But where I shined was in the combination of the two. I was stronger than regular acrobats and more flexible, and more agile than a run-of-the-mill strong man. I did an act once where I was the base for a pyramid of other acrobats standing on top of an elephant." There was a light in her eyes that told me she missed that life.

"That must have been a sight to see. Why did you give it up?"

"Lots of reasons, but like I said, mostly because I was tired of being on the road. I'm still performing for tourists down at Cairn's Point. The money is decent. I keep a roof over my head and food on the table, but in the winter I'm usually late on the rent and eating soup for weeks on end."

"Is that the motivation for pursuing this case, the money I mean?"

Her mouth turned down. "I'm not going to lie. Having a little extra money would be nice. If I'm entitled to it. My lawyers think I am, I would just like to hear from them why they think I'm not. Is that too much to ask?"

"I don't think so, Miss Grimm, not at all."

•••••••••

I met with Oliver Chancellor that afternoon and he went over the file. He wasn't an expert on British inheritance law and succession, but he knew a guy in Boston, and they talked on the phone a bit. We also looked up the firm that had been working for Grimm to begin with. Not exactly what one would call powerhouse attorneys, and certainly not in a position to battle members of the British aristocracy. That afternoon I learned more about the laws concerning marriage and inheritance than I should have. We delved deep into the idea of marriage between people of unequal social ranks, so-called morganatic marriages, in which the bride and children have no expectation of an inheritance. We also discussed the relative importance of legitimate and illegitimate heirs with relevance to the Legitimacy Act of 1926. Chancellor had a relationship with a law firm in London and we asked them to do some investigating for us. It took them two days to get back to us with the details we needed and a reference with which we could build our case. Thus, it was on Thursday that I contacted the Brightholme Family and invited them to a meeting at Griffith House, promising an arrangement of mutual benefit if they attended, and legal action if they failed to show up.

I had set the meeting for two in the afternoon but had Jane show up an hour earlier so that I could go over some details and coach her on how to remain calm. She was a quick study—a benefit of her occupation, I supposed. She was as much of a performer as she was an athlete. She had worn the outfit I had suggested, a plain suit that was not too flashy, but conveyed a respectful demeanor. I sat her to the side and back, where the light was dim. Not to hide her or her features, but to create the illusion that she was not entirely present, that she was in a way taking a backseat to these proceedings.

When the Brightholmes arrived, I was somewhat surprised. William Brightholme was rather disheveled with an ill-fitting suit that could have been better cut to hide his weight, and a rather messy head of hair that seemed not only unkempt, but unwashed. There was also an odd smell. There had been an attempt to cover it up using cologne, but that was obviously not entirely successful. In contrast, his sister Cordelia was well dressed, in a woman's charcoal suit over a silk top. Her hair was expertly coiffed in a large bun just to one side. A large broach at her throat accented the thin oval of her face. Where William's eyes appeared dull, Cordelia's were bright and somewhat wicked.

As they sat, I offered drinks. William opened his mouth, but Cordelia's hand darted out to touch him on the leg and he frowned a little but never said a word.

"Thank you for coming, I know your time is valuable, so I'll get right to the point."

Before I could continue Cordelia was speaking. "Before you go any further, our father has asked us to represent the family in this matter. It is our position that the claim of that woman," she cast a distasteful glance into the shadows at Jane Grimm, "is invalid. She is not a legitimate heir to the Jermyn line and has no claim to the baronetcy, its lands, or monies."

"I see. And on what facts do you base that position?"

This time it was William who spoke. He wasn't as elegant as his sister, but he made his points. "There are a number of factors, primarily the lack of legitimacy. Alfred Jermyn already had a wife and child, and he was not divorced when he married Winifred Grimm. That makes their child illegitimate." He cast another look of scorn at my client. "She has no legal claim to the title." He seemed pleased with himself. "Even if she did, Arthur died in 1913, fifteen years ago. The baronetcy was declared dormant in 1918. The Brightholmes have been managing the lands for more than a decade."

I nodded, "A position you obtained through the marriage of Amelia to Robert Jermyn."

"Yes, Amelia was still alive when Arthur took his life, and in lieu of any heirs inherited the entire estate. When she passed in 1921, Jermyn House was incorporated into the Brightholme Estate."

"And now the Brightholmes reside in Jermyn House do they not? And do not the Jermyn lands form a significant portion of the annual income for your family?"

Cordelia was suddenly offended. "Not that it is any of your business, but you are correct on both accounts. However, restoring Jermyn House after a hundred years of neglect cost the family a substantial amount. And making the Jermyn tenant farms and the timber on the property profitable was also our doing."

"So, you would lose your home and a substantial amount of income if a legitimate heir were to be found?"

Cordelia's face turned red. "Highly unlikely, but yes."

I smiled, "Thank you for humoring me. A question, who was Alfred Jermyn's mother?"

"No one knows," offered William. "Nevil brought the child to Jermyn House and told the family that the mother had died."

I nodded. "Would it surprise you that our agents have not been able to find a record of marriage for Nevil Jermyn, or a record of birth for his son Alfred?"

"Your point?" Cordelia snapped.

"Alfred Jermyn was likely illegitimate."

"Irrelevant," Cordelia smiled wickedly. "After Robert killed Nevil and his brothers, Alfred was the only heir. His legitimacy was secured by his primacy."

"Yes, yes. Absolutely. Tell me, what was Arthur's mother's name?"

William sighed. "I really don't see the point to all these questions about family history. Magwitch, I think, yes Dorothy Magwitch."

"Would it surprise you to learn that our agents can find no record of marriage between Alfred Jermyn and Dorothy Magwitch?"

William again opened his mouth, and this time got as far as making a single sound, but once more Cordelia's hand on his knee shut him down. When the Brightholme family finally responded to my question, it was Cordelia that spoke.

"You are mistaken."

"Actually, we aren't. In fact, we've managed to locate Miss Magwitch's sister. She's rather old, a little dotty, but she's signed a document attesting that her sister never married Alfred Jermyn. She couldn't, she was already married to another man—a man named Godwin Kearns." I let that sink in for a moment. "Let me put it to you another way. Alfred Jermyn never married Dorothy Magwitch. Arthur was his illegitimate child. Alfred's marriage to Winifred Grimm was not only legal, but it was his first and only marriage. Jane Grimm is the legitimate Jermyn heir."

Cordelia's tone was suddenly very flat. "I doubt what you've said is true, but even if it was, the point is moot. The baronetcy is dormant, it would take a supreme effort to bring it back through a legitimate claimant, and I assure you that the British peerage are not fond of Americans."

"Our consultant in Boston agreed, Miss Grimm should have made her claim years ago. But she didn't know she had a claim. That's a valid mitigating circumstance. But you knew that didn't you?"

"I'm sorry?" William was obviously annoyed.

"Oh, maybe not you William, but your family. Winifred Grimm wrote to the Brightholmes back in 1915. She told you about her daughter, asked if she could meet her distant cousins."

"That woman is no cousin of mine!"

There it was the vitriol I was looking for. I had thought that baiting William would draw it out but was truly surprised that it was Cordelia that broke face. She quickly regained her composure. "None of these issues matter. Jane Grimm has no claim to the title and will not ever be recognized by the British Court, not if we have anything to say about it, and I assure you we Brightholmes are quite influential."

"So, you acknowledge that Miss Grimm has a legitimate claim to the title and property and your family has specifically failed to acknowledge a potential heir in favor of your own claim to the property?"

"Yes," Cordelia almost hissed. "But as I suggested, we shall endeavor to keep any claim she makes from ever reaching the Court."

I had had enough; it was time to lay the cards on the table. "Why is it you hate her so much? Is it because her great-great great-grandmother, Sir Wade Jermyn's wife, was Portuguese?"

William opened his mouth, Cordelia's hand shot out to stop him, but it was too late. "She wasn't Portuguese, and you know it, she wasn't even human." William nearly spat the words out. The prim and proper lady grimaced at the sentence.

"Because she was African? Is all this because Wade married a negro? I thought you were supposed to be more enlightened than this."

Again, William began to speak, his sister tried to stop him, but he pushed her hand away and stood up. "No! Not because she was a negro, but because, as I said, she wasn't human." He was angry, spittle was forming on his lips. "Wade Jermyn committed an affront to God. He carried out the rite of marriage and had relations with an inhuman thing, a female of the species that was subhuman, more ape than man. Their child Phillip and all descendants should have no part in human society. When Arthur burned himself alive, we thought that was the end of the line. That thing," he pointed at Jane, "is an affront to humanity. If I had my way . . ."

Jane had finally had enough, "How dare you!" She rose from her chair and stalked across the room pushing furniture out of her way as if it weighed nothing.

"Miss Grimm!" I reined her in and pointed her back into a seat. "Please, all of you, remain civil." I sighed to emphasize my point. "Let me see if I understand this. You're suggesting that Sir Wade's wife was what—a gorilla?"

Cordelia smiled that vicious smile. "Before the Royal Anthropological Institute took it away, Aunt Amelia saw the shriveled and mummified thing that Verhaeren sent back from the Congo. She saw it, just as Arthur did. It drove Arthur to take his own life, Aunt Amelia was of stouter fortitude. It comes from breeding. She knew what it meant for that anthropoid thing to bear far too great a resemblance to Arthur and his father Alfred, and why it wore the Jermyn arms in a golden locket around its neck. She knew the truth when she saw it, and only went a little mad. But even in her madness she made sure that the family would benefit. Jane Grimm may be a descendent of the Jermyns, but her lineage is tainted by inhuman blood. She has no legal standing."

"And you do?" Jane sneered.

"By right of marriage, yes." Cordelia seemed pleased with herself. "I'm sure that you wouldn't want to air this in public."

"No, of course not," I agreed, "but neither would you—and you have much more to lose than Miss Grimm. Given your precarious legal position."

Now she and her brother looked confused. "What are you babbling about now?"

I stood up and walked behind Jane, putting my hands on her shoulders. "Your final contention is that Miss Grimm has no legal standing because she isn't entirely human, a position that most courts would find ludicrous, but let us for the sake of argument, stipulate to that position. If Miss Grimm has no legal standing because of her—questionable ancestry, then it would seem that such standing would stretch back to the first in the line of issue. In this case, Wade's son Phillip, and all of his descendants."

Cordelia folded her arms, "Your point?"

"If Jane has no standing as a human being because she is descended from Phillip, then neither did Arthur, or his father Alfred, or Nevil, or even Robert. Any contractual agreements they entered into would be void, sales of property, inheritances, even marriages." I paused and let things sink in. "If Robert Jermyn, as you suggest, wasn't human, then his marriage to Amelia Brightholme wasn't legal. Which would void your claim to the property."

Cordelia Brightholme wasn't happy, neither was her brother. "I'm not going to listen to any more of this." He stood up and made to leave.

"Sit down, William." He did as she was told. "An interesting strategy, but there is no point. With our connections the case will never reach the courts."

"Maybe not in Britain, but here in the States? Somehow, I don't think your influence is the same on this side of the pond. How much is the house in Kingsport worth? What about the one in Palm Beach? You have extensive timber holdings in Georgia. I'm sure I can convince a judge that those rightfully belong to Jane."

"We will fight you," muttered William.

"Of course, you will," I admitted, "you might even win. But in the meanwhile, assets and bank accounts in the States will be frozen. Life might become very difficult." They were both silent. "Unless . . ."

Cordelia's eyes brightened a little. "Unless what?"

I walked over to the desk and picked up a file. "It's all outlined in this contract. You support Jane Grimm in regaining the family title. You return Jermyn House and its immediate grounds, say one hundred acres, to her control. The remaining properties will be held in partnership. Jane and any of her descendants will be a silent partner in the Brightholme Family business. For this she will earn a minimum of twenty-five percent of all profits but never less than one hundred thousand dollars annually."

This time William did stand up.

"You're insane." He grabbed his hat and stalked out.

His sister sat there quietly for a minute, thinking. When she finally stood up, she took the file. "Does she have legal counsel? Someone we can negotiate with?"

I nodded. "Oliver Chancellor, here in Arkham. His card is in the file."

She didn't say another word as she followed her brother out the door.

I checked the window and made sure that they had walked out the back gate. Then I collapsed in my chair. "That went better than expected."

"Better than expected?" questioned Jane. "They didn't agree to anything."

"She took the file and wanted to know who to talk to. I would bet money that they meet with Oliver tomorrow." I grabbed a bottle of gin from the cart. "Care for a drink?"

We both had two before she left, feeling very much reassured.

··········

I was right about them contacting Oliver. They did it that afternoon, and he sat down with their lawyer the next morning. It took most of the day, and Jane had to settle for seventeen percent with a lower limit of eighty thousand dollars, but she also received an initial lump sum of twenty thousand dollars. She also agreed to allow the Brightholmes to stay in Jermyn House for another decade while they refurbished the family seat. For this she would be paid a substantial amount of rent. In the end she was a very rich woman, or soon would be.

I wasn't surprised when she came around that evening with a check in one hand and a bottle of champagne in the other. The check was from Delapore, and was for more than I had expected. Jane said it was a bonus for resolving things in an expeditious manner. The champagne was just for celebrating, and just for us girls. I made sure to address her as Dame Grimm. She almost choked when I said it.

It took her three glasses to work up the nerve to ask me about the details I had uncovered. "How come nobody ever mentioned that Alfred and Arthur weren't legitimate?"

I shrugged, "Were they?"

Jane nearly dropped her glass. "You were bluffing?"

I filled another glass and drank it quickly. "I was making an educated guess. Our agents spent a few days looking but couldn't find anything in any of their files or in the respectable churches. It was a bluff, which could have been called if they wanted to take the time to do their own research. The threat of legal action here in the States lit a fire to make them negotiate to protect their own interests."

She raised a glass to me. "It was one hell of a risk, but it paid off." She drank the glass dry. "What about that other stuff, that Sir Wade's wife wasn't human. Do you think there's any truth to that?"

I took a moment to think about what I would say to her. I thought about what I had seen: the wonders and horrors, and what I knew to be real, and what I suspected to be true about the world and the people living in it. "Does it matter to you?"

She thought about it for a moment. "I suppose not. The Greeks and Romans had tales of demi-men that were monstrous and yet still civilized. Chiron was half horse and the tutor to Heracles. The cyclops were the servants of Vulcan and master forgers." She paused for a moment. "It's probably just idle gossip. A convenient legend to explain away their racism, their fear of the different and foreign."

"And if it's not a legend?"

She laughed a little. "If it's not a legend, if I'm really only partly human? That makes me special. Unique. A demi-human, the civilized and savage ape-girl. That would look great on a banner: 'The Civilized and Savage Ape-Girl!'"

I couldn't argue with her. "What would you do for an act? Sit in a tree dressed in leopard skins and drink tea?"

"Do you think people would pay to see that?"

I laughed a little, "Probably not, but if you were in a cage surrounded by chimps dressed in tuxedos and you were all drinking tea. Then yes, people might pay to see that."

Jane Grim laughed a little louder. "Megan, I think *I* would pay money to see that."

We laughed some more, and then when things got quiet, I turned to her and asked a more serious question. That question evolved into a discussion, and within the hour we had papers out and language formulated. By midnight we had a plan.

But that is for a later discussion.

THE ELDRITCH EQUATIONS

PART FOUR

AN ERROR IN BIAS

Sixteenth Report

Frank Elwood

It was more than two weeks after I had been injured that I finally felt capable of leaving Griffith House on my own. Megan Halsey had been quite kind in letting me stay while I fully recovered and old Mrs. Kreitner buzzed around me like the most horrible fusion of mother and nurse ever concocted. If it were up to her, I would still be in bed and still be eating something that she claimed was chicken soup but tasted like old socks that had been buried in the dirt. I am not sure what was the more rapid cure, her soup or my desire to stop eating it.

It had been made clear to me that I was welcome to stay at Griffith House for as long as I needed. Of this I was appreciative. But at the same time, I had been instructed that physical exercise would aid in my recovery. To this end I had begun a daily regimen of walking around the house and up the stairs, slowly increasing my activity until at last I was walking around the entire block several times a day. This vigorous activity also helped with my somnambulism and the outré visions I often perceived in my dreams. There was a growing difficulty in determining what was reality and what was phantasm, and on several occasions I found myself wandering the house or grounds with no clear idea of how I had escaped my room. Once, I woke to find myself in my bed clothes several blocks from Griffith House. I had to make my way back, running through melting snow in my bare feet. My only consolation in all of this was that Brown Jenkin, the rat-thing that had served as familiar to Keziah Mason and had been so instrumental in the death of my friend Walter Gilman, had only ever visited my dreams that one time. For this I was extremely grateful.

The similarity of my situation to that of Gilman did not go unnoticed, and more than once I found myself reviewing the notes I had made regarding his reported visions and "sleep travelling." It was frustrating to realize that I appeared to be undergoing the same sort of trials and tribulations that Gilman had, albeit at a much slower pace. That difference in rate was also curious to me. Was my more moderate rate caused by the differences in our mental capacity, with me being the mentally weaker candidate and therefore slower to master the appropriate techniques? Alternatively, was it the lack of a guide that mediated my progress? Both Keziah Mason and Brown Jenkin had served as guides to Walter, but I had no one to show me the path I should be taking to master the abilities that I manifested. Did I even want to master them, or did I want to suppress them, and if so, how? I did not even understand the source of these abilities. I suspected that they were the result of the equation that Gilman had written on the chalkboard that day, but I didn't understand how simply seeing that jumble of numbers and symbols could do this to me. And not just to me, but to Leroy Beaumont as well. How could math engender such mutations in human beings?

This idea embedded itself in my psyche and I spent hours each day dwelling on the matter, trying to understand the mechanism behind what had happened to Gilman, Beaumont and myself. But no matter how hard I tried I couldn't devise a satisfactory conclusion. In the end I needed help, and I realized there was only one person I could turn to who might have the capacity to understand what I was talking about and perhaps guide me to a conclusion. Thus, on Wednesday, February twenty-seventh, I found myself at the front of Professor Upham's home and nervously rapped on the door.

To my surprise, young Alexander Murry answered the door, though his mother was only a few steps behind him. They ushered me in and after taking off my coat I was shown to his laboratory, while they went and got the professor. It was little changed from the last time I was there. The desk was still covered with papers. Stacks of books teetered precariously, leaning on each other like ancient rock towers on the verge of collapse. The chalkboards were still covered with vast mathematical formulae that seemed illogical. It was as if mathematical rationality had been banished from the room.

Bored, I went over to one of the huge pieces of slate and tried to follow the progression of terms that were written there. Even on closer inspection the reasoning was not only flawed but completely nonsensical. I shook my head as I moved along the floor and continued to read, my suspicions about the man's mental state confirmed.

It was only when I reached the pages that had been taped up over the board that I realized the truth. I lifted those pages up casually, gently, at first so that they could be let go and fall easily back into place, but then I saw what they hid. In anger I tore the pages off the black slate and revealed the chalk scribblings underneath. There—and I assumed it had been there the whole time—was Walter's formula, the one that he had spontaneously written in class, the one that seemed to have been the root of the murder of my classmates. There it was, as clear as day, rewritten in Upham's own hand.

"I see you've found my little secret."

Enthralled by my discovery, I hadn't heard Upham roll into the room in his wheelchair. He pulled the door shut behind him and I was suddenly panicked.

"I'm sorry—I'll have to come back—I have an appointment I forgot about," I stammered as I took a step toward the door.

Upham looked at the equation and then glanced at the door I was heading for. Suddenly—impossibly—he was out of his chair and floating between me and my escape, his legs dangling beneath him like two shattered branches.

"No, no Mr. Elwood, I insist you stay." He was sneering as he spoke. "It will save me the trouble of hunting you down." His head twisted sideways in an impossible manner. "I really should thank you. After all, you did a fair amount of work for me. Particularly, I should thank you for killing Beaumont. I had been watching him for weeks, and of all my students he was the one I thought the most powerful. How did you ever accomplish that?"

I was backing up slowly. "I didn't, Miss Halsey shot him."

He smiled wickedly. "Ah, the meddling Mrs. Peaslee, I should have guessed. No matter, once I dispatch you, I'll take care of her and her husband, permanently."

I made a dart toward the other door, but he cut through the air like a speeding bullet and blocked me once more. As I stumbled back, I knocked over a pile of books and a whole chain reaction ensued. The piles clattered across the floor like a roll of thunder.

I backed into the desk. "Why?"

He put his hands out in a queer, offering gesture. "I would have thought that obvious. This power, it's something man was not meant to have. To be in one place and then another in the blink of an eye, traveling without moving, it's an abomination. It will destroy us, our whole society, our civilization, perhaps even our species." He glanced at the equation, and then back at me. I felt the hair on the back of my neck rise and dove across the room. Something on the desk where I had been standing exploded and disintegrated. In its place was a queer crystalline structure that hadn't been there before.

Upham growled, and floated higher into the center of the room. "There's only two of us now, and once I kill you and the Peaslees it will be only me. And once I am gone the world will be safe."

"Safe from what?" I was edging along the room.

His eyes narrowed. "What do you mean?"

We were rotating slowly, I was working my way behind the desk, almost standing in front of the equation. "You said that we would be safe. Safe from what?"

He cocked his head in haughty agreement. "I'm sorry, my memory isn't what it once was. Safe from those outside and inbetween. Safe from the hounds and the masters and the things that fumble and dance at the threshold. They're all around us, you know. Seen but unseen, so far away and yet close. What does distance matter to those such as us?"

He looked at the blackboard again and I had that queer feeling, like a premonition. Instead of dodging, I embraced it. I folded myself dup and traveled owen. It was easy, traveling without moving. Without effort I teleported to the far side of the room, behind Upham. But it was only for an instant.

"Stay still, damn you."

He picked up a book from a shelf and threw it at me. I dodged again, this time apparating back to where I had been before. This seemed to annoy him. He craned his neck trying to do something and then in frustration flung another book in my direction. I slid left.

"That's better," his eyes shifted to where I had been standing and then shifted back.

I could feel him opening a small gate and letting something in. Something sharp and solid. I twisted sideways, his eyes shifted back and forth again, and once more I had to dodge as a crystalline dagger cut into reality.

While twisting sideways, I noticed where his eyes kept looking, and I remembered what he had said—his memory isn't what it once was. He was looking at the equation. He wasn't able to hold it in his memory. He had to keep looking at it to keep it fresh in his mind.

Another attack came. This one was different. A small hole opened up and began trying to suck me in. While I dodged this, he cast another crystal at me. He was escalating, pulling more tricks out of his hat. As I rolled, a third object cut across my back, and I screamed in pain.

"This would be easier if you would stop fighting."

I took a deep breath and surveyed the room. Then I folded in on myself and reappeared in front of the door. But only for a moment, just long enough to draw his attention. Then I was gone again, back to where I had once been. I was standing right in front of the equation, with my back to Upham.

He cursed me again. "Get out of the way damn you!"

But I didn't, at least not right away. I was too busy using the eraser, wiping out what was written there. Only when I had eliminated five or six components did I fade away to a position behind him.

He was screaming as he rushed forward and tried to rewrite what I had removed. He was desperately scratching chalk to the board trying to fill in the gaps from memory, but I could tell he was getting it all wrong. Even worse, he thought it was right.

He finished inscribing the last few lines and seemed satisfied with himself. He turned and looked at me.

"Now, Mister Elwood, you are going to die."

He clenched his fists and jaw. His eyes filled with a dark light. A terrible, pulsating aura of purplish light emanated from him, staining the air around him. There was a sound, something akin to a train as it tore through a station that it was not stopping at. That was what told Upham that something was wrong, the sound. That roaring, tearing thunder that shook the room and shattered the windows and brought the chandelier crashing down from the ceiling.

Upham was screaming again, his throat torn up and broken, but he was still screaming. And then the light went out from his eyes, and the aura vanished. He hung there for an instant, his mind still processing the formula, still allowing him to deny the law of gravity, one of the immutable rules of the universe itself. But then his memory failed, and he fell from the air and landed on the floor in a crumpled-up ball of human frailty. I went over to him. It might seem odd—this man had killed, and more than once, but I recognized the truth. The formula, Gilman's equation, had driven him mad—but now it was gone. He may have become a ruthless monster, but now he was powerless. At least until he remembered. Until then he was deserving of pity, perhaps even sympathy. I knelt by him and cradled his head.

His eyes looked up at me, they were full of tears. When he opened his mouth, a dribble of blood flowed out. "You have to kill me, Elwood, and then you have to die too."

I shook my head, "No, not today."

I don't know where the knife came from, but it was suddenly in his hand, and for that I am grateful. For it was at that moment that the police broke through the door. If they hadn't seen that tableau, that scene of me trying to fight off Upham as he tried to plunge the knife into my throat, they might have come for me. After all, I was a young and healthy man, and he was old and confined to a wheelchair. It would have been a fair conclusion. Thankfully, the young officers pulled him off me and restrained him as he began to rant about killing me for the sake of humanity.

While I sat there, my back bleeding, my face and body bruised, the cops carrying Upham out as he struggled madly against them, a most curious thing happened. Young Alexander Murry wandered in. I thought perhaps he was coming to tend to me, but I was mistaken. Instead, he went over to the blackboard and examined the equation Upham had tried to rewrite. He shook his head.

"This isn't right."

He took his sleeve and erased something, only one component, and then rewrote it. It was still wrong, it still wasn't Gilman's formula, but he somehow seemed happy with it.

And then he wandered toward the door. He turned back for a moment and looked again. Then his gaze turned to me, and he said a single word.

"Tesseract."

He said this and nothing more. He lingered a moment longer, staring at me, then turned and walked out the door and I was left to pick myself up and wonder what had just happened, and how I and the detectives at Halsey, Peaslee and Lydecker could have overlooked the one man who now seemed the most obvious suspect.

Seventeenth Report

Robert Peaslee

As I write this in the last few hours of Saturday, the second day of March, I cannot deny that I wish I had better news to report. The household is in chaos. Megan and Lydecker have had words—a serious incident, considering that one is dependent on the other for his very survival. As for our guest—I'm sorry, let me start from the beginning.

Prior to writing this, I submitted to the files notes provided by Frank Elwood on the events that occurred between him and Professor Upham that ended in the professor's arrest for the murders of Elwood's classmates. We were correct in our assumption that the primary impetus for the murders was the generation of Walter Gilman's mathematical formula for building what he called a bridge to the stars, and what Upham refers to as the Eldritch Equations. What we didn't understand was that there was a secondary event that triggered Upham. The stress of the eldritch equations had taken a toll on the professor, so much so that he suffered a minor stroke and during the end of October was hospitalized in St. Mary's. There he witnessed our Frank Elwood engage in a physical conflict with what can only be described as a trio of maniacs. During this conflict Elwood was able to vanish and reappear at will. This, according to Upham, was Elwood subconsciously using the equations, and it was then that the professor realized how dangerous they could be. And in response he went "a little mad." Those are my brother's words, not mine. Wingate has volunteered to treat Upham, feeling a kind of responsibility to his fellow faculty member, who has been confined to the Sefton Asylum.

This is an important point. Yesterday, there was a very rushed and very private meeting between Judge Hand, the Chief of Police, and the university's lawyer. I and Oliver Chancellor were also at this meeting, representing Elwood's interests, but strictly in an advisory manner. There was much deliberation as the reputation of the university, its faculty, and the local police force were on the line. It took many hours and some protestation on our part before agreements between all parties were reached, and Judge Hand signed off on a number of binding documents.

From our point of view, the least of the concessions were payment by the university of Chancellor's legal fees and our consulting fees. We had told Elwood that his case would be handled gratis, but there was no reason to tell Judge Hand. Of more import to us was the granting of Frank Elwood his degree with honors, and a letter of recommendation from the Department Chair. All involved agreed that the poor man had been through enough and this was the least they could do.

Frank Elwood didn't see it that way. He was more interested in what was going to happen to his former professor. When I told him that the Judge had ruled him insane and unfit for trial, he assumed that lifetime incarceration in an asylum was the result. With some difficulty, I explained that the exact opposite was true. Upham was only incarcerated until his doctors deemed him fit to return to society. Indeed, his involvement in the murders was being kept quiet, for both his sake and that of the university. Not even the relatives of the eight people he had killed were being notified. Those cases would be quietly closed and marked as unsolved with no leads. None of the victim's families would ever know the truth about what happened, what Upham had done.

This did not sit well with Elwood. I tried explaining how making things public might only make things worse for him. There would be too many questions, questions that would have to be answered—about him, and Megan, and that weekend at Crowninshield Manor. But he wouldn't listen.

"That's not fair," he mumbled, "That's not fair at all. All those students—he killed them all. He should be held accountable."

"But he was insane, he's not responsible."

"Who says so?"

"What?"

"Who says he was insane? He knew what he was doing, and he knew it was wrong. That's why he hid it from us. He could have told us outright on the first day, but he knew that killing was against the law."

"In his mind, he thought that the formula, the thing that allows you to do strange things with time and space, he thought of that as a threat to humanity, to the world."

Elwood looked at me with his jaw clenched and his eyes set in anger. "But that wasn't his call. He set Gilman and I on this path. It was because of him we first read about Keziah Mason. If we hadn't learned about her, read about her, studied her, maybe she and her familiar would have left Walter alone. Maybe he wouldn't have thought up that formula, maybe he would still be alive." He paused and caught his breath. "But once Walter came up with the formula, once it was made available to the world, it wasn't up to Upham to take it away. You can't tell students to search for truth and then when they find the truth—even a very inconvenient truth—take it away. Knowledge is a genie, and once released you can't put the genie back in its bottle. One man doesn't get to declare that there are things man was not meant to know and go on a killing spree." He was ranting. "That's not the way the world works."

I closed my eyes for a moment and sighed. "Unfortunately, Frank, in my experience that is exactly how the world works."

He stormed out of the room, signaling the end of the discussion, but my night of arguments was just getting started.

Downstairs in the laboratory where Megan kept the equipment used to sustain Lydecker's head the two were having a related discussion. The old man was berating my wife for not being professional while she continued to apologize profusely.

"You are not just investigating for yourself Megan, you are my eyes and ears, and Robert relies on you as well." In the laboratory, hooked up to a pneumatic pump, he didn't wheeze as much as he did in public.

Megan threw her hands up in frustration. "I know that, Doctor, but it was Upham's intent to deceive and make us think he was crippled."

"Well, he *is* without the use of his legs, so technically he is crippled. That should not have eliminated him from our list of suspects." Lydecker sighed. "You of all people should know that looks can be deceiving."

Megan glared at the head as it sat in its support cradle on the laboratory bench. "What is that supposed to mean, exactly?"

I swear Lydecker rolled his eyes. "It means that we—you, me and Robert—are engaged in a most daring of subterfuges. I pretend to be a great detective in a paralyzed body, Robert pretends to be alive, and you—you pretend that this is more than just a distraction, hoping that nobody notices that you are simply a dilettante, an idle rich girl with nothing better to do than play investigator!"

Megan was seething. "If it weren't for me, you would have been left to rot on the slopes of Sentinel Hill."

"Yes," the head hissed, "and if it weren't for me; Robert would have died while you dithered over what to do. You have the intellect, Miss Halsey, the skills, the tools, everything you need to accomplish the tasks you set before you, and yet somehow you lack commitment. It takes a certain amount of will to do this job, perhaps you aren't up to the task. Perhaps you might consider a different line of work."

"Then who would take care of you?" She shot back. "Who would be here to buy the chemical components, to mix them together, to make sure you were properly dosed? Without me you would have to get a job in a freakshow."

He smiled, "I've thought about that. Considering my talents and condition, I think I would excel at being a businessman, the head of some multinational conglomerate, perhaps even a politician or a director of a secret government agency."

"That would be grand. Sir Eric Clapham-Lee, Director—No, *Head*—of the Cabinet Noir—the Black Chamber."

"That is where we differ, Megan. You see it as a jest, but I can see the value in such a thing. Could you imagine it: an entire corps of the bodiless set to the task of cryptography and interpreting intelligence? I can see that, see the rows after rows of great men—great minds—that continue to serve long after their appointed lifespans. It would be magnificent."

Megan shook her head. "It would be grotesque, and dangerous. The undying in such positions would inevitably seize power and twist things to serve their own needs, sustaining themselves *ad infinitum*. Our nation would become one run by the dead, a necrocracy!"

"A necrocracy is a government that adheres to the directives of a now dead leader. I believe the proper term you are looking for is thanatocracy, meaning rule by the dead, though this term itself is imprecise. Technically the reanimated are not dead."

Megan slumped into a chair and started to laugh. "Are we really going to debate the technical points of a government run by the reanimated?"

"I've been thinking about it for a while now." I couldn't tell if he was joking or not.

They were so wrapped up in their argument that they never saw me, and I didn't bother to interrupt them. Instead, I went back up the stairs and sat in the kitchen drinking a glass of warm tea and thinking about the events of the last few weeks. I apparently had much to think about, for when I heard a noise in the hallway I glanced at the clock and saw I had been sitting there for hours, my tea long gone cold.

That disturbance came from none other than Frank Elwood, coming down the stairs with his suitcase. He stood there, staring at me. It was clear that he hadn't expected to encounter anyone.

"You're leaving." I made a gesture to his bag.

"I can't stay here," he said morosely. "I appreciate all you've done for me, and I understand how you were fooled by Upham. Even I was fooled by him. That isn't the issue."

"You can't see the man go unpunished. He's not. He's getting psychological help, and I assure you that the asylum he's going to is not a resort. On the contrary, it holds some of the most violent people in all of Miskatonic Valley."

"No—while I don't agree with that, there's nothing I can do about it. What I can't tolerate is how you and Megan can agree to that arrangement." He paused and put on his coat. "It's your right, I suppose, but I don't have to tolerate it, and if I stay here, if I take advantage of your hospitality, that means I'm condoning your actions." He bent down and picked up his suitcase. "I may not be the wealthiest of people, but I can still afford the courage of my convictions."

"Where will you go? Back home?"

"No," he opened the front door. "I'm not ready to go home, not until I figure out how to control what is happening to me. I thought that Upham might have been able to do that, but obviously that didn't work out. My choices are limited now, but I think there are still one or two individuals who might be able to help me. Even if I do find them rather distasteful."

And then he stepped out the door and closed it behind him.

I wanted to go after him, to explain things, to help him find someone he could trust to teach him to control whatever was going on in his head. But that wasn't my job. Frank Elwood was a grown man, able to make his own decisions. And by walking out that door ha had made it clear that he no longer wanted our help. A shame, really. If he could gain control of his ability, he might have made an excellent addition to our little group.

It wasn't until much later that I began to wonder to whom he was referring to when he talked about finding someone to teach him to control his powers. "... one or two individuals ..." he had said. Not people, but individuals. Why had he phrased it like that?

That notion has been keeping me up for hours. I wonder which would be worse: not knowing who he chose as a teacher, or finding out?

The Restitution Society

Roman Lydecker

It is not every day that your enemy walks into the office and asks for your help, but that was exactly what had happened, and so I found it prudent to pay attention.

It was Monday, May the eleventh and Phaedra Whateley was sitting in the chair opposite mine. Over Phaedra's right shoulder, several yards back, stood Megan, who was obviously uncomfortable. Over Phaedra's left shoulder, leaning against the wall, was Robert trying not to look like he was going to shoot our prospective client. Phaedra sat there looking almost demure. I say almost because her stature and facial features did not really allow her to assume a countenance that one might interpret as reserved or shy. Phaedra Whateley was an imposing woman, not unattractive in an exotic manner. Like her mother she was an albino and wore her white crinkly hair in a long braid down her back. Her skin was the color of milk and her lips an unnaturally pale pink that matched her eyes. Those eyes were set farther apart than normal, which gave her a kind of feral cast. Unlike her mother's side of the family, she had a strong chin with a powerfully set jaw line. She was wearing gloves and a rather long coat that had gathered around her boots. The coat was made out of sections of fabric that had the same pattern but were alternating in either black or white, such that her left sleeve was entirely dark, while the right one was a match for her skin. Even with the coat being closed and her blouse buttoned up to the top of her neck you could see that she was a strong woman. Her neck was thick, her shoulders wide, her thighs thick but fluid as they moved. I had read the report on her encounter with Mariah Lieberman at the university library and was appreciative that she had kept her coat on and buttoned tight. I also recognized that she was taking a risk coming here. There were some who wanted to take her into custody, not that they could. I'm not sure that even we had the ability to restrain her if we wanted to.

"Miss Whateley, to what do we owe this highly unexpected visit?"

She seemed hesitant to speak; indeed, I thought for a moment that she was going to leave. She had that look about her, the one that suggested she was only now aware she was making a grave tactical error. This was the last opportunity for her to not involve us, to keep whatever issue she had entirely private. She was, after all, not without her own resources. She might not need us at all, but as Toussaint Delapore had noted when he had hired Robert, sometimes those resources can be costlier than hiring our firm, even considering the prices we charged and the expenses we accrued.

Finally, she opened her mouth and spoke. "I find myself in the position of being a target of theft. I want you to prevent it." Her voice was deep and unearthly, like thunder rolling in the distance that only sounded like words.

"Your choice of words is peculiar, Miss Whateley. Am I to understand that you anticipate being robbed?"

She nodded. "Perhaps I should explain."

"It would make our job easier."

"As you know, I recently sold a significant portion of the Whateley Family library to Miskatonic University. What you don't know is that I retain a small collection of select books, volumes that the university did not want, or which I held back for my own uses. This included a copy of Richard Verstegan's *A Restitution of Decayed Intelligence*, which was published in 1605. It is a rather uncommon book and has been in the family for many generations. Family lore holds that only a single copy was brought over by the Whateleys, but that it was copied many times by others, including members of the Potters, Curwens, Carters, and Waites. So prized were these books that their owners organized the first bindery in the region so as to repair and preserve their copies." She paused and made sure I was paying attention. "Of late, I have been made aware of two events that led me to be concerned. The first was last month's vandalism of the Providence Athenaeum, at which the Ward Family collection is held, which included the Curwen copy. I have contacted the library directors and they have been unable to locate their copy. The second was a similar event last week at the Carter Mansion just outside town. Once again inquiries have confirmed that the volume in question is missing. The Potter copy was lost to a fire along with the rest of that family's library a few years ago. In my mind, that places my copy and that of the Waite Family at risk for theft."

"You said you had been made aware of the thefts. How was that?"

She reached into her pocket and withdrew an envelope. "Someone sent me these newspaper clippings. The book title is written in the margins of each article." She handed the clippings to Megan.

"Interesting," I blinked and then blinked again. "Is there a particular reason that someone might want to steal these books?"

"Other than for their historical value, not that I know of."

"And where is your copy of this book right now?"

"On a shelf in my study, surrounded by hundreds of other books."

"Hidden in plain sight, then."

"As you say, though I would prefer this to be a temporary state. It would be significantly more pleasing to me if you were to take possession of the book and keep it safe for me."

"And what about the thief? Are we to be concerned with his apprehension?"

She rolled her head oddly, in a gesture that was not a nod but not a shake, either. "I am not concerned with justice, Mr. Lydecker, only with protecting my property."

"But are you opposed to it?" I offered.

"I don't get your meaning."

"The theft of the book from the Athenaeum and from the Carter Mansion are crimes, Miss Whateley; they can be used as leverage. If a suspect is identified and can be linked to the previous two thefts, the perpetrator could be arrested and incarcerated. In this manner your copy would be protected."

"I understand." Again, with the queer head rolling. "I'm not opposed to such a course of action. If you can restrain the would-be thief, then do so. As long as my copy remains out of his hands."

"And what of the other copy, that belonging to the Waite Family—do you know where that is?"

"The last I heard was that it was still amongst the collection of the Innsmouth Waites. Given the current situation in Innsmouth, if it is still there, it might be considered well-guarded."

I hissed disapprovingly. "I doubt that the Federal agents occupying the town would concern themselves with preventing petty theft. I would consider that copy vulnerable, if it was still there."

"Where else would it be?"

My eyes went to Megan, who caught my non-verbal cue. "Asenath once told me that, before he died, Ephraim Waite had much of his property put into crates and placed in warehouses in Kingsport and Arkham. There is a good chance that the library has been packed away. Asenath might know where it ended up."

I smiled. "Do you have any objection to us extending protective services to Miss Waite's copy?"

She looked at me strangely, "Old Ephraim had a daughter? That must have come as a great inconvenience to him." Her comment seemed rather cryptic and rude.

"What do you mean by that?"

"Hmm? Oh, nothing. If you wish to involve Waite in this, feel free. But let me be clear, I am hiring you to protect my copy. First and foremost, I am your primary client. I will not have the security of my property compromised because you involved someone else who has different concerns and priorities. Is that understood?"

The smile vanished from my face. "Perfectly clear. Now, as to the matter of our fee. Mr. Peaslee?"

Robert took a moment to write something out on a piece of paper and then crossed the room to hand it to her.

She took it and glanced at it only for a second, then her eyes returned to me. "For that rate, I could hire one of your competitors for an entire week rather than just a day."

"Feel free, Miss Whateley. But if you were looking for routine services you wouldn't be here. We offer specialized skills for discerning clients, for that we expect to be compensated fairly. Our prices are non-negotiable and fully guaranteed. If, while we are in your employ, we fail to keep your property safe, then you will pay us nothing."

"An equitable arrangement, but I'm not after equity. If you fail, I will be without my property."

"We are not an insurance agency, Miss Whateley, and you should realize that that equity comes at a risk to us as well. If we lose your property, we will not only be out any expected profits, but expenses as well." She opened her mouth, but I continued, "Additionally, loss of the book will probably entail damages to our property and potentially injury to our staff. Both of these would no longer be your concern."

"They were my concern before?"

Robert reached over her and pointed to the lower line below our daily rate. "Plus, expenses," he grunted.

"I see." She purred.

"As I have said, Miss Whateley, you aren't yet bound to us in anyway. You are free to walk right out the door."

"Your reputation does you justice, Mr. Lydecker. I think these terms might be acceptable." She stood up and offered me her gloved hand, but then withdrew it awkwardly. "Let me think about it, and if I agree I'll be back with the book this evening."

"No!" I did my best to roar.

"I'm sorry?" She was genuinely startled.

"I said no, Miss Whateley. You will sign a contract, you will provide us with a check for a retainer for one week, and then you and Mr. Peaslee will travel in his car to go get the book and bring it back here. If you decline, then the offer of our services will be revoked."

"Really!"

"Please, Miss Whateley, I am not a fool, and I know that you aren't one either. You wish to retain our services; we have agreed to help you. Let us be done with the formalities and get on with it."

You could see the change in her face as she dropped the act. "I'll need a pen."

It only took a few minutes for Robert to fill out the blank places in the contract and for Miss Whateley to sign it. In the meanwhile, Megan had brought the car around to the back. We did not want this woman traipsing through the house to the front door.

After the two of them had left, Megan sat down in the same chair that Miss Whateley had occupied. "Do you trust her?" She asked me.

"No."

"She's lying about something."

"Yes, yes, she is, but she also isn't telling the whole truth. I'm not sure which is more important."

"You know we have a copy of this book? We retrieved it during the Potter Incident back in October. It's on the shelf in my private library. It's a rather mediocre text on the resurrection of the dead."

"As you say, a mediocre text—and yet, young Mr. Potter was able to put it to spectacular use."

Megan looked back at the door. "Do you think Robert will be safe?"

I looked her in the eyes. I could see that she was worried about her husband.

"I don't think she means to harm him. If she wanted to hurt us, she could have done so any time after she walked in the door." I paused, suddenly frustrated. "Why did you do that?"

"What?"

"Let her through the door."

"I didn't. I thought Robert did."

"No, Robert came down from upstairs after she was already here, and you brought me out of the lab."

"I didn't bring you out of the lab. I thought Robert did that." She stopped. "Do you remember me bringing you out?"

"No. In fact, I don't remember anything that happened this morning before we began our conversation with Miss Whateley, and neither do you, I'll wager."

"Now that you mention it, there is a rather large hole in my memory." She picked up the contract and looked at the signature. "Phaedra Whateley, an interesting name. Greek, right?"

"Yes, Phaedra was the daughter of Minos and Pasiphae. She was married to Theseus, but fell in love with her stepson Hippolytus. When Hippolytus spurned her, she told Theseus that the boy had raped her. Theseus then cursed his son, and the horses the boy was riding dragged him to his death."

"Lovely," commented Megan. "This Phaedra seems to be something of a bitch."

"Yes," I said, "it ran in the family. Her half-brother was no charmer, either."

"Who was he?"

"The cannibal-monster they called the Minotaur."

Megan threw the contract back down on the table. "We're in trouble, aren't we?"

I didn't have the heart to tell her no. She wouldn't have believed me anyway. "It might be best if you were to get out the big guns and make sure that they were loaded."

She almost laughed. "Robert will like that; he so rarely gets to use them." Then she began walking toward the door.

"Miss Halsey," I called after her.

She turned and for a moment I could still see the schoolgirl that I had once taught. "Yes?"

"You might ask Misses Kreitner to put on some tea. I have a feeling it's going to be a long day."

She glared at me. "You do remember that you don't have a stomach, right? You can't drink tea."

I was tempted to not respond. She was technically correct, but how do I explain to one such as her about the sensuality of tea? She still possessed the ability to drink, to taste, to swallow, to feel the neuro-chemical response to caffeine and theanine. All of this I was denied, condemned as I was to wallow in the artificial chemical haze of the reanimation reagent that sustained me. When it came to pleasures of the flesh there was so little that remained for me. Scent was one of the few primary mental stimulants that I could still access, and there may be nothing more refreshing than the crisp odor of a good pot of Darjeeling brewing. How could I explain that to a woman who still lived, still had all that she had been born with?

"Please, Megan," I pleaded, "it would mean so much to me." And I left it at that.

· · · · ● · · · ·

Robert did return in about an hour, carrying a small wooden case that had been stained a dark, warm red, with a brass handle and hinges. I, of course, wanted the book opened immediately, but there was an order to things, and I had questions for the man. "You followed Miss Whateley home?"

He frowned and nodded. "I followed her to a house. It could have been her home. There was some mail on the entryway table; it was addressed to her using a post office box, but there were no bills, just private letters."

"So, nothing official?" Megan was stating the obvious.

"No. The house is south of the Pike, on the far side of where they are planning to build the Reservoir, just on the edge of Billington's Wood. Not a mansion, but not a shack either. A saltbox design, grey-colored clapboards, red doors, and a central brick fireplace. The front door was three inches thick. The windows on the first floor have grates installed over them. It's not a fortress, but it's not particularly vulnerable either."

Megan seemed perturbed, "Not what I expected. I was sure she lived in a crumbling castle, an abandoned amusement park, or even perhaps even a decommissioned steamer."

I ignored her vitriol. "What about her library?"

"An interior room, no windows, very heavy door with a large lock. Modest, comparable to ours in size, so about five hundred volumes built around a painting of her ancestor Zabdiel Whateley and an urn with his name on it, presumably his ashes. A few locked cabinets. I casually looked inside—she has a Mather and a Reverend Phillips, but the vast majority consists of British and European History with some philosophy thrown in. She has a small section of autographed editions, again mostly British writers. She showed me a Dickens, a Barrie, and a Defoe, but I also saw a Parsons, and a Goldsmith. There were several volumes by Diogenes Small, and a whole shelf devoted to Kara Ben Nemsi. There was a fat volume entitled *The Night Always Gives Way to Dawn*, though I'll admit I'm not exactly sure who wrote that."

"A rather obscure volume of poetry by Étienne de Marigny, supposedly written under the influence of the composer du Hond. I met the man once during the war," I paused, but then asked Robert to elaborate. "Did you notice anything else?"

"I asked for a glass of water and followed her into the kitchen. It was rather bare, and there was no garbage in the bin."

Megan snorted, "She's either meticulous or she doesn't use the kitchen much."

"Or, she isn't really living there," added Robert.

There were other possibilities, but I saw no reason to go into them. "You can find this place again?"

Robert agreed. "It's a little off the beaten track, but I know where to turn off on the Pike. After that, it's just following the right track through the woods. Not many places to make a mistake."

"Good. Now let us take a look at the cause of all this concern."

Robert placed the case on the desk and snapped the latch open. The inside of the box was lined in blue velvet and into what appeared to be a custom void sat the book wrapped in a delicate white cloth. Robert withdrew the carefully encased volume and removed the cloth. In the process he reveled a rather unassuming but handsome quatro volume. It was bound in brown leather with inlaid silver along the spine identifying the author. Even without opening the book you could see that the binding was younger and in better condition than the sheaves that encompassed the page block. With care, Robert cracked opened the volume to reveal the endpapers. These too were relatively new and were of an ornate design reminiscent of Celtic knotwork. A turn of the page revealed a piece of onion skin covering a frontispiece of the Tower of Babel. This page was significantly older than the binding.

Before we went any further, Robert closed the book entirely. "I just want to check something." He then reopened it to the back endpapers. Here again was the detailed Celtic knotwork, but instead of covering the entire age, it encircled a box that included some text printed in a long-forgotten typescript.

Rebound by
The Restitution Society
Arkham, Massachusetts
1714

Megan was looking over Robert's shoulder. "We've seen the name of that organization before."

"Yes, in the Potter Incident—and Jane Stanley said their name just before she set fire to the collection of grimoires hidden underneath the Tabularium," Robert reminded us.

"I hadn't realized just how old they were," I sighed. "I'm surprised they are still active today."

"Are they?" queried Megan.

"Yes, they were the ones soliciting for funds to repair the Whateley Collection."

"Doesn't that seem like too much of a coincidence?" offered Robert.

"Indeed. Perhaps, Robert, a trip over to the university to inquire about their nature and activities is in order." I turned my eyes to look at Megan. "In the meantime, you might ask Miss Waite to come pay us a visit this evening."

"Should she bring her copy of the book?"

"If it's readily accessible, yes, but I would prefer not to wait to speak to her." Given their assignments, the two began to move toward the door.

"Miss Halsey, before you go, would you please take me back to the lab, set the book up in the reader and put the radio on? I want to see if there is anything in this book that might explain why someone is so desperate to steal copies of it." It was the least she could do.

··········

It was about a half-hour before Asenath Waite was to arrive that Megan moved me out of the laboratory and back into the receiving room. Robert had come home and had research to share concerning the Restitution Society. They sat there, drinking coffee as I listened to his report.

"According to records found in the university library, the first mention of The Restitution Society is recorded around 1710. It was apparently organized by a man named Edward Hutchinson. Their goal seems to have been to preserve the volumes that made up the Miskatonic University Library. To this end they solicited funds for two efforts. The first of these was the creation of a bookbindery staffed with craftsmen skilled in book repair and preservation. The second was to then regularly examine the books in the library and have those in need of repair sent to the bindery. They were successful on both accounts with a man named Elias Von Kronenschieldt as the manager of the bindery." He flipped a page in his notebook. "Elias was the black sheep of the family and reverted to the Danish form of the name. The anglicized version the family uses is Crowninshield."

Megan coughed. "As in Crowninshield Manor?"

Robert nodded. "Apparently. The Crowninshields are considered founding members of Arkham, even though they weren't British. Other branches of the family have become notable for public service and maritime activities. Here in Arkham they made their fortune in trade with the British, and were loyalists during the war. They fled to London with William Franklin, which is when the Griffiths took possession of the manor as a payment for undisclosed debts." He flipped another page. "By all accounts, Elias was a skilled craftsman and ran the shop as a subsidiary of the Restitution Society quite efficiently. He also apparently trained some of the people he was supposedly working for. There are notes in his diary about sessions with S. Orne, E. Hutchinson. J.

Curwen, Dr. C., and E. Waite. He employed about five people full-time, and by 1718 their skill in repair and rebinding had become widespread, rivaling the book printing business that had flourished in Philadelphia. Books from all over the colonies were sent to Arkham for repair, and several apprentices quit the society and began their own company, one specifically designed for publishing religious tracts and books for divinity students.

"In 1720, the founding members of the society resigned and began moving out of the area. With the withdrawal of their primary source of support, the bindery began to flounder. This sparked an exodus of the craftsman as well, the most famous of which was George Gamwell, who set up a printshop in Philadelphia and once employed a young Benjamin Franklin. Gamwell was apparently loyal to his home town, and established ties with the bindery and set up a fund for with which to continue the 'good work' as he called it.

"By 1730 the Restitution Society had been reincorporated as a charitable organization that still exists today, with essentially the same goals as the original. They don't have their own bindery any longer, but they still accept books from all over the country to have them repaired or rebound by a few shops throughout the Miskatonic Valley. The society is chaired by a local man named Timothy Corey, a retired naval doctor, with several other local members serving as the board. Donors are mostly local, and include the Phillips, Howards and Smiths. There are, however, a few international donors, including a man in Prague named Nadek and a Transylvanian nobleman," he looked at his notebook and flipped through it until he found the right page. "Baron Ferenzcy."

"That's it?" Megan snorted. "No scandals or dark deeds?"

"Not that I can find. The staff at the library were very helpful. As far as I could see, the Restitution Society is a legitimate organization."

There was a tone in his voice that I couldn't ignore. "But you suspect something?"

He shrugged. "The warehouse of books I found underneath the Tabularium; it would make sense for that to be related to this."

"Perhaps, perhaps not. Let us operate under the idea that it is distinct, but evaluate any evidence in the light of both possibilities." Megan frowned at my suggestion but didn't say anything.

It was then that the doorbell rang, and a few moments later Megan showed in her old friend, and my former student, Asenath Waite. It had been a few years since I had seen her, but frankly she had changed little. Perhaps, there was a new sense of worldliness about her, but that might simply have been a result of her no longer wearing the Hall School uniform. That she was wearing a three-piece suit, much in the manner that Megan often does, did not surprise me. Nor was I surprised by the large case that she carried in her left hand, which I surmised contained her copy of the book.

I greeted her politely, "Good evening, Miss Waite. I hear congratulations are in order."

"Thank you, Mr. Lydecker. I do hope you will be able to attend the ceremony."

"Perhaps, if the weather is good. Given my health, it is difficult to make such commitments."

"I understand. It's fortunate that you have Megan to look after you." She nodded to her friend. "But we're dancing around the matter at hand, aren't we?" She lifted her case and placed it on the desk. "For what possible purpose would you need this particular book?"

"I'll explain in due time, Miss Waite. But first, could you tell us what you know about the Restitution Society?"

She looked at me as if she had just seen a ghost.

"I haven't heard that name in a long time. Father told me about them once, when he was talking about our family history. It was his Great Grandfather Efraim, for whom he was named, that helped create the Restitution Society." She suddenly looked uncomfortable. "Father said it was a trick, perhaps one of the greatest tricks ever perpetrated."

I saw Robert perk up, and I urged her to continue. "Go on."

"At the beginning of the eighteenth century there weren't that many printers in the colonies, and most of what they produced was on cheap paper and not really meant to last. The books that were being used in the University had all been from private donors, and almost everything was from either Great Britain or Europe. Books weren't being produced in any real quantity in the colonies, and certainly not enough to educate the public. The Restitution Society was founded to make sure the books we did have were properly cared for, and—when need be—restored and rebound. But what nobody told the people who sent their books to be rebound was the fact that they were actually being copied. The society employed a team of expert printers who were very dedicated and very skilled. They would do the job they were asked for, but at the same time the relevant texts would be laid out and rapidly reprinted."

"You would need a small army and a dozen printing presses to make that work," commented Megan.

"Haven't you ever wondered why there are so many printing houses in Arkham? The Miskatonic University Press, Arkham House, Witch Hill, just to name a few. How many newspapers do we have in the area? Five, I think. It's because we have a long history with lots of printing equipment laying around from the work that started with the Restitution Society."

"But the cost would have been exorbitant."

Asenath shook her head. "The original was returned, and the extra copies, all without any publication marks, sold to discriminating clientele for their own usage, or to colleges that were willing to turn a blind eye to a rather dubious source. There were also the fringe benefits."

She was being deliberately vague, "Which were?"

"On rare occasions something truly rare would be sent in for repair, usually quite discreetly. In such cases the Society would still make copies, but they would have to be cautious about whom copies were offered to, and the price of these volumes could be quite spectacular. Imagine having a copy of a book that there are only five known copies of, and then you make five more. How much are those worth? How much could you sell them for?"

"Interesting," I was being politely noncommittal, "And this book in particular?"

She patted the case at her side. "More of a family heirloom than anything else. One of five that the society restored back in 1715."

"Are you sure about that date?" Megan asked.

"Yes, absolutely. There is a plate on the back page with that year on it." She fumbled with the lock. "I can show you if you want."

"That won't be necessary Miss Waite. We have reason to believe that someone is stealing copies of this book. We have been asked to keep one copy guarded until the danger has passed. Would you be interested in partaking in a similar service?"

A questioning look drifted across her face. "Are you seriously suggesting that someone out there is trying to steal copies of *The Restitution of Decayed Intelligence* and that someone else is paying you to keep their copy safe, and that you want me to pay you as well?"

"Normally we protect people, but we are more than willing to protect valuables as well. It is our profession. There have been thefts of other copies in the last few weeks."

"Interesting, but the problem is I don't particularly care. The book isn't that valuable, at least not to me, and I'm not going to pay for someone to protect it against theft." She stood up and turned to go, "I'm sorry but you've wasted your time, and mine."

I spoke before she could move. "Miss Waite, would you consider leaving the book here, at no charge? I would like to examine it at length."

She mulled the request over and then set the case on my desk. "As I've said, I don't have a particular attachment to this volume. Would a week be sufficient?"

"More than enough," I told her.

She nodded, and Megan showed her out.

"I'm not sure I understand this case," commented Robert.

"Indeed," I responded, "it does seem to be the most curious of circumstances. One woman fearful that someone will steal her book. Another one completely nonchalant concerning the issue."

"Which one do you think is telling the truth?"

My eyes fell on the case that Waite had left behind. "Both, perhaps. Maybe neither. I think we won't know until the last card has been played."

·····•••·····

I spent the rest of that night in the laboratory comparing the texts of the two books. Given my condition, one might assume such an activity would be difficult for me. However, I had at my disposal several mechanical page turners, modified from those used by musicians, which are usually activated by a foot pedal. I used a much more sensitive mechanism that was activated by my tongue. Though this was a rather slow and somewhat messy method, it worked, negating the need for someone to sit with me and carry out that menial task. The limitations of the design meant that I had to proceed from page to page slowly, as there was no means by which I could skip ahead. So, while I intensely wanted to compare the end pages and the dates contained there on, I was instead forced to peruse the pages in sequential order.

It was in this manner that a side-by-side comparison of each page was meticulously carried out. I examined page layout, numbering, the block of text, the length of sentences, and even the words themselves. It was almost dawn before my tedious task was finished, and it was only then that I turned to the last page and noted the slight differences in the two books. The most obvious difference was as, Asenath Waite had said, the year of repair, which differed by one year between the two. It was as I was staring at these pages that I realized that there was another difference. While both books featured a Celtic knotwork design for their endpapers, each used three-cord plaits—but of different styles. This I found interesting, for according to J. Romilly Allen's book on Celtic art, there were only eight basic knotworks used in such pieces. Of these, six were four-cord plaits, and only two were three-cord plaits. That the artisan had picked such slightly different styles seemed odd and bore further investigation. It was then that I noticed that, buried in the knotwork of Miss Whateley's copy, were small symbols in a color slightly different from that of the rest of the work. I looked at Miss Waite's copy and did indeed find similar symbols—similar but not identical. At first, I thought the symbols to be some kind of letters, but they weren't from any of the alphabets that I was familiar with. These were the only differences that I could detect in the two volumes, and it seemed all had been inserted during the rebinding process.

Not long after I finished examining the two books, Megan came into the laboratory and began my morning process, which is a rather lengthy procedure that exists to keep me in the best health my condition allows. First, my connections to the hydraulic pumps that move nutrients and reagent through my system are removed and clamped shut. I am dried with sterile towels and my tissue examined for evidence of infection. It has been my experience that the reanimated are quite resistant to saprotrophic organisms; however, there are several species of fungi that, while relatively easy to treat in the reanimated, can develop strains that are highly virulent in the living and resistant to treatment. I am then attached to my mobile system, which is a smaller and quieter version of the reagent pump, and an air pump that rhythmically passes air through what remains of my throat and mouth. This apparatus simulates my breathing, a biological function that I do not actually require; but this creates an illusion that comforts the people I interact with. Additionally, this flow of air passes over my vocal cords, and allows me to speak, albeit in a rather wheezy manner. Once I am properly connected, I am then strapped into the mannequin that rests in the wheelchair. The clothing on the mannequin is adjusted and then an ascot is put in place around my neck to further hide my connection and provide some additional support for keeping my head in place. The straps are rigid and highly durable, and even if I were to be turned over, I would likely remain in the chair and connected to my false body. The entire routine takes about half an hour, and only after this am I rolled out of the laboratory and into the study through the hidden door in the back of the elevator. The real elevator door is designed to stay closed until the hidden door is shut. It was around eight in the morning when I rolled out into our offices.

Robert was there drinking a cup of coffee in a porcelain cup. I am not fond of coffee, preferring a variety of teas. Still, I did enjoy the rich aroma that was lingering in the room. On the desk in front of me were the morning papers which Megan and I routinely shared. Robert, being more of a man of action, only occasionally read the paper. After we had settled, I explained what I had discovered and suggested that the two of them make copies of the symbols and take them over to the university to see if anyone could identify them. This entailed some risk. First, it relied on transcribing the symbols, which could induce error and thus lead to an improper translation. Additionally, it could work to inform someone that we possessed the books and increase the risk of theft. The chances of either of these occurring, in my opinion, were low enough that I was willing to take the risk. Both Robert and Megan agreed with my assessment and Megan went to transcribe the symbols while Robert set up the newspaper in yet another mechanical page turner.

I am a thorough reader of the papers, starting with the *Boston Herald*, then moving to the *Providence Journal*, *The New York Times*, and finally the *Arkham Advertiser*. While I read, I listen to a local radio station playing classical music, and I often find myself setting my reading pace to whatever piece of music is being played. Much of the day's news seemed to focus on varying opinions concerning the recent pronouncements by the Federal Reserve Board and the Advisory Council that had warned about the dangers of speculative loans. Most seemed to think that the Board was being alarmist, but a few articles bolstered the conservative position. There was also an article on the findings of the Italian commission on the Italia airship expedition to the North Pole, which laid most of the blame on team leader Umberto Nobile. There was also an article concerning the sudden cold snap that struck France at the end of the previous month, which had apparently led to the deaths of more than two thousand individuals. The rest of the papers were focused on the recently inaugurated Herbert Hoover and his attempts to get Congress to work on a farm relief bill. Thus, it was more than two hours later that I finally picked up the local paper and found within, at the bottom of the third page, a small article concerning the arrest of a man in connection with burglaries of books from libraries throughout New England. This man, who used the name Graham Ward, had been caught stealing from the Haverhill library and had led investigators to his home in Newburyport, where they discovered hundreds of books from dozens of institutions. The article went so far as to name several of the institutions that had been involved, including the Athenaeum in Providence. I read this piece with a small sense of elation. It seemed that the danger Miss Whateley felt her book was in was now not only in the past, but had probably never really existed in the first place. It did make me wonder who it was that had warned her of the possibility of theft, and why a such a woman as Phaedra, who possessed her own significant capabilities, had bothered to retain us in the first place.

I had to wait to share this information with my colleagues until they returned home, and even then, I was delayed further as they had their own information to share.

Robert related the first part excitedly. "The symbols you found embedded in the two books are actually only one set of symbols, just inverted in one copy.

They are a crude cipher, common among pre-colonial craftsmen who wanted to sign their work but were forbidden to do so by the men they worked for. An assistant professor and folklorist found an old monograph on the subject, and we were able to identify the signature as belonging to Zabdiel Whateley."

I connected the dots. "The ancestor that Phaedra has a portrait of in her library."

"And whose ashes sit in an urn below," added Megan. "He was a rather interesting character. Not one of the founders of Arkham, but in the second wave of colonists, and the entire Whateley clan can be traced back to him and his three wives. Records say he emigrated out of Warwickshire. Apparently, his claim to the family name was somewhat suspect, deriving through a child born in 1583 to a woman named Anne Whateley, who refused to name the father. The problem with this is that, besides a rather curious entry granting her a marriage license, the Whateley Family tree has no record of such a woman, or indeed the entire branch that Zabdiel claimed descent through."

"Which means what?" I wondered aloud.

"Zabdiel's family name was probably not Whateley," suggested Megan. "It was likely changed to hide who he really was, essentially restarting his life anew in the American colonies."

"Alternatively, but less likely," added Robert, "is the idea that he was using his birth name, but the woman he descended from, Anne Whateley, was the one who created the false lineage."

"What do we know about Zabdiel?"

"Not much," suggested Robert. "He came to the area around 1655 as a young man and worked for the Latimers out on Witch Hill. He was married three times, losing his first two wives in childbirth. Seven children reached adulthood, but all of these left the village between 1688 and 1691, moving northwest along the Miskatonic River and founding New Dunnich, now known as Dunwich. Zabdiel stayed behind, turning the day-to-day operations of his carpentry shop over to his nephew, but still drawing a small percentage of the profits. He became involved with the Restitution Society as a kind of gentleman's distraction, and then trained under Elias Von Kronenschieldt before becoming an expert in restoration and binding. He died in 1717 when a horse threw him on the road to Kingsport." He flipped through his notebook. "He was buried in Dethshill Cemetery."

"Buried, not cremated?"

Megan nodded. "That's right, cremation wasn't a common practice in Europe and the United States until about fifty years ago. In some places it was even illegal or considered a punishment for heretics who the church refused to bury in consecrated burial grounds." She paused and let what she had said sink in. "It's possible that Zabdiel was disinterred in 1894 when the cemetery underwent considerable renovation. His remains could have been cremated then and just never returned to the earth or placed in a mausoleum. Given the financial state of the Whateley Family, it seems likely they couldn't afford to have the remains properly interred."

"Or they have an alternative motive," suggested Robert, who knew a thing or two about raising those long dead from their ashes, as opposed to Megan, whose skill set was limited to using a reagent to raise the recently deceased. Useful skills, particularly in Arkham, but unused of late.

It was at this moment that I decided to reveal to my partners the newspaper article concerning the book thief. They were as surprised and elated as I was, and together we called Miss Whateley and made arrangements with her for the return of the book and its case. Robert would drive it back to her home that afternoon. A few minutes and another phone call later we had made a similar arrangement with Asenath Waite. Robert would make both deliveries, first to Whateley and then to Waite.

I thought that was the end of the matter, but I couldn't have been more mistaken.

·····•·•····

It was shortly after midnight when Megan burst into the laboratory with news that Phaedra Whateley had just phoned in a panic. She had apparently been roused from her sleep by a crashing noise, which had turned out to be the door to her library being broken open. She ran out and discovered a man in her hallway fumbling with the lock. Before she could do anything, the man opened the door and ran off into the woods. She asked that Megan and Robert come out to the house and protect her while she surveyed the damage and had someone out for repairs. It was a fair request, but I urged both of them to be careful, not only when it came to the burglar, but also with Miss Whateley. I reminded them that while all our encounters with her had been routine, we had evidence that she could invoke forces that might be beyond our ability to handle. Megan agreed and left in a hurry, promising to return as soon as possible.

That turned out to be more than six hours later, when the two of them returned very tired and rather dirty, covered, it seemed, with some kind of gray soot. It wasn't just on their clothes, but was caked in their hair and skin. I asked them about it, and they just stared at me as if I had offended them. Then they sat down and began to tell their story.

"First off," chided Megan, "it took us more than an hour to get out there. Robert couldn't find the turn."

Robert shrugged, "Things look different in the dark."

"When we got there, Phaedra met us wearing a housecoat and cradling a shotgun. The front door was intact, but the door to the library had been forced. Looking around the room I couldn't see any gaps in the shelves, and her copy of *The Restitution of Decayed Intelligence* was on her desk. I asked her outright if anything had been stolen, and she pointed at the mantle beneath the portrait of Zabdiel Whateley."

"Someone had stolen the ashes," I suggested.

Megan was dumbfounded. "How did you know?"

"I've had several hours to think about what happened. The library door was forced from the inside, yes?"

Robert nodded but said nothing.

"And the lock for that door requires a key to open it, even from the inside, correct?"

"Exactly," said Robert.

"What happened next?"

The two of them looked at each other knowingly, and then Megan said, "Phaedra Whateley accidentally exposed herself."

"What? What did you see?"

"Nothing," said Robert. "I mean, everything—I mean, what you would expect to see. A woman," he moved his hand up and down uncomfortably, "her private stuff."

Megan laughed, "What he means to say is that she has breasts and pubes just like a normal woman. Nothing at all like Miss Lieber had described."

"Really?"

She nodded, "In fact, she explained the whole thing to us. Apparently, her grandfather had been trying to use Lavinia to produce a monstrous hybrid child for years, and as we know from our interview with Miss Lieber, Wilbur Whateley was not the first result—that was Phaedra. But at birth, the girl appeared perfectly normal. Unsatisfied, old Whateley sent the girl to live with relatives in Ashborough. A mistake on his part. Phaedra finally manifested some semblance of her father's nature in her teens, after she began to experience puberty. For five days each month, her body becomes possessed by energies that she doesn't understand. She becomes very manipulative, and highly attractive to other people, but at the same time her torso is replaced by what can only be described as a portal for sounds, lights and energies she has little control over. Fortunately, a heavy coat is sufficient to suppress most of the activity."

"That explains why she needed our help; her powers are unreliable."

"She admits that she can manifest these abilities at other times of the month, but not on command, and usually with debilitating pain."

"Interesting."

Robert moved the conversation in another direction. "It was just about then that the wind in the woods suddenly rose up and began whipping through the trees. Thunder rolled and there was a strange whistling coming from a spot in the distance. As usual, I drew my gun and ran headlong into the heart of things, with Megan hot on my heels. As we worked our way through the woods, I caught sight of a pale light and motioned Megan to be quiet. Together we crept up behind some low shrubs and caught sight of three men standing in a small clearing. One was of average height with a few extra pounds on his frame, wearing a fashionable yellow coat with its hood pulled over, effectively hiding his face. The second man was a little shorter, and dressed in an outfit that was a few years out of date but still respectable. I didn't notice until Megan pointed it out, but he only had one arm. In front of them both, the third man knelt on the ground, naked save for a ragged beard and wild shock of grey hair. I couldn't see his face, but what I could see was the urn that lay open and empty by his side. There was no doubt in my mind that this was Zabdiel Whateley returned from the dead. What was more, is that I was almost as sure that the one-armed man was the so-called dust vampire I foiled weeks ago in Bolton." He paused and took a deep breath.

"I wanted to rush them, and I was sure that together we could take them before this went any further, but then one in yellow spoke. 'Joseph, we're not safe here. You've got the invocation. Let us return to my home and finish this there.' The other man, the one with one arm who had been called Joseph, growled back, 'Tis easy for you ta say, yer whole and living, while I'm little more than an aggregate of mixed parts, some of which I've lost.' He waved the sleeve of his missing arm about. 'We do this here and now, and when I'm whole and alive then ye'll be done with me, but until then Kamog shut yer mouth!' Having some concept of what was happening, I motioned for Megan to provide me some cover while I dealt with the situation as best I could."

This is where Megan took over the conversation, "I moved over a few yards and then when I was in position stood up and opened fire. It wasn't my intent to hit any of them, but just to keep them off-balance. The ground at their feet erupted in clouds of dirt as my bullets kicked up the frozen earth into fist-sized clods, while Robert began reciting the incantation that would turn these things back into dust. They tried to run, but I used some well-placed shots to keep them in one place. I heard Robert start his incantation to turn them back into dust, but so did they. Before he could finish, a strange word issued forth from the man called Kamog: 'Shushurra!' This was accompanied with a strange hand gesture, and in response the whole forest went silent, including Robert. I could see his mouth moving but no sound was being produced."

Robert took over. "The man called Kamog and the other one called Joseph made to leave, but the third man, Zabdiel, refused and they left him there. Megan took a few shots to try and keep them in place, but they just kept going. I gave chase but lost them in the queer silence that they had summoned over the wood. After ten minutes I returned to where Megan was standing guard over Zabdiel."

He was talking the whole time I was watching him, almost chanting I think, but I couldn't hear anything. Then as Robert returned the spell lifted. Zabdiel was reciting the spell that would turn him back to dust. He smiled when he heard his own voice and looked at us. 'Damn the Restitution Society,' he said, 'damn them all to Hell.' And then he said the words and the lightning struck and the wind blew, and he exploded over us like an ancient wave of ash."

"So, the gray stuff all over your clothes and in your hair and on your face is . . ."

"Human remains."

"And you never saw the other men, Joseph and Kamog, again?"

"The explosion knocked Megan and me on our butts, and by the time we recovered they were well gone."

"And Miss Whateley?"

Megan looked at Robert and he at her. "We've made arrangements for her to stay with a friend, at least temporarily. If she likes it there, she might stay permanently. It would be good for her to not be alone."

"I see, are we in agreement that Joseph Curwen and this Kamog person were likely the ones to have sent the letter with the newspaper clippings?"

"Yes, and likely instigated the robberies in the first place," added Megan.

"And the goal all along was to gain access to the Whateley library, so as to steal Zabdiel Whateley's ashes."

"The book was just a red herring."

"Yes, Miss Halsey, a distraction—but I'm still concerned about one thing."

"What's that?" asked Robert.

"How did the thief get into the library?"

There was an uncomfortable silence that was finally interrupted by Robert. "I think I know. As ash he was slid under the door and then reconstituted. It was only because he was carrying the urn that he had to bust the door down."

I let this thought mull around in my head. It was satisfying in a way, but at the same time seemed incomplete. But, unable to offer up any alternative, I reluctantly agreed. "Of course, a simple solution."

Of course, it wasn't that simple, and it would be months before we learned the truth.

The Wedding of Asenath Waite

Robert Peaslee

It had been three months since we had a client call. As a resident of Arkham I found that comforting, but as a detective I would have preferred something—anything—to do. Is there anything worse than an idle investigator? We grow inquisitive, some might even say paranoid, and begin sticking our noses into things that we should leave alone, things we haven't been invited to. It's a dangerous condition, and it will fester if left too long uninterrupted. It's bad for one, but worse for two, and almost impossible for three. I honestly don't know how Lydecker doesn't go mad from inactivity.

Even the papers were boring, with reports filling the columns with the most mundane of subjects. The university was reporting that the wireless station they were building on Kingsport Head, with significant participation from financier Edward Howland Robinson Green, was nearing completion. Megan and I took a week in Kingsport to visit my sister, take in the sea and march up Kingsport Head to see the towering steel structure. As impressive as it was, I could not convince Megan to stay out and observe the facility as it was lit after dark. She had an aversion to being on the cliff at night. When I pressed her on it, she refused to speak of why, just saying that as a youth she had spent one night in the misty woods and had no desire to do so again.

Given the paucity of interesting events the papers soon began reporting on the most speculative of subjects. There was an entire half-page devoted to the visit of British tycoon Edward Eliot who was in town apparently looking at property to buy for some new venture. Rumor had it he was secretly buying up parcels on the outskirts of Innsmouth and looking to make a move on the besieged little village itself. Megan could only partially confirm this gossip. She had met with the directors of Griffith and Son to finalize the sale of Crowninshield Manor to Edward Derby, giving him and his future bride, Asenath Waite, a residence to return to after their nuptials. Megan said that they negotiated a fair price, but I couldn't help but wonder about the truth of that. Having known Asenath at the Hall School in Kingsport, Megan was somewhat excited by being invited to the wedding and dismissed me each time I reminded her that we had not been invited but hired to be there. The marriage between the two was not without its opponents. Some considered Asenath too young for Derby, while others voiced concerns over her reputation as a decadent amongst the Bohemians, or even her familial background—old Ephraim after all did have a rather dark history in the region, one that Asenath did nothing to dispel. Asenath and Edward did not expect anyone to make trouble—physical or verbal—but felt that our presence would act as a deterrent to anybody that might step out of line.

Not that there were many people to be concerned about on the list of invitees. The invitations had gone out to two very different groups of people, divided almost strictly along lines of groom and bride. Certainly, there were family members, most of which were on the Derby side, with the Waites being represented by just a few distant cousins. Friends of the groom were mostly drawn from the old families of Arkham and many of these were considerably older than Edward himself, which suggested that they were more friends of his parents than of himself, including Uptons, Pickmans, and Carters. In contrast, the guests of the bride were much younger, primarily students or recent graduates, with a smattering of unusual individuals from up and down the coast. Perhaps most surprising were some members of various performing troupes including the infamous freak show der Zirkus L'Avenza. Even if there were no fireworks, the wedding was going to be a significant event, something to break up the boredom and give the closing weeks of classes at Miskatonic University a party that a select few wouldn't soon forget.

The ceremony was to be held at a private home along the road that ran from Arkham to Cairn's Point, the owner of which, a Doctor Hu, was not well known in Arkham, but was apparently a friend of Asenath's, and his fifty-acre estate had long been the envy of the more horticulturally-minded of Arkham's citizens. About half the grounds had been left as virgin forest, fifteen acres served as a small gentleman's farm, and the remaining ten acres had been transformed into a formal English garden complete with a small lake, a stream leading to the river, and even a folly in the form of a faux tower ruin made of local stone and festooned with a number of crumbling gargoyles. Rumor had it that Hu had once been an advisor to the Korean Court but following the death of Empress Min had fled the occupying Japanese forces for California, before finally moving to Arkham. What he was a doctor of was unclear; some said it was of medicine, others of astronomy, and even more said he held a degree in engineering. Hu himself never talked about his past and had a tendency to deflect inquiries and discuss matters botanical instead. It was a subject he seemed to be quite well versed in—particularly, as one would expect, when it came to the vegetation of northeast Asia. Oddly, his garden was almost entirely comprised specimens native to the region of New England, though maintained in such a way as to make them an almost ethereal sight. It was a fine place to hold a wedding, even if the weather had turned.

The forecast from the Weather Bureau had been pleasant enough, but that mid-June morning there was something in the air that almost anybody could recognize as an ill wind. The predominant breeze was from the north, and while not a cold wind, it was gently cooling and pleasant. On occasion, and more frequently as the morning progressed, the wind shifted to the east and from this direction it was colder, more blustery, and tinged with just a hint of the strange petrichor that loiters in the air suggesting precipitation isn't far off. I didn't believe it would interfere with the ceremony, which was to be in the east garden beneath two ancient oaks. Nor did I believe it would intrude on the reception, which was being held in the house itself and on the east terrace. I didn't believe these things, but I packed my coat, and Megan's, just in case.

We arrived at the Hu estate around noon to find the preparations for the wedding in full swing. The grounds were decorated tastefully with white bows and velvet rope. Folding chairs, set up in the traditional rectangles separating the bride's guests from the bridegroom's, sat neatly in the shade of the two oaks that would serve as the setting for the ceremony. A small dais and trellis had been set up to form an elevated stage and backdrop. A long white carpet ran from the dais though the divided chairs and toward the house. Doctor Hu was acting as a coordinator and met us happily after we parked the car. We were each given a list of guests and were asked to stay at the main gates of the property making sure those arriving had actually been invited.

As we walked back the way we had driven in I smiled and made a sarcastic comment. "We're not even ushers, we're glorified security guards."

Megan was annoyed. "We are getting paid, Robert, and after we check everybody in, we can make our way back for the ceremony."

I laughed and scanned over my guest list. Several names were checked off, indicating that they were already on the grounds. This included a specified number of unnamed staff, the Sargents who worked for Asenath, and man named Embry Grimes, whom I didn't know, but was a guest of Asenath. The list seemed pretty standard, but it did contain one surprise that I hadn't expected—there, on the Groom's side, was the name Frank Elwood. We hadn't seen him for months and we had thought he had left town. To see him here on this list was rather pleasant, for it told us he was well, but it also meant that there was a potential for conflict. Thankfully, Megan pointed out that his name was checked off, meaning that he was already here, and we might be able to avoid an argument.

It was long after that, with the ceremony scheduled for two, that guests began to arrive, and we started ticking them off the list. I handled the groom's guests, and Megan dealt with those of the bride. There were, of course, problems. The Goreys had been joined at the last minute by their daughter Hester, but their invitation had not made allowances for a third. Thankfully, Raoul Frump, an art student at the university, had arrived alone and was more than pleased to take the rather charming young woman as his companion for the afternoon.

As the clock ticked past one-thirty I checked in the last person on my list, a young man named Addams, and then looked over at Megan. She hadn't been quite as successful, and was still missing several parties, including the Courts from Kingsport, and the Fishers from Newburyport. Despite this, we both felt that our duties at the gate had been accomplished and slowly began the walk back to the house. Megan took the opportunity to ask about the dress of my attendees.

"Nothing out of the ordinary," I said. "Pretty standard wedding attire, I think."

"I think I know why we are here," she said.

And then, just a few moments later, I caught sight of the gathered guests, and the division between them. The groom's side was as I expected: older, genteel, dressed in respectable suits and dresses befitting the upper class of Arkham from which they had been drawn. More than a few of the gentlemen wore green carnations, but there was nothing particularly rebellious about that. Certainly, there were a few rebels, one woman wore a yellow ribbon, and one man a pink band around his hat. There was even a young man who had the audacity to wear shoes without spats, showing off his paisley socks. But for the most part the groom's side of things were as expected. The bride's side, however, was something else altogether. For certain, there were guests that would be considered normal, but these were in the extreme minority. Others wore normal respectable outfits but were possessed of features that were far from normal. Some of these were mere physical quirks such as a single eyebrow or an extremely receding hairline, while others might have been classified as conditions or deformities, including a man with ichthyosis and a woman who seemed to have no hair whatsoever. While my eye was drawn to these human abnormalities, the dominant attraction on the bride's side was the variation in dress. One might describe it as a riot of color, but also of fashion. I saw two saris and at least one kimono. Sometime in the last few hours Doctor Hu had adopted the formal dress of a Chinese mandarin, including a large, ornate hat that reminded me of a bicycle seat.

Besides the international range of fashion, there was also a temporal one; while some of the outfits were of the latest style, others seemed to date back by more than fifty years. One woman was wearing a large red gown with a massive silk petticoat in a style that had been worn just after the Great War. It seemed entirely impractical and prevented her from taking anything but the smallest of steps, and yet her movements were fluid and graceful, as if she hadn't any feet at all, but rather was floating across the grounds. Another woman, who was short with flaming red hair piled high in a kind of wild pompadour that would have made Charles Dana Gibson shudder, had decided to wear a men's style suit, but cut from bright green silk and sporting a purple paisley print. She had done her makeup in the same colors, which accented her rather extreme cheeks and large eyes. Her companion was a tall and lean African with skin so dark it seemed almost midnight blue, and her sharp features were accented by her short haircut and the oddly cut gown she wore, which seemed to draw inspiration from the ancient Moors. But the sartorial splendor was not limited to women. There was a man wearing what appeared to be a suit cut in the most recent of styles, but made out of white cotton and printed with text that relayed Baudelaire's poem "Au Lecteur," the preface to his collection *Les Fleurs du Mal*. There was another man who had taken great care in the preparation of his hair and mustache, coating them in lacquer so that they did not move in the slightest, but his suit seemed three sizes too big for him, and ballooned in odd places as he walked. The entire effect made him appear as a kind of a doll that was not a man, but only the idea of a man, made manifest for a child to play with.

"Where should we sit?" I asked Megan.

"Have you ever met Edward Derby?"

"No," I answered, "have you?"

She shook her head no.

"Then we should sit on the bride's side."

"This is going to be fun," she said, but I wasn't sure if she was being serious or sarcastic, but I noticed her hand had unconsciously checked for her gun. A reflex I understood but didn't see the need for. We were at a party, and these were just people having a good time. There was nothing to be afraid of.

Two steps later the crowd shifted, and I saw our former client Frank Elwood standing there looking pale and tragic in a charcoal gray suit talking to an older man in an older suit with a long beard and dark glasses. Elwood looked over and saw both of us. His gaze lingered long enough to draw the attention of the man he was talking to. Where Elwood seemed disturbed to see us, the other man seemed elated. He grabbed Elwood by the arm, whispered in his ear and then dragged the student over to meet our path.

"It is good to see you again Mister Peaslee, Miss Halsey." His tone was subdued. "It is my duty to introduce Professor Embry Grimes. Professor Grimes, Robert Peaslee and his wife Megan Halsey."

The older man took my hand in his and shook it vigorously. "Mr. Peaslee, it is such a pleasure to finally meet you, and you too Miss Halsey, though my friend Frank here told me that the two of you were married?" His accent was strange; it seemed British, but I was unfamiliar with the dialect.

Megan grimaced. "We are, but I prefer my family name. Are you on the faculty at Miskatonic, Professor?"

He smiled but only with his lips. "No, though I am working there. I'm consulting with young Wilmarth on some genealogical studies in the area." He paused and took our looks as a cue to explain. "I'm an historian. I specialize in pre-revolutionary American history. I'm doing an article on the folklore of the region, its historical origins, and the process by which the truth was corrupted into legend."

"For example?" I must admit I was curious.

He thought for a moment, and then seemed to hit on an example. "There's a persistent tale that Arkham was founded by people fleeing the Salem witch trials. Now, this is patently untrue. Arkham was founded many years before the trials began, but the rumor is there because the town did provide a refuge for many who would have likely fallen victim to Salem's religious zeal."

"But Arkham did have its share of witches, didn't it? It's nicknamed 'Witch-haunted,'" countered Megan.

"Yes of course, we all know about Keziah Mason. She is the most famous, but few people seem to remember that she had sisters that grew just as notorious as Keziah." He paused. "The appellation you used—'witch-haunted'—that might be better applied to the entirety of the Miskatonic Valley rather than just Arkham. Why, I could name more than a score of people from Dunwich to Kingsport who would have been considered witches by their neighbors."

"And some rightfully so," I suggested.

"I suppose, though it depends on your definition of witchcraft. Sometimes all it took to be accused was an open mind and the possession of books that others couldn't understand. Much of the science taught and practiced at the university would have looked and sounded like witchcraft to the people who settled this land, which included ancestral Halseys and Peaslees." He smiled strangely. "Rather prudish people if I recall—at least, that is how they appear in contemporary documents."

"Interesting," said Megan. "How do you know Frank?"

Grimes glanced at the young man, "We met through Asenath. I knew her father from back before she was born, and Frank here has been studying with Asenath, reviewing some rather interesting philosophical and metaphysical concepts. Did you know that Asenath is quite adept?"

"I did," said Megan. "Asenath was quite the spectacle back at the Hall School. Her work as a spirit guide was always entertaining at parties."

His attention was suddenly elsewhere, "I think Doctor Hu would like us to take our seats. The ceremony is about to start."

As we walked over to the chairs, I made sure that Megan and I held back, separating ourselves from Elwood and Grimes. While they moved to sit further up, we sat in the outer seats in the last row. Just in case we had to get out quickly and deal with something. It only took a minute or so for the rest of the seats to fill, and the two of us were just grateful that the woman with the pompadour hadn't been seated in front of us. Hu walked down the aisle and then took his spot on the dais. As he settled in, looking all official, a small four-piece ensemble that I hadn't noticed before began playing. It was then that Edward Derby appeared and strutted through the crowd with two groomsmen. He looked familiar, and I whispered so to Megan.

"You're right," she said. "I think we have met him before, but I can't remember where."

"What do you think about Elwood 'studying' with Asenath?"

"I'll talk to her about it. She's not much older than he is. I can't see how she could be in any position to help him."

With a musical flourish the doors to the house opened and out stepped the bride. She was a stunning figure in a cream satin dress that went to just below her knee. It was brocaded around the waist and shoulders with detailing that trailed down the arms and then exploded around her wrists with intricate cuffs. Around her neck was a string of pearls with an oversized tear-shaped centerpiece that hung down further than the rest. She wore no veil, but on her head she wore a tight-fitting piece that let almost no hair be seen. It was like a half-helmet or skullcap, decorated with semiprecious stones that glittered in the sun. From the back of this headwear trailed a wispy lace-like train that reached all the way to the floor and a few feet after that. A few people gasped, but I couldn't tell if they did so because they thought the ensemble beautiful or because they thought it in poor taste. After an appropriate pause she continued down the aisle toward the dais, walking slow enough to let everybody get a good look and admire her.

It was just then that the music was interrupted by the raucous sound of a badly tuned car pulling up the drive. Megan frowned in disappointment, and I quickly jumped from my seat, patted her on the shoulder and left her behind to enjoy the ceremony while I dealt with the new arrivals. Running through the grass I waved at them and motioned for the driver to cut the engine, which he did, leaving the car parked in the middle of the drive. With the car stopped, the doors were suddenly flung open and out poured more than six occupants in various styles of dress. It was as if children had been given free rein to raid their parent's closet and try on their finery. Not that any of the six were children, but they had dressed that way, and in exiting the vehicle behaved that way as well. I motioned for them to be quiet and make their way over to the ceremony. In hushed tones I asked for the driver's keys and told him that I would park the car for him. He handed them to me and never said another word.

I did not restart the engine, but rather put the car in neutral and pushed the car along with one hand while steering through the open window with the other. It was not the easiest of chores, and in fact it was rather slow and tedious, but I accomplished my goals: the car was parked safely, and the ceremony had not been further interrupted. I know this because by the time I finished and began making my way back toward the lawn I heard a joyful cheer and the music rose. I hadn't been gone that long, but apparently the couple had decided on a short ceremony. Not that I minded; the sooner we got inside the better. The weather was definitely turning.

The rest of the evening went off without so much as a single incident. Certainly, there were a few unsettling glances between those representing Arkham's upper crust and the university bohemian set, but nothing came of those. At one point I grew concerned when two men pulled out some knives, but these were obviously juggling knives, and used as part of a rather boisterous dance that I had never seen before. Young Addams, one of the two men involved, claimed it to be a generations-old tradition amongst his family. It was all in good fun, and the party went on well into the night, even with the rain coming down in torrents. It was after midnight when the band finally ended their last set and began packing up. Asenath and Megan were chatting and laughing at a table while I made sure a few stray guests made it to their cars. When I came back Megan had my coat and Asenath was putting hers on.

"They are leaving tonight for Maine," she told me. "I thought for sure they would be going someplace like Paris or London, maybe even the Palm Beaches, but they're going to a little cabin in Chesuncook, Maine."

"I prefer the peace that comes from the wilderness," came an unfamiliar voice.

I turned and came face to face with Edward Derby. He was older than Asenath, by ten or maybe fifteen years, I would guess, and a little plump, which made him look soft around the edges. He was an attractive man, in his way, certainly not my type, but not homely by any means. I was staring, because I suddenly knew where I had seen him before, and a quick glance at Megan told me she was having the same revelation.

He stuck his hand out and introduced himself. "Edward Pickman Derby. Asenath has told me a lot about you, and your wife. I must admit I'm rather jealous of you."

I looked at him confused, "You are?"

"Yes," he was exuberant, "Asenath and I may both be rather liberal in our thinking, but we've been unable to shake off some of the trappings and traditions that old families insist on. Megan keeping her name and providing financial support, while the two of you play at being detectives. It really is quite droll."

I couldn't stop staring at his coat. "I'm sorry?"

He rolled his eyes at me, "Anyway, Asenath dear, we really must get going. We have a long drive tomorrow and I want to get an early start."

"Of course, you're right." She grabbed her clutch from the table. "We'll talk when I get back, Megan."

"I look forward to it." The tone in my wife's voice was suddenly very cold.

As the two of them walked away, Megan and I watched with rapt attention. It was only after the door closed that I noticed Megan's hand was under her own coat and resting on her gun.

We waited a few minutes and then left the house, got in the car, and drove home. We were only a few blocks from Griffith House when I couldn't bear it anymore. "His coat," I said, "his coat was yellow."

She nodded ever so slightly. "He was the man in the woods outside Phaedra Whateley's house. The one called Kamog."

"Yes, I'm sure of it. What do you think we should do?"

Megan turned and looked at me, and then in a calm and rational voice told me what she thought our next course of action should be. "They'll be on their honeymoon for two weeks. Let them enjoy it. Asenath said she would phone me when they got back into town. They'll be living in Crowninshield Manor then. I'll give them another week and then suggest we have dinner together. When the opportunity arises, we talk about Edward's extracurricular activities and find out exactly what is going on. And I better like the answers he gives."

"And if you don't."

"Then we kill him and burn the house to the ground."

"What about Asenath? You two have been friends for a long time."

"I'm hoping that she doesn't know anything about this."

"And if she does?"

My wife looked at me, and for the first time in a long time I was afraid of her—of what she might be capable of.

"That just might be the cost of doing business."

I didn't say anything after that, and neither did she.

THE ELDRITCH EQUATIONS

PART FIVE

THE REMAINDER

Looking for a Ghost

Megan Halsey

It was in the late evening when my husband noticed that I was getting dressed to go out.

"Going somewhere?" he inquired.

"I have a case."

"A case? We don't have any clients right now." He glanced at me over the top of his book. "Anything I should be concerned about?"

"Haven't you seen the papers? The articles about the disturbances in French Hill?"

He put his book down. "The ghost wandering on Parsonage Street?"

"And on Pickman and College Street as well. Witnesses describe a ghostly figure that moved silently through the streets as if its feet never even touched the ground. Some of the locals think it's the ghost of Keziah Mason."

"The residents of French Hill are an uneducated and superstitious lot. They see ghosts and witches and the ghosts of witches on every mist-shrouded corner, and in every old building."

I gave him an incredulous look. "Weren't you involved in a case in that neighborhood? The missing boy, what was his name?"

"Ladislas Wolejko." There was a touch of melancholy in his voice.

"Yes, that's him. You dealt with his killer, Mary Czanek, didn't you?"

"You know I did, and I ended up on leave in Kingsport because of it. You know all this, Megan. Why bring it up now?"

I wandered over to him and kissed him on the forehead. "You are a good man Robert, a very good man. Yes, you've done some terrible things, but you've done good as well. I just thought you should be reminded of that. All things considered."

"What things?"

I kissed him again. "We'll talk more when I get back." And then I left.

Arkham after dark is much like Arkham during the day—quiet, clean; a quaint New England town with secrets hidden just beneath a veneer of normalcy. I walk these streets, not as often as Robert, but often enough.

The streets of Arkham at night have their own inhabitants. There are the usual suspects—rats, of course, and cats and dogs. The cats and dogs come in all shapes and sizes: some thin and feral, others plump household pets slumming it for the evening, a few somewhere in between. There are other citizens, the night people, some revelers and dairymen, junkmen, even a few policemen. Then there are things you don't expect, things that you catch out of the corner of your eye. Things that sometimes pass for men and others that could pass for something canine. Some of these half-seen specters resemble a large dog or a wolf while others share a semblance with leaner canids, like a coyote or a jackal. You catch a glimpse of them in the shadows of mausoleums and crypts and old bridges and the openings to forgotten sewers. You turn to look, and they're gone, but their stench still lingers. That dry dusty stink of rot betrays them, and you hurry on your way, afraid that they might come back and this time they might not fade into the darkness, and you might find out exactly what they are.

Arkham is like that, full of ghosts and ghouls and yes, the occasional witch, but nothing that I can't handle with the proper application of firepower and knowledge.

It seems odd when I think about it. We've faced a variety of threats: mostly human, some alien, some supernatural, but, almost always, the proper application of guns, explosives or fire has always resolved things. It is rare that a bullet doesn't solve things or have the potential to solve things. This might be because for the most part the things we have encountered have been firmly rooted in understandable physical laws. The reanimated, despite their strength and resistance to pain, are still just biological organisms. As are the various human hybrids and weird animals we've encountered. They eat and breathe; they have organs and muscles. Break them and they will fall. You just have to know how and be capable of it. Some have nearly impenetrable hides, and others are so large a few bullets wouldn't make a difference. But they are all made of recognizable matter arranged in systems that conform to the laws of physics and ecology and biology. It's the other things I worry about, the things that aren't made of matter and don't conform to known laws. That is when our tactics will fail us. The dust vampires that Robert has seen worry me. As do some of the things that are described in the ancient texts that we have gained access to. The semi-protoplasmic things that seethe and change—Lydecker calls them Shoggothim—terrify me the most. A close second are the so-called Fungi from Yuggoth which—like the whistling polypous things—seem only partially made of normal matter, and phase in and out of our reality as they move through it. We hadn't actually encountered any of these things, and for that I was grateful, but I still worried about how we were going to deal with them if we did. I have some ideas, though, and that's why I still keep vials of reanimation agent in my pocket, and why Robert still practices the incantation for raising and putting down things from their ashes. Good alternatives to have besides the usual mayhem.

Parsonage Street wasn't far from our home, and once I arrived, I took a few minutes to familiarize myself with the area and find a place to set up shop for the night. It wasn't a great neighborhood, and as it sloped down the hill to the river it got progressively worse. The shops and homes and apartments weren't as well maintained. The wood on many homes was rotting away and the paint was just whitewash that barely protected the intact wood, let alone hiding the damaged wood. You couldn't help but see the decay and blight that was devouring this section of town. Broken fence posts, unkempt lawns, broken glass, dogs—feral, mangy, and emaciated—roaming the street, and far too many cats lounging on porches and windowsills. These were no contented and fat housecats; they were mutated from that proud breed by a poverty that left them lean, hungry, and mean, waiting to pounce on an unwary passerby. And, of course, there are the rats, there are always rats, and more than anything else, these are the things that you see out of the corner of your eye. The pale brown things that skitter along the edges, seeking cover in the shadows that most people don't look at, not because they don't want to, but because they don't have to. That's the way of most people, I think, and maybe how people can live in Arkham without noticing all the madness and horror that surrounds them. They aren't ignoring it; they've been trained not to see it. It might be an evolutionary trait that developed to keep people sane and safe. If you don't see the monsters, then they can't drive you mad. Sure, a few will be killed, but the rest will survive. Is that a horrible way to think about mankind? Maybe. It's just a working theory, though it is one that seems to explain so much of the world.

I was there for just over two hours and growing bored with doing the Carnacki-bit when I decided to call it a night. I was disappointed, but also hungry for a piece of Mrs. Kreitner's brisket. Why had I thought that I might resolve this issue in one night? It seemed suddenly ridiculous. The thing had only been spotted a handful of times in the last few weeks, and never in the same place twice, nor in consecutive evenings. That I thought I might have success in just one try was a testament to my arrogance. It was as if I was a deer hunter who walked down a game trail only once and expected to fell a ten-point buck. Possible, but highly unlikely. So I began walking back home, back up the hill along Parsonage, passing College Street and inevitably falling into the shadow of the Witch House, now condemned and boarded up by the town.

The ghost was waiting for me.

I had never considered that instead of hunter I might be hunted, but there it was, standing on the corner—a pale luminous figure, waiting for me, a sad and loathsome look on its face. A face I knew quite well, but one that I hadn't expected to see again, at least not in this part of town.

"What are you doing here, Miss Halsey?" asked Frank Elwood, his voice lonely and tinged with anger. He was standing there in the overgrown grass and weeds that filled the front lawn of the Witch House. There was a fog about him, something wispy and insubstantial, and within it he shone, just a little, like sliver moon on a cloudy night. He wasn't much of a man anymore. He was barely there, and almost unrecognizable, but I knew who he was, though perhaps given what was left of him I had no right to.

"I was looking for a ghost," I told him, "One that walks these streets at night, scaring the locals."

He looked longingly out over the houses and shops that lined the road. "Are they scared? Perhaps that is for the best. I wish perhaps I had been a bit more frightened when I lived here before. It might have helped me avoid the horrors I've endured for the last year." There was something dark and shadowy moving around his feet.

"Before?" I had caught an off handed comment. "You're living here again, where?"

He smiled, "In my old room, in the Witch House."

I looked at the crumbling old building with its cracked windows, flaking paint and crumbling edifice. "The place is condemned. It's not safe to go inside, let alone live in."

He laughed and shook his head. "No one seemed to mind before Walter died. It was good enough for us back then and it's good enough for us now." There was something dark and furtive slinking in the luminous fog.

"Us—who is us?" I took a step forward.

He took a step back, "I've said too much. You need to leave now, Miss Halsey. You need to leave us alone. We don't want you here. We don't want to see you anymore. Not today, not tomorrow, not ever." He moved and the shape at his feet reared up.

I pulled out my gun and took aim.

"That won't help, Miss Halsey," said Elwood. "He isn't really here. I'm surprised you can even see him. You must be sensitive, gifted."

"I've never thought of it as a gift, but yes. Now, what is it, that shadow that lurks at your feet?"

"You know his name, you and your husband. Once he was Keziah Mason's companion. He wanted to teach Walter, and have him take Keziah's place, but he's perfectly happy to teach me instead."

"Brown Jenkin," I spat the name out of my mouth. "But he killed your friend. Why would you ally with him?"

Elwood shrugged. "I've watched a respected professor kill his own students and get away with it. Yes, he'll go to the asylum, but you and I both know that he'll be out in a year or so, and Miskatonic University will cover it up. Murder isn't the crime that it used to be. In fact, I'm growing quite understanding of the practical applications of killing people. Particularly those that get in my way."

I moved forward angrily. "I thought you were supposed to be working with Asenath?"

And then he looked at me and spoke words that cut me to the bone, words I didn't understand but haunted me as I walked all the way home.

"Asenath? You expect me to study with that . . . but you don't know, do you?" He opened the door to the Witch House and stepped inside. "Everything she's ever told you, everything you thought you knew about her, is a lie."

Then the door closed, but I could still hear him as he said one last thing.

"Asenath Waite is dead. She has been for a very long time. In fact, I don't think you ever knew her at all."

The Last Case

Roman Lydecker

Part One: Dubious Gifts

It was Monday, June the twenty-fourth when the beginning of the end began to suggest itself. We didn't know it then, didn't recognize it for what it was, but it began with the delivery of a present, a large planter of flowers. The planter was done up in style to imitate a Han Dynasty soul jar, with a phoenix in an intricate design raised up off the celadon-glazed surface. It was rather large, two gallons at least, and had been filled with shards of pumice that supported a large post made of what appeared to be teak. Around this post was a thick layer of living moss through which an orchid had been trained. The orchid itself was delicate and leafless with a green steam and several pale white flowers with long petals that reminded me of frogs. There was a custom glass case that fit over the plant and onto the rim of the vase which was held in place by three evenly spaced screw clamps. A note attached to the vase provided instructions for the care of the plant, which was named as a Ghost Orchid, *Dendrophylax lindenii*. Also present had been a handwritten card with one word written on it, "Congratulations." The card was unsigned, and the delivery man had no information on its origin.

"It must be from Vargr," suggested Robert. "He has a mania for these kinds of plants."

"Perhaps," agreed Megan, "but what is he congratulating us for?" She gave Robert a coy look.

"I haven't said anything. I haven't spoken to him in months—you know that he's been busy renovating that brownstone on 35th Street in New York." Robert seemed embarrassed by something, but I wasn't going to pry.

"Do you think he'll really go into private practice?"

"He says that he always wanted to, but then that's what Chan has always said, and I don't ever see him leaving the police force, not since he got married.

He's too comfortable. Nick, on the other hand—there's a man ready to retire. He's been on his own for a few years, ever since he quit Continental, and doing quite well. He's got quite a reputation in both New York and San Francisco. But ever since the Gorilla Man Murders, he's been shadowed by reporters, and that makes it hard for him to find work. Thankfully, he's fallen for a rather well-to-do socialite Nora Forrest. If he can seal that deal, he'll never have to worry about working again."

"Did you just say, 'seal the deal' in reference to two people falling in love and getting married?" Megan was slightly incredulous.

"I did." Desperate to change the subject, Robert looked at me and asked about the week's news.

"American diplomacy seems to be triumphing this week. Morrow has negotiated a peace between the Mexican government and the Catholics, essentially allowing the Vatican to renew operations again, albeit with government oversight. Meanwhile Dawes, the ambassador to Britain, is calling for a conference on naval disarmament. It seems that despite the rough start, the powers that be have finally found a way to turn the economic boom into prosperity for all. The twentieth century might actually go down as a century of peace."

Megan looked at Robert and he back at her. I knew that they did not share my optimism. Just days earlier Megan had signed paperwork selling off her family businesses. As of this day she was no longer a businesswoman, just a very wealthy private detective. But that also meant that she had no regular source of income. The savings would have to last. She also had decided to ask my advice and had taken the money out of the bank and any investments that she could earn a return from. She kept the cash in a safety deposit box in a bank in Portland, Maine. She planned on buying property, but where exactly she would not say. I thought perhaps she didn't know.

It was just then that the doorbell rang. Our appointment was on time, if not a few minutes early. It only took a few seconds for Robert to return with a potential new client.

"May I introduce Doctor George Cardigan."

Cardigan was a tall, balding man with a stern face and an average build. He was dressed in a smart black suit. He carried with him a slim valise that had seen better days. I met him once before, quite some time ago, before the war, when I was a different person. I recalled that he had been friends with West and Cain, or at least a fellow student under Allan Halsey, Megan's father. He was British, and rather formal in his attitudes.

"How can we be of service?" I asked.

He sat down and seemed reluctant to speak, but only for a moment. He was looking around the room, surveying it. He focused on the ghost orchid. "A lovely specimen," he commented. Before anyone could say anything he suddenly began to speak quite insistently. "I'm afraid I've misled you a tad. I am not here to seek your services, but rather to deliver some things that I think belong to Miss Halsey-Griffith."

Megan bristled at the use of her full name, "It's just Halsey, please, or Misses Peaslee."

He nodded his head like a lizard in the sun. "As you wish. You see, I've taken a position as a records archivist at the Sefton Asylum, only temporary of course. I'm setting up my own surgical practice out in California and things aren't quite ready out there yet. The asylum needed a qualified medical man to organize their records, and as I had no patients here, I thought it would be both interesting and beneficial to my financial state to take on the position. The previous archivist had died a few months back and nobody could make sense of his filing system. So, I've been tasked with going through years of files, including on cases that have long been closed. That is when I found your file Miss Halsey-Grif—Miss Halsey."

Robert looked puzzled, "I didn't know you spent time at the Asylum. Megan?"

She shook her head. "Mother took me there to have me evaluated. I was having bad dreams, and I was rebellious. I saw several doctors; it was then that they figured out I was something of a prodigy. Not long after, they sent me to the Hall School."

Cardigan withdrew from his bag a large file and a phonographic record in browned sleeve. "The doctors who examined you, they made some rather interesting notes. Observations and diagnoses that might be best kept private, if you understand what I'm saying."

Robert reached out his hand for the file, but Cardigan clutched both it and the disk to his chest. "These are official records Mr. Peaslee, I couldn't just hand them over. I could get into a significant amount of trouble."

Peaslee reached into his suitcoat and took out his checkbook. We all sat in silence as he wrote something out and then signed it with a flourish. He tore the check out and handed it to the unscrupulous physician. "I think you should be happy with that amount, Doctor Cardigan." He almost spat the last two words.

Cardigan looked at the slip and his eyes grew wide. "Yes, this will do, this will do quite nicely."

Robert took the file and the recording. "I'm sure you can find your own way out."

Cardigan stood and cocked his head as he smiled. "A pleasure doing business with you." Then he strode out of the office and as he left slammed the door.

Robert handed the file to Megan and laid the record on the table. "So that's how that feels."

Megan was flipping through the pages of her file. "How what feels?"

"Being blackmailed." He sighed. "Anything interesting in there?"

Part Two: The Resignation of Abraham Pierce

Doctor Winchester,

While I am sure that it comes as no surprise, decorum requires that I inform you that I am resigning my position as your assistant and will no longer be in service to you in private practice or at the Sefton Asylum. I assure you, Doctor Winchester, I am not a man of weak will; the horrors that can be inflicted on and endured by the human body and mind do not particularly disturb me, and there was little at your hospital that I had not seen before. It was not the state of the patients in your asylum that caused me to flee in terror, but rather something else, something that I only understood through the correlation of unconnected facts and events that no one else had access to. The horrors of the natural world hold no terror for me, Doctor, but what I learned that day goes beyond the natural and hints at something in defiance of all that modern science has deemed possible. If what I suspect is true, then something preternatural exists, not within the walls of your sanitarium, but rather outside them—a part of the general populace that stands blissfully unaware of the monstrosity that walks among them.

I suppose I should explain, but where do I begin? There is of course the girl. Most of your patients are hysterical women, alcoholic businessmen and nervous professors shattered by years of monomaniacal research, but amongst them was the startling child prodigy you had no clue on how to treat. Megan Halsey-Griffith was ten years old, though she looked older than that. According to her file, she had done exceedingly well on the newly promulgated Stanford-Binet intelligence test, but despite her intelligence she was wracked by bouts of fancy, and in particular by recurring nightmares that she was frustratingly vague about. At your request I met with the young girl and found her personable, even likeable. She was, as I expected, bright, but also charming. She knew that she was smarter than her peers, and even smarter than her mother, but attempted to avoid situations in which she would be forced to embarrass others via her knowledge and intelligence. All in all, she seemed rather well adjusted as geniuses go, though she did complain about her dreams. She had terrible dreams, not the usual nightmares, but more existential complaints that disturbed not only her but also her mother as well.

Those dreams, the ones that disturbed her, often imprisoned her in a terrible place that she called the White Room, an impenetrable, featureless oubliette, whose walls, floor and ceiling were like clouds, soft, white and inescapable. In these dreams Megan was not her normal self, but rather a kind of animal, trapped in a cage she not only didn't understand, but also couldn't even fathom. More importantly, the dream had evolved over time, and on occasion would now include visits from you, Doctor Winchester. It would seem you were something of a foil to her dream self, poking and prodding her with needles and various other bits of equipment. It was, as I wrote in my notes at the time, that the genius child's dream-self represented her desire to escape and be free, while the room itself symbolized the bonds placed on her not only by society, but more importantly by her mother. The occasional appearance of you, Doctor, was little more than a reflection of actual events, meaning the various tests that you administered during the course of your study of her psyche. It was, I believed, a variant on Jung's Electra complex, modified by the death of both the child's father and stepfather, and I made suggestions toward that diagnosis in my notebook.

If only things were that simple. If only I had paid more attention to the girl and her dreams.

The other facet of this story, I know only a fragment of, and revolves around the thing hidden within the walls of the Sefton Asylum. Decades ago, Arkham was besieged by a terrible plague that struck the city and decimated its populace. With the plague came the Arkham Terror, a plague-demon, a degenerate creature the origin of which was entirely unknown. The creature stalked the disease-ridden streets of Arkham, doling out murderous rampages on almost a nightly basis. There were suspicions—hopes, really—that it was some kind of animal, an ape of some sort, escaped from a travelling circus, but all such hopes were dashed when it was finally captured. That it was, or at least had once been a man, was clear, for upon its capture it bore all the hallmarks of humanity, but only in the most primitive of ways. The authorities, in their wisdom, had the simian thing locked away in Sefton Asylum, behind iron doors and padded walls, where the only harm it could do was drive young researchers mad with its incessant shrieking and weird, almost impossible physiology. As you well know, Doctor Winchester, the heartbeat of that thing is barely detectable, its blood bears little resemblance to ours, and the behavior of its brain and nervous tissues is inhuman. The appearance of that thing is entirely superficial; whatever it is that is imprisoned inside those padded walls could hardly be defined as human. The opportunity to study the Arkham Terror was just one of many possibilities that I considered all those months ago when I took the position as your assistant. The creature is legendary amongst the students of the Miskatonic University medical school, and few are ever lucky enough to see it, let alone actually study it. Thus, when you granted me access to the thing during the second week of my night shifts at the sanitarium, I jumped at the chance to examine the creature and even test its responses to various stimuli, all with fascinating results. So intrigued was I by my progress that night I barely slept the next morning and went into the offices exhausted and unprepared.

It was in this unfit condition that I sat down with young Miss Halsey-Griffith, and she opened our discourse with a most chilling statement: "I saw you last night, in my dreams." I was not surprised by such a revelation. To tell the truth, I had been expecting it. I had become an authority figure in her life, and it was only natural for me to be inserted into her dream world. "You hurt me with your tests, your needles, stealing little samples of my blood and flesh. It's not a nice thing to do, Doctor Pierce."

I agreed with her, of course, and then redirected the conversation towards her relationship with her mother. We talked for some time about her mother, and her aunt, and about the difference between turtles and tortoises. Then we spoke of the White Room and what it could mean. It was a meandering conversation that, despite my best efforts, never went exactly where I wanted it to go, but rather seemed to be diverted into nonsense by Megan. In the end I left feeling confused and frustrated with the session, as if it were I that had been the subject of interrogation rather than the interrogator.

That night marked the beginning of the fever that overtook me and laid me low for three straight days. Whether the fever was the source of the dreams, or the dreams brought the fever I can't say. What I do know is that whenever I closed my eyes, I could see that strange girl staring back at me with her huge eyes. Eyes so deep that you could be lost in them. Eyes so deep that they hid a shadow. It was a shambling thing that lurked just beyond the threshold of being clearly seen. It howled and gibbered back there, hidden by the veil of her retina. I tried to cast more light on the thing that shuddered there. With my hands, I grasped her iris and pulled the pupil wider, but no matter how much light filtered down into the back of that little girl's eye the shadows just grew larger, ever larger. The more I looked, the more I searched, the more I tried to understand, the more the shadows spread, and the less I could see. In the end I was left standing in twilight, on the edge between darkness and light with something shadowy and unseen shuffling and wailing in the darkness. As if it wanted to be seen but was at the same time forbidden.

And then the fever was gone, and I was myself again.

That first night you wouldn't let me go to the asylum. Do you remember that? You told me to rest up, to gather my strength, to start fresh the next day. It was a kindness, I suppose, and it left me feeling refreshed and ready to tackle the cases I had been assigned at the office. It was a rather uneventful morning, and a similar afternoon. I spoke with five patients that day, but there is only one that I can recall.

Little Megan Halsey-Griffith came to see me around three in the afternoon. She was talkative, more talkative than normal, and I suspected right away that something had happened, that there was something she wanted me to know.

"It's good to see you, Doctor Pierce, so very good to see you. It's been four days since I last saw you. I haven't even seen you in my dreams."

I smiled, "Not even in the White Room?"

Her eyes grew wide and wild. She opened her mouth to say something, but then closed it again. I could tell she wanted to reveal something, to tell me a secret, but was hesitant to do so.

"You can trust me, Megan." I suppose in my mind I was telling the truth, but it was just another lie that adults tell children because they don't know any better. It takes a long time for children to learn that adults lie.

"The White Room," she finally blurted out, "it's gone. Well, kind of. It's different now."

I pressed for details. "How?"

The walls are blue and there's a window near the ceiling. In the corner of the window there is a bird's nest, a robin, I think. In a way it's kind of beautiful."

I supposed it was. Given the history she had, any change would have been welcome, and we spent a good hour talking about the symbolism of blue, and the window, and the robin. It was a good session, with real progress, and when she left that evening, I had the feeling that the girl was on the verge of a breakthrough, and that at last I was doing some good in this world.

It was the last time I ever saw her. And God help me, I never wish to see her again.

I had dinner in the kitchen of the asylum before I did my rounds. It was a cool summer evening and the staff of the hospital had opened some of the windows to let the winds blow through the dusty old building. It made the place a bit cooler than I preferred, but at the same time seemed to revitalize some of the patients, who had been rearranged into new cells so as to allow them to benefit from the cooling breeze. The rearrangement of my patients made the undertaking of rounds a little more difficult. It was well after midnight before I finished administering to my regular patients and was able to finally sit down and labor at the paperwork that had accumulated over the last few days.

It was in the wee hours of the morning when a familiar howling roused me from my focus. I knew immediately that something was out of place, for the source of that terrible vocalization was a lot closer than it should have been. It was then that I realized that it wasn't only the non-violent patients that staff had rearranged. The howling man, the Arkham Terror, had been relocated into one of the cells in the area of the asylum not far from the offices of the administration. This realization came with a sense of fear, for the cells in this section were not as secure as others. With a sense of urgency and some trepidation I made my way briskly toward the source of the wailing that had not only disturbed me, but many of the patients as well.

As I stalked down the halls I picked up two orderlies and sent a third to make sure that the Arkham Terror's normal cell was prepared to receive him. The two men that came with me were large, muscular attendants who were accustomed to handling the patients of the Sefton Asylum, but I could see in their eyes that even they were nervous about dealing with this patient. As we approached the door the two men equipped themselves accordingly, one in a heavy padded coat with a hood, and the other with a control stick—a long, heavy rod with a loop on one end, not unlike those used by dogcatchers and other animal handlers.

Once we were suitably prepared, I took a deep breath and opened the door to the cell. The man in the hooded jacket rushed in and tackled the occupant, sending both orderly and prisoner crashing to the floor. As they flew through the air one or the other had collided with the pendulum lamp, setting it swinging back and forth like its namesake and putting in motion a frightening tableau of careening light and shadow. The man with the loop waded in next, and I in my foolishness followed. The two combatants were rolling about on the floor, the prisoner screeching like some kind of enormous cat, and his jailor huffing from both fear and exhaustion. It took a moment of violence but in due course the orderly placed our patient into a headlock, and his partner was able to slip the loop over the thing's neck and assert control.

Thinking the matter well in hand I let down my guard. Given the flashing light and shadows cast by the swinging lamp, what happened next I can't exactly be sure of, but without warning, something heavy impacted me in the chest and I ended up being thrown backwards against the far wall. As I lay there trying to catch my breath the two orderlies inquired after me, but I waved them off and ordered them to move the prisoner back to his regular cell. I watched as the first man removed the heavy coat, retrieved a second loop, and then working together they moved the monstrous subhuman thing down the hall.

I took a moment to regain my senses. Whatever had hit me—and I suspected it was the butt end of the control pole—had caught me in the left side just a few inches below the heart. The area was tender to the touch, definitely bruised, and I winced and held my breath as I checked for broken ribs. Finding none I relaxed and exhaled, staring at the ceiling as the bulb began to slow its wild and pendulous motion.

It was then that I saw the glimpse of moonlight that was filtering through the high window, and the thing that sat just there on the ledge of the frame. Even in the pale moonlight, I could see it. It was such a simple thing, and yet it filled me with such a feeling of dread and frightening wonder. I turned my head to stare at the walls, to confirm the terrible suspicion that had crept into my mind. With suspicion turned to confirmation I ran from the room and then down the hall in a blind dash, careening in a mad attempt to escape from that horrible place.

I don't remember when I began screaming, only that when I burst from the building and onto the front lawn, my throat was raw and the incoming morning staff looked at me with such faces. They must have thought the most abhorrent things about me, but I don't care. What I saw that morning in that cell shook me to the core, and I could care less what other people think. I only know that I shall never return to Sefton Asylum, or Arkham, ever again.

That was many days ago, and I'm much happier and calmer now that I have returned to my home in coastal Maine, but I still wake in a cold sweat, with the bedclothes soaked and my hands shaking when I think of the eldritch horror that I encountered, sat with and spoke to. Tell me, Doctor Winchester, how did she know? When the Arkham Terror was moved, and I sat there alone, I caught sight of the moon through the window, and the small bird's nest on the ledge, and then as the light stabilized and my eyes saw the room the thing had been living in, I saw that it was blue. The room was blue; there was a high window, and a bird's nest. How did she know? How did the child know all those details about where the Arkham Terror had been moved?

The inescapable White Room that young Megan Halsey-Griffith dreams of isn't a fantasy, or a metaphor, or some symbol for her psychological condition—it's the view the Arkham Terror has of his cell. It's how he comprehends his world. It's the world through his eyes! When that little girl dreams, she sees through that thing's eyes. How is that possible? Tell me, Doctor Winchester, what terrible bond exists between these two? How is it that a child like that sees with the eyes of a monster? What is she, Doctor? What kind of monster is she?

No, never mind! Never write to me again, please, I beg of you. Don't tell me, I don't want to know!

Part Three: The Sound of Silence

"I remember him," sighed Megan, "he was nice, polite. He meant well." There was sadness in her voice as she laid the pages on the desk. "Why would Cardigan bring that here? Dredging up old memories. What was the point?"

"He wanted money, Megan, that's all," Robert answered. He could see his wife was upset. "He wasn't trying to be cruel. He was just greedy, that's all, just greedy."

She didn't say anything after; she just walked out, not in anger or sadness but as if she had just turned herself off, shut herself down.

Robert sat there in silence for a moment just staring after her. "I'm sorry, Lydecker . . . Eric. She's rather emotional right now. It comes with the territory." He stood up. "I should go after her, see if she needs anything."

"What about the recording, Robert?"

He picked it up and took it out of its paper sleeve. "Requiem Mass by Du Hond, performed by the orchestra of the Opera Populaire in Paris. Recorded in 1920 in memory of the war dead. Why would Cardigan . . ."

I stopped him mid-sentence. "It doesn't matter, Robert. I haven't heard that one. Could you put it in the phonograph please?"

Robert did as I asked. The disk was scratchy, but as soon as the sound started the crackling didn't matter anymore. I was enraptured with the atonal beauty of du Hond's composition. I barely noticed that Robert had left. There is something about du Hond, something that other composers lack, or perhaps it is the other way around. Perhaps it is not what du Hond brings to his compositions, but rather what he doesn't. Like Debussy, the influence of Russian and Asian musicians was rather apparent, but these had been developed into innovative harmonies that most conductors and orchestras eschewed. Performing a piece by du Hond was no easy task; there were often many parallel chords that were supposedly meant to develop into harmonies, but usually turned into anything but, and therefore were difficult for many musicians to perform, and harder still for a conductor to manage. Though I do remember thinking that the man on this piece was particularly talented, guiding his charges through a variety of rather difficult turns and changes that lesser performers might have fumbled. The recording reached a crescendo, filling the room with a series of crashing explosions first from the brass, but then from the strings and the winds as well. Below it a drum beat out a gentle almost melodic thread completely out of character with the rest of the composition. It was both jarring and comforting to hear that beat, to latch on to it and hold it, to find comfort in that simple bass and use it to float through the rest of the cacophony that swirled around and flooded my senses. And then the music waned, and a voice came in. A beautiful voice, invoking an ethereal quality, a sense of the spiritual, of the eternal, of the resurrection. And then it began speaking, and I heard words that I hadn't heard in a long time, but still knew very well. Words that drove fear into my metaphorical heart and chilled me to the few bones I had left.

"Y'AI 'NG'NGAH, *YOG-SOTHOTH* H'EE—L'GEBF'AI THRODOG*UAAAH!*"

Through the room there suddenly blew a terrible wind, cold and fetid. The lights sputtered, and a gloom crept into the room, growing from the corners as the lamps failed and only the very faintest of glows came from around the corner. There was an odor as well, something exotic, that reminded me of my time spent in Persia, India and China, and the forbidden delights that were partaken there. There was smoke, too, a billowing blackness that was tinted green. It arose from the ghost orchid, or more accurately from the stones held in the Chinese pot beneath it. I should have guessed the danger it posed from the phoenix that it had been decorated with. The wind grew stronger and the smoke thicker. Papers flew from the desk into whirlwinds and were joined by the dust and debris of the room. Books tumbled from their shelves, a chair shifted, a lamp fell and crashed.

And I could do nothing but sit there, helpless in my chair.

There was a form, a shape, a man who had not been there before. His features were rough, ancient, older than they had a right to be, and he only had one arm.

He spoke, and as he did, I could see inside his mouth and the horrible, yellowed teeth that dwelt there.

"Good evening, Doctor. I apologize for not making an appointment, but I didn't think you would see me, not after the encounter I had with your compatriots at the wedding."

I had not been there, but I had an inkling of who this was. "Embry Grimes, Asenath's friend."

He cackled—he actually cackled. "Asenath, no, never met her. I'm a friend of her father, Ephraim."

"Were," I said. "You mean you were a friend of her father's."

"How quaint. No, not what I meant at all."

There was a sudden explosion of noise—a shot rang out and a glass mirror shattered.

"Could you take a moment to explain it, Mister Pulver?" demanded Robert. He had come down the stairs and drawn our intruder's attention as the elevator door opened and Megan snuck in behind me. She was pulling me back, slowly, into the safety of the lift itself.

"I haven't used that alias for months now. How is it you know it?"

"I was a cop, assigned to investigate what happened at the asylum. I followed your trail to the farmhouse. I cleaned up one of the messes you left behind."

"And here I thought that I only owed you retribution for foiling me in Bolton and outside the Whateley place."

"Now you know I've been on the case for much longer, and I know exactly how to deal with your kind."

"Did you think after Bolton I wouldn't be prepared?" He pulled something out of his pocket and threw it. I never saw it, for just then Megan closed the door between us and sent me moving toward the main floor, but I heard it. It was a piercing siren of a sound, one that would have drowned out any voices, and would have forced me to clutch my head if I had hands.

With each second the elevator climbed the shaft, and the sound grew more distant. There were other sounds. Crashing furniture, breaking glass, what could have been a body being thrown against a wall. I strained to hear, to make sense of what was going on, but then the door opened, and Mr. Kreitner was there.

"We've got to get you out, Sir," he said as he pulled me through the hall. "Miss Megan said it wasn't safe for you, or us."

The old handyman rolled me out of the house and down the drive. He stopped at the gate where his wife was waiting. She hugged him, and he kissed her, a true display of undying affection if I had ever seen one. Then he turned and made to head back toward the house. His wife clutched at him, but he tore from her grasp and took one, maybe two steps before we heard the terrible noise ring down from the clouds above us. That pause was all the old woman needed. She grabbed her husband and pulled him back, and in doing so probably saved his life.

They were arguing. He was desperate to go back inside to help the young couple who they had both served so faithfully, but the rumbling thunder came again, and the sky cracked open, and lightning crashed down into the house. The fire started immediately, fed by the exposure of so much timber and debris from the explosion. It spread quickly, from one wing of the house to the other. Through the windows I could see the flames jump from room to room, climbing up the stairs and into the library. Smoke both black and gray stained the sky dark and coated the stones with soot. It was in a way an awesome thing to watch as the inferno devoured my home. I would not have thought it would go so quickly. But the flames seemed insatiable, and they devoured Griffith House hungrily. By the time the fire department arrived there was little left to save—only some crumbling masonry, the tower façade and a chimney or two, and these, deprived of the structures that had supported them for years, didn't last much longer. They crumbled, falling into the pit that had opened inside the house itself where the cellars had once been, where I had once lived, where Megan and Robert presumably were still.

Halsey, Peaslee and Lydecker was over. Destroyed by fire and swallowed up by the earth itself. It seemed somehow appropriate and ironic at the same time, and I couldn't help but laugh a little as the men came and loaded me into the ambulance.

I thought they were from the hospital. Imagine my surprise when I was brought here. It has been a rather pleasant stay, though I wish you hadn't kept me waiting so long. Two days without news is rather disconcerting.

No, I'm not surprised that you didn't find any bodies. No, I didn't know about the nursery. I had my suspicions, though, but I never did broach the question. They would have told me when they were ready. Of course, I don't know where they are, and no, I don't think they're dead. How they got out is their own secret. Let them have it. But I'm sure we shall hear from them again someday, they are, after all, not the kind to stay quiet. They are adventurers at heart, I don't think this, or a child, will keep them out of business for very long.

As for your proposal, I find it intriguing. Tell me more about this organization you work for, Doctor Dexter. What did you say the name of it was?

Afterword

A Week Later

Robert Peaslee climbed up to the upper deck where his wife and the others had gathered. He had spent the last few hours in bed, where he had spent much of the last few days, trying to heal the wounds he had suffered in the battle that destroyed Griffith House. Megan had applied reagent, and that was helping, but he would still have a scar, one that would run the length of his chest. As he reached the last rung of the ladder Megan came to help him. It wasn't necessary, but it was a nice gesture. In all fairness it was he who should be taking care of her. She didn't want to admit it, but she was starting to show, and she was feeling sick in the morning. Soon she wouldn't be able to hide it anymore, and Robert would have to talk to her about settling down and taking things easy until she had the baby. After that, they would have to have another talk. He certainly didn't want her working while they had a young child, but he wasn't entirely sure that she would agree to that. She was who she was, having a child wasn't going to change that.

Up on the deck, the sea breeze felt good. It had been a long time since he had been to sea, and never on a ship of this size. It was a luxury yacht more than four hundred feet in length, built by the Gibbs Brothers just the previous year. Toussaint Delapore had bought it on the cheap from the previous owners who felt it was too small for their needs. It was certainly large enough for the five people who now occupied it, and those who crewed it.

Toussaint put his hand on Peaslee's shoulder as he sat down next to Jane Grimm, the Lady Jermyn. He was still tall and thin with that dark olive-colored skin, while she was just as tall, but muscular and broad. They looked good together, odd but good, almost striking. She put her hand in his and smiled, and he smiled back. They were happy together, and Robert liked to think that he and Megan were responsible for some portion of that, though the two of them had known each other before. The money helped too. All combined, the wealth they now held between them was more than that of some small countries. It was an ongoing discussion as to what they were going to do with it.

"Robert dear, Jane has an idea. She's heard all our stories about our adventures, and apparently Toussaint has had a few of his own, but she's been sheltered for most of her life. Not entirely, but no experiences like we have had."

I could see where this was heading. "Go on."

Jane leaned forward. "Well I was just thinking that we could pick up where you two left off, but except on a grander scale."

"A grander scale?"

Toussaint took a sip of his drink. "You've been thinking too small. Helping people in and around Arkham is all fine and good, but there's a bigger world out there, we're proof of that. They need us."

"Us?" Suddenly there was an "us."

"The five of us," suggested Megan.

"Five?"

"For now." She gave me a look. "We can talk about expanding when the time comes."

"So, the four of you are way ahead of me on this, aren't you?"

Toussaint shrugged, "You've been down for the count the last few days, but you have to admit that if Megan hadn't called Phaedra, we wouldn't be having this conversation. You need more help."

I nodded. "And I suppose you have a name picked out already?"

"Well, we were talking . . ." hemmed Jane. "Megan told us about the group you used to work for during the war, and we found it rather auspicious."

"The Inquiry? Why is that auspicious?"

Toussaint laughed. "This ship. The previous owner was a law firm, defense attorneys. They named it *The Inquisition*."

"You've got to be kidding me."

They shook their heads.

"The Inquiry has a kind of ring to it, official but private. It will give us gravitas," Megan grinned as she said the word.

"Gravitas," I was being railroaded, but in a good way. "You three are doing a lot of talking. Phaedra, what do you think?"

Phaedra Whateley had been standing at the rail, looking at the sea, at the horizon, at the birds floating in the air.

"There's a storm coming," she said wistfully as she turned back to the table. The wind caught her white hair and her black dress, and both fluttered playfully, almost innocently. "The world isn't ready for what is coming. We need to be prepared. We need to prepare them, prepare the world." She sat down at the table and picked up her tea. "At least some of them."

I sighed. "This is what you all want to do?" I looked at their faces. "It won't be easy, or safe. We've been lucky so far, avoided losses. But our luck can't hold forever."

Megan squeezed my hand. "What you call luck, I call training, and skill, and planning. Luck is no substitute for that."

Toussaint pulled an open bottle of champagne from the ice and poured five glasses. "We're with you Robert, we've all agreed. Somebody needs to do this work, it might as well be us."

The glasses were passed around, but Robert's sat on the table. He was reluctant to start something without thinking it through, but it seemed that he had no real choice. These fools were going to do this with or without him, and with him they might just survive.

He picked up the glass, "The Inquiry," he announced.

"The Inquiry," came the voices of his companions as one.

In the air above, the gulls screeched and called their cackling laughs as if they were deriding the events they had just been witness to. As if those ancient semi-saurian brains knew the futility of things. The world would turn no matter what they did. Men would be born, men would die, monsters would rise, monsters would fall, gods would ascend to the heavens or plunge headlong into the pit, and the world would turn beneath the sun, and the moon, and the stars, with or without them, as it had done for millennia and would do so for millennia more, no matter what they did.

Acknowledgments

I must thank my family who gave me the most precious of all things, time to write. I hope I haven't disappointed you.

As much as *Reanimatrix* was an homage to Vera Caspray's *Laura*, so too is *The Eldritch Equations and Other Investigations* my homage to Rex Stout's long running Nero Wolfe series, particularly the novel *The League of Frightened Men*. I also owe a debt to August Derleth and Fritz Leiber, who were inspirations in their own unique way.

The idea for this novel came in part from listening to *Dreams in the Witch House: A Lovecraftian Rock Opera*, produced by the H. P. Lovecraft Historical Society. Significant amounts of text were produced while listening to the album, and I probably owe everybody involved a drink.

Finally, I must thank my dear friend, Sal Ciano, whose patience, advice and editorial skills made this book infinitely better than it would have been without him.

About the Author

PETER RAWLIK is a writer and book collector living in Florida. In 2000, his research for a history of the Miskatonic River Valley laid the groundwork for what would eventually become the *Reanimators* (2013), *The Weird Company* (2014), *Reanimatrix* (2016), and *The Peaslee Papers* (2017). He edited *Legacy of the Reanimator* (2015, with Brian Sammons), and *The Chromatic Court* (2019); his short story collection, *The Strange Company and Others*, was released the same year. In 2021, he continued exploring the characters of *Reanimatrix* in *The Miskatonic University Spiritualism Club*, a novella published by Jackanapes Press. He is a regular member of the *Lovecraft eZine* Podcast and a frequent contributor to the New York Review of Science Fiction.

MEGAN AND ROBERT
WILL RETURN
IN

GHOSTS
-OF THE-
MISKATONIC

AS FOR LYDECKER—
ONLY TIME WILL TELL

From Peter Rawlik, Author of *Reanimators*
- A new novella in his *Reanimatrix* series -

- ARKHAM, 1928 -

HALSEY, PEASLEE, & LYDECKER, CONSULTING DETECTIVES

Arkham's newest detective agency doesn't handle philandering spouses, missing relatives, kidnappings or even murders. Even so, they aren't looking for work—if anything, they would appreciate some time off, to rest and recuperate.

THE MISKATONIC UNIVERSITY SPIRITUALISM CLUB

Dilettantes playing at ghost hunting—but the university knows better. If the club wants to borrow university equipment, they'll need someone to chaperone them—someone that can handle themselves against the living, the dead—and whatever else the universe might throw at them.

THE KRAG

The crumbling mansion squats abandoned on a New England cliff, overlooking the cold, dark sea. They say its owner, a professor broken by tragedy, had spent years trying to contact the dead—only to vanish from behind the locked doors of the house itself. Nearly a decade later, the place remains untouched, and the caretaker won't spend the night.

THESE ARE THE PLAYERS. THIS IS THE PLACE.
IT'S CHRISTMAS. AND A GHOST STORY IS JUST THE BEGINNING.

"The coolest, most gifted Lovecraftian writer working today."
—W. H. PUGMIRE, Author of *Witches in Dreamland*

AVAILABLE NOW!

www.JackanapesPress.com
www.facebook.com/Jackanapes-Press

GOT WEIRD?
DON'T FORGET YOUR SHOGGOTH

From horror / sci-fi / cyberpunk legend JOHN SHIRLEY, author of *Demons*, *Wetbones* and *Lovecraft Alive!*—a unique collection of stories, organized into four sections. The first section is *Really Weird Stories*. The second is *Really, Really Weird Stories*. The third is *Really, Really, Really Weird Stories*. The fourth is—oh yes—*Really, Really, Really, Really Weird Stories*. Each section is weirder than the last, doubling its strangeness a section at a time. The collection starts out disquieting; it becomes disturbing, then it gets outrageously weird—then *mind-bending*.

The updated edition of *RRRRWS* is one of the most impressive feats of sustained and varied weirdness since Harlan Ellison's landmark *Dangerous Visions* anthologies. This edition contains four new stories, including the Lovecraftian Antarctic adventure "A Boy and His Shoggoth," and, published here for the first time, "The Whisperer Made Visible"—a tale of secret treaties with horrors eldritch and invisible.

> "A landmark collection from one of speculative fiction's wildest and greatest talents. What a joy to see it back in print!"
> —PETER ATKINS, writer of *Hellraiser 2-4* & *Wishmaster*

AVAILABLE NOW FROM

www.JackanapesPress.com
www.facebook.com/Jackanapes-Press

Also from Jackanapes Press

AVAILABLE NOW

Past the Glad and Sunlit Season: Poems for Halloween
by K. A. Opperman / Illustrated by Dan Sauer

October Ghosts and Autumn Dreams: More Poems for Halloween
by K. A. Opperman / Illustrated by Dan Sauer

The Withering: Poems of Supernatural Horror
by Ashley Dioses / Illustrated by Mutartis Boswell

The Voice of the Burning House
by John Shirley / Illustrated by Dan Sauer

The Ettinfell of Beacon Hill: Gothic Tales of Boston
by Adam Bolivar / Illustrated by Dan Sauer

Book of Shadows: Grim Tales and Gothic Fancies
by Manuel Arenas / Illustrated by Dan Sauer

The Miskatonic University Spiritualism Club
by Peter Rawlik / Illustrated by Dan Sauer

Really, Really, Really, Really Weird Stories
(A New Edition with Four New Stories) by John Shirley

Not a Princess, But (Yes) There Was a Pea
and Other Fairy Tales to Foment Revolution
by Rebecca Buchanan

I Awaken in October: Poems of Halloween and Folk Horror
by Scott J. Couturier

Halloween Hearts
by Adele Gardner

COMING IN 2023

Darker Than Weird: Fourteen Tales of Horror
by John R. Fultz

www.JackanapesPress.com
www.facebook.com/Jackanapes-Press